G000079471

Women, Authorship and Literary Culture, 1690–1740

Other books by Sarah Prescott

WOMEN AND POETRY, 1660–1750

Women, Authorship and Literary Culture, 1690–1740

Sarah Prescott
University of Wales
Aberystwyth

© Sarah Prescott 2003

All rights reserved. No reproduction, copy or transmission of
this publication may be made without written permission.

No paragraph of this publication may be reproduced, copied or
transmitted save with written permission or in accordance with
the provisions of the Copyright, Designs and Patents Act 1988,
or under the terms of any licence permitting limited copying
issued by the Copyright Licensing Agency, 90 Tottenham Court
Road, London W1T 4LP.

Any person who does any unauthorised act in relation to this
publication may be liable to criminal prosecution and civil
claims for damages.

The author has asserted her right to be identified
as the author of this work in accordance with the
Copyright, Designs and Patents Act 1988.

Published by
PALGRAVE MACMILLAN
Houndmills, Basingstoke, Hampshire RG21 6XS and
175 Fifth Avenue, New York, N. Y. 10010
Companies and representatives throughout the world

PALGRAVE MACMILLAN is the global academic imprint of the Palgrave
Macmillan division of St. Martin's Press, LLC and of Palgrave Macmillan Ltd.
Macmillan® is a registered trademark in the United States, United Kingdom
and other countries. Palgrave is a registered trademark in the European
Union and other countries.

ISBN-13: 978–1–4039–0323–5

This book is printed on paper suitable for recycling and made from fully
managed and sustained forest sources. Logging, pulping and manufacturing
processes are expected to conform to the environmental regulations of the
country of origin.

A catalogue record for this book is available from the British Library.

Library of Congress Catalog Card Number: 20020815

I Idloes Roberts, gyda chariad a diolch

Contents

List of Figures

Acknowledgements

Some material on Penelope Aubin in Chapters 1, 2 and 3 appeared as 'Penelope Aubin and *The Doctrine of Morality*: a Reassessment of the Pious Woman Novelist', *Women's Writing*, 1.1 (1994): 99–112. I am grateful to Triangle Journals for permission to use this. Part of Chapter 6 is a revised version of my 'Provincial Networks, Dissenting Connections, and Noble Friends: Elizabeth Singer Rowe and Female Authorship in Early Eighteenth-Century England', *Eighteenth-Century Life*, 25 (2001): 29–42. I am grateful to the editor for allowing me to reproduce that material.

In the course of writing this book I have received enormous help from a variety of sources and individuals. My colleagues at Aberystwyth have supported me in many ways. The first debt of gratitude is to Diane Watt, whose support, guidance, intellect and friendship have proved invaluable throughout. I would also like especially to thank Claire Jowitt for her constant encouragement, and David Shuttleton for his invaluable comments on drafts of various chapters of this book. I have also benefited from the advice and support of Jane Aaron, Peter Barry, June Baxter, Damian Walford Davies, Helena Grice, Andrew Hadfield and Paulina Kewes. I thank Patricia Duncker for her optimism and belief in me. The Departmental Research Committee at Aberystwyth granted me study leave which enabled me to work on the book in earnest. I am grateful to the College Research Fund for financial assistance. The staff at The British Library, the Bodleian Library, and the National Library of Wales have all been especially helpful.

I would also like to express my appreciation of the community of scholars working in the area of women's writing and eighteenth-century studies. Jane Spencer deserves special mention for her inspiring supervision while I was a doctoral student at the University of Exeter, and for her continuing friendship and interest in my work. Ros Ballaster, Brean Hammond, Jacqueline Pearson, Marie Mulvey Roberts, Valerie Rumbold, Ashley Tauchert and Janet Todd have all been generous with their time and expertise at different stages in the book's evolution.

I owe many debts of gratitude to my family. Elizabeth Moon has, as ever, been a constant inspiration as well as a source of practical and emotional support. Cliff Moon and Jane Hudson have provided a steady supply of sound advice in moments of stress. Faye and Abbie have been a frequent source of delight. Mae fy nyled pennaf i'm gŵr am ei gariad a'i gefnogaeth, sy'n golygu cymaint imi. Cyflwynaf y llyfr hwn iddo ef.

Introduction: Relocating Women's Literary History

This study offers a challenge to existing models of women's literary history by investigating a variety of different contexts in which women wrote and published from the 1690s to the 1740s. One of my main aims is to revise the urban, professional and fiction-oriented model that has so often been used to describe early eighteenth-century women writers.[1] Instead of focusing exclusively on novelists, the present study includes analysis of writers in both poetry and fiction. Furthermore, rather than concentrating solely on the impact of a professional print culture on women's writing practices, I suggest that multiple contexts for writing and publication coexisted at this time. Throughout this study, I relocate women's relation to literary culture in two ways. First, I complicate the way in which we can understand the authorial modes women practised at this time by expanding the current critical templates we have at our disposal. I suggest that factors such as political allegiance and religious belief as well as individual economic circumstances and class positions all affected women's relation to their authorial identities and their publication practices. In this respect I am relocating women's literary history in a conceptual sense by rethinking and expanding the theoretical categories used to describe women's relation to literary culture and authorship. Through an analysis of a broad span of women writers, I take into account a wide range of contexts for writing and publication; from sociable literary circles, the patronage system, and subscription publication to the commercial world of the London booksellers.

The second way in which I relocate women's literary history takes a more literal interpretation. A central argument here is that provincial literary culture, and women's place in that culture, have been severely neglected in studies of this period. One of my main aims is to locate the history of female authorship away from an exclusive focus on metropolitan literary life. By looking at the careers of writers such as Jane Brereton, Mary, Lady Chudleigh, and Elizabeth Singer Rowe, who all lived away from London for the majority of their writing lives, it is clear that provincial culture was not only vibrant and productive but also enabling for many women writers. However, I do not want to continue the impression that the provinces existed in polar opposition to London. Rather, I argue that there was a vital interaction between province and metropolis in this period. Therefore, to view the provincial woman writer as automatically distanced from mainstream literary life is overly schematic. Life in the provinces did not necessarily imply isolation from literary culture or critical recognition. In fact, in many cases a provincial existence could actively enable a woman's literary career. By the same token, even in London itself, literary culture was not only based on a professional author–bookseller relationship. Metropolitan literary culture was also diverse and included patronage networks, literary circles and friendly encouragement in much the same way as provincial culture. Literary London was not just 'Grub Street' and to be a London-based author did not automatically classify a writer as a mercenary hack. Overall, then, this study redefines current conceptions of women's participation in literary culture by arguing for a broader and more inclusive interpretation of female authorship, as well as a more fluid conception of both the metropolis and the provinces as sites of literary production. What I am arguing for is a move away from limiting polarities towards what I term a 'pluralist' model of women's literary production. Such a model would attend not only to women's participation in the literary marketplace, but also take into account the impact of religious, political and regional identities on women's experience of authorship.

In order to situate my own approach it is necessary to outline briefly some of the dominant paradigms used to describe the literary culture of the late seventeenth and early eighteenth centuries and the place of women writers in that culture. This period in history is commonly acknowledged to mark the first substantial development of a commercial literary marketplace and a culture of professional authorship. More and more writers, both male and female, entered print as poets, novelists, dramatists, political satirists and as contributors to periodicals, to name only a few of the avenues explored by writers in this period. As the development of the literary marketplace gathered momentum in the early years of the eighteenth century, the traditional idea of authorship as a pursuit of leisured learning came face to face with newer conceptions of the writer as professional, commercial and market-oriented.

Various scholars have attempted to explain the effects of these changes on the practice and conception of authorship in this period. Critics such as Alvin Kernan and Mark Rose, for example, have emphasized the modernity of early eighteenth-century literary culture.[2] In Kernan's view, the emergence of a literary marketplace freed 'the writer from the need for patronage and the consequent subservience to wealth, [...] through a copy-right law that made the writer owner of his own writing'.[3] In contrast to this emphasis on the rise of the modern author, Dustin Griffin and Margaret Ezell, amongst others, have argued that the early eighteenth century was a period of transition. These scholars see print culture and the literary marketplace as existing alongside, and often being shaped by, the authorial practices and contexts of production which critics like Kernan deem to be outdated and moribund: patronage systems, manuscript culture and the conventions of amateurism.[4]

Critical approaches to the study of gender and authorship complicate these discussions even further. Brean Hammond, for example, has made the point that the eighteenth-century male writers most studied today, such as Alexander Pope, are those 'who contrived to have themselves perceived as least professional, who evolved a *raison d'être* for the writer's career that most artfully concealed the profit motive, and who created an art that could plausibly be seen to transcend its material conditions'.[5] In direct contrast, scholarship on female authorship has tended to privilege those writers who were the most blatantly professional: Aphra Behn, Delarivier Manley and Eliza Haywood. Aphra Behn is, of course, the most famous example of this celebratory treatment of female literary professionalism. Although Behn herself wished for a measure of critical esteem as well as popularity, it is her professionalism and survival in the literary marketplace that prompted much of the initial feminist interest in her as a writer in the 1970s and early 1980s, often to the detriment of in-depth analysis of her texts.[6] As Catherine Gallagher notes, 'No other author has the very fact of her initial market success so prominently in the forefront of her reputation that it often obscures everything else about her works.'[7] Similarly, the writers from the early eighteenth century who are gaining the most critical interest are those who are seen to be the most obvious successors to Behn's style of authorship: Eliza Haywood and Delarivier Manley again. In contrast, writers like Elizabeth Singer Rowe and Mary, Lady Chudleigh, who do not fit the 'professional' template offered by Behn, remain relatively underexplored.

The recent focus on those women who represent professional female authorship is predicated on narratives of women's literary history which view the fact that women could make money from writing as, in part, a feminist act and as an unequivocal advance for women writers. One of the earliest and most influential author-scholars to articulate this view was, of course, Virginia Woolf in *A Room of One's Own* (1928). Woolf makes great play of the connection between writing for money and the mental freedom to write. Of Behn, she declares: 'She made, by working very hard, enough to live on. The importance of that fact outweighs anything she actually wrote [. . .] for here begins the freedom of the mind.'[8] In effect, women writers can only be taken seriously if they had a professional attitude to their writing, and if they received payment. As Woolf states, 'Money dignifies what is frivolous if unpaid for.'[9] Woolf's privileging of professionalism for women writers as a positive gain directly affected early studies of Behn who was, for a time, known primarily as the first woman writer to make a living by her pen.[10] This treatment of Behn has impacted on the broader paradigms of women's literary history we currently tend to take for granted. The model of female authorship which has arisen out of the emphasis on the professional woman writer is one based on a sexualized image: the familiar anti-feminist trope of the woman writer as whore. On the other hand, there is the image of the woman writer as genteel amateur; a style usually represented by Behn's contemporary Katherine Philips. In contrast to Behn's image, this conception of female authorship emphasizes the woman writer's modesty and sets her apart from the commercial context of the literary marketplace. This process of assigning feminine characteristics to different modes of authorship – the scandalous professional versus the modest amateur – stems from what Kathryn King has recently termed the 'moralized taxonomies' which have haunted women's literary history of this period in particular.[11]

Nancy Cotton was one of the first critics to describe women writers in terms of moral dichotomies. In her book on women playwrights, Cotton describes Philips as 'the model for the authoress as graceful amateur'. In contrast, Behn represents 'the model for the commercial woman writer outside of the circle of propriety'.[12] Janet Todd's description of the scene of women's writing in the Restoration and early eighteenth century is one example of the way in which these taxonomies have since been reified. With reference to Behn and Manley, Todd writes:

> While an aura of naughtiness might sell books, it still remained scandalous, and two poles of women's writing were speedily formed: the

modest and the immodest. The first was personified in the professional and flamboyant Aphra Behn as 'Astrea'. [. . .] The second was
typified by the refined, retiring poet and playwright of heroic tragedy,
Katherine Philips, or 'Orinda', isolated in Wales but at the centre of
a network of platonic friendships 'as innocent as our Design'.[13]

Todd goes on to contrast Philips' 'retreat from publicity' and reluctance
to publish with 'Behn's hunger for financial success'.[14] As such, Behn
represents a professional model of authorship for women which is motivated by economics and centred firmly in the literary marketplace of
London. By contrast, Philips is 'isolated in Wales' far from the centre of
print culture, relying on a circle of close friends to circulate her coterie
verse in an amateur context.

These opposing images of Behn and Philips have been extremely
influential for the critical treatment of early eighteenth-century women
writers. In effect, these two writers have come to represent models of
authorship which are either rejected or assimilated by women writing
immediately after them. Marilyn L. Williams, for example, structures
her study of women writers from 1650 to 1750 around the perceived
dichotomy between Behn and Philips. She enforces the impression of
polarity by describing eighteenth-century writers as either 'Daughters
of Behn' or 'Daughters of Orinda'.[15] In her influential essay, 'The
Daughters of Behn and the Problem of Reputation', Jeslyn Medoff
signals that Behn is the standard by which later writers have to be compared and contrasted.[16] In his *Popular Fiction Before Richardson*, John
Richetti also discusses early eighteenth-century women's fiction in
terms of this notion of two conflicting images of the woman writer. His
chapter on Eliza Haywood explores 'The Erotic and the Pathetic',
whereas his chapter on Penelope Aubin, Jane Barker and Elizabeth
Singer Rowe is titled 'The Novel as Pious Polemic'.[17] In such accounts,
a woman writer's life and reputation are constantly conflated with the
type of writing she was seen to produce and the style of authorship she
adopted. As a result of such constructions, the overall picture of
women's participation in literary culture after Behn and Philips has been
coloured by the models these writers are seen to represent. For example,
Paula Backscheider describes the early eighteenth-century woman writer
as being 'forced into one of two classes: the new position of the shame-
less, crass, fallen woman jostling with men and willing to live by her
illicitly gained sexual knowledge, a place in stark contrast to the other,
which was the long accepted practice of the aristocrat writing for herself
and her circle and tastefully circulating manuscripts'.[18]

In her extended critique of the conventions of women's literary history, Margaret Ezell notes the way in which these polarities have since become the dominant method of theorizing early modern women's literary history:

> In our current theoretical models, we are thus offered two paradigms for the early woman writer. She can forfeit all social respectability to enter the arena of male commercial literature and be crushed, or she can suffer injustice privately without challenging the rules of social decorum and be vindicated through her posthumous publications.[19]

As Ezell and others have noted, such models of women's literary history are based on a distorted view, not only of Behn and Philips themselves, but also of women's participation in literary culture in general. Elaine Hobby's work on seventeenth-century women writers, to give only one example, demonstrates the way that the perceived choice between decorous amateurism or cut-throat professionalism obscures other factors which shape women's writing, such as religious belief and political affiliation.[20] More recent studies of Restoration and early eighteenth-century women writers have focused on individual authors as a way of complicating existing perceptions about women's relation to literary culture. Jane Spencer's investigation of Aphra Behn's ongoing influence in the eighteenth century has revised the Woolfian image of Behn as a warning to other women writers.[21] Kathryn King's study of Jane Barker similarly overturns Barker's previous image as a 'daughter of Orinda' and pious polemicist by focusing on her Jacobitism, her Catholicism and her interactions with the literary marketplace.[22] Broader studies of women's place in literary culture have also extended the context for thinking about women and authorship in the late seventeenth and early eighteenth centuries. Carol Barash's groundbreaking work on women's poetry of the period 1649 to 1714 has not only shifted the emphasis away from fiction but has also recast women's poetry of this period – including that of Katherine Philips – in terms of its immediate political context.[23] From a different perspective, Paula McDowell's study of *The Women of Grub Street* moves away from literary genres such as the novel and poetry, to look at women's interventions in the print trade as well as the popular political culture of their day.[24] On an even broader level, studies such as Margaret Ezell's most recent book on *Social Authorship* have presented the relationship between manuscript and print culture in the early eighteenth century as mutually informative and coexisting authorial choices rather than as starkly opposing modes of literary production.[25]

My study builds on these recent revisionist accounts of women's literary history and early eighteenth-century literary culture. However, my adoption of a 'pluralist' model for describing women's place in literary culture does not mean that I neglect the role played by the literary marketplace in shaping women's approaches to, and experience of, authorship. The book as a whole is centrally concerned to trace the way in which the economics of authorship affected women writers' self-perception as well as their reception and promotion by the literary critical establishment. As in my general approach, I take a broad view of the role of economics in relation to women's literary careers. On the one hand, I investigate how women novelists negotiated the fact that their chosen genre was, almost by definition, a commercial commodity and how this affected their self-representation as writers. In addition, I look at the marketing strategies used by the London booksellers to make women's fiction attractive to a broad readership. However, I am also concerned to emphasize the way in which women novelists attempt to deflect attention away from economic motives. Far from being blatantly professional in approach, many women novelists adopt a deferential persona of the poor, suffering female forced to make a living from her pen due to reduced circumstances. As well as examining these more conventional manifestations of economic authorship, I explore women's use of patronage and subscription as alternative ways of generating income. Both these systems represent very different kinds of economic networks than direct negotiations with booksellers. The book therefore argues for a more nuanced and inclusive approach to the economic side to authorship in this period. One salient fact which emerges from this broad exploration of authorship and economics is that, contra Woolf, writing for money in the early eighteenth century did not equate with freedom of mind. Rather, economic considerations crucially shaped, and in some instances severely limited, women's approach to publication and authorial self-promotion.

The problem of how to disguise the commercial aspects of writing in the early eighteenth century has been less of a prominent issue in discussions of women poets; especially those of provincial origin. Although there has been much important work on women's poetry, there is still an overall sense that women poets were less likely to be professional than their novelist counterparts. There is a certain amount of truth in the view that poetry was less lucrative than fiction as a way of making money from writing. However, it is not the case that women poets were separate from the literary marketplace and the commercial appeal of the woman writer in general. In terms of the conventional taxonomies of women's literary history, the woman novelist is seen as professional, commercial, and as having a sexualized image. By contrast, the woman poet is portrayed as modest, virtuous and amateur. I break through these particular categories by not only placing both women poets and novelists in a commercial context, but also by suggesting that the image of the modest woman writer who eschews economic gain was, in fact, commercially motivated. I argue that the market value of a particular woman writer could depend as much on her reputation for virtue as her 'scandalous' participation in the literary economy. In the case of Elizabeth Singer Rowe, for example, it was precisely her image as non-professional, provincial and virtuous that constituted the terms of her popular appeal. In other words, an emphasis on morality, provinciality and an amateur status could itself be an effective marketing ploy, not a symbolic retreat from the literary marketplace and literary culture in general. To rephrase Todd, an aura of morality could also sell books.

The fifty years from 1690 to 1740, the focus of this study, represent an important transitional period in the history of authorship. By the mid-eighteenth century literary culture had changed dramatically from the latter years of the seventeenth century. In the 1690s the novel was barely recognized as a serious branch of literature. In contrast, the post-1740 novel was reified as the dominant genre in literary culture. As population, literacy and leisure increased, so did the consumer demand for reading material which, in turn, enabled a rise in the number of authors. Following the steady increase in authors from 1700 onwards, the second half of the eighteenth century witnessed a massive increase in writers of both sexes who could claim authorship as a respectable profession. From the 1760s onwards, women writers entered the authorial ranks on an unprecedented scale. Judith Phillips Stanton claims, for example, that the number of women becoming authors actually started to exceed population growth and estimates that 'Their numbers increased at around 50 percent *every decade* starting in the 1760s.'[26] In the years immediately preceding my period, from approximately 1649 to 1688, there were early stirrings of an increase in women's literary activity. Elaine Hobby highlights the 1650s as an especially productive year for women's published writing when over 70 women produced approximately 130 texts.[27] In the period from 1649 to 1688 as a whole, Hobby notes that work by more than 200 women was published on a range of topics and in a variety of genres.[28] However, as she goes on to acknowledge, 'Well over half the texts published by women between 1649 and 1688 were prophecies.'[29]

How does the period from 1690 to 1740 compare? The early years of the eighteenth century do not show the dramatic increase of the post-1760 literary marketplace. However, as Stanton indicates, 'the numbers of women starting to write, decade by decade, increased steadily but slowly from the 1660s to the 1730s'.[30] Despite the critical focus on the eighteenth-century woman novelist, statistics suggest that poetry was in fact the most popular genre for women. In the years 1690 to 1699, according to Stanton, ten women began practising as poets compared to only one novelist. In 1730 to 1739 the ratio rises to thirteen poets as opposed to only four women who published fiction.[31] The 1720s are anomalous in this respect. Due to Eliza Haywood's vast output the number of novels published by a woman rises dramatically in this decade.[32] Yet even without Haywood, the 1720s saw five women begin their careers as novelists. Such figures underline the argument that this decade marks the first important cycle of eighteenth-century fiction and that women were instrumental in this development.[33] In contrast to the radicalism of the later seventeenth century, and the predominance of religio-political works by women at this time, the period from 1690 to 1740 sees a move in favour of the more literary genres of fiction and poetry, although religious works do come a close third. Although the years from 1690 to 1740 do not match the figures of the later eighteenth century, this period is important if we are to understand the basis on which the subsequent explosion of women's writing occurred. The period focused on in this study is crucial for realizing the terms on which later women writers presented themselves and were received by their public. Many of the patterns I have been describing – the significance of provincial culture, the marketing of virtue as a saleable commodity, the emergence of the highly public yet respectable woman writer – were absolutely necessary for the remarkable success of women writers on the late eighteenth-century literary scene. Without an understanding of the years 1690 to 1740, we cannot comprehend how and why the explosion in women's writing could and did occur in the final decades of the eighteenth century.

Although I have emphasized the period from 1690 to 1740 as a time of transition, my focus in this study is primarily on print culture and women's published writings. However, throughout the book I also explore how manuscript culture and coterie styles of authorship impinge on women's public personae and publication practices. Indeed, it is apparent that in the formative years of its development, the literary marketplace relied on older writing practices to conceptualize the idea of the author in print.[34] For example, the miscellany and the periodical, two of the most popular and also innovative types of publication at this time, are based on notions of manuscript circulation and modes of social authorship associated with coterie circles. Therefore, despite my primary interest in women's published writings, I do not suggest that print and manuscript cultures are separate modes of authorship at this time. I am not so much interested in manuscript and print as 'competing technologies', to use Margaret Ezell's phrase, as in how the two modes of writing interact and complement each other in the period under discussion.[35] Given the close relation between manuscript and print cultures in this period it was possible, as Elizabeth Singer Rowe's modes of authorship amply demonstrate, to participate in both authorial practices either simultaneously or at different stages in a single career. This is one further example of my wish for a 'pluralist' model of women's literary history; a model which allows for such fluidity and sense of process rather than one which fixes women's literary experiences into rigid and often oppositional categories.

The book is structured so as to be both general and detailed. I have included sections which offer broad-based discussions of women's relation to the literary culture of the period as well as more closely focused discussions of individual writers. The book is divided into three parts each comprising two chapters. The first two parts are broad in focus. Part I, 'Women and Authorship', discusses the circumstances and multiple contexts from which women wrote, published, and presented themselves as writers. Chapter 1 provides a survey of the literary careers of some representative poets and novelists from the 1690s to mid-century, concentrating on both the provincial and the metropolitan contexts in which women were writing. The professional novelist, the aristocratic poet and the middle-class provincial woman publishing through the periodical press are all discussed here. The chapter also focuses on the diversity of literary culture within London. I argue here that, even in London, women's literary production was predicated on sociable exchange and the interaction of coterie-style literary circles. Chapter 2 deals with the way in which some key writers negotiate their positions as authors. The first section of the chapter discusses the way in which women novelists, such as Eliza Haywood, Mary Davys and Penelope Aubin, negotiated the commercial context of the market for fiction through the prefaces and dedications to their work. The second section of this chapter focuses on the way in which women poets disassociate themselves from commercial literary culture by employing

Horatian conventions of retirement to authorize themselves as writers. By casting themselves in the Horatian mode, women poets could suggest that they were uninterested in literary fame and that their poetry was merely a leisured accomplishment. I argue here that it was this image of the virtuous, amateur and provincial woman poet which was not only to become the most influential model of female authorship, but also the most marketable. I end this chapter with a discussion of the Welsh poet Jane Brereton who uses the conventional trope of Horatian retreat in her work and inflects it through her invocations of the Welsh landscape. My discussion of Brereton further extends the scope of this study by focusing on alternative sites of production and authorial identities outside an exclusively English context.

Part II, 'Authorship and Economics', concerns the marketing of women writers and the economic realities of authorship for women. Chapter 3 includes discussion of the different marketing strategies used to promote the woman novelist as well as exploring the commercial role played by posthumous editions of a writer's work. In the 1720s, the dominant method used to market a woman novelist was to emphasize her sexuality and passion. However, the woman writer could also be presented to the public as an ideal of feminine virtue and morality. I argue that Elizabeth Singer Rowe played a key role in this development. In order to demonstrate Rowe's influence, I read her posthumous biography alongside another biographical account from the early 1740s, that of Jane Brereton. Chapter 4 looks at three different ways women could make a living from writing in the period: sale of copy to the booksellers, the patronage system, and subscription publication. The focus here is on the various ways women interacted with the broader systems of literary culture to make a living as writers and to construct their authorial identities. In this chapter I trace women's relations with particular booksellers as well as exploring women's use of subscription publishing. The chapter also examines a much neglected aspect of women's involvement with literary culture in this period: their engagement in, and use of, the patronage system. The chapter concludes with a detailed analysis of Mary Barber's problematic experience of publishing her only collection of poetry by subscription.

The final part is an extended case study of the career of Elizabeth Singer Rowe. I chose to focus on Rowe not only because she was one of the most popular and influential women writers of her day, but also because her career complicates the narratives of women's literary history I have been discussing here. Rowe was a provincial woman with close links to aristocratic patrons. She also circulated a large proportion of her poems in manuscript, many of which were only published after her death. However, her position as an extremely popular published writer who showed an active interest in printed versions of her poetry, letters and fiction complicates the traditional view of Rowe as a modest and retiring amateur woman poet. An in-depth study of a writer like Rowe – extremely successful in her day yet relatively neglected in modern criticism – throws new light on our overall understanding of women's relation to literary culture. Furthermore, her example offers some fresh ways for thinking about woman and authorship from 1690 to 1740. As I discuss in these final two chapters, Rowe's religious nonconformity, her Whig politics, her virtuous reputation, together with her commercial success and her provincialism, offer a very different set of configurations than those offered by conventional women's literary history.

In conclusion, this book argues that the model of the woman writer offered by Elizabeth Singer Rowe was, in fact, more representative of, and enabling for, the majority of women writers than the more well-documented image of the scandalous urban professional. Moreover, as one of the most popular and influential writers of her day, Rowe's varied career signals the ways in which we can attain a fuller understanding of women's place in literary culture. The 'pluralist' approach advocated here provides a conceptual model which brings us closer to achieving such an understanding. By redefining and relocating the dominant paradigms of women's literary history, this book provides the means to reach a fuller appreciation of women writers, their experience of authorship, and their significance for the literary culture of their time.

Part I
Women and Authorship

1
Authorship for Women: Careers and Contexts

Why did women choose a literary career in this period and what effect did factors such as economic necessity and place have on the career paths and publication patterns they chose to follow? This chapter provides some broad categories for thinking about how material circumstances and geographical location affected the careers of women writers. Although one of my overall aims in this study is to contest the assumption that the professional 'Grub Street' writer was the dominant model for women writers at this time, part of my project here is to reassess those writers whose literary careers were indeed shaped by economic pressures. Despite the popular image of the professional woman writer as a literary prostitute, many authors conventionally known for their morality, such as Jane Barker and Penelope Aubin, were as concerned to make their writing pay as their more 'scandalous' counterparts, such as Eliza Haywood. Therefore, although literary professionalism for women at this time was undoubtedly a difficult route to follow, this is not to say that all women who earned money for their writing were the objects of scorn and derision.

From the 1690s onwards, many aspiring women writers chose to gravitate towards London as the centre of print culture and as the obvious location for the literary professional. Writers such as Eliza Haywood and Penelope Aubin all spent most of their writing lives in the capital city. What is also clear, however, is that many women moved between capital and province as their circumstances and/or fortunes changed. After her original move to London from Ireland, Mary Davys lived temporarily in the provincial city of York, which is where she wrote a play, *The Northern Heiress*, based on her experiences there. Jane Barker's fictions also draw on her experience of different locations. *A Patch-Work Screen for the Ladies* (1723) and *The Lining of the Patch-Work Screen* (1726)

15

both feature a heroine, Galesia, who moves between London and the provinces, just as Barker herself did when her circumstances changed in the early eighteenth century. Even for those women writers whose publication patterns relied to some extent on a London context, the provinces played a significant role in their lives and their writing. In addition to those women who moved between metropolis and province but tended to be London-focused, there were also writers who were firmly based in a provincial location. Elizabeth Singer Rowe is the most famous example of a writer who was frequently linked to her home town, but many other women in the period wrote from, and were associated with, their provincial contexts. Although relatively ignored in studies of the period, I suggest that the model of the provincial woman writer is crucially important for our understanding of women's literary careers and publication patterns. Indeed, a provincial identity did not automatically mean social isolation for the woman writer but could, in fact, actively enable women's literary production and publication. Furthermore, although critical attention has mostly focused on literary professionals such as Haywood, the majority of women in this period did not write primarily from economic motives nor did they spend the majority of their writing lives in London.

The image of the 'scandalous' woman writer or 'prostitute of the pen' owes much to the popular conception of late seventeenth- and early eighteenth-century London literary culture as a cut-throat environment filled with predatory booksellers and grasping hack writers. This is London as 'Grub Street' where, as Pat Rogers has phrased it, 'topography serve[s] as moral symbolism'.[1] By focusing on areas of London and aspects of London literary life which do not conform to the 'Grub Street' model, where all women writers are figured as sexualized drudges, I aim to complicate our perception of the significance of London literary culture for women writers of the time. My analysis of Mary Astell's habitation in Chelsea, for example, offers a significant corrective to the construction of the professional London woman writer as scandalous and sexual as well as demonstrating that the London literary world at this time did not simply mean 'Grub Street'. Rather, London could offer aspiring writers a variety of contexts and conditions in which to produce their work. The involvement of Eliza Haywood and Martha Sansom in the literary circle surrounding Aaron Hill in the 1720s reinforces this point. The intricate relationships and mutual systems of support within what was, in effect, a coterie group suggest that, in the case of the Hill circle at least, metropolitan writers operated in very similar ways to their provincial counterparts. In the career of Eliza

Haywood in particular, this sociable and integrative element to women's literary production has often been downplayed in favour of a model of the professional female author as solitary, embattled and exclusively driven by commercial and economic motives.

In fact, the model of the sociable woman writer – be she aristocratic, middling or labouring class, provincial or metropolitan, professional or amateur – was a crucial component of the authorial practice of many women writers and formed the basis for a number of important literary careers. My final section on woman and poetry emphasizes the sociability of the provincial contexts in which many women poets produced their work. From an analysis of the careers of women from a range of economic backgrounds, it is clear that provincial literary networks proved extremely enabling for the woman writer. Just as there were connections between London-based writers and provincial literary culture, provincial writers also interacted extensively with writers, printers and booksellers in the metropolis. Authorship for women in the late seventeenth and early eighteenth centuries, then, was not exclusively based on a metropolitan, professional and fiction-oriented model. Although this model was influential, especially for women who wanted to earn a living from their writing, a variety of women writers from various backgrounds also wrote poetry from non-metropolitan locations, and found that these provincial contexts offered an enabling environment for their literary careers.

Writing for money: professional contexts

Women novelists and the literary marketplace

While I want to avoid a crude professional/amateur dichotomy, it is nevertheless possible to make a distinction between those women whose writing career was primarily motivated by economic necessity and those who did not have to make a living from their writing; although they may, at points, have received payment for their work. Cheryl Turner's sub-division of professionalism into those 'authors for whom payment was a concomitant but inessential accompaniment to publication' and those 'who used writing as a means of earning a living' is a useful distinction.[2] Turner labels this second group 'dependant professionals' and it is this group which forms the initial focus of my discussion here. Even within this narrow category there are marked divergences between individual careers and different decades, although one common denominator is the extreme difficulty women experienced in making a living from the pen. The stories of these 'dependent' careers are often ones of financial hardship and lack of familial support. As Frank Donoghue has argued in relation to the later eighteenth century, 'The most common excuse for publishing used by women writers was that financial distress (typically occasioned by the absence of a husband and a stable home life) had forced them to earn their own money.'[3] In some cases these pleas of poverty may indeed have been rhetorical gestures to deflect attention away from literary ambition or mercenary motive, but in a number of cases, from what we know about the writers, financial distress was the genuine reason why women entered print in the absence of alternative options.

In the 1690s the main commercial literary activity for women was drama. Building on the success and example of Aphra Behn in the 1670s and 1680s, Mary Pix, Catherine Trotter and Delarivier Manley all had plays performed in the 1690s and, in the cases of Trotter and Manley, into the 1700s. The launching of the careers of these three writers can be directly traced to one extraordinary theatre season. The 1695–6 season was unprecedented in that 'over one-third of all the new plays that season were by women or adapted from women's work'.[4] This season, then, presented a very particular and enabling context for the debuts of Pix, Trotter and Manley as a time when women playwrights were actively encouraged to participate in literary life. Furthermore, in addition to the opportunities represented by the newly competitive environment, Pix, Trotter and Manley also benefited from a more general sense in the 1690s that women were important consumers of drama and needed pleasing as much as the male audience.[5] As well as witnessing women's increased visibility as dramatists, this decade also marks a significant progression in the ongoing debate about the place and role of women in society. Women such as Mary Astell, Sarah Fyge Egerton and Judith Drake all argued for the right of women to education and variously complained against the unequal status of the female sex in order to claim recognition for women's intellectual capacities.[6]

Although the 1690s and early 1700s offered women unique opportunities as playwrights, drama did not continue as the most profitable genre for the dependent professional. Whereas the market for fiction increased in the early eighteenth century, the theatre suffered a relative decline. Robert Hume notes that, 'as far as we can tell, no one was making a living by writing plays in the mid-1720s'.[7] In contrast, by the end of the 1720s, the main commercial genre for women was the novel. The spectacular success of Eliza Haywood's *Love in Excess; or, The Fatal*

Enquiry (1719–20) initiated a vogue for fiction throughout this decade, and many women were to capitalize on Haywood's successes.[8] Given her rapid rate of production and high commercial profile, it is not surprising that Haywood has been seen to exemplify dependent professional female authorship in the eighteenth century.[9] She started professional life as an actress in Smock Alley in Dublin and the theatre continued to be an important part of her life and work.[10] However, her main output in the early eighteenth century was fiction, although she did diversify into translation, drama, periodical journalism and scandal narratives as well as producing an anti-Walpole political fiction in 1736: *The Adventures of Eovaai*. By the 1720s, the theatre was no longer the main route for literary professionals and Haywood appears to have turned to fiction and translation as an alternative way of making a living from her writing. In a letter to a patron dated 5 August 1720, concerning the subscription publication of her translation *Letters from a Lady of Quality to a Chevalier*, Haywood gives precisely this reason for her change of career: 'The Stage not answering my expectation, and the averseness of my Relations to it, has made me Turn my Genius another Way.'[11] Indeed, although Haywood's early connections with the theatre must have helped her as a novelist, it is clear that by 1720 Haywood is shrewdly adapting her practice and production to other areas of market interest. In the 1730s, when women's fiction fell out of fashion, Haywood returned to her previous career in the theatre.[12]

Haywood's career was also affected by her socio-economic and familial circumstances. Like many other women writers, Haywood was without the support of family or husband. In a letter from around 1728 to an unknown patron Haywood makes it clear that 'necessity' has turned her literary inclinations into a means of making a living, due to the loss of the male figures in her life: 'the Inclinations I ever had for writing be now converted into a Necessity, by the Sudden Deaths of both a Father, and a Husband, at an age when I was little prepar'd to stem the tide of Ill fortune'.[13] In what seems to be a later letter to another patron Haywood also suggests that, even before the death of her husband, she found herself without male support and solely responsible for the care of her two children: 'an unfortunate marriage has reduced me to the melancholly necessity of depending on my Pen for the Support of myself and my two Children, the eldest of whom is no more than 7 years of age'.[14] Although these claims are difficult to adjudicate, in that they could be exaggerated appeals to a patron, it is nevertheless clear that Haywood needed to use her writing as a means of earning a living.

The other main producers of fiction in the early eighteenth century were Penelope Aubin, Jane Barker and Mary Davys. Despite their different individual circumstances and origins, all three women wrote fiction from financial motives. Penelope Aubin's main output was in the 1720s, when she published seven novels between 1721 and 1728. In addition, she produced four translations from French texts, edited a translation of a French moral treatise, and had a comedy performed in December 1730. Given the relatively high output of her production and the length of her career, Aubin was obviously commercially successful as a writer; successful enough for her booksellers to reprint her fiction in three volumes after her death in 1739.[15] Furthermore, Aubin's remarks in her prefaces make her economic motives explicit. In the preface to *The Strange Adventures of the Count de Vinevil* (1721), she demonstrates an awareness of the marketplace in which she pitched her work: 'if this Trifle sells, I shall conclude it takes, and you may be sure to hear from me again', she declares hopefully. Like her female contemporaries, Aubin was driven to writing for economic reasons, but not this time because of the death of a husband. Contrary to William McBurney's guess that she took up a literary career because of widowhood, Abraham Aubin, a second lieutenant in the army, actually outlived his wife.[16] Mr Aubin was retired on a half pay of approximately £55 per annum in 1712.[17] It is therefore more likely that Penelope Aubin wrote to supplement her husband's income rather than to replace it.

Even a writer who was married and as successful as Aubin may not have been able to sustain a living from her writing. By the late 1720s, Aubin was obviously diversifying into other areas to supplement the money she made from her novels. In 1729, a year after the publication of her last novel, Penelope Aubin was preaching at her own oratory in the York Buildings, near Charing Cross. In an issue of the *Universal Spectator* for 16 August 1729, 'Henry Stonecastle', the pseudonymous editor, mentions what was presumably an ongoing debate between Aubin and John 'Orator' Henley.[18] Stonecastle states that he will not 'Interfere at all between the wonderful Mr Henley and that other Candidate for the Town's Applause, Mrs Aubin, or so much as Hint an Opinion which of them excels in Oratory'.[19] Aubin's participation in oratory has conventionally been read as an extension of the 'preaching' in her novels, but this activity can also be seen as financially motivated.[20] The Abbé Prévost certainly thought so. In his periodical *Pour et Contre*, he claimed that Aubin capitalized on her novelty as a woman writer to make money and attract crowds to her performance. He states that her oratory was enacted to make money as her novels were falling out of fashion and hints that she cynically 'turned her sights to heaven' to further her finances.[21] Prévost's comments on Aubin's economic standing are contradictory. He claims she was poor, but then goes to suggest that she died rich as a result of her oratory. Two years after his attack on Aubin in 1734, he again stressed her poverty and the way in which she used her position as a writer to make money. In volume ten of *Pour et Contre* he claims that she was forced to give a manuscript copy of a 'histoire galante' to ward off creditors.[22] Whatever the veracity of Prévost's assessment of Aubin, she was obviously not able to live off the success of her 1720s fiction. By the early 1730s she was trying another way to make money from her literary talents. In 1730 she appeared on stage to speak the epilogue to her comedy *The Merry Masqueraders*. The play lasted only until the second night, and her career as an author ended here. The advertisement for the second performance of the play on Friday 11 December 1730 states that the proceeds of the play would benefit Aubin directly, despite it not reaching the traditional author's benefit on the third night.[23] Aubin died in 1731. The evidence of her attempts to make money late in her career from other activities than novel writing suggest that she died in a state of financial necessity, despite the longevity of her writing career and her relative success as a writer.

Traditionally, Penelope Aubin and Jane Barker have not been seen as professional writers, but rather as 'pious' alternatives to writers such as Manley and Haywood, and therefore somehow outside of the literary marketplace and a commercial context.[24] This is clearly an inaccurate assessment of Aubin's writing life. Furthermore, despite the pious reputations which have hitherto been seen to exclude them from the 'scandal' of women's involvement in professional literary life, both Aubin and Barker can be seen to participate confidently in print culture. As Kathryn King's work on Jane Barker has demonstrated, it is clear that by the 1720s Barker was writing fiction in the hope of financial reward. Barker's prefaces to her two 'patchwork' narratives from the 1720s point to her awareness of the marketplace. In *The Patch-Work Screen* preface from 1723, Barker implores the reader to 'buy these *Patches* up quickly', which, she says, 'will greatly oblige the *Bookseller*, and, in some degree, the *Author*'. In the dedication 'To the Ladies' of the *Lining of the Patch-Work Screen* (1726), Barker ends by again asserting her wish for commercial success: 'Since you have been so kind to my Booksellers in favour of the *SCREEN*, I hope this *LINING* will not meet with a less Favourable Reception from Your Fair Hands.' As King argues in relation to the earlier preface, here Barker is 'very much a woman of 1723 [. . .]

She belongs, indeed, to the new breed of writer, the novel-writing woman who casts a commercial eye on that new breed of reader, the novel-buying public.'[25] King and Jeslyn Medoff's biographical work on Barker's life provides evidence for the reason she turned to a more commercial mode of operation in the 1720s. From 1714 onwards, Barker faced considerable financial difficulties as a result of a lawsuit brought against her by her niece.[26]

Barker's career not only spanned the centuries, starting with the publication of her poems as *Poetical Recreations* in 1688, but also two very different modes of authorship. Barker began her literary life as a provincial coterie writer, producing work in manuscript for a prescribed and known audience or community of readers and writers. These communities ranged from the Cambridge-based male poets who encouraged her early work to the political community which formed the exiled court of James II, of which Barker was a member.[27] In 1704 Barker returned to Wilsthorp, a rural village in Lincolnshire where she had spent her youth, but she probably left in about 1717, either to live abroad or in London.[28] Barker is fascinating precisely because she exemplifies the transitional nature of this period where manuscript circulation and publication could coincide and coexist with print culture. In the 1670s and 1680s, when Barker produced her early poetry, the first mode of authorial practice was dominant and her first fiction, *Love Intrigues*, was probably originally intended for a coterie audience, as was her Jacobite romance, *Exilius; or, The Banish'd Roman* (1715).[29] From her early beginnings as a coterie poet, Barker developed her style of authorship to include a more professional and commercial approach to writing and publication. However, although her career exemplifies broader changes in literary culture, Barker's life also demonstrates that economic necessity was often the reason why women chose to adopt a professional stance towards their writing and why they decided to take advantage of the opportunities the literary marketplace could offer.

Mary Davys' career demonstrates the extreme difficulty of making a proper and sustained living from the pen, especially if the writer lived in the capital where the cost of living was substantially higher than the provinces. Davys was an Irishwoman who moved to London in about 1700, after her husband died in 1698. She was therefore left as a widow in an alien city and a foreign country, forced to make a living from her wits. Like many of the writers already discussed, writing substituted for the support of a husband or family. Davys only half-succeeded as a literary professional. She was probably writing quite continuously from about 1700 onwards, but only managed to publish twice between 1700 and 1716. *The Amours of Alcippus and Lucippe* was published in 1704, and *The Fugitive* in 1705. As a result of this relative lack of commercial success, Davys moved to the provincial town of York from lack of finances rather than any shrewd career move.[30] But York proved fertile ground for Davys and provided her with a firm basis for her future economic survival. Davys made the acquaintance of some notable York families who were to subscribe to her later fiction. Furthermore, while in York, Davys wrote her comedy, *The Northern Heiress; or, The Humours of York*, which was performed at Lincoln's Inn Fields in 1716. As a result of the third night benefit, Davys earned enough money to open a coffee house in Cambridge where she lived for the rest of her life and from where she published her later more well-known fiction as well as her collected *Works* by subscription in 1725.[31]

Davys was very open about the fact that she wrote to augment her income but, as was the case with Barker, she also operated in what can be described as a coterie context where the Cambridge undergraduates who visited the coffee shop encouraged, read and subscribed to her work. Overall, however, Davys' career shows us that she found it impossible to survive only on her writing. Despite her professional approach, she did not produce material at the same rapid pace as Haywood. Her 1720s publications must have added to her income mainly through using subscription as a mode of publication, but her main business was her coffee house. By the early 1730s Davys was in poor health and the 1732 reprint of her novel *The Cousins* (1725) as *The False Friend* was most likely published to provide some money when Davys could no longer run her business. She died in poverty in 1732.[32] Davys' business venture was a result of her inability to sustain a living from writing, but her use of alternative sources of income is not an isolated case. In the 1730s, for example, a little-known writer, Elizabeth Boyd, published her novel, *The Happy-Unfortunate: Or, The Female Page* (1732), by subscription in order, as she states in her 'Advertisement', to open a shop selling 'Papers, Pens, Ink Wax, Wafers, Black Lead, Pencils, Pocket Books, Almanacks, Plays, Pamphlets, and all Manner of Stationary Goods'.[33]

For the dependent professional female author it is clear that, despite some isolated stage successes, the main genre for earning money from writing was fiction. Even then, and even if one were as productive as Haywood, the rewards were not enough to produce a secure income. Indeed, Haywood is exceptional in that she managed to sustain a career almost solely from her writing. Even after her 1720s successes in the fiction market, Haywood too was forced into other areas of literary production.[34] Unlike Haywood, many other women writers used writing only as a temporary relief from poverty and did not continue with their writing careers. What is also clear from an analysis of these careers is the difficulty of surviving as a dependent professional author in London. Although London was the centre of print culture in this period, many women began their careers in a provincial context or moved away from the capital as their circumstances changed. Therefore, although London was the obvious focus for dependent professional women writers, it is also clear that, for various reasons, many women moved between the provinces and the capital and produced their work in a variety of contexts and locations.

London literary circles

Mary Astell and the Chelsea context

Mary Astell's career provides an example of a young woman who moved from the place of her birth, the provincial town of Newcastle, to live in London for the rest of her life. To an extent, Astell's motives for moving to London were the same as those experienced by Eliza Haywood and Mary Davys: London was the obvious location for any writer who wished to make a living from her work and Astell's circumstances meant that there were very few options open to her. In fact, her life starkly represents the limited professional choices available for women at this time. Astell's father died when she was twelve. After his death, the family, comprising her mother, a maiden aunt and her brother Peter, were dependent on loans and gifts from the Hostmen's Company, her father's trade guild.[35] Although, as Ruth Perry suggests, it is likely that Astell's relatives funded her brother's apprenticeship to the law, there was no such support for Astell herself. There were no similar career routes for the daughter of the family. With the conspicuous lack of a dowry, Astell's chances of marriage were also reduced to nothing. Not surprisingly, Astell decided to live on her writing and to do so she had to go to London. What is remarkable, however, about Astell is that she managed to sustain herself as a single woman in the city until her death in 1731. Furthermore, not only did part of her income stem from her writing, but she also achieved a high level of respectability as well as literary renown.

Mary Astell is, of course, most famous for her *Serious Proposal to the Ladies* (1694), which was the most influential of the 1690s proto-feminist debates about women's education and established her fame as a literary figure. Rather than trace the reception of this text, what I want to focus on here is how Astell managed to survive as a woman of few means in a strange city. Some key factors explain her survival. First, is the particular area of London she chose to live in: Chelsea. Astell's life in Chelsea provides a useful reminder that London was not just 'Grub Street' or Drury Lane, and that living in London did not necessarily mean being at the centre of the London literary scene. As Ruth Perry has shown, late seventeenth-century Chelsea was like a small town with a high proportion of respectable rooms to rent at a relatively cheap rate. Chelsea was, therefore, the ideal choice for Astell and due to its town-like qualities was not that different from the provinces she had left: 'Any of these advantages might have drawn Mary Astell to Chelsea. The lower prices suited her means, the wealth and respectability of the local population suited her conservative attitudes and her social origins.'[36] In a sense, then, Astell managed to combine all the advantages of living in London while avoiding its dangers. In addition, many wealthy noblewomen also lived in the area and Astell came to the attention of four women in particular: Lady Catherine Jones, Lady Elizabeth Hastings, Lady Ann Coventry and Elizabeth Hutcheson. These women provided Astell with a close circle of similarly bookish female friends who were, importantly, also influential and rich. As well as giving Astell access to social circles higher than her own, and to other aristocratic literary women such as Lady Mary Wortley Montagu, Lady Hastings also helped Astell financially. As Perry notes, 'There are records in Lady Betty's bank account of a draft of £8.1.6 to Mary Astell in 1714, £33 in 1718, £25 in 1720, and so on – until the last entries in August 1730, which amounted to £55.15.00.'[37] Astell spent her final days in the comfort of Lady Hastings' home, where she died in 1731.

Astell's relations with this circle of wealthy and respectable Chelsea women not only reveal how she maintained herself, but also show how the particular area that she lived in contributed to her style of career and her reputation as a literary lady and respected figure on the literary scene. Astell's Chelsea friends show the importance of networks of friendship and patronage within London itself. She also had direct contact with her booksellers as well as a more straightforward experience of patronage. Shortly after arriving in London, Astell approached the archbishop of Canterbury, William Sancroft, for assistance. Her choice of patron was directly informed by her high Anglican views, which, in turn, must have strongly influenced Sancroft's generous response to her demands. From an undated letter which Astell sent to Sancroft, it is clear that she was in dire financial need. She appeals to Sancroft's charity and alludes to biblical parable to enforce her claims:

'I am a gentlewoman & not able to get a liflyhood, & I may say with ye steward in ye gospelle worke I cannot & to beg I am ashamed, but meer necessaty forces me to give yr grace yt trouble hoping yr charity will consider me.'[38] Sancroft responded by giving Astell money, but also by encouraging her writing. Astell sent him a manuscript copy of her poems in 1689 as a token of her gratitude.[39]

Astell's choice of bookseller, Richard Wilkin, was also informed by her personal and religious principles. Wilkin was at the conservative end of the publishing world and had a good reputation. He may have helped Astell financially as well as publishing her books. Astell's good fortune in finding a sympathetic bookseller in Wilkin helped her entry into print considerably.[40] The choice of bookseller can, therefore, be seen as another crucial factor in a woman writer's career. Rather than signifying the scandal and impropriety of a woman's entry into print, Astell's connections with the publishing world enforced rather than undermined her respectable reputation and conservative attitudes. However, this was also largely connected with the sort of texts she published. Although she was a dependent professional woman writer, she never published any novels or plays and, in fact, actively spoke out against these genres. Nevertheless, Astell experienced the same financial difficulties as Haywood, and used the same routes to alleviate her hardship, appealing to influential patrons and publishing through the booksellers. She also survived as a writer in London without independent means. Astell's circumstances and career pattern add another dimension to our sense of the dependent professional urban woman writer. Her location in Chelsea, her circle of wealthy female friends, and her choice of patron and bookseller, reveal a very different configuration of influences and networks of support than the usual construction of the dependent professional as isolated and at the mercy of a cut-throat literary marketplace.

The Aaron Hill circle in the 1720s

In the mid-1720s, the critic, poet and dramatist Aaron Hill was a prominent figure in London and acted as a patron and supporter of a number of aspiring writers and artists.[41] The group of writers who gathered around Hill included Eliza Haywood and Martha (Fowke) Sansom, as well as a number of male figures, such as James Thomson, Richard Savage, David Mallet and John Dyer. Hill and his circle could provide the means of support and acceptance for aspiring writers as well as offering a number of professional advantages and connections. For example, Hill wrote the epilogue to Haywood's play *The Fair Captive* in 1721. The presence of Haywood and Sansom in this literary circle provides important evidence about how women participated in what have often been seen as exclusively homosocial literary networks in this period. What is also significant about the literary circle cultivated by Hill, is the way in which this group styled itself along the lines of the sort of coterie inhabited by provincial writers. Like these coterie groups, Hill's circle addressed each other through the use of romance pseudonyms with Hill acting as the focus of amatory attention for both Haywood and Sansom. For example, Haywood wrote a number of effusive love poems to 'Hillarius'; and Sansom's posthumously published autobiography, *Clio; or, A Secret History of the Life and Amours of the Late Celebrated Mrs. S-n-m* (1752), written in the form of an extended letter to Hill, frequently eulogizes him in terms such as 'The Monarch of all my Soft Desires'.[42] In addition, John Dyer painted Sansom's portrait, and Hill and Richard Savage wrote complimentary verses to both Sansom and Haywood. Savage's poems were also used in the marketing of Haywood's novels. His poems in praise of Haywood appear as commendatory verses for both *Love in Excess* (1719–20) and *The Rash Resolve* (1724). This exchange of poetry was clearly based on the manuscript circulation of poems predicated on membership of a select literary circle. Even at the heart of London literary culture, it can be seen that writers styled themselves as part of coterie groups at the same time as they were involved in the commercial world of the literary marketplace. The poems exchanged are based on an ideal of romantic friendship dedicated to passionate expression of feeling. Thus, despite its metropolitan status, the Hillarian style of authorship also incorporated what have been seen as older, and by now outdated, forms of sociable literary interaction and manuscript culture. While this fusion of traditions and developments is beginning to gain recognition in the work of provincial writers, its place in the London literary world is often neglected. In the case of Eliza Haywood in particular, her role within this social and literary circle is often overlooked in favour of her image as the consummate professional.

Although their lives intersected through Aaron Hill, Sansom's career followed a different pattern to that of Eliza Haywood. The main difference between the two women is that Sansom had an independent income, whereas Haywood had to use her writing to support herself. Sansom was born into the well-established family of the Foulkes. Like many of the women discussed here, she lost both parents relatively early in life. Her mother died when she was sixteen, and in 1708 her father was murdered.[43] It is probable that after the deaths of her parents,

Sansom received a settlement which gave her the freedom of financial independence. Before her marriage to Arnold Sansom in the mid-1720s, she lived alone in London or with various family friends and relatives. Early in her career Sansom published poetry in periodicals such as *The Delights of the Ingenuous* (1711), and many of her poems were later printed in the *Barbadoes Gazette*.[44] Her epistolary exchange with William Bond, *The Epistles of Clio and Strephon*, was published in 1720, close on the heels of Haywood's *Love in Excess*. Sansom's poems also appeared in a variety of miscellanies as well as in the publications connected to Hill's circle. By the late 1720s, however, she had disappeared from the literary scene and was apparently in debt when she died in 1734.[45]

Hill's literary circle directly affected the authorial practices of Haywood and Sansom. I focus here on three publications which demonstrate the way in which such a specific social and literary group could shape a woman's entry into print. A number of poems by Sansom and Haywood appeared in *Miscellaneous Poems and Translations. By Several Hands. Publish'd by Richard Savage, Son of the late Earl Rivers* (1726). This volume was published by subscription and, as Savage states, the material was provided by his friends, most of whom were members of the Hillarian group. The subscribers include John Dyer, Hill, Sansom (two books), Edward Young, Richard Steele and David Mallet and includes, almost exclusively, poems by Savage, Hill, Dyer, and Sansom and 'Miranda' (Hill's wife). The volume was sponsored by Hill and published to benefit Savage and to further his claims that he was the illegitimate son of Earl Rivers, as the title suggests. Although a commercially motivated project, the basis of its contents and the identities of the contributors stem directly from the Hill coterie. For example, the collection includes the following poems: 'To Mrs. *Eliza Haywood*; by Mr. *Savage*', 'To Eliza' by Hill, '*Grongar Hill*; by Mr. *John Dyer*', 'The Choice; to Mr. *John Dyer*; by A. *Hill*, Esq', 'To Mr. *John Dyer*', 'To Mr. *Savage*' by Clio (Sansom's pseudonym), as well as poems by various pseudonymous contributors (Evandra, Miranda, Daphne, Aurelia and Lysander). What is also significant about this group is that it is not exclusively homosocial nor is it provincial. Sansom and Haywood occupy a central place in the collection, and the contributors are all London literary figures associated with the Hill circle.

The second publication, Anthony Hammond's *A New Miscellany of Original Translations and Imitations. By the most Eminent Hands* (1720), follows a similar pattern, and the title-page boasts that the poems are 'now first Publish'd from their Respective MANUSCRIPTS'. Hammond was associated with the literary circle which grouped around the deaf and dumb prophet Duncan Campbell.[46] Phyllis Guskin records that 'the group included Anthony Hammond, Richardson Pack, Philip Horneck, William Bond, George Sewell, John Philips, Susanna Centlivre, and Eliza Haywood'. Although these writers were not, in Guskin's view, 'the lower class of hacks', they were certainly not figures of major literary renown. In its inclusion of poetry by Manley, Centlivre and Sansom alongside that of Lady Mary Wortley Montagu, Matthew Prior and Alexander Pope, Hammond's collection is an attempt to bridge the gap between the sort of middle-brow writers represented by the Campbell coterie and higher-status writers. The *Miscellany* included a good proportion of Sansom's work. The poems 'Clio's Picture', 'Thoughts to a Friend, On the MASQUERADES', 'To Cleon's Eyes' and 'On Cleon's Letters' all appeared there.

The representation of the Hillarian group in print was more extensive in the third of Hill's literary projects discussed here: *The Plain Dealer*, a periodical which Hill edited in 1724. *The Plain Dealer* has two major pre-occupations: praise of women writers and the vindication of Richard Savage's claims to be the illegitimate son of Earl Rivers, despite his 'unfair' treatment by his supposed mother, Lady Macclesfield. The periodical included extensive discussion of, and included a number of poems by, a variety of women writers. Lady Mary Wortley Montagu is praised in number 30 for bringing the smallpox vaccination back from Turkey. Number 53 printed a poem on the death of Delarivier Manley (Delia) by 'Cleora', and number 79 published extracts from Elizabeth Singer Rowe's elegy on the death of her husband. Number 15 presented a poem by Savage on Dyer's portrait of Sansom, 'To a Young Gentleman, a *Painter*: Occasion'd by seeing his *Picture* of the *Celebrated* CLIO'. The periodical also served to market the production of Savage's *Miscellany*, which was advertised in number 69 as being available by a subscription of half a guinea to be sent to Button's coffeehouse in Covent Garden. The poem on Manley is interesting on two counts. First, because here Manley is being praised as a good example for women writers in the 1720s, when by this date her image is usually seen in a negative light. The poem is styled in terms of a coterie tradition of female friendship and the subject is praise of Manley as a friend and example to other women writers. Cleora asks, 'Where shall my Muse *another Delia* find?', and goes on to praise Manley as an angel amongst women. The second point of interest is the identity of the author, whose name is only given as 'Cleora'. The periodical is teasing about the identity of this lady, saying only that her poetry is 'rich in Beauties' and her eyes full of 'fire'. Guskin suggests that Sansom was the author of this poem, but as Sansom is always referred to as 'Clio', this seems unlikely. It is more probable that 'Cleora' is Haywood, for, as Dorothy Brewster has noted, in Hill's collected works, the references to Haywood as 'Eliza' are changed to 'Cleora'.[47] What is significant here is that Haywood is a writer who is usually seen to eschew such coterie names in her professional approach to publishing her name on the title-page of her novels. By contrast, the use of the name 'Cleroa' is direct evidence of Haywood's involvement in a coterie group, using a romance pseudonym as part of a coterie-style exchange of verses. It is not only apparent, therefore, that print culture was, to an extent, based on literary coteries and circles of writers, but also that these coterie-based groups were influential for the career of a woman writer who is viewed as the typical dependent professional, geared only to the exigencies of the commercial marketplace.

Provincial contexts and the woman poet

While those women who wrote for the stage and/or published fiction in the years from 1690 to 1740 did so primarily for economic reasons, the reasons why women wrote poetry reveal a more diverse picture. Although statistically poetry was the most attractive genre for women writers in this period, it was even less lucrative than fiction in terms of making a living from writing. Poetry was not the first choice for a dependent professional and was seen to be less directly oriented to commercial print culture than the novel.[48] As a result, poetry attracted a wider class range of writers than fiction, and included a broader range of authorial practices. As Carol Barash has argued, 'poetry remains, at once, both a more élite genre (in the sense that ideologically it is often considered as separate from the market-place, even when published through booksellers) and a more popular one, in that virtually every woman who kept a diary or commonplace book wrote or copied verses now and then'.[49] The view that poetry was non-commercial, amateur and part of a woman's usual accomplishments, helps to explain why those women writers who gained the most prestige and recognition from the male literary establishment were primarily poets, not novelists.

Despite the ideological construction of the woman poet as amateur-ish and 'private', the careers of women poets did intersect with the literary marketplace and the publishing world albeit through strategies usually associated with older traditions of production and transmission. Many sixteenth- and seventeenth-century women writers wrote from very specific literary contexts or 'communities'.[50] Often these communities were court-based and, as such, women's poetry often used praise of the monarch as a frame for their poetry and authorial personae. This context for women's literary production was therefore predicated on a known group of writers and readers who circulated poems in manuscript and who usually shared political affiliations with the court. Women, like their male counterparts, did not have literary careers in the sense of their professional successors in the marketplace, but instead produced their writing in response to particular events at court or political developments. However, for women, this community of writers and readers was often based on the idea of female friendship, which was used as a trope in poetry to signify shared political sympathies as well as providing a context for their work in addresses to specific women friends. A common approach which emerges from this context is women's use of pastoral and romance pseudonyms to signify their writing identities, their place within certain social and literary circles, and their political sympathies.

Only one of the women I discuss in this chapter actually inhabited such a court culture: Anne Finch. Nevertheless, the creation of symbolic literary coteries based on the court model served a useful purpose for women writers in that it shaped their careers through older traditions of sociable authorship rather than by a commercial context. Writers as diverse as Mary, Lady Chudleigh, Anne Finch, Elizabeth Singer Rowe, Jane Brereton and Mary Leapor, all used coterie pseudonyms as part of their authorial identities. In addition to this symbolic use of coterie culture, many women did inhabit and benefit from different kinds of literary circles. These range from close-knit provincial literary groups, often based around literary-minded female friends, to broader networks of friends and acquaintances which included male literary figures, patrons and the London booksellers. In the careers of many women poets all these elements are important not only for the publication of their work, but also the content of their poetry. Miscellany publication, for example, was one of the main ways in which women poets first entered print, and these collections were often based on the exact coterie circles within which the poems were originally written. At the same time, the miscellany was one of the most fashionable and prestigious forms of publication in the eighteenth century, produced by the most high-profile publishers of the day, such as Tonson, Dodsley and Lintot.[51] The coterie production of women's poetry also explains that aspect of eighteenth-century poetry which seems particularly alienating to modern readers. A large proportion of verse written in this period was in response to particular events and written to specific people, either on a grand scale, such as the deaths of monarchs or addresses to patrons, or on the more intimate or familiar level of the epistle to a friend or verses on the death of a child or family member. It is not surprising, therefore, that the most common titles for poetry collections in this period were variations on 'Poems on Several Occasions' or 'Miscellany Poems'.

Literary ladies and social authorship

The career of Mary, Lady Chudleigh (1656–1710) exemplifies some of the trends I have been outlining: the way in which the provinces interacted with London, the support of male literary figures, coterie provincial networks, symbolic communities of women, and a high-profile reputation in print. These factors are often seen as mutually exclusive but, as Chudleigh's career and circumstances show, these elements could all be present in a single career. Although she did not publish until late in her life, she nevertheless produced a substantial body of printed texts: *The Ladies Defence* appeared in 1701, followed by *Poems on Several Occasions* in 1703 and *Essays Upon Several Subjects in Prose and Verse* in 1710. As Margaret Ezell notes of Chudleigh, 'In the patterns of authorship she followed, she shows the typical pattern of writing first for a select coterie audience and later for a commercial public, a pattern which can be seen in the careers of many of her contemporaries, both male and female.'[52] Mary Lee was born in Devon in 1656 and after her marriage to George Chudleigh in 1674 she continued to live in the county for the rest of her life, moving to the Chudleigh family seat, Place Barton, in 1688.[53] Conventionally, her provincial life has been read as one of retirement and solitude, but it was from within this context that she engaged fully in both local and national literary culture.

Chudleigh's literary aspirations were helped considerably by her class status. She had access to a good library and connections with other literary figures as well as relatives living in Chelsea who provided a link to London life. Chudleigh was also related by marriage to the influential Clifford family at Ugbrook Park which was close to Chudleigh's home.[54] The female members of the Clifford family may have formed part of Chudleigh's provincial literary circles. Lord Clifford was a well-known patron and 'the Clifford household also included several women who may have shared Chudleigh's literary tastes and formed part of her literary circle, including Clifford's wife Anne Preston, a contemporary of Mary Chudleigh, and at times three of his unmarried sisters'.[55] This literary circle exchanged verses under pastoral pseudonyms. Chudleigh herself used the name 'Marissa' to refer to her poetic persona and her poems are often addressed to this coterie under the names of 'Cleanthe', 'Lucinda', 'Clorissa', and 'Eugenia'.

Chudleigh's career offers some important precedents for later women poets and provides what was to become a clear career pattern for women poets of all classes. Although her poetry was initially produced in a provincial context for a select group of mainly aristocratic readers, she also managed to make connections with mainstream London literary culture, publishing most of her work with the high-profile publisher Bernard Lintot. She also maintained correspondences with Mary Astell, Elizabeth Thomas and John Norris. Chudleigh also benefited from her inclusion in one example of the literary circles which often met in the country houses of aristocratic patrons. It was at Ugbrook Park that her work came to the attention of John Dryden, who was a frequent visitor. Dryden admired Chudleigh's poetry and even carried her manuscript poems from Devon to London to introduce her work to Jacob Tonson.[56] At the time of her death, Chudleigh had achieved a high level of critical acclaim and visibility as a published author. Far from restricting her career as a writer, Chudleigh's provincial circumstances proved an enabling context for her writing and did not stop her from interacting with the London literary world of printers and booksellers.

Anne Finch was another aristocratic woman who did not publish her work until late in her career. Before her marriage to Heneage Finch in 1684, Finch had been a Maid of Honour to Mary of Modena, and then lived at court with the Duchess of York. She later became a Lady of the Bedchamber to Queen Anne. Finch's early poetry was produced from a court-based community of learned royalist women which shaped her poetry and her sense of herself as a poet. Her first poetic productions were pro-Stuart panegyric which were either circulated in manuscript or published in miscellany collections of poetry, although she did publish a poem in 1701 on the death of King James.[57] Finch's circumstances soon changed, however. After the revolution of 1688, her husband refused to take the oath of allegiance to William III. As a result, the Finches were politically exiled from the court and financially insecure. After this date, they lived at Eastwell in Kent, and it was from within this context of a provincial country house that Finch wrote most of her mature poetry and began to publish her work. It was at Eastwell, too, that Finch's husband began compiling the manuscript of her *Miscellany Poems* which were to be published in 1713 by John Barber.[58] Finch also moved between London and the provinces and maintained connections with both contexts. By 1708, the Finches were back in London in Cleveland Rowe near St James's Palace. This is the period in Finch's life when she began participating more fully in the literary world as she began to have more direct contact with London literary figures and printers. During her time in London, Finch published a number of poems in miscellany collections. In 1701 'The Spleen' appeared in Gildon's *Miscellany*, and in 1709 three of her pastoral poems were printed in Tonson's *Poetical Miscellanies*. A poem also appeared in Steele's *Poetical Miscellanies* (1714).[59]

Finch's career spans the late seventeenth-century court-based literary world and early eighteenth-century modes of authorial practice. Like Chudleigh, Finch initially benefited from the support of literary provincial circles and the support of her female friends and family. Like Chudleigh again, she also received the support of other literary figures including Elizabeth Singer Rowe, Alexander Pope and Jonathan Swift. Swift in particular encouraged her to print her work, and it was Swift's printer, John Barber, who produced Finch's 1713 poems. Finch also enjoyed a high literary profile which was furthered by her appearance in prestigious miscellanies, such as those by Tonson and Steele where she appeared with prominent male literary figures of the day. Despite her period of enforced exile in the countryside after the revolution, it is clear that she was far from isolated and secluded as a poet. She was also helped considerably by the emotional and practical support of her husband and benefited considerably from her aristocratic connections. Although Finch's social and class status may have limited her public role as a woman poet, and made her more circumspect about the content of her printed work, Finch's authorial practices and her career pattern, as well as her literary reputation, were useful models for the aspiring middle-class woman poet in the eighteenth century. Many middle-class women poets were to acknowledge Finch as an influence, and many women from this social class also followed her style of authorship: publishing in miscellanies, creating literary pseudonyms, and fostering supportive networks and literary friendships with both men and women.

Middle-class poets and the periodical press

The careers of Chudleigh and Finch demonstrated to other women writers that women's poetry could be acceptable, admired and respected, not only by female readers, but also by the male literary establishment. As the court's influence on literary culture diminished, poetry became less of an aristocratic practice and more women from the middling and lower ranks of society began to write and publish. From the early eighteenth century, we can detect a shift away from the idea that poetry was often the preserve of aristocratic women to a more middle-class model of the woman writer, epitomized, as I will be discussing at a later stage, by Elizabeth Singer Rowe. Although the class base for women poets was considerably broadened in the early years of the eighteenth century, and included labouring-class women such as Mary Collier and Mary Leapor, many women continued to use some of the main practices and poses previously used by women poets higher up the social scale. Whatever their class background, for example, women poets almost uniformly adopted pastoral-sounding pseudonyms and drew on their own social circles as topics for their verses. However, there are also significant differences between the authorial practice of a poet like Finch and one like Rowe. One major difference was the middle-class woman's increasing use of the periodical press. Women had, of course, used periodicals as a way of entering the literary sphere in the late seventeenth century, as shown by Rowe's appearance in *The Athenian Mercury* in the 1690s (the subject of Chapters 5 and 6). As the eighteenth century progressed, however, more and more women reached a wider audience through the pages of periodicals which, in turn, came to rely increasingly on the contributions of women.

The 1730s proved to be a fruitful decade for women's poetic production and this development was partly due to the success of Edward Cave's *The Gentleman's Magazine*. The journal began in 1731 and, despite the masculine bias of its title, was especially instrumental in publishing and promoting women's poetry.[60] In a similar way to the miscellany, the periodical format represents a sociable context for authorship which builds on previous contributions and forms connections between writers and readers. As such, the carefully controlled editorial policy and the impression given of a well-defined textual community of readers and writers which the periodical format fostered, must have seemed attractively safe for the fledgling woman writer. Various women did indeed take advantage of the welcoming environment *The Gentleman's Magazine* seemed to offer and provincial women in particular used this periodical as a way of showcasing their work.[61] Furthermore, after their connections with *The Gentleman's Magazine*, many women poets went on to publish collections of verse, having used the journal as a launchpad for their future publications.

Jane Brereton is one such middle-class provincial woman poet who benefited from the support of Edward Cave and *The Gentleman's Magazine*. Jane (Hughes) Brereton was brought up in Mold near Flintshire but, after her marriage in 1711 to Thomas Brereton of Brasenose College, Oxford, it is likely that she lived in London. Her husband was also a writer. Thomas Brereton 'pursued a literary career in London, publishing verse and two unacted plays, as well as a periodical *The Criticks* in 1718'.[62] Brereton herself published two poems in this period: *The 5th ODE of the 4th Book of* Horace, *imitated, and apply'd to the King* (1716) and *An Expostulary Epistle to Sir Richard Steele upon the Death of Mr. Addison* (1720); the latter poem suggesting connections with, or aspirations to join, the London literary world. Brereton moved back to Wales with her two daughters in about 1721 as a result of her separation from her increasingly violent husband. She settled in Wrexham and shortly after her move Thomas Brereton died: he was drowned in the incoming tide at Saltney in February 1722.[63] Brereton must have been both financially insecure as a widow with two daughters as well as in a precarious social position due to her failed marriage.[64] Despite these inauspicious circumstances, Brereton continued to write, and from the content of her poetry it is clear that she relied on a circle of literary-minded female friends and a lively provincial literary culture. Many of her poems are addressed to women friends in Wales and Brereton fashioned her poetic persona through the use of a pseudonym, 'Melissa'. Melissa is the name of the good sorceress in Ariosto's *Orlando Furioso*, who leads Bradamante to Merlin's cave.[65] This name stemmed from the publication of Brereton's *Merlin: a Poem* in 1735. From 1734, Brereton had also used the pseudonym in her regular contributions to *The Gentleman's Magazine*.[66] In 1734–6 she was part of a three-way debate in the magazine between 'Melissa', 'Fido' and 'Fidelia'. Unbeknown to Brereton, 'Fido' was actually Thomas Beach, a Wrexham neighbour.[67]

Cave's influence can be seen again when he published Brereton's *Poems on Several Occasions* in 1744. Brereton had died in 1740 and this volume had been available by subscription from 1741 onwards to benefit her two daughters, Charlotte and Lucy. Although the project did not attract many subscribers, the list of 120 names did include that of Elizabeth Carter, whom Cave had introduced to Brereton in 1738.[68] Brereton's career serves to broaden our conceptions of female authorship in this period. She is an interesting example of a middle-class Welsh woman who published verse in English and contributed to a major periodical. She represents a new model of the relatively obscure middle-class woman poet who lived apart from the capital city for most of her life, but did have literary connections and did publish her verse. Furthermore, as I discuss more fully in the next chapter, for Brereton, her Welsh identity and the Welsh context in which she produced her writing were central to her construction of herself as a writer and provided her with the major themes of her poetry.

Patterns of women's literary careers

While it is clear that women writers increasingly turned to professional authorship as the eighteenth century progressed, it is equally clear that this was not a straightforward advance for women's writing. A career as a dependent professional was extremely difficult to maintain and many women simply could not make a sustained living from their work. In this sense, then, a writer like Eliza Haywood, who is often taken as the template for the professional woman writer in this period, was an anomaly: and even she could only survive by producing a large volume of texts in rapid succession and by diversifying into other areas of literary production. Diversification was, in fact, typical of the pattern of a dependent professional career in this period. As I have shown, a number of women writers tried different sorts of activities to augment their income which could range from trying their luck as dramatists to starting their own oratory or opening a coffee-house. Many women also drifted into and out of professional authorship as their circumstances changed. Therefore, the image of the professional woman novelist triumphantly succeeding in the eighteenth-century literary marketplace has been over-emphasized in accounts of women's literary history. To be sure, women writers at this time became increasingly aware of the opportunities offered by commercial literary culture and learned how to engage with it, but it is certainly not true that writing could provide women with a comfortable or secure income.

In many cases the writing careers and publication histories of women writers in this period do reveal the growing significance of the literary marketplace for women. However, what these careers and histories also demonstrate is the continuing importance of social modes of female authorship, both in London and the provinces. Metropolitan writers as much as provincial ones benefited from their inclusion in literary circles and many women received the support of their male contemporaries. It is not the case, therefore, that all women writers were fighting against a hostile male literary establishment and were therefore excluded from literary networks usually characterized as exclusively homosocial. In many cases, women were, in fact, the direct beneficiaries of male support and encouragement, whether these male figures were relatives, other writers, or influential editors of popular periodicals. Just as the role of male encouragement and social modes of authorship have been downplayed in favour of an emphasis on commercial literary culture, so too has the importance of the provincial woman poet been relatively ignored. As the careers of Chudleigh, Finch and Brereton demonstrate, a provincial identity did not automatically translate into obscurity. Rather, a provincial location could help a woman's literary career and certainly did not prevent her from interacting extensively with the London literary scene.

The significance of provincial literary culture and the way in which London and the provinces intersected and influenced each other has emerged as an important pattern in the careers of the women writers discussed here. The work of social historians such as Peter Borsay have pointed out that the relation between London and the provinces in the eighteenth century is often interpreted through a 'dominance model', whereby the cultural developments originating in London are then marketed to the provinces and consumed uncritically by the provincial population.[69] As Borsay notes, despite some overwhelming evidence of London's cultural dominance and the indisputable fact that London was the centre of the publishing industry, this is not always an accurate representation of the metropolitan–provincial dynamic. He argues that to understand the interaction between metropolis and province, what is needed is a 'pluralist' model that 'accommodates the vitality and resilience of provincialism and reflects the complex reality of cultural exchange'.[70] A similarly inclusive model is needed to describe women's relation to literary culture in this period, both metropolitan and provincial. Certainly, as the careers of the women discussed here demonstrate, the cultural and literary exchange between capital and province in the period 1690 to 1740 was considerably more fluid than a 'dominance model' allows for. A 'pluralist' model, on the other hand, which takes into account the full range of authorial practices, textual choices, geographical locations, and literary networks operating in the period will come closer to recognizing the scope and diversity of women's relation to literary culture. Such a model is what the remainder of this book will explore.

2
Negotiating Authorship: Women's Self-Representations

Genre and geographical location combine in the early eighteenth century to shape women's self-images. Moving from the broad survey offered in Chapter 1, the present chapter considers how the different contexts and the different genres in which women were writing informed their self-representations. For women novelists, the commercial and metropolitan world in which they pitched their work was central to their authorial pronouncements. In the many prefaces and dedications which accompany women's fiction at this time an often expressed anxiety concerns the blatantly commercial basis of the novel as a genre. This anxiety manifests itself in a number of ways, from the demonstration of a heightened awareness of public expectations about fiction to the adoption of a variety of authorizing strategies which attempt to deflect attention away from any economic motive behind publication. However, what connects women novelists together is an anxiety about audience. This anxiety is a direct result of the mainly urban and anonymous readership created by an impersonal and diverse metropolitan literary culture. As J. Paul Hunter points out, 'Readers were more likely to be urban than rural in 1600, even more likely to be so in 1675 or 1750. Those with the ability to read [. . .] were concentrated in the most highly populous areas, especially London, and were more likely to have urban concerns, attitudes, and tastes.'[1] Awareness of the need to please this readership directly informs women novelists' authorial self-fashioning. In the early stages of the novel's development, women novelists had to negotiate the competing demands of respectability, marketability and possible hostility to the novel as a culturally low genre, as well as justify their precarious positions as women in a predominantly male literary culture.

Genre and geographical context also combine in the work of many women poets of the period. Some of the most popular poetic forms of the time were familiar epistles or letters. Such forms were predicated on an acknowledgement of the influence of sociable literary groups or private friendships rather than a marketplace context. In direct contrast to the anonymous and alien readers of commercial fiction, much poetry of the period includes a sense of a direct addressee to whom the particular poem is written. In the self-presentation of the two poets I discuss here, Mary, Lady Chudleigh and Jane Brereton, it is clear that the provincial and rural contexts in which they wrote provided a framework and rationale for the particular poetic forms they chose to use. Many of their poems are addressed to members of their local community, immediate circle or, more commonly, a particular female friend who is either addressed directly by name or through the use of a pastoral pseudonym. What I suggest here is that appeals to a specific readership, or indeed reader, allowed women poets to circumvent the problem of addressing a wide and unspecific audience and enabled them to disassociate themselves and their poetry from the commercial side of literary life.

In contrast to the professional negotiations of their counterparts in the fiction market, then, poets like Chudleigh and Brereton rely upon a sense of themselves as amateurs. Due to their physical as well as moral distance from the London literary marketplace these poets can present themselves as eschewing both economic gain and literary ambition. An important part of this approach was, of course, women's use of the Horatian epistle. As Claudia Thomas has noted, the 'good-natured sociability' of the Horatian persona particularly attracted women poets as it avoided the harsh invective of Juvenalian satire.[2] Moreover, the Horatian trope of virtuous retirement from public life was ideally suited to women writing in a provincial context. The Horatian model of authorship, popularized in the early eighteenth century by Alexander Pope, provided provincial women poets with a recognized template for their writing identities. Like the use of female friendship, the Horatian mode allowed a public rejection of economic motives or thirst for fame. Many provincial women poets did, however, interact extensively with London literary culture, as shown by the careers of both Chudleigh and Brereton. In many ways, then, the Horatian mode of authorship and the concomitant play on provincial retirement cannot be taken at face value as an actual retreat from literary life or the commercial culture of the London marketplace. Rather, anxiety about the propriety of professional female authorship necessitated a range of strategies which deliberately worked to create an alternative authorial model for women based on provincial amateurism and private virtue. This model, I suggest, should not be read merely as a capitulation to cultural expectations of proper femininity – a physical and moral retreat to virtue – but also as a deliberate piece of self-fashioning which aligned the author with older traditions of coterie as opposed to commercial production. What is also clear is that this alternative model of female literary production is as much to do with marketing the woman writer to a broad audience as it is about retreating from public visibility. As I go on to argue at a later stage, the image of the provincial woman poet living in virtuous retirement was to become an extremely useful model upon which many women writers, both professional and amateur, were to found the basis of their respectability and acceptance.

Jane Brereton's example further extends the context for thinking about women's literary production in the early eighteenth century and suggests some ways in which national difference, as well as a metropolitan–provincial distinction, could inform women's authorial identities. Brereton's poetic use of her geographical location in Wales incorporates generalized invocations of provincial circumstances to denote retirement and modesty, but she also specifically uses her Welsh roots to frame her literary persona and authorize her literary production. Brereton's use of her Welshness is not a straightforward enunciation of national distinctiveness from the English, however. As Linda Colley has argued, 'acknowledging that England, Wales, and Scotland in 1707 differed sharply from each other is not the same as saying that ordinary men and women in each of these countries were invariably possessed by a single and overwhelming sense of their own distinctive identity [. . .] Most of them were not.'[3] In keeping with Colley's perception, Brereton's self-representation as the 'Cambrian Muse' clearly signals her Welsh origins, but her authorial identity is also strongly marked by a stout allegiance to the Hanoverian monarchs. Brereton's location within Wales, at Wrexham near the border with England, also partly explains her English orientation and sympathies. Her poems frequently praise Queen Caroline and the Brunswick line in general. Moreover, her representation of Welsh history demonstrates a decidedly pro-English bias. Despite her mixed allegiance, Brereton's attempts to negotiate her loyalties to the House of Hanover alongside her commitment to her native land demonstrates how images of retirement – in this case the cultural and geographical 'obscurity' of the 'Cambrian Muse' – could enable an articulation of political allegiance and national pride.

Professional images and the novel

Mary Davys

In her ironic preface to *The Amours of Alcippus and Lucippe* (1704), Mary Davys provides a humorous insight into early eighteenth-century expectations of a printed book:

> I should have saved myself the Trouble of writing a Preface, had I not know the expectation of almost all Mankind, which is very much disappointed without one, and will no more allow a Book complete without a Preface, than a Lady fine without a Furbeleau Scarf; or a Beau without a long Peruke.[4]

Davys' comic glance at the expectations of the book-buying public signal her awareness of the commercial codes which dictate the material appearance of a text. Albeit in an ironic way, Davys suggests that her novel must also conform to the whims of a modish reading public. Just as fine gentlemen and ladies adorn themselves with fashionable accessories to enter society, so too must Davys' novel appear properly dressed in public. In the act of satirizing public expectations, Davys reveals a shrewd awareness of the mechanics of commercial print culture. Her remarks suggest that, although ostensibly superfluous, the preface performs an important function in marketing a work of fiction.

Davys' satirical remarks clearly indicate the status of fiction as a modish commodity. In this formulation books are not learned repositories of knowledge or demonstrations of high artistic ability, but components of a material consumer culture which relies on a fashionable, and implicitly urban, audience to succeed. Despite the satire, Davys manages to pinpoint one of the central anxieties facing the early eighteenth-century novelist: how to make fiction both popular and respectable. Prefaces to novels performed a very specific marketing function in this respect by acting as the initial interface between author and reader. However, it is precisely the openly commercial frame of such prefatory statements which could undermine attempts at legitimization. As Laura Runge explains, 'Because many prefaces incorporate blatant attempts to seduce the reader into purchasing the text, the inferior status of the novel is compounded by the commercial grounds of its construction.'[5] The problem facing women novelists, therefore, was not just how to authorize their sex and their status as professional writers for pay, but also how to justify the genre in which they were writing.[6]

Mary Davys employs a range of strategies to authorize herself and her fiction. In her various prefaces and introductory comments to her novels she relies on a combination of classical precedent, her own status as an impecunious widow, and appeals to specific readerships to present her work in the most acceptable light. One familiar method Davys uses to authorize her fiction is to insist on its modesty and therefore its suitability for female readers. In the preface referred to above, Davys makes an appeal to 'the ladies', her target audience, based on the decorum of her work: 'as it is chiefly design'd for the Ladies, so the most reserved of them may read it without a Blush, since it keeps to all the strictest Decorums of Modesty' (p. xiv). At the same time as Davys is openly admitting the commercial impetus behind her text she is providing a means for its justification on moral grounds in relation to specifically feminine codes of modesty and decorum. Her women readers provide Davys with a way of defending her text and her role as a writer.[7] Appeals to 'the ladies' were a conventional way of authorizing fiction. On one level, such constructions could be read as limiting female authority, in the sense that invocations of a female readership could automatically be tied to notions of proper femininity and decorum.[8] However, Davys extends this convention to insist upon the discernment of her women readers as well as their modesty, and she uses this sense of women's critical judgement to make further claims for the worth of her writing.

In the preface to her collected *Works* (1725), for example, Davys reveals an anxiety about the way in which 'those Sort of Writings call'd *Novels* have been a great deal out of Use and Fashion', and suggests that the 'Ladies' to whom she dedicated *The Reform'd Coquet* are more likely to buy 'History and Travels' than 'Probable Feign'd Stories'.[9] Davys suggests that the reason for the public turning away from novels is due to the inferior nature of most fiction, against which her own novels, of course, are favourably judged. Accusations are directed at the 'insipid' nature of some texts, repetition of very similar themes and formulae, and those novels which are 'offensive to Modesty and Good-manners' (p. 87). What Davys seems to mean by a 'novel' here is the French romance. She mentions French 'novels' which 'pretend to write true History', but in reality invent most of the action and convert history into 'all Fiction and Romance' (p. 87). In contrast, Davys suggests that her 'novels' use the 'Advantage of Invention' in the proper manner; that is, 'to order Accidents better than Fortune will be at Pains to do' (p. 87). She claims to have applied Aristotle's theory of dramatic unity to fiction writing by only having 'one entire Scheme or Plot' to order events in her novels. Not only is her fiction formally based on classical rules but, as a result, the content is also more improving than the majority of novels: 'The Adventures, as far as I could order them, are wonderful and probable; and I have with the utmost Justice rewarded Virtues, and punish'd Vice' (p. 87). This claim for moral purpose and didactic efficacy was to become an important part of how many early novelists presented their work. Like male writers, such as Daniel Defoe and William Congreve, Davys confronts the problem of combining fiction with moral probability and therefore with 'truth'.[10] Unlike Defoe's statements in the prefaces to *Robinson Crusoe*, *Moll Flanders* and *Roxana*, however, Davys openly asserts that her work is based on fictional invention not hard fact. But she makes it very clear that her reliance on her own imagination actually makes the morality of her fiction stronger through her adherence to probability and her control of the moral justice meted out to her characters.

Davys' use of the prefatory space, then, indicates her awareness of the marketplace into which she pitched her literary productions. Davys authorizes herself by appealing to classical precedent and contemporary moral expectations, as well as acknowledging the economic power of the reader as supporter, or 'patron', of her work. But Davys' self-authenticating strategies are also gender specific. She is, of course, not only authorizing herself as a writer, but defending her position as a female author publishing for money. One of the ways in which she does this is very familiar: she simply pleads poverty. Davys' main justification for entering print is her widowhood and she emphasizes her respectability by reference to her husband's profession in the clergy. In the preface to *The Reform'd Coquet* (1724), Davys stresses the fact that she has male support and encouragement to publish, but she also suggests that subscription to her work is tantamount to a charitable act. As such, she reconfigures the economic transaction, and her own skill as a writer, as an act of charity on the part of respectable gentlemen towards a clergyman's widow:

When I had written a Sheet or two of this Novel, I communicated my Design to a couple of young Gentlemen, whom I knew to be Men of Taste, and both my Friends; they approved of what I had done, advised me to proceed, then print it by Subscription: into which Proposal many of the Gentlemen enter'd, among whom were a good number of both the grave and the young Clergy, who the World will easily believe had a greater view to Charity than Novelty; and it was

not to the Book, but the Author, they subscribed. They knew her to
be a Relict of one of their Brotherhood, and one, who (unless Poverty
be a Sin) never did anything to disgrace the Gown.   (p. 5)

Similarly, in the preface to her *Works* published the following year,
Davys reiterates her status as the widow of a clergyman. She uses her
widowhood and her late husband's occupation as a way of defending
the publication of her writing as well as the content of her work:

Perhaps it may be objected against me, by some more ready to give
Reproach than Relief, that as I am the Relict of a Clergy-man, and in
Years, I ought not to publish Plays, &c. But I beg of such to suspend
their uncharitable Opinions, till they have read what I have writ, and
if they find any thing there offensive either to God or Man, any thing
either to shock their Morals or their Modesty, 'tis then time enough
to blame.   (p. 88)

Davys reconfigures the rewards of professional writing as charity by
playing on her widowhood to deflect attention away from any crude economic motive. Those who do not buy (or subscribe to) her book are
uncharitable and lacking in pity. As she adds to the *Works* preface, 'And
let them farther consider, that a Woman left to her own Endeavours for
Twenty-seven Years together, may well be allow'd to catch at any Opportunity for Bread, which they that condemn her would very probably
deny to give her' (p. 88). In the preface to *The Reform'd Coquet*, Davys
had also presented her writing as standing in lieu of her ability to provide
monetary aid to those in need. Here she declares, 'tho I must own my
Purse is (by a thousand Misfortunes) grown wholly useless to every body,
my Pen is at the service of the Publick, and if it can but make some
impression upon the young unthinking Minds of some of my own Sex,
I shall bless my Labour, and reap an unspeakable Satisfaction' (p. 5).
Davys thus uses her poverty both to authorize the publication of her
work for sale and to add to the moral purpose of what she is writing. In
the opening paragraphs of *The Reform'd Coquet* itself she is more candid
about the connection between money and writing. She admits that she
writes for money, but is also concerned about her reputation as a writer
and the critical reaction to her work. Davys then directly contests the
idea that commercialism inevitably means bad art, and that writing for
money implies a lack of artistic integrity: 'The most avaricious Scribbler

that ever took Pen in hand, had doubtless a view to his Reputation, separate from his Interest. I confess myself a Lover of Money, and yet have the greatest Inclination to please my Readers' (p. 11).

Davys' description of these readers in the opening of *The Reform'd Coquet* is partly a satire on male social stereotypes, from the classical pedant to the tradesman, but it also serves to signal her awareness of a male audience as well as a female one. Davys dismisses certain types of male readers in order to narrow down the kind of man she will please through her novels. The pedant is said not to be content with any book, 'unless it appears in the World with *Greek* and *Latin* motto's', and she adds that 'a Man that would please him, must pore an Age over musty Authors, till his Brains are as worm-eaten as the Books he reads, and his Conversation fit for nobody else'. As a result, Davys declares, 'I have neither Inclination nor Learning enough to hope for his favour, so lay him aside' (p. 11). The 'Dogmatical Puppy', 'the busy part of our Species, who are so very intent upon getting Money, that they lose the pleasure of spending it', as well as the 'Philosopher', are also dismissed as unlikely readers, again because of their own foibles and Davys' ignorance of their professions and interests. After rejecting these different types of male readers, she chooses instead to 'face about to the Man of Gallantry', whose knowledge of love makes him an ideal reader for her novel, especially as her book deals with the story of 'a fine young lady' (p. 12). In contrast to the man of letters, the tradesman, the dogmatic politician and the philosopher, the man of gallantry is her target reader; a man who is implicitly feminized by his interest in fashion and affairs of the heart.[11] In keeping with her chosen type of reader, Davys chooses the theme of her novel because it is fashionable and commercial:

> Love is a very common Topick, but 'tis withal a very copious one; and would the Poets, Printers and Booksellers but speak truth of it, they would own themselves more obliged to that one Subject for their Bread, than all the rest put together. 'Tis there I fix, and the following Sheets are to be fill'd with the Tale of a fine young Lady.
>
> (pp. 11–12)

Davys' use of the phrase, 'Poets, Printers and Booksellers', clearly demarcates literary culture as a three-way exchange between writers, the printing industry and the bookseller. Davys authorizes her work by foregrounding the importance of the commercial marketplace, and by carefully drawing attention to her place within it as well as showing her familiarity with its operation and her awareness of audience. Her self-image as a writer is, therefore, a complex amalgam of a display of commercial savvy, a claim to be a moral commentator, an innovator of fictional form based on classical models, and the poverty-stricken 'relict' of a clergyman in receipt of charitable support from her readers and subscribers. Davys can be seen to play with different expectations about her readership, both male and female. By pre-empting their responses and their composition, often in a satirical way, she attempts to neutralize any adverse criticism about either herself or her fiction.

Penelope Aubin

Penelope Aubin's reputation as pious and respectable has diverted attention away from her professional identity and the commercial context in which she was writing. The view of Aubin as a virtuous opposite to writers such as Eliza Haywood and Delarivier Manley has become a commonplace in criticism on early eighteenth-century female novelists. What has been neglected in discussions of Aubin is the way in which her authorial self-representation is centrally informed by her wish to sell her novels and her awareness of a commercial readership. In this respect, Aubin's authorizing strategies can be directly compared to Mary Davys'. Aubin also makes a bid for morality to authorize herself and the genre in which she is writing. She is also very aware of the fashions in reading tastes and pitches her work accordingly. Like Davys again, she frequently addresses her work to a female readership. The preface to *The Noble Slaves* (1722), for example, demonstrates her awareness both of fashions in reading tastes and the advantages of a woman writer being associated with women readers, as the following comment illustrates: 'Books of Devotion being tedious, and out of Fashion, Novels and Stories will be welcome. Amongst these, I hope, this will be read, and gain a Place in your Esteem, especially with my own Sex, whose Favour I shall always be proud of.'[12] In the preface to *The Life of Charlotta du Pont* (1723), Aubin offers another careful response to the commercial context she is writing in by indicating her wish to engage in more serious genres than the novel, while at the same time making it clear that she has adapted her writing in line with what her booksellers believe will sell. She employs the familiar strategy of distancing herself from her female contemporaries as a way of defending her own position, implying that the style of most female-authored novels is as 'careless and loose' as the behaviour of her contemporaries:

> My Booksellers say, my Novels sell tolerably well. I had designed to employ my Pen on something more serious and learned; but they

tell me I shall meet with no Encouragement, and advised me to write more modishly, that is, less like a Christian, and in a style careless and loose, as the Custom of the present Age is to live. But I leave that to the other female Authors, my Contemporaries, whose lives and Writing have, I fear, too great a resemblance.[13]

Aubin plays here on the anti-feminist conflation of a woman's writing with a woman's scandalous personal life; the other side of the image of the woman writer which insisted upon chastity and virtue in life and in writing. Aubin does not contest this conflation of life and writing, but builds on it to her own advantage, suggesting that her own virtue and her Christian principles are reflected in her novels. In this respect, Aubin can be said to have it both ways. Ostensibly she refuses to give in to fashion – to write more 'modishly' – yet she does not reject fiction as her chosen genre. Aubin thus achieves respectable status for the novel as a genre and by doing so buttresses her own position as a commercial player in the literary marketplace.

Throughout the prefaces to her novels Aubin expresses particular anxiety about the 'unknown' nature of a commercial readership, particularly a fashionable London readership. As a result she is very concerned to control the effect her novels could have on her readers and worries about how this authorial supervision can be achieved. At the end of *The Life and Adventures of Lady Lucy* (1726) she declares, 'The few Good and Virtuous will, I am sure, read this with pleasure; the Vicious I do not strive to please, but to reform.'[14] In effect, Aubin divides her readers into two types and tries to impose a schematic framework on the otherwise amorphous reading public for which she is writing. J. Paul Hunter's analysis of didactic fiction is useful for making sense of Aubin's anxieties about genre, as well as for an understanding of her concerns about a general marketplace readership:

The potential of novels to guide was seen by many moralists – not just rationalized by novelists eager to justify themselves – as a powerful force for good. But what could guide could also misguide, sometimes with the best of intentions, and again the problem of sending words out into the cold world where unknown and alien readers might make something of them quite unintended became crucial.[15]

In the preface to her first novel, *The Life of Madam de Beaumont* (1721), Aubin is indeed crucially aware of potential misreadings of her work:

In this story I have aim'd at pleasing, and at the same time encouraging Virtue in my Readers. I wish Men would, like *Belinda* [the heroine], confide in Providence, and look upon Death with the same Indifference as she did. But I forget that this Book is to be published in London, where Abundance of People live, whose Actions must persuade us, that they are so far from fearing to die, that they certainly fear nothing that is to come after dying.[16]

She directly attacks the morals of a London readership by suggesting that the immoral behaviour of the rapidly expanding urban populace signals a general social decline and a turn away from proper Christian values. Aubin's novel therefore acts as a social monitor which, through the fictional adventures of the heroine Belinda, teaches readers to emulate virtue and trust in a providential God. Aubin thus deftly undermines the idea that fiction could lead to moral decline.[17] In a direct reversal of the view that novels were morally reprehensible, Aubin declares that fiction is actually instrumental in improving the moral fibre of the nation.

In *The Life of Madam de Beaumont*, Aubin utilizes a morally inflected sense of place to reinforce the idea that her novels will reform a profligate London audience. Her construction of a moralized topography in this novel not only draws on the familiar trope of city vice opposing country virtue but also offsets English immorality and extravagance against Welsh bravery, loyalty and courage. In the preface Aubin directly contrasts the rural nature of Wales with the urban vice of England, specifically London: 'Wales being a place not extremely populous in many Parts, is certainly more rich in Virtue than *England*, which is now improved in Vice only' (p. vii). Wales is set up as a geographical and metaphorical retreat which symbolizes traditional virtues and Christian loyalties. Belinda and her mother, the titular Madam de Beaumont, have lived for over fourteen years in a cave 'NOT far from *Swansey*, a Sea-Port in *Wales*, in *Glamorganshire*' due to Madam's exile from France as a result of religious persecution and inter-familial wrangling. Belinda's virtue is directly linked to her social and geographical obscurity. She declares to her mother: 'Can there be any Pleasures in the World exceeding those that this sweet Retirement gives us? How often have you recounted to me the Miseries and Dangers that attend a Life led in crowded Cities, and noisy Courts' (pp. 13–14). Much of the text is concerned with the dangers Belinda faces as she is forced to leave the retirement and isolation of her cave. The seduction plot surrounding the heroine parallels the London–Wales opposition as the virtuous lover is one Mr Lluelling of Swansea and the villainous libertine is Mr Charles Owen Glandore. Although a relative of Mr Lluelling, Glandore has been perverted by city life and transmuted into 'a lustful *Londoner*'. Aubin comments that 'he, like most Gentlemen of this Age, had forgot the noble Principles, and virtuous Precepts, he brought to Town with him, and acquir'd all the fashionable Vices that gave a man the Title of a fine Gentleman' (p. 56).[18] By contrast, the admirable characters are all associated with the moral virtues of country retirement and these are the characters the reader is asked to esteem and emulate: 'let us imitate their Virtues, since that is the only way to make us dear to God and man', the narrator comments in the conclusion to the novel. Although set in Wales, Aubin's first novel is specifically directed at a London audience. Through the symbolic representation of Wales as London's virtuous opposite, Aubin asks her readers to rise above the majority and reject the immorality of their urban contemporaries. Again, she has it both ways. She attracts the crucially important London consumers by attacking the extravagance of the commercial culture which they inhabit yet simultaneously provides a template for their reformation.

Aubin's novels have recently been seen as playing a key role in the early eighteenth-century market for fiction. William Warner, for example, has placed Aubin's fiction alongside that of Daniel Defoe in terms of sales appeal and projected reading practices. The work of both writers, Warner argues, provided 'an ethical alternative to prevailing patterns of reading for entertainment' and offered a substitute for the amatory fiction of Eliza Haywood in particular.[19] Aubin's self-authorizing strategies are more easily understood if we take this competitive environment into account. By presenting herself quite deliberately as a virtuous opposite to her female contemporaries she can carve a market niche for herself and suggest that her novels offer something different from the rest of the female-authored fiction being sold at that time. Her own fiction attempts to combine the narrative pleasures of both Defoe and Haywood: most of her novels include a providential plot, various shipwreck and captivity narratives as well as a thematic emphasis on seduction and amatory intrigue.[20] Like Defoe, Aubin suggests that her fiction is specifically designed to reform the morals of her readers. However, unlike Defoe, the question of Aubin's gender is of central importance to her attempts to make her novels artistically serious, morally responsible and popular. Aubin's self-authorizing strategies are firmly based on a notion of female virtue whereby the woman writer is justified by her difference from her less than reputable contemporaries. In this sense, the market competition between

Haywood and Aubin becomes less a question of ostensibly different narrative attractions and more a matter of the perceived moral and social respectability of the author. Although Aubin and Mary Davys attest to the artistic and moral seriousness of their chosen genre, what is perhaps even more crucial for both these women is that, as authors, they appear to be as moral and respectable as the novels they publish. Far from being removed from a competitive commercial context, the image of the virtuous woman writer was, as I go on to discuss in the next chapter, a marketing triumph. For woman novelists, a virtuous image was valuable in a directly commercial sense. Although the construction of a respectable persona, as worthy widow or pious Christian, deflected attention away from the commercial market for fiction, a woman novelist's respectability and perceived distance from this market was, paradoxically, her strongest selling point.

Women's poetry and the conventions of amateurism

Early eighteenth-century fiction was explicitly geared to the marketplace. By contrast, it was much easier for poets to claim a distance from commercial concerns. While the novel was perceived to be lacking in literary status, poetry was a much more established and respected genre.[21] Poets did not embark on the strenuous justification of their choice of genre in the same way as novelists. The women poets I discuss here were, for the majority of their writing lives, also physically distanced from the London marketplace and a London readership. Mary, Lady Chudleigh and Jane Brereton did not have professional literary careers in the manner of Penelope Aubin, Mary Davys or Eliza Haywood. Nevertheless, like their professional urban counterparts in the fiction market, Chudleigh and Brereton were directly engaged in negotiating their roles as women writers in relation to a potentially critical literary environment. Furthermore, although they are not explicitly dealing with a commercial audience, both Chudleigh and Brereton are highly aware of the importance of their readership and reception. What I suggest here is that Chudleigh and Brereton utilize the fact of their provincial backgrounds for their own advantage as authors. One method of doing this was by employing the Horatian trope of rural retirement as part of their self-representation. By using the Horatian mode, women could justify their literary aspirations by framing their writing within a context of virtuous retirement which would automatically distance them from the commercial and professional world of London. The Horatian mode of authorship would also mark their poetry as concerned with the higher pursuits of learning and contemplation rather than popular entertainment.

In keeping with this Horatian model, both Chudleigh and Brereton are at pains to construct themselves as literary amateurs who have no view to public fame or reward. However, in contrast to male appropriation of the Horatian mode, as practised by Pope, for example, Chudleigh and Brereton ostensibly reject both a male readership and a male literary culture. Their poems are addressed mainly to female recipients and seem to exclude a male audience either through fear, indifference or a mixture of both. For male poets, retirement from public life could be seen as an integral part of an overall conception of authorship – having served his country, the poet now retires to contemplative life. For women, this trope could have the very different implication of a virtuous feminine retreat to a domestic and circumscribed existence beyond the sphere of the London literary world, which, it is implied, is no place for a woman. On the surface, then, this model of female authorship could be said to construct the newly restricting terms that critics have identified as facing women writers by the early eighteenth century.[22] As an alternative to the increasingly public visibility of the professional woman writer an emphasis on amateur production and rural retirement could been seen as a backward step for women writers.

To an extent, the Horatian model of retirement was indeed reshaped by women poets as a gendered model of feminine virtue and amateur accomplishment. It is also clear that many women themselves used the retirement theme in this way to distance themselves from their professional counterparts and the commercial world of the London booksellers. However, what we also have to take into account here is a new model of female authorship that is emerging in this period: the middle-class, provincial woman writer who does not write from the London literary marketplace nor attempts to have a professional literary career, but who nevertheless publishes her work and views herself as a serious writer. The Horatian trope of retreat from urban life was very useful for women writing from this context. This literary convention provided a framework for the provincial literary circles within which many women poets worked and circulated their poetry. The Horatian mode worked as a way of authorizing women's non-professional status, while simultaneously endorsing their positions as serious writers. Therefore, women poets' use of the trope of rural retirement is not as innocuous or reactionary as it may initially seem. Furthermore, as I show in my final section on Jane Brereton, the image of the woman poet as an obscure amateur could also serve as a way of authorizing explicitly political poetry. Far from being a simple retreat to private domesticity, then, the model of the writer as provincial amateur could provide a range of authorizing strategies which actually enabled and increased women's participation in literary and also political culture.

Mary, Lady Chudleigh

Not surprisingly, given her provincial life in Devon, Chudleigh was particularly drawn to poetry of rural retirement. In her *Poems on Several Occasions* (1703), Chudleigh included a poem which is an exercise in the generic conventions of Horatian poetry. 'The Happy Man' is a conventional rendering of the main tropes of the Horatian mode where the male subject of the poem is praised for his reason and his rejection of worldly ambition.[23] In keeping with convention, the man is seen to prefer rural pleasures to the bustle of the city: 'Both Business, and disturbing Crouds does shun,/Pleas'd that his Work is with less Trouble done:/To whom a Grove, a Garden, or a Field,/Much greater, much sublimer Pleasures yield'.[24] The poem demonstrates Chudleigh's attraction to Horace and the way in which the *beatus ille* theme resonated with her own circumstances. However, Chudleigh does not simply reproduce Horatian ideals in her poetry, she also uses these ideas to explore her own position as a woman poet. Another poem in the collection, 'To *Clorissa*', more directly concerns Chudleigh's own position as a poet. As the title suggests, the poem is framed as an epistle to a female friend, and praises the excellencies of female friendship through the use of pastoral pseudonyms: 'To your lov'd Bosom pleas'd *Marissa* flies;/That place where sacred Friendship gives a Right,/And where ten thousand Charms invite' (1–3). The admiration of the female friend serves as an introduction to Chudleigh's rejection of ambition and power: 'Let others Pow'r and awful Greatness prize;/Let them exchange their Innocence and Fame/For the dear Purchase of a mighty Name' (4–6). The second stanza of the poem presents Chudleigh's conception of herself as a writer within the context of this female-centred retreat. Here she figures 'Marissa' as content in her retirement as it gives her space to write and think:

> When all alone in some belov'd Retreat,
> Remote from Noise, from Bus'ness, and from Strife,
> Those constant curst Attendants of the great;
> I freely can with my own Thoughts converse,
>   And cloath them in ignoble Verse,

'Tis then I tast the most delicious Feast of Life:
There, uncontroul'd I can my self survey,
    And from Observers free,
    My intellectual Pow'rs display,
And all th' opening Scenes of beauteous Nature see   (2.20–9)

In keeping with her Horatian precedent, Chudleigh figures her persona, 'Marissa', as having more liberty in her solitude and retreat than if she were at the centre of business and power. Chudleigh presents the trope of the poet eschewing the world as enabling for 'Marissa' as it allows her to write in an unselfconscious way, free from male expectations of the woman writer and any criticism which her writing may invite. For Chudleigh, solitude and retreat are metaphors for intellectual and literary freedom: 'And from Observers free,/My intellectual Pow'rs display'. As the emphasis on female friendship and female company suggests, the poem also presents a specifically gendered version of the Horatian mode. 'Marissa's' contentment is based firmly on her relation with her female friend and primary reader, 'Clorissa', who is described as combining 'all the Graces of the female kind' (3.61). Chudleigh's retreat is one based on moral virtues centred on an ideal of female friendship; as she declares to 'Clorissa': 'Love, Constancy, and spotless Truth I bring,/These give a Value to the meanest Thing' (4.65–6).

In the preface to *Poems on Several Occasions*, Chudleigh describes the writing of her poems in very similar terms to her poetic portrayal of the woman poet in 'To *Clorissa*':

> The following Poems were written at several Times, and on several Subjects: If the Ladies, for who they are chiefly design'd, and to whose Service they are entirely devoted, happen to meet with any thing in them that is entertaining, I have all I am at. They were the Employment of my leisure Hours, the innocent Amusement of a solitary Life. (p. 44)

Chudleigh figures her writing as the 'innocent Amusement' of her 'leisure Hours' and, therefore, positions herself as a poet in the amateur mode who does not write for fame or money, but instead for the entertainment of her female readers. This stance was to be extremely influential for a number of women poets writing after Chudleigh as it enabled women to distance themselves from the dangers of being associated with the literary marketplace, and shielded them from suggestions of unfeminine behaviour. In the preface to *Essays Upon*

Several Subjects in Prose and Verse (1710), Chudleigh reiterates her earlier stance, stating that 'The following *Essays* were the Products of my Retirement, some of the pleasing Opiates I made use of to lull my Mind to a delightful Rest, the ravishing Amusements of my leisure Hours, of my lonely Moments', and adds, ' 'Tis only to the *Ladies* I presume to present them; I am not so vain as to believe any thing of mine deserves the Notice of the *Men*' (pp. 246–7). Unlike Aubin and Davys, Chudleigh actively repudiates a male audience in favour of an exclusively female one. This construction of a gender-specific readership makes the idea of an unknown audience more palatable. In effect, Chudleigh uses her female coterie audience as a template for her address to a broad readership. She therefore avoids confronting the kind of anxieties expressed by Aubin, for example, and carefully detaches herself from the commercial implications of her engagement in print culture.

Chudleigh's claim that her writing is mainly for a female audience might seem at first to be a conventional modesty trope. However, these statements must also be read in the light of the content of much of her work which, in the tradition of Mary Astell, repeatedly stresses the intellectual capacities of women. As she states in the *Essays'* preface, 'My whole Design is to recommend Virtue, to perswade my Sex to improve their Understandings, to prefer Wisdom before Beauty, good sense before Wealth, and the Sovereignty of their Passions before the Empire of the World' (pp. 247–8). Therefore, as well as being the product of a retired woman's leisure hours, Chudleigh's printed texts are also presented as having a didactic purpose as their primary aim. In this way, Chudleigh can add a moral dimension to her own retired life of solitude and contemplation, as well as gendering the Horatian mode as specifically feminine, and furthering the argument for female virtue as a life of intellectual rather than worldly pleasures. Chudleigh's stance in her prefaces have some interesting parallels to women novelists' attempts at self-authorization. Although Chudleigh's statements make no mention of financial motive, it can be seen that the claims for morality in fiction, and a didacticism specifically aimed at female readers, are, to some extent, similar to Davys' authorizing strategies. It must also be remembered that, despite her presentation of her work as the product of a leisured amateur, Chudleigh did have to deal with the world of the London booksellers. In the *Essays'* preface, for example, Chudleigh claims that her poem *The Ladies Defence* (1701), was written 'with no other Design, but that innocent one of diverting some of my Friends; who, when they read it, were pleas'd to tell me they lik'd it, and desir'd me to Print it, which I should never have had the Vanity to have done, but in a Compliment to them' (p. 248). This statement fits in with Chudleigh's overall self-presentation as a provincial coterie writer, but it must also be read in the context of her dealings with the London marketplace. In the second edition of her *Poems* from 1709, Lintot had printed *The Ladies Defence* without Chudleigh's consent. As Chudleigh explains, the poem appeared without 'both the *Epistle Dedicatory* and the *Preface*; by which means, he has left the *Reader* wholly in the Dark, and expos'd me to Censure' (p. 248). Chudleigh is worried that without her own statements on the text the poem will be misinterpreted as 'an Invective on Marriage' rather than, as she claims it is, 'a Satyr on Vice' (p. 249). Here Chudleigh betrays an anxiety about her literary reputation, and it is in her role as a public author that her claims to write only for amusement must also be read. Chudleigh's authorizing strategies relate to her own retired circumstances and provincial circle of friends, but also engage with her role as a public author that characterized her later years. Far from being a straightforward enunciation of feminine modesty, Chudleigh's complex use of the Horatian mode and conventions of amateurism were to prove enabling for subsequent women poet's self-representations in print. Furthermore, her example was to set an important precedent for future negotiations of the figure of the woman poet.

Jane Brereton

One example of the influence of Chudleigh's mode of authorial representation can be found in the poetry of Jane Brereton. Like Chudleigh, Brereton was conversant with Horatian precedent. In 1716, for example, she published a poem to King George I entitled *The 5th ODE of the 4th Book of* Horace, *imitated, and apply'd to the King*. Another poem, 'Epistle *to Mrs* Anne Griffiths. *Written from* London, *in* 1718' includes a traditional *beatus ille* theme.[25] In this poem Brereton presents Horace as:

> [. . .] blest with all an Epicure could charm!
> His Flocks, his Herds, and his delicious Farm;
> His bounteous Patron, and his noble Friends,
> And every Joy that Luxury attends.   (47–50)

She goes on to compare the fate of Terence with that of Horace, and suggests that if Horace had also lost favour with his patrons and 'noble Friends', 'His sprightly vein he ne'r cou'd have maintained' (46). On one level, Brereton praises the Horatian values of wise retirement, but she is also critical. As a woman of substantially less means than Chudleigh she is very aware that the *beatus ille* is an ideal construction which glosses over any sense of the material wealth and patronal support necessary to support a literary career. She remarks of Horace: 'But had he once to Poverty been brought,/The Bard had wanted many a brighter Thought!' (55–6). In terms of authorial self-fashioning, Brereton's clear-sighted treatment of the Horatian model demonstrates a rather oblique stance on her part which, although admiring, reveals a shrewd equation of prosperity and ease with the possibility of literary achievement:

> A plenteous easy Life, and prosp'rous State,
> Gay smiling Mirth and chearful Thoughts create:
> Those Gifts, tho' to a mod'rate Genius join'd,
> Brighten the Fancy and elate the Mind.   (57–60)

As well as being dissimilar in terms of class status and economic security, Brereton differs from Chudleigh in that she spent at least ten years of her life in the capital city. From 1711, the year of her marriage, to 1721 she lived in London, at which date she returned to Wales. Brereton's use of the theme of retreat in her poetry from the 1710s is therefore framed by her status as a Welshwoman living in London who looks back with longing to her native land. In contrast to Chudleigh, she is not praising the virtues of retirement from within a rural context. Rather, her position is that of looking back from London to her previous life in Wales. The poem 'Epistle *to Mrs* Anne Griffiths' is an extended exploration of Brereton's circumstances and her status as an author, mediated through the Horatian ideal of virtuous retirement. After her invocation of Horace at the start of the poem, Brereton figures herself as aspiring to be with Anne Griffiths, whose friendship is directly linked to the Welsh landscape:

> Oh, how I long with you to pass the Day,
> Sedately cheerful, innocently gay!
> Where *Alyn* glides, to breathe my native Air,
> To view our pleasant Hills, and dear *Moelgaer*.*
> *A mountain in Denbighshire.   (95–8)

Brereton constructs rural Wales as a place where she can fulfil her role as a poet in the Horatian mode. The connected tropes of rural retreat and female friendship have a particular force. In addition to describing the Welsh landscape, in a similar manner to Aubin, as a place of innocent joy and rural pleasures, Brereton also, like Chudleigh, describes her poetry as private verses exchanged between female friends. Unlike the women novelists, then, Brereton authorizes herself by stressing that she does not write for fame or profit, but for amusement only and the private entertainment of a female friend in the country. Far from courting a broad readership, Brereton's poetry is presented for the eyes of only one reader, Anne Griffiths:

> For me, who never durst to more pretend
> Than to amuse myself, and please my Friend:
> If she approve of my unskilful Lays,
> I dread no Critic, and desire no Praise. (91–4)

Even though Brereton is writing from a London context, it would seem here that her authorial persona is based on the evocation of a provincial coterie world of female friendship which avoids both literary professionalism and commerce. However, later in the poem Brereton reveals her apprehension about the censure women writers may receive, and betrays a greater anxiety about the public side to female authorship. She ventriloquizes the words of a London critic who takes offence at her presumption to write and to claim a measure of literary fame:

> BUT should some snarling Critic chance to view
> These undigested Lays design'd for you;
> The surly Blade, methinks, would storm and fume;
> 'How dares this silly Woman thus presume,
> 'In her crude, injudicious Lines to name
> 'Those ancient Poets of immortal Fame?
> 'The Women now forsooth! are Authors grown,
> 'And write such Stuff our Sex would blush to own!' (61–8)

Brereton's authorial self-representation is informed by her sense of how she will be perceived by male critics as a scandalous scribbling woman who desires fame as a writer on equal terms with men. Although she describes the critic as 'snarling' and 'surly', she does not openly contest his image of the woman writer. Instead, she carefully distinguishes her persona from her professional counterparts by presenting herself as an amateur writer of private epistles to a female friend in the country. As such, she circumnavigates the dangers of the potentially hostile literary culture she inhabits:

> That I am dull is what I own and know;
> But why I mayn't be privileg'd to shew
> That Dullness to a private Friend or two,
> (As to the World Male Writers often do)
> I can't conceive:– Dullness alone's my Fault;
> Guiltless of impious Jest, or obscene Thought!
> None e'er can say that I have loosely writ,
> Nor would at that dear Rate be thought a Wit. (69–76)

Brereton ironically aligns her virtue as a poet with her dullness: she may be dull but at least she isn't scandalous. Chudleigh had made a similar move in the preface to *Essays Upon Several Subjects*, where she draws attention to 'the Incorrectness of my Stile', which she puts down to her retired life: 'Politeness is not my Talent; it ought not to be expected from a Person who has live'd almost wholly to her self, who has but seldom had the Opportunity of conversing with ingenious Company' (p. 247). For Brereton, dullness is associated with a retreat from the 'World' into a 'private' space comprising a 'Friend or two'. In these lines she constructs a moral and gendered scheme for authorship. Women writers are associated with a private mode of authorship which, because it is removed from fashionable society, means that the author herself is 'Guiltless of impious Jest, or obscene Thought'. By contrast, male authorship is seen in terms of the 'World', as a public style of professional writing which is witty but profane. Brereton makes a sly comment about dullness being as prevalent in public male writing as it is in private female-authored epistles. Nevertheless, her self-presentation here is firmly based on a sense of the author as private, amateur and without ambition.

As well as making a distinction between male and female styles of authorship, Brereton also directly sets herself against the model of female authorship as marketplace professional. She names Behn, Manley and Haywood in this context as a 'motley Train'. All three are seen to have brought women's writing into disrepute:

> Fair Modesty was once our Sex's Pride,
> But some have thrown that bashful Grace aside:

> The *Behns*, the *Manleys*, head this motley Train,
> Politely lewd and wittily profane;
> Their Wit, their fluent Style (which all must own)
> Can never for their Levity atone.   (77–82)

In contrast to this group of dependent professionals, which also includes Eliza Haywood, Brereton constructs an alternative female poetic
lineage based on those women poets who had reputations for virtue,
and who also appeared to reject a professional mode of authorship:
Katherine Philips (Orinda), Anne Finch, Countess of Winchelsea and
Elizabeth Singer Rowe:

> But Heaven that still, its Goodness to denote,
> For every Poison gives an Antidote;
> First, our *Orinda*, spotless in her Fame,
> As chaste in Wit, rescued our Sex from Shame:
> And now, when *Heywood*'s soft seducing Style
> Might heedless Youth and Innocence beguile,
> Angelic Wit, and purest Thoughts agree,
> In tuneful *Singer*, and great *Winchelsea*.   (83–90)[26]

By association, Brereton aligns her own poetic image with Philips, Finch
and Rowe. These writers cancel out the pernicious effect of Behn,
Manley and Haywood by acting as the 'antidote' to their 'Poison' which,
like the previous description of male writers, is a poison of polite lewd-
ness and witty profanity. Furthermore, in contrast to the urban careers
of Behn, Manley and Haywood, Philips, Finch and Rowe were at various
stages in their careers writing from a provincial context. In addition,
the latter three were, in the 1710s, primarily known for their poetry. By
contrast, Behn, Manley and Haywood were mainly associated with the
professional and commercial genres of the novel, drama and politically
motivated scandal fiction. Brereton therefore makes a concerted effort
to distance herself from the mode of urban, professional authorship suggested by Behn, Manley and Haywood, in order to align herself with
the idea of the woman poet as amateur, private, provincial, modest and
non-profit oriented.

The Cambrian Muse

Jane Brereton's self-representation could be viewed as contributing to
a narrow view of female authorship. The attributes which Brereton

assigns to her ideal image of the woman writer are those of the stereo-typically virtuous female paragon of the early eighteenth century: modesty, chastity, innocence and purity. However, it has been seen that Chudleigh's professions of modesty actually served to authorize her entry into print culture and that, for her, virtuous retreat could sym-bolize intellectual freedom from male expectation. Brereton's use of her self-image is also more than just a passive capitulation to eighteenth-century expectations of domestic femininity. Despite her careful creation of a modestly retiring persona, many of her poems reveal a strongly politicized voice which is closely tied to her Welsh identity and her staunch Whig allegiances. Brereton's only collection, the posthu-mously published *Poems on Several Occasions* (1744), is a representative mixture of occasional verse on birthdays, marriages and deaths, but it also includes some strongly pro-Hanoverian verse mainly addressed to Queen Caroline, the former Princess of Wales. The collection also includes many poems which strongly assert Brereton's identity as a Welsh poet and were mostly written, unless otherwise indicated, after her move from London to Wrexham in 1721. Brereton was widowed in 1722.[27]

In her poem 'To Miss W——s, Maid of Honour to the late Queen', for example, Brereton begins by singing the praises of the 'glorious Race' of Wales, and she uses the Celtic tradition of Merlin's bard as a way of framing Welsh history and representing a Welsh tradition of poetry:

> Long they maintain'd their Country free,
> Nor yielded but to Fate's Decree.
> Subdu'd at last the Homage paid,
> And *Saxon* Kings and Laws obey'd;
> 'Twas then a Bard from *Merlin* sprung,
> Thus to his Harp prophetick sung.   (13–18)

Here Brereton depicts a positive image of Welsh resistance. The freedom of the Welsh as an independent nation has been steadfastly maintained until the eventual subjection to the Saxons. Despite this subjection, resistance resurfaces in poetry as Merlin's song prophecies the return of Welsh glory in the shape of 'Miss W——s', the Cambrian Venus:

> 'From *Cambrian* Race a Nymph shall rise,
> 'Bright as yon *Venus* of the Skies;
> 'Whence *Romulus* or *Brutus* came,
> 'Who gave to *Rome* and *Britain* name'.   (19–22)

Brereton alludes here to the Galfridian myth about the founding of Britain which was notoriously popular with the Welsh. According to Geoffrey of Monmouth in his influential *Historia Regnum Britanniae*, Britain was founded by Brutus the Trojan. According to this narrative, the present-day Welsh were the direct descendants of the Ancient Britons. Brereton reinforces this myth by making an analogy between the founding of Rome by Romulus and the founding of Britain by Brutus. Her use elsewhere of the term 'Cambro-Briton' as a self-identifying marker chimes with her support for the Galfridian myth of origins. Brereton's engagement with these debates are also self-authorizing, of course. The representative of the Welsh nation is a woman, 'a Nymph', who, as maid of honour, will bring the glories of the Welsh race to the attention of court and monarch. Brereton's poems addressed to the king and queen re-enact this process. The poetry of the 'Cambrian Muse' is raised from obscurity to reassert the importance of the Welsh nation as well as show allegiance to the Hanoverian succession. As a result, Brereton is able to authorize herself to speak on matters of national pride as well as political importance.

Despite the celebratory tone of this last poem, Brereton's use of her Welsh identity as a way of authorizing her political views is far from straightforward. Another poem, 'On Reading some Dissertations, in the Reverend Dr. FOULKES's modern Antiquities', returns, as the title indicates, to the subject of Welsh history as a topic suitable for a '*Cambro-Briton*' (11). Brereton's stance is complex in this poem as she attempts to negotiate competing loyalties to Caroline and the Hanoverian dynasty as well as to the Welsh nation.[28] Although Brereton uses her Welsh identity to authorize herself as a poet, at times she capitulates to stereotypes of the Welsh being 'civilized' by the Romans and the English. She declares that 'our warlike Fathers' were 'prov'd' to be 'Fierce as their Wolves', and 'as our Rocks unmov'd' (13–14). Furthermore, 'The *Roman* Arts' (16) are praised for subduing the 'Fierceness' of the Welsh, and restraining Wales from 'savage Liberty' (18). Her invocation of Edward I as 'great' and 'glorious' similarly reveals these conflicting loyalties:

> Still honour'd by our Sex, still dear to Fame,
> Be the first *Edward*'s great, and glorious Name!
> Who abrogated that unrighteous Power,
> By which our Sex enjoy'd nor Land nor Dower.
> No Wonder for this Prince the much lov'd Wife
> Should risque her own to save his dearer Life! (19–24)

Edward's victory over Llywelyn at Gruffudd in 1282, has traditionally marked the end of an era for Wales. As Gwyn A. Williams argues, after 1282, 'The Welsh passed under the nakedly colonial rule of an even more arrogant, and selfconsciously alien, imperialism.'[29] In this context, Brereton's praise of Edward I may seem to be at odds with her position as a Welsh woman, although her stance is in keeping with Colley's claim that many of the Welsh, especially in the border lands, were Anglo-identified. As Geraint Jenkins has also argued, 'Welshmen nursed ambivalent views regarding their assimilation with the English. [. . .] Although many Welshmen cherished a passionate nostalgia for the heroic, distant past, they no longer entertained dreams of recovering Welsh independence. Indeed, there was a strong tradition of loyalty to the English Crown.'[30] Brereton's sex further complicates her politics, however. What Brereton is referring to in this poem is how Edward's importation of English law to Wales may have actively empowered women, widows in particular. Although the traditional Welsh laws of Hywel Dda – *cyfraith Hywel* – have been seen as enabling for women, there were two ways in which Edward's changes to the Welsh legal system could have changed the position of women in the ways Brereton suggests.[31] As R. R. Davies notes, 'on two substantive issues of land law Edward introduced English customs which ran contrary to long-established Welsh practice: he allowed a widow to enjoy a third of her late husband's lands as dower (whereas dower in much of native Wales had hitherto been confined to moveable goods), and permitted females to succeed to land where the male line had failed'.[32] Given Brereton's status as a widow these inheritance laws must have particularly caught her attention, as she notes later in the poem, 'Let Fame to latest Times his virtues tell;/And own his Laws our *Howell Ddas* excell!' (27–8). Brereton therefore uses her widowed status to authorize her to speak on legal matters which directly pertain to her situation. The reference to Edward's wife, Eleanor of Castile, possibly refers to the fact that Eleanor followed Edward to the crusades in 1270. Brereton uses Edward's reputation as a loving husband to further her portrait of him as a friend to women. Given her efforts to name Caroline as her inspiration and her whiggish commitment to the Hanoverians overall, such negotiations of Welsh history to accommodate positive views of an English monarch's conquest of Wales can be seen as an attempt by Brereton to gain favour with her chosen patron. Such efforts on Brereton's part also display the contradictions involved in her presentation of herself as a poet based on her 'Cambro-British' identity. She is caught here between her wish to emphasize her identity as Welsh and her, perhaps stronger, need to present herself to Queen Caroline in a way that fully articulates her whiggish sympathies and wish for royal approval.

Brereton continues the construction of herself as a Cambro-Briton dedicated to singing the praises of the nation in her long poem 'The Dream', an imitation of the second and third books of Chaucer's *The House of Fame*. This poem is a version of the seventeenth-century satiric genre in which various writers compete to be crowned with the laurels and awarded with immortal fame by Apollo.[33] An eagle picks up Brereton's poetic persona and takes her to 'The House of Fame', where she is asked to 'suspend thy female Fears for Shame!' 'Fame' declares that Milton and Newton are 'Justly' bove all my Sons approv'd', but she seems more interested in scandal than poetic worth. The poem ends by the speaker rejecting fame in a very similar way to Brereton in 'Epistle *to Mrs* Anne Griffiths'. As she stands watching the proceedings, someone whispers in her ear, 'How didst Thou to yon Place ascend?/ Thou wilt not, sure! To Fame pretend?' (695–6). To which Brereton's speaker replies:

> No; – let me have but a good Name;
> I will not make pretence to Fame.
> Would Heaven, indulgent to my Pray'r,
> Relieve my Mind from anxious Care;
> A mod'rate Competency give,
> Obscure, unknown, I'd chuse to live. (697–702)

This seems a conventionally Horatian rejection of worldly fame which endorses the idea of the poet eschewing public duty for obscure and private contemplation. Brereton's persona here expresses a preference for a respectable reputation and a life free from financial care as opposed to fame and riches. Brereton therefore reiterates her stance as lowly and insignificant, especially in relation to male giants such as Milton and Newton. Such sentiments can be read as an expression of Brereton's acceptance of her exclusion from the male literary tradition and her wish for obscurity. However, when read in the light of some of Brereton's further constructions of her authorial voice there is another dimension to this ostensibly limiting self-representation.

In her poem to Queen Caroline 'On the *Bustoes* in the *Royal Hermitage*', Brereton constructs herself as a 'Cambrian Muse' in very similar terms to the 'rejection of fame' passage just quoted:

How shall a *Cambrian Muse*, obscure, and mean,
The lowest, latest of the tuneful Train,
Too weak her Wings, too tardy in her Flight,
Amongst their Sterling Coin, dare to present her Mite? (5–8)

The 'Royal Hermitage' refers to a pavilion which Queen Caroline commissioned to be built in Richmond Park.[34] Inside the structure was a series of busts celebrating some of the key Whig figures of religion, learning and ideology: Locke, Newton, Samuel Clarke, William Wollaston and Robert Boyle. In the previous poem, Brereton had emphasized her insignificance in comparison to Milton and Newton. Here she constructs herself again as 'the lowest' of Caroline's 'Train' whose wings are not strong enough to raise her to the heights achieved by such male worthies. Although phrased in the conventions of modesty and weakness, this introduction of the poet actually serves to authorize Brereton's praise of Queen Caroline as 'learned', 'wise' and as a 'Patroness of Science'.[35] Brereton fuses her national identity with her praise of a female queen through her description of herself as the lowly 'Cambrian Muse'. The allusion to the biblical story of the widow's 'Mite' is significant in this respect. In Luke 21.1–4, Jesus watches the rich men in the temple throwing money into the treasury but his attention is drawn to 'a certain poor widow casting in thither two mites' (2). Jesus then draws the moral that even though her contribution is relatively meagre, the widow 'hath cast in more than they all' because unlike the rich men the poor widow 'hath cast in all the living she has'.[36] Brereton appears to be undermining her position as poet by contrasting her weak offerings to the 'Sterling Coin' of Locke, Newton et al. What she is really doing here is using biblical example to suggest that it is precisely her obscurity and insignificance which make her contributions so important. By careful reference to a particularly apposite biblical allusion, Brereton again uses her widowhood as a way of framing her identity as a poet and authorizing her political comment.

Brereton's use of the retirement trope is not an admission of feminine retreat or limit, but instead a way of making political and national allegiances clear. Furthermore, she makes sense of her gender and her geographical origins by fusing her identity as a Cambro-Briton with her status as a woman poet. All these strands come together in *Merlin: a Poem*, which was written in 1733 and inscribed to Queen Caroline in October 1735.[37] In this poem, Merlin is described as trying to find a Welsh bard who can bring him to the notice of the Queen. He looks around but can only find 'Melissa', Brereton's pseudonym from *The*

Gentleman's Magazine: 'But since the *Cambrian Bards* neglect the Muse, *melissa*'s humbler Strains I'll not refuse' (46–7). Brereton makes positive use of the demise of the Welsh bardic tradition. 'Melissa' is chosen by Merlin, Brereton suggests, precisely because of the dearth of any suitable male Welsh poets. It is because of the lack of male competition that Brereton can elevate her own position to that of the Welsh nation's bard.

Brereton's position as a Welsh woman gives her a different perspective on questions of self-representation and literary authority. She uses the obscurity of the Welsh tradition as a way of explaining her own lack of access, as a woman, to the seat of (English) power, both political and literary. Paradoxically, this obscurity also serves to authorize and make visible her position as a 'Cambrian Muse'. Brereton's poetic identity and her use of the conventions of retirement further complicate the models of female authorship that currently shape our perceptions of women's writing in this period. In this instance, a consideration of geographical location as an influence on women's literary production alerts us to an important but often neglected context for understanding the variety of ways women could present themselves as writers. Brereton's example is an especially clear demonstration of how genre and geography combine to shape women's literary practice and of how individual circumstances could directly inform a woman's authorial self-image.

Part II
Authorship and Economics

3
Marketing the Woman Writer: Commercial Strategies

As women writers became increasingly visible in print culture, the various marketing strategies employed to present their work to the public became correspondingly more sophisticated. Publishers of women's writing in this period used a range of tactics to promote the sales of female-authored texts, from collected editions to the use of portraits of the author, encomium poems, biographies, advertisements and prefaces. All these techniques combine to construct the particular image of the author which the bookseller deemed to be attractive to the book-buying public. In contrast to women novelists' self-representations, the most common marketing strategy used by the print trade was to conflate the woman novelist with the amatory themes of her fiction. Various commendatory poems connect the woman novelist's literary abilities with her representations of passion. The success of such an image, which plays on the reader's curiosity about the 'real' woman behind the text, is shown by the way in which this formula is repeated between different novelists. The image of the woman novelist as an expert in affairs of the heart was used as a way of suggesting that there was an identifiable trend in women's fiction, and that all women novelists fill the same template. As such, readers were led to expect a very similar reading experience from any novel written by a woman, whatever her particular agenda or approach might be.

The commercial appeal of the early eighteenth-century woman novelist as a seductive purveyor of amatory fiction has been well-documented.[1] Yet there was an equally influential alternative circulating at this time: the moral and virtuous woman novelist exemplified by the persona of Penelope Aubin. Aubin's commercial appeal lay in her virtuous difference from her 'scandalous' sisters, not in her emulation of them. The image of Aubin as a pious alternative to her female contemporaries was set in place by her own authorial pronouncements in the 1720s, as discussed in the previous chapter. In 1739, the preface to Aubin's posthumous collection of novels, published in that year, reified this construction of the novelist by strenuously disassociating Aubin from her contemporaries in the fiction market. The 1739 collection of novels was an attempt by Aubin's publishers to elevate her work above the majority of female-authored fiction. The way in which this was effected – through a posthumous edition of Aubin's work and a retrospective account of her character and life – was part of a developing trend which used posthumous publication and a biographical account of the author as alternative ways to market the work of women writers.

As a novelist, Aubin was exceptional at this time in being presented as a model of virtuous piety. For women poets, writing in more respectable genres, the image of the woman writer as an exemplar of virtuous femininity was more easily applicable and became increasingly widespread. The popularity of this image of the woman writer is shown by the growing trend for posthumous editions of women's poetry, often compiled by the friends or relatives of the deceased poet. By the early eighteenth century, posthumous publication had, of course, a long history and, as recent feminist work on earlier periods has shown, was especially common for the printing of women's texts which had previously only circulated in manuscript form.[2] Just as posthumous accounts of Renaissance women's lives were characterized by their subject's saintliness, the biographical accounts of Elizabeth Singer Rowe and Jane Brereton from the late 1730s and early 1740s testify that women writers were increasingly being presented in almost hagiographic terms. In contrast to Renaissance lives of exemplary women, however, these biographies are literary; specifically designed to present the *writer* as well as the *woman* in the best possible light.[3] As such, these eighteenth-century lives of women writers have a commercial edge lacking in their sixteenth- and seventeenth-century precedents. When placed in the context of a rapidly expanding print culture, the biographies have a similar function as prefaces to novels. Positioned at the front of the printed book, the account of the author attracts readers to buy the literary product which the exemplary life endorses and frames. Furthermore, the material presentation of these posthumous editions is remarkably similar to that used for women's fiction in general. Portraits, commendatory verses and glowing praise of the woman behind the text continue to be integral to the packaging of the woman writer and serve an equally commercial purpose. However, the ideological construction of the female author promulgated by these posthumous editions presents a very different image than that assigned to writers such as Haywood and Manley. Ultimately, it is the style of authorship suggested by Jane Brereton and Elizabeth Singer Rowe, which was to prevail and prove itself to be the most commercially successful and culturally viable way of marketing the woman writer in the eighteenth century.

Marketing fiction

Material strategies

Given the uncertain generic status of fiction in the early eighteenth century, it is perhaps inevitable that the marketing of fiction in this period mimicked the material presentation of other, more established, genres such as drama and poetry. The marketing of the woman novelist had to justify not only the genre of the text but also the gender of the writer. An important precedent which combined both these desiderata was the fiction of Aphra Behn. As Jane Spencer has noted, the publication of Behn's fiction constituted 'some of the earliest attempts by publishers to market the novel in England as a distinctly modern form, one that could be the basis of an authorial oeuvre'.[4] Although examples of Behn's fiction had been published by William Canning as early as 1688, it is the 1696 publication of her *Histories and Novels* which marks a watershed in the presentation of her fiction. In contrast to previous editions, this collection had all 'the trappings of authorial canonization, a preliminary biography and [. . .] an engraved portrait'.[5] Although the trend for collected works of male dramatists had a long provenance, Behn's 1696 collection marked the first attempt by publishers to present an author primarily through their fiction.[6] The presentation of Behn's fiction provided just the sort of double justification publishers of women novelists needed. The 1696 collection demonstrated that a female author, and the genre of fiction, could be presented in a way that suggested literary status as well as market appeal. The marketing of Aphra Behn provided publishers with rich suggestions about how to package the growing band of women novelists in the early eighteenth century.

One direct result of the presentation of Behn's fiction was the subsequent trend for presenting the work of women novelists via collected editions of their work. In the early eighteenth century, the work of Penelope Aubin, Jane Barker, Mary Davys and Eliza Haywood all appeared in collected editions. Although some of these editions were cross-generic – Haywood and Davys's 'Works' included poems and plays – the primary focus of these collections were fictional texts. Parallels can be made here with the marketing of professional male dramatists in the late seventeenth century. *The Works of Mr. John Dryden*, a two-volume edition of John Dryden's plays and poems, was published by Jacob Tonson in 1691. Collected editions of the plays of Thomas Otway, Nathaniel Lee and Thomas Shadwell appeared almost immediately in an attempt to emulate the collected Dryden.[7] As Paulina Kewes has demonstrated, 'Such sets were made up of left-over quartos and marketed under the name of an individual writer. Each set was composed of old stock which the publishers were hoping to vend at reduced rates.'[8] From a purely practical perspective, then, these 'nonce collections' were 'basically a way of peddling old wares' (p. 199). However, on a conceptual level, 'the notion that old plays would sell better if bound together and marketed as the 'Works' of a Dryden or a Shadwell shows that the names of these authors had acquired high publicity value. They had become commercial assets' (pp. 199–200). I suggest that the collected editions of the works of eighteenth-century women writers served a similar canonizing and commercial function. The appearance of the collected 'Works' of authors like Aubin, Barker, Davys and Haywood represent an attempt by publishers to claim a higher literary status for the commercial genre of the novel and add a veneer of seriousness to texts which could easily be perceived as ephemeral entertainment. Furthermore, by appearing as authors of a corpus of writing worthy of collection, women could be seen to have canonical standing and literary importance as well as commercial appeal.[9]

The first woman to have her fiction collected in the eighteenth century was Jane Barker. In 1719 Edmund Curll published a revised edition of her earlier fiction *Love Intrigues* (1713) and *Exilius; or, The Banish'd Roman* (1719) in two volumes as *The Entertaining Novels of Mrs. Jane Barker*.[10] Barker's name is clearly signalled in the title of the collection as is the genre in which she is writing. Mary Davys capitalized on this trend when the two-volume edition of *The Works of Mrs. Mary Davys: consisting of plays, novels, poems and familiar letters* were printed in 1725 'for the author' and published by subscription. By organizing the publication of her own work in a collected format, Davys could raise her status as a writer, make some money by reprinting revised versions of her earlier fiction, and print some of her work here for the first time.[11] Eliza Haywood had two collections published within two years. In 1724 Daniel Browne and Samuel Chapman published *The Works of Mrs. Eliza*

Haywood in four volumes. Although the volumes include Haywood's plays, *The Fair Captive* (1721) and *A Wife to be Lett* (1724), as well as her *Poems on Several Occasions* (1724), the majority of the work is fiction. *Love in Excess; or, The Fatal Enquiry* (1719–20) comprises the entire first volume and the other texts printed include *The British Recluse; or the Secret History of Cleomira, Suppos'd Dead* (1722), *Idalia; or, The Unfortunate Mistress* (1723), *The Injur'd Husband; or, The Mistaken Resentment* (1723), *The Rash Resolve; or, The Untimely Discovery* (1724), *Lasselia; or, The Self-Abandon'd* (1723) and *Letters from a Lady of Quality to a Chevalier. Translated from the French* (1721).[12]

Considering that Haywood had only published her first piece of fiction in 1719, her publishers were very quick to capitalize on her success by reissuing what they claimed were new editions of her fiction. The presentation of Haywood's works here is slightly different, however, from that of Jane Barker. Haywood's *oeuvre* is presented as 'Works' rather than 'Entertaining Novels', adding a extra cachet to her productions. The term 'Works' implies the result of an entire literary career of a distinguished literary figure. Haywood's publishers are here attempting to present the work of only five years in the context of a high-profile literary achievement. It was perhaps the audacity of Haywood's publishers in presenting her in this way that led, in part, to Pope's famous vilification of her in *The Dunciad*. Pope's attack on Haywood in this poem is usually seen as a reaction to her scandal novels, particularly *The Court of Caramania* (1727), which lampooned Henrietta Howard.[13] However, Pope's derogatory portrait of Haywood can also be seen as a reaction to the claims for canonical authorial status suggested by the publication of her *Works*. Indeed, it is this collection which was the main focus of Pope's vitriol.[14] Haywood's seeming claim for literary greatness through the publication of her *Works* must have seemed to Pope a disturbing manifestation of what could be seen as dunce-like self-importance, especially as Pope's own *Works* had been published in 1717. Like Haywood in 1724 , Pope was only beginning his career in 1717 and could, therefore, quite reasonably be suspected of authorial vanity in the early promotion of his 'classic' status.[15] Although the two collections are very different – Pope's *Works* were printed in quarto, folio and large folio – both Haywood and Pope are young authors being deliberately presented in public as canonical figures at an early stage in their careers. The publication of Haywood's *Works* must have worried Pope, especially in the light of his vigorous efforts to disassociate himself from the literary marketplace and writers such as Haywood. Events like the appearance of Haywood's *Works* must have seemed, to Pope, to blur the line between high culture and popular entertainment.[16]

Browne and Chapman obviously benefited enough from this strategy to repeat it a year later. In 1725 they published the *Secret Histories, Novels and Poems, By Mrs. Eliza Haywood*, again in four volumes, but this time with a portrait by George Vertue (who also engraved Pope's portrait in 1717) as a frontispiece (see Figure 1).[17] *Love in Excess* again served as the opening text, but the collection did not just recycle old texts. *The Surprise; or, Constancy Rewarded* (1724), *The Fatal Secret; or, Constancy in Distress* (1724), *The Force of Nature; or, The Lucky Disappointment* (1725), *Fantomina; or, Love in a Maze* (1725) and *The Masqueraders; or, Fatal Curiosity* (1724) were all new additions. The overall title of this collection has a different effect than the previous use of *Works*. Although none of the texts presented here is a scandal narrative in the style of Delarivier Manley, the publishers highlight the term *Secret Histories* to suggest that Haywood's fiction may include a dimension of scandal and reference to the private lives of real people. This use of *Secret Histories* can be seen as a ploy to grab the attention of the reader, and to play on the popularity of scandal narratives and inside gossip about high-profile society figures or members of the government. Therefore, although some of the texts in each collection overlap, the ways in which Haywood's fiction is marketed shifts from an attempt to represent the author through a serious collection of her *Works* to a presentation of Haywood, and her fiction, as potentially scandalous and salacious. Of course, the generic labels used to describe fiction in this period are notoriously slippery, and novels and histories could often be used to describe the same text. Nevertheless, I would argue that the use of *Secret Histories* was a deliberate attempt to make Haywood more commercial and there is evidence to suggest that this method of marketing was indeed more successful than the 1724 attempt. The *Secret Histories, Novels and Poems* were reprinted in 1732 and 1742, while the *Works* were not reprinted.[18] Haywood herself capitalized on this presentation of her work by publishing two scandal narratives: *Memoirs of a Certain Island Adjacent to the Kingdom of Utopia* (2 vols, 1725–6) and *The Secret History of the Present Intrigues of the Court of Caramania* (1727).

The material presentation of Haywood's collected editions, as with those of her contemporaries, serves to elevate Haywood's status in the marketplace and testifies to the popularity of her fiction and her name as a selling point. The 1725 collection also demonstrates Haywood's continuing popularity and market presence. The publication of her portrait with this later collection can be seen as an attempt to capitalize on

Figure 1 Frontispiece portrait of Eliza Haywood, from *Secret Histories, Novels and Poems* (1725).

Haywood's growing public reputation as a novelist and as a ploy to raise curiosity about the writer behind the popular novels. Such a move is also in keeping with the canonizing and elevating function of collected editions of women's fiction in general. Barker, Davys and Haywood are all raised above the status of mere 'hacks' and instead seen as identifiable authors of a definable body of literary texts. Novels by women, it is implied, could attain commercial success and possess literary merit. By contrast, the novels of Daniel Defoe received no such treatment in their day. On one level, Defoe's pose as an anonymous editor of his fictional texts ruled out any chance to present his novels as part of an authorial *oeuvre*. On another level, and ironically given his centrality in the modern canon, Defoe's style of authorship precluded any attempt to elevate him to canonical status. As a writer, he is a shadowy figure who resists categorization in terms of an identifiable authorial persona. As a professional, Defoe was primarily known for his journalistic activities which, although bringing him wealth, marked him as separate from the world of serious literature and letters.[19] The difference in treatment between male and female novelists was also, of course, predicated on gender. A male writer like Defoe simply did not have the novelty value of an Eliza Haywood or a Penelope Aubin whose sex could, albeit in different ways, dictate the terms of their public presentation as authors.

Commendatory verses

Nowhere is the distinction between male and female writers clearer than in the various poetic compliments which preface women's literary offerings in the early eighteenth century. The use of commendatory verses on the author to introduce works of fiction is another example of the importation of marketing strategies from other genres, such as poetry and drama. Such verse tributes could be applied to men as well as women. The various verses which preface women's fiction, from the late 1710s to the early 1730s, however, pay ostentatious attention to the sex of the author. These verses tempt the reader to buy the novel through an association of the life of the woman writer with the amatory content of her texts. Although commendatory verses obviously say little about the actual circumstances of women's authorial production, they can tell us something about the public perception and reception of women writers. The verses can also reveal how a writer's public reputation could be shaped by the intervention of the booksellers, often in ways at odds with the author's own conception of their status and role. Jane Barker's *Love Intrigues* (1713), published by Edmund Curll, is an early example of the use of commendatory verses to validate a work of fiction.[20] The poem on Barker's novel, 'To Mrs. Jane Barker', was provided by Dr George Sewell, one of Curll's hack writers.[21] One key function of commendatory verses to the author was to conflate the woman writer with the heroine of her text. This construction is immediately apparent in Sewell's poem.[22] The first line names Galesia, the heroine, and draws an implicit connection between Galesia and Jane Barker: 'Condemn me not, *Galesia*, Fair Unknown'. Furthermore, although Barker was in her sixties in 1713, the novel is advertised on the title-page as 'Written by a Young Lady', a tactic which deliberately raises curiosity about the 'Fair Unknown' lady novelist.

Sewell's poem draws out the implications of the title-page. His opening remarks refer to the expectations raised by presenting the text as a young lady's romantic outpourings. However, his poem also works to refine these expectations as the text is also praised for its plainness, naturalness and the appearance of truth. Unlike romances, Sewell declares, Barker's tale is 'so well, so naturally dress'd,/At once with Wit and Innocence express'd,/So true appears, so just, and yet so plain,/We mourn thy Sorrows and we feel thy Pain' (26–9). Here Sewell suggests that the reader vicariously feels the sorrows and pains of the heroine, and, by implication, suffers with the young lady who has written the novel. On one level, then, Sewell's poem serves to authorize the genre of the novel by disassociating it from the 'Poor dry *Romances* of a tortur'd Brain' (7). His poem works to unsettle the connection between romances and the writing of a young lady. However, his praise of the novel is also predicated on the assumption that young ladies are qualified to write about love in more 'natural' way than the 'stiff affected Vein' (15) of the romances. Barker's novel is presented as attractive to the reader because it seems to offer an insight into the hearts of women, and Galesia's personal history in particular. Sewell's poem entices the curiosity of the reader to know the details of Galesia's 'pain and sorrows'. Fools and madmen may be satisfied with the idealized love of romances, but Barker's text offers a 'real' account of the pains of love where the reader gains knowledge of the following emotional truths:

> The Charms of Nature, and those painted true;
> By what strange Springs our real Passions move,
> How vain are all Disguises when we love;
> What Wiles and Stratagems the Men secure,
> And what the tortur'd *Female Hearts* endure;

> Compell'd to stifle what they feign would tell,
> While Truth commands, but Honour must rebel. (19–25)

Sewell's identification with Galesia suggests a similarly sympathetic response from the projected reader with the particular torments women endure in love. He also plays on the prurience of the reader by implying that Galesia's story is a true account of female suffering which would have usually been kept secret because of the dictates of honour and social codes governing women's behaviour in courtship: 'Compell'd to stifle what they feign would tell'. Although this is indeed one of the themes of Barker's novels, Sewell's poem capitalizes on the vogue for secret histories about real people by drawing particular attention to the biographical elements in the text. At the end of the poem Sewell underlines his association of author and heroine by suggesting that Sewell himself is not immune to Galesia's charms:

> And yet the perjur'd Swain, *Galesia* spare,
> Nor urge on Vengeance with a hasty Pray'r;
> Tho' much He merits it, since all agree
> Enough He's punish'd in losing Thee. (32–5)

Many of the strategies used by Edmund Curll to market Jane Barker's fiction were also employed in the presentation of Eliza Haywood's novels. The first part of *Love in Excess* (1719) was anonymous. Haywood's bookseller, William Chetwood, acted as a mediator between the 'young Lady' author and the patroness he had chosen for her. Chetwood himself supplied the dedication to Ann Oldfield, a famous actress of the day. He thus acts as a kind of buffer between the 'young Lady' novelist and a potentially censorious public. The marketing of Haywood soon moved from the presentation of the author as a modest young lady to an open acknowledgement of her identity. The second complete edition of *Love in Excess* for 1719–20 is clearly marked as 'by Mrs. Haywood', and was accompanied by two poems praising Haywood and her writing.[23] The main thrust of these poems is to praise, in extravagant terms, the descriptions of love in Haywood's novel. The poem 'By an Unknown Hand, To the most ingenious Mrs. Haywood' describes how the male speaker ('an Atheist to Love's Power declar'd'), is converted by the force of Haywood's prose, and also, it is implied, by the author herself:

A Stranger Muse, an Unbeliever too,
That Women's Souls such Strength of Vigour knew!
Nor less an Atheist to Love's Power declar'd
Till YOU a Champion for the Sex appear'd!
A Convert now, to both, I feel that Fire
YOUR Words alone can paint! YOUR Look inspire!   (1–6)

The conflation of the 'fire' in the words and the 'look' of the female author, herself the site of desire generated by the text, is continued by the poem, 'Verses wrote in a Blank Leaf of *Love in Excess*': ''Tis Love, *Eliza*'s soft Affections fires,/*Eliza* writes, but Love alone inspires' (8–9). Likewise, Richard Savage's poem, 'To Mrs. Eliza Haywood on her Novel, call'd *Love in Excess*', equates the skill of the author directly with her ability to inspire love and passion in the reader: 'What Beauty ne'er could melt, thy Touches fire,/And raise a Musick that can Love inspire' (7–8). Similarly, in James Sterling's panegyric, 'To Mrs. Eliza Haywood on Her Writings', which appeared with her *Secret Histories, Novels and Poems* in 1725, Haywood is figured as the 'Great arbitress of passion!' (21), and the male reader is said to 'melt in soft desires' (26) raised by the author.[24] The connection between the woman and her work is even more striking in a 'letter' which was published in *The Ladies Journal* on Thursday, 16 February 1727. The author of the letter, who styles himself as 'Love More', encloses verses which are supposed to have been written on 'a blank leaf of a Lady's *Love in Excess*'. Here Haywood's personal knowledge of the pleasures and sorrows of love is directly linked to her proficiency in writing on amatory themes:

Ingenious *Haywood* Writes like one who knew
The Pangs of Love and all its raptures too;
O cou'd I boast that more than common Skill,
Which guides her Fancy and directs her Quill.   (1–4)[25]

These promotional techniques were also used to advertise Haywood in the newspapers. Haywood's *Works* were advertised in the *Daily Journal* for Monday, 12 August 1723 as comprising three volumes, and again on the 17 August. The four-volume edition was advertised on Friday, 31 January 1723/4 as 'The Works of Mrs. Eliza Haywood Consisting of Novels, Letters, Poems and Plays', and included a quotation from William Walsh which served as an epigraph for the printed text:

> ——Go, and to the World impart
> The faithful Image of an am'rous Heart:
> Those who Love's dear, deluding Pains have known,
> May in my fatal stories read their own.
> Those who have lov'd, from all its Torments free,
> May find the Things they never felt by me:
> Perhaps advis'd, avoid the gilded Bait
> And warn'd by my Example, Shun my Fate.

The quotation succinctly outlines all the major effects of Haywood's fiction which are obviously perceived as marketable by the booksellers: the pains of love, the conflation of the woman writer's personal experience with the sufferings of the heroine, the vicarious pleasures and the implicit warning to the reader to avoid the fate presented to them. The extract provides a summary of all the themes and provides the tone of the commendatory verses that would be attached to the novels. In the 1720s, Haywood's publishers certainly believed these strategies to be the best way to market her fiction and attract a broad readership.

'A new Eliza writes': niche marketing

In some oft-quoted lines from his poem 'To Mrs. Eliza Haywood on Her Writings' James Sterling contributed to the growing sense of a female tradition of women writers:

> Read, proud usurper, read with conscious shame,
> Pathetic Behn, or Manley's greater name;
> Forget their sex, and own when Haywood writ,
> She closed the fair Triumvirate of Wit.   (45–8)

The use of Aphra Behn and Katherine Philips as precursors to a recognizable tradition of women's literature was something of a commonplace in commendatory verse written to women writers. What is interesting about Sterling's use of a female lineage of writers is that he replaces Philips with Manley, who is obviously seen as the more appropriate comparison to make with Haywood. Although Sterling places Haywood above both Behn and Manley, there is an obvious attempt here to create a recognizable grouping of particular women writers who would appeal to certain readers. This set of writers came to represent an anti-model of female authorship against which later women writers were keen to disassociate themselves. However, when this poem is set in a commercial context, it is more appropriate to see Sterling's combination of Behn, Manley and Haywood as another marketing strategy designed to promote sales of an author's work. Sterling's poem works as an eighteenth-century version of niche marketing for women's writing. When seen from this commercial angle, it is clear that Manley's name was more useful than that of Katherine Philips as a way of popularizing Haywood's image.

In fact, far from being negative examples for other women writers to avoid, in the late 1710s and early 1730s both Manley and Haywood were used to market the work of other women. Their success in the market provided useful ideas for introducing other women writers to the public. Manley's value as a commodity worked to introduce another woman writer published by Edmund Curll in the 1710s: Mary Hearne. In 1718 Curll published *The Lover's Week; or, Six Days Adventures of Philander and Amaryllis* which was prefaced with a dedication to 'Mrs. Manley' signed 'M. H.' This was swiftly followed by a sequel, *The Female Deserters*, in the following year, also published by Curll.[26] Like Barker's earlier novel, *The Lover's Week* was advertised as 'By a Young Lady' which suggests that, whatever the real age of the author, this was an effective marketing ploy.[27] In the dedication to *The Lover's Week*, Hearne makes it clear that she is using Manley's name to authorize and market her own production by associating herself with a famous author, a known quantity in the literary marketplace. As Hearne declares: 'Writers deal like Strangers in these Cases, who when they are to try their Fortunes in a new Country, contrive to fix upon a standard Name and Reputation to assist their Hopes at their first Appearance.'[28] Hearne plays on Manley's reputation as 'mistress of the art of love', and uses this image to back up her treatment of amatory themes in the text: 'Your Name Prefix'd to anything of LOVE, who have carry'd that Passion to the most elegant Heighth [sic] in your own Writings, is enough to protect any Author who attempts to follow in that mysterious Path' (p. 1). Manley's reputation for passion and intrigue in her writing is not seen as a negative aspect of her fame. Instead, Hearne uses this image as a way to carve out her own market niche and to appeal to those readers who enjoyed Manley's work. As Hearne acknowledges, 'You, MADAM, may lend a portion of your Light to cast a Lustre over these Pages' (p. 2).

In 1732 Elizabeth Boyd published *The Happy-Unfortunate; or the Female-Page: A Novel. In Three Parts* by subscription. The novel uses a quotation from Manley's *Atalantis* on the title-page.[29] As was the case with Hearne's fiction, Boyd's text is presented in a way that would appeal to and attract readers who had enjoyed Manley's productions. The connection with Manley therefore figures as one obvious selling point. Furthermore, after the list of the subscriber's names, two commendatory verses are printed, addressed to Boyd, through her pseudonym Louisa, as '*the Ingenious Author of the* The Happy-Unfortunate'. One of these poems, 'On Louisa's NOVEL, call'd *The Happy-Unfortunate*', specifically evokes Eliza Haywood as a model for Boyd's writing:

> Yeild *Heywood* yeild, yeild [sic] all whose tender Strains,
> Inspire the Dreams of Maids and lovesick Swains;
> Who taint th'unripen'd Girl with amorous Fire,
> And hint the first faint Dawnings of Desire. (1–4)

In keeping with the presentation of Haywood in the poems affixed to her novels, Boyd is figured as raising desire in her readership. The appeal is to readers of Haywood's fiction, and the novel is presented as being in the style of Haywood's work. The panegyrist places great weight on the themes of love and pastoral romance, most famously employed by Haywood herself:

> A new *Eliza* writes_by her the Young
> Instructed, shall avoid the busy Throng;
> Retire to Groves, by murmuring Fountains sigh,
> Expire in Vision, and in Emblem die. (7–10)

Like the power of love in Haywood's novels, Boyd's writing is seen to lead statesmen away from affairs of the nation to hang over 'a gilt Romance' and play the pastoral lover. The panegyrist ends with a fanciful vision of the whole of London becoming amatory lovers through a reading of Boyd's work:

> Methinks I see the crowded *Mall* in Pairs,
> Breathing soft Vows, and hymning am'rous Airs;
> *Whigs, Tories, Cits,* and *Courtiers,* swell the Train,
> And good *Sir Gill* becomes a very Swain. (29–32)

The dominant marketing strategy for promoting the work of women novelists, from the 1710s to the early 1730s was to associate the woman writer with the amatory themes of her fiction. As I argued in Chapter

2, many women writers were themselves alert to the commercial value of presenting their work through an emphasis on its amatory content. A key approach in the presentation of a woman's novels to the public was to play on the associations between the passionate content of the texts and the desirability of the writer herself. The success of such an approach is suggested by the fact that those writers who had reputations for writing on amatory subjects could be used to promote the work of other women novelists. The reputations of Manley and Haywood in this context were obviously perceived as extremely marketable. Although later women writers strenuously avoided associations with Manley and Haywood, in the years between 1710 and 1732, at least, it is clear that their names, and the style of authorship they came to represent, had considerable market value.

Marketing virtue

In 1739 some of the publishers of Aubin's previous novels from the 1720s decided to print a posthumous three-volume collection of her fiction. This edition was presented in order to distinguish Aubin's fiction from the novels of her female contemporaries. The different approach taken for Aubin is immediately apparent in the title of the three-volume collection: *A Collection of Entertaining Novels and Histories designed to promote the Cause of Virtue and Honour.* Rather than imply a scandalous element to the fiction presented, the publishers here draw attention to the moral intentions of the author and the didactic nature of her fiction. Just as Haywood's publishers attempted to market her work as a type of 'secret history', Aubin's publishers here make a deliberate ploy to market their author as moral and virtuous. Although an emphasis on sexuality and passion is typically seen to be the main way in which women novelists were marketed in this period, this collection suggests that virtuous femininity was an equally commercial selling point for the woman novelist. The preface to this collection is presented as a plural endeavour. This could suggest that it was written by the publishers themselves, who boast that 'We present the Publick with a Collection of Novels, written by the late ingenious Mrs. PENELOPE AUBIN, and published by her, at different times, singly, and with no small success' (p. 2). As well as building on Aubin's previous success, the preface also carefully distinguishes their writer from the majority of female-authored fiction. Aubin is described as 'preserving that Purity of Style and Manners' in her fiction, whereas the unnamed female contemporaries are 'like fallen Angels, [whom] having left their own Innocence, seem, as one would think by their Writings, to make it their study to corrupt the Minds of other[s], and render them as depraved, as miserable, and as lost as themselves' (p. 3). By contrast, Aubin is presented as having 'a far happier Manner of Thinking and Acting'. The writers of the preface claim that, 'Our Design is not to attempt to establish this Collection at the Expence of others, or, indeed, on any other Footing, than that of its own Merit' (p. 3). Yet it is clear that they are creating a particular market niche for Aubin as a respectable woman novelist precisely at the expense of other women writers. These other writers, the most prominent of whom would have been Manley and Haywood, are attacked through a conflation of their lives and their writing. As a result of their personal depravity they write fiction which will corrupt and destroy their readers. Aubin's aims and the effects of her fiction, as constructed by the preface, are directly opposite to the perceived dangers of novels by other women writers. Rather than corrupting the reader, Aubin's texts serve to increase the nation's morality. The writers of the preface validate their own publishing enterprise by constructing the market opposition as not only morally defective but actively pernicious. Aubin's contemporaries from the 1720s are carefully edged out of the marketplace by being deemed unsuitable reading matter.

In this edition of a woman's collected fiction, the woman novelist is constructed as a virtuous exemplar. Aubin's life and character are seen to endorse the moral tone of her fiction. She is presented as superior to the majority of her sex, not only because of her innate ability but also due to her associations with persons of a higher class than herself: 'She had no contemptible Share of Learning, surpassing what is usual in her Sex. She had excellent natural Talents, which were improved by Reading and Observation, as well as her conversations with Persons as much distinguished by their Rank as for their good understanding' (p. 3). The later section of the preface prints carefully selected extracts from Aubin's own prefaces and dedications which particularly demonstrate the image of Aubin put forward here. In order to reinforce their image of Aubin, the preface specifically names Elizabeth Singer Rowe as a way of endorsing Aubin's respectability:

> *The Life of Charlotta du Pont* she dedicates to the celebrated Mrs. Rowe, with whom she had an Intimacy, as we there see, and may farther reasonably infer from the Tenor of both their Writings, for the Promotion of the Cause of Religion and Virtue, and from that Affinity and Kindred of Souls, which will always make the Worthy find out

one another, and create stronger Ties of Union and Friendship than those of Blood. (p. 5)

It is far from certain than Aubin ever knew Rowe on a personal level.[30] Furthermore, the dedication to *Charlotta du Pont* does not necessarily refer to Mrs Rowe the author. The connection between Aubin and Rowe, a well-known female exemplar, is deliberately used here to justify Aubin's writing and character. The writers of the preface draw an implicit parallel between the writing and characters of Rowe and Aubin in order to forge an alternative tradition of women's writing based on 'Religion and Virtue'.

Through its carefully controlled presentation of Aubin as a moral writer, the preface betrays anxieties about the genre of the novel. It has been suggested that the author of the preface was Samuel Richardson.[31] Richardson also attempted to distinguish his fiction from Behn, Manley and Haywood, and frequently claimed a higher moral purpose for the novel as a genre. Furthermore, the booksellers involved in the publication of Aubin's collection of novels were known to Richardson personally through the trade. Charles Rivington, Arthur Bettesworth and Thomas Longman, in particular, who had all been involved with Aubin's previous publications, were Richardson's associates in business.[32] It is therefore likely that these booksellers could have asked Richardson to supply a preface to their collection, particularly as Aubin's pronouncements on her fiction chimed with Richardson's claims a year later in the editorial commentary for *Pamela*. In addition, as Wolfgang Zach has argued, there are many stylistic and theoretical parallels between the 1739 preface and Richardson's commentary on his own fiction.[33]

Whoever was behind the preface, it is clear that these bookseller associates chose Aubin's fiction to validate the project of the novel along reformist lines. Indeed, the endorsement of the novel and the justification of the woman novelist are directly linked. The preface enumerates five 'rules' for the writing of novels which emphasize that fiction should demonstrate a 'purity of style', a sense of social duty, as well as the punishment of vicious characters and the reward of virtuous ones. Lastly, fiction should also have 'an Air of Probability, that the Example may have the greater Force upon the Minds it is intended to reform' (p. 3). Aubin's fiction is said to demonstrate all these qualities, but what is significant is the way in which her example, and the 'rules' set down in the preface, are then used to elevate the novel, and women's writing,

from its disreputable position. In relation to the 'rules', the preface
declares:

> If these, among others that might be enumerated, may be said to be
> the indispensable Requisites of a good Novel, we must confess, with
> Concern, that they have been too seldom observed by those who
> have undertaken this species of Writing, insomuch that it has
> brought a Disreputation on the very Name. And we are still more
> sorry to have Reason to say, That those of the Sex, who have gener-
> ally wrote on these Subjects, have been far from preserving that
> Purity of Style and Manners, which is the greatest Glory of a fine
> Writer on any Subject.   (p. 3)

As William Warner has suggested, this may be an attempt by Richardson
to pave the way for the publication of *Pamela*.[34] It is also apparent that
the 'bad' novel, as it were, is specifically female. It is the female sex
who have given the novel a bad name. At the same time, however, the
preface uses a female novelist as a way of authorizing a different
type of novel, one based on purity and didacticism. The work of
women writers such as Aubin and Rowe, act as antidotes to the poison
of those 'fallen Angels', the majority of other women novelists in the
marketplace.

Aubin's example, and her fiction, may have been serving another
purpose here: namely, to authorize Richardson's forthcoming publications, if indeed he did write the preface. What is more significant for
my argument here, however, is that Aubin is being carefully distinguished from her female contemporaries to provide another way of
marketing the work of a woman writer. Under such instructions, most
readers would be keen to disassociate themselves from the fiction and
the writers who are typed as disreputable. Furthermore, the image of
the woman novelist as moral and virtuous serves to authorize the genre
of the novel in a broader sense. Although fiction is still gendered
feminine, it is the alternative values of proper female conduct that are
emphasized here, rather than the stress on scandal and sexuality. As the
century progressed, the use of feminine virtue as a marketing strategy
was to outpace the sexualized image of the woman writer as a way of
selling women's writing to the reading public. Despite the popular
success of Eliza Haywood in the early eighteenth century, it was the
alternative image of the woman writer as virtuous and respectable
which was to prove the most enduring, influential, and commercially
viable.

Literary biography as marketing strategy

The most usual format for presenting the work of women poets in the late seventeenth and early eighteenth centuries was to use a variation on *Poems on Several Occasions*. Such collections allowed women to include a range of miscellaneous poems in one volume and often included a life of the author, a selection of her letters, and some verses on her work. Another prominent way in which women poets were represented was through posthumous collections. In 1739, Richard Hett and Robert Dodsley published *The Miscellaneous Works in Prose and Verse of Mrs. Elizabeth Rowe* in two volumes, complete with a portrait of the author by George Vertue (Figure 2), various commendatory verses, and a 'Life' which was begun by Henry Grove, a family friend, and completed by the poet's brother-in-law Theophilus after Grove's death. Four years after her death in 1740, the collected poems of Jane Brereton were published by subscription, and were also prefaced by a biography of the author. Another, slightly later, example of a woman's posthumous publication was Catherine Trotter Cockburn. Her works were collected by Thomas Birch in 1752 as the *Works of Mrs. Catherine Trotter, Theological, Moral, Dramatic and Poetical*. This collection also included a biography of the author written by Birch. Earlier examples of this publication method include Anne Killigrew's *Poems by Mrs. Anne Killigrew* (1686), and Mary Monck's *Marinda. Poems and Translations upon several Occasions* (1716). Killigrew's poems included the famous commendatory ode on the author by John Dryden. Both collections were the result of the intervention of the fathers of the two writers who were responsible for the printing of their daughters' previously unpublished poetry.[35]

Posthumous collections of women's poetry became increasingly popular from the late 1730s onwards. The collections are carefully tailored to present the woman writer as a virtuous exemplar and, in many cases, to present her life as one of retirement and her poetry as the result of her leisure hours. In the case of Rowe and Trotter, the male editors do not include the early works of the author which are described as youthful follies or juvenile indiscretions. Rowe's editors do not mention her 1696 *Poems Written by Philomela*, nor do they mention her early incarnation as the *Athenian Mercury*'s 'Pindarick Lady'. Her political verse from the 1690s, the focus of Chapter 5, is similarly omitted. For Cockburn's *Works*, Birch chose only one of her plays, *The Fatal Friendship*, and left out her fiction *Olinda's Adventures; or, The Amours of a Young Lady*. The title of Cockburn's *Works* foregrounds her theo-

Figure 2 Frontispiece portrait of Elizabeth Singer Rowe, from *The Miscellaneous Works in Prose and Verse* (1739).

logical and moral work and makes no mention of her fiction. By the late 1730s and into the 1750s, it can be seen that the collected works of women writers no longer capitalized on the commercial appeal of fiction, but instead focused on different genres which seemed more appropriate to the particular image of female authorship being presented.[36] Although the material format of such collections remained constant, the content is carefully adapted and any text or piece of information which may seem at odds with the image of respectable female authorship being promoted is deliberately left out.

In order to gauge the model of female authorship which these editions construct it will be useful to focus on the representation of two women poets through the posthumous biographies which preface their work. 'The Life of Mrs. Elizabeth Rowe', with which I begin, sets some key precedents for subsequent biographical commentary and provides the parameters for later constructions of female authorship. The influence of Rowe's biography as a template for other treatments of the woman poet can be seen by the parallels between this text and 'An Account of the Life of Mrs. Brereton', which prefaced Brereton's 1744 collection of poems. What I trace here is the way in which these biographical accounts shape conceptions of female authorship through particular tropes such as the retired provincial woman poet, the amateurism of women's writing, and the presentation of the woman writer as fulfilling expectations about respectable femininity. Overall, I suggest that this model of female authorship should not be dismissed simply as a conservative reaction to the image of the woman writer offered by Haywood's booksellers, for example. Rather, I argue that the construction of female authorship as an appropriate occupation for a respectable woman is another way in which the work of women writers could be successfully marketed to the reading public.

'The Life of Mrs. Elizabeth Rowe'

'The Life of Mrs. Elizabeth Rowe' acts as a preface to Rowe's *Miscellaneous Works*.[37] The biography manipulates the reader into assessing Rowe's work through the careful presentation of the author's life. The reader must digest the biography before reaching Rowe's own writing and is thus prepared to read her texts in the light of the exemplary portrait. It is difficult to read the 'works' without being influenced by the 'life'. Throughout the biography, Rowe's life and works are intimately connected. A devout Christian life provides the particular template for ideal female authorship. Henry Grove mentions Rowe's 'fine writing' and the 'amiable qualities of her heart' (p. iv) in the same sentence. Theophilus Rowe completes the association, carefully choosing which of Rowe's works best illustrates his point:

> Her writings give a faithful picture of her soul. Her profound humility, and supreme affection to God; her faith in his promises, and dependence on his providence; her zeal for glory, and love to the holiness of his laws, appears in the strongest light in her works; and particularly in her *Devotions*.   (p. lxxxiv)[38]

The stress on Rowe's piety connects this literary biography to spiritual biographies of women popular in the sixteenth and seventeenth centuries. As Suzanne Trill has observed, exemplary lives, such as Philip Stubbes' memoir of his wife Katherine, *A Crystall Glasse, for Christian Women* (1591), 'sought to define the character of the ideal Christian woman'.[39] Such an exemplary Christian woman would, like Katherine Stubbes, have suitably feminine virtues, such as 'wisdom, piety, humility, meekness, love, constancy, charity, good household government and godly devotion'.[40] Stubbes' memoir continued to be printed up to 1700 and his version of exemplary Christian femininity obviously resonates with the 1739 portrait of Rowe. Like Katherine Stubbes, Rowe has 'profound humility', deep piety, 'zeal for glory' and a trust in God's providence. As dissenters, it is extremely likely that both Grove and Theophilus Rowe were familiar with the writings of the Puritan Philip Stubbes. Rowe's zealous style of religious worship is thus another connection between the eighteenth-century writer and her sixteenth-century counterpart. As well as being a model of domestic virtue, Katherine Stubbes, like Rowe, is also characterized by 'her fervent zeal' and religious devotion.[41] What is different about Rowe is that her Christian virtue serves to authorize her as a writer. Paradoxically, but also in a similar way to which spiritual biographies endorse women's religious utterance, Rowe's humility as a Christian legitimizes her as a published author. In effect, an older model of exemplary femininity is being adapted to create an ideal image of the woman writer whose work reinforces her piety and Godliness. As her brother-in-law states: 'Her writings give a faithful picture of her soul.'

Such an image, however, depends on a careful foregrounding of appropriate texts from an author's *oeuvre*. In contrast to the emphasis on her later religious writing, Theophilus only gives a very brief mention of Rowe's first publication, *Poems on Several Occasions Written by Philomela*. These poems were published by the entrepreneurial bookseller John Dunton as a result of Rowe's dealings with his periodical the *Athenian Mercury*, which I discuss in my final two chapters. Theophilus completely avoids discussing the then Elizabeth Singer's connections with a London bookseller and reconfigures the publication of her poems as an offshoot of coterie encouragement: 'In the year 1696, the 22nd of her age, a collection of her poems on several occasions was publish'd at the desire of her friends' (p. xv). These early productions are said to have been troubling for the mature Rowe. Although Theophilus stresses that they were 'consistent with the strictest regard for the rules of virtue' (p. xvi), his anxiety that the early poetry may contradict the image of Rowe he is presenting is palpable. His 'editing' of Rowe's life is reflected in the editorial choices of the collection. The 1696 poems are not included in the *Works*, except for those poems which appeared in various miscellanies in the early eighteenth century.[42] Theophilus states that it would be 'violating the respect due to Mrs. *Rowe*' to 'endeavour to revive the memory of her first attempts at poetry, which, as juvenile follies, she thought only worthy of perpetual oblivion' (p. li). Many of the poems Theophilus excludes are of an overtly political nature; a part of Rowe's authorial identity which does not fit easily with the ideal image created by the biography.

The 'authorized' biography may have also been written, in part, as a corrective to an unauthorized edition of Rowe's poems, published by Edmund Curll in 1736. The fact that Curll saw fit to reproduce a collection of Rowe's 1690s poems in the mid-1730s demonstrates the commercial value of her name and reputation. The collection was titled *Philomela; or, Poems by Mrs. Elizabeth Singer, now Rowe, of Frome in Somersetshire* and was completely ignored by Theophilus Rowe. However, his insistence that the 1696 poems be forgotten suggests that he was responding, albeit covertly, to this recent reprint and to the commercial context Rowe was placed in by Curll. As a further insult, Curll included an 'Account' of Rowe's 'poetical life' in the dedication to Alexander Pope. In contrast to the 1739 biography, Curll unearths Rowe's dependence on the Athenians at the start of her literary career: 'Among their *numerous* Correspondents, this Lady was *One*, under the Name of PHILOMELA. Several of her Productions were published by these our *English-Athenians*' (p. iv). Curll also reprints examples of the verses to Rowe which had appeared in the *Mercury*. For example, he includes a long poem dedicated 'To the Author, known only by Report, and by Her Poems'. As in the commendatory verses on Eliza Haywood, 'Philomela' is seen to inspire love and devotion in the male reader: 'In vain, alas! In vain our Fate we shun;/We read, and Sigh, and Love, and are Undone' (p. xi).[43] This image of the woman writer as amatory heroine who inspires love and passion in her male reader through the force of her poetry is precisely the kind of construction the 1739 biography is trying to avoid. In this instance, Henry Grove and Theophilus Rowe were more astute than Curll in creating an image of the woman writer which would appeal to the popular imagination in the late 1730s. It is their version of Rowe which was to prove both enduring and extremely influential, not only for Rowe's own reputation, but also for many women writing in her wake.[44]

To further the virtuous image of Rowe, the biography uses the ideal of retirement from worldly pleasures as a way of contextualizing her literary production. After the death of her husband, Thomas Rowe, Rowe is figured as being able to indulge her 'unconquerable inclinations to solitude' when she left the 'town' in order 'to conceal the remainder of her life in absolute solitude' (p. xxxiii). It is true that Rowe did leave London after her husband's death for Frome in Somersetshire, but in the biography this fact attains a symbolic status which provides a Christian framework for her life and authority for her writing. Rowe's provincial context and her poetic talent are yoked together as evidence of her virtuous character: 'The love of solitude, which seems almost inseparable from poetic genius, discovered itself very early in Mrs. *Rowe*, and never forsook her but with life itself' (p. lvi). The link between literary talent and provincial retreat feeds into the image of the modest woman writer. The biography places great stress on Rowe's lack of vanity and the absence of 'art' in her writing. Rowe is not presented as a professional or learned author, but through a gendered model of authorship based on notions of feminine accomplishment and amateur coterie amusement:

> She read no critics, nor could her genius brook the discipline of rules: And as the pains of correcting appeared to her some kind of drudgery, she seldom made any great alteration in her composures from what they were when she first gave copies of them to her friends. For she did not set so high a value on her work, as to employ much labour in finishing them with the utmost accuracy; and she wrote verses through inclination, and rather as an amusement, than as a study or profession, to excel in which she should make the business of her life. (p. liv)

Here Rowe is firmly placed in opposition to a professional model of female authorship: 'inclination' and 'amusement' are carefully balanced against writing as a 'profession' or 'business'. Although this construction owes something to eighteenth-century notions of the poet as a natural genius, when applied to a woman writer this trope quickly assumes the connotations of lack of pride in achievement and the absence of professional labour in composition. The biography uses Rowe's lack of professionalism as further evidence of her modesty and discretion.[45]

Rowe's provincial context is used again to authorize her prose works *Friendship in Death* (1728) and *Letters Moral and Entertaining* (1729–33). It is stated that Rowe composed her 'most celebrated works' in the 'recess' of Frome (p. xxxiv), thus continuing the equation of virtuous retreat and respectable female authorship. Like the commentary on Penelope Aubin's novels, the biography here draws an implicit parallel between Rowe's virtuous character and the moral message of her writing, as well as assuaging any anxieties about the fact that Rowe wrote fiction:

> The design of both of *these* [. . .] is, by fictitious examples of the most generous benevolence and heroic virtue, to allure the reader to the practice of every thing that ennobles human nature, and benefits the world; and by just and lively examples of the sharp remorse and real misery that attend the false and unworthy satisfactions of vice, to warn the young and unthinking from being seduced by the enchanting name of pleasure, to inevitable ruin; the piety of which design is the more worthy of the highest panegyrics, as it is so uncommon.
>
> (pp. xxxiv–xxxv)

As well as stressing the piety of Rowe's fictional texts, the biography also insists on Rowe's reluctance to publish. Her *History of Joseph* (1736) was only printed because of the 'importunity of some of Mrs. *Rowe's* acquaintance' (p. xxxv); the author herself is said to have shown 'real reluctance to suffer it to be made public'. Theophilus Rowe quotes from a private letter where Rowe asserts that she 'had no other view in their publication but the profit, or innocent entertainment of the reader' (p. li). Furthermore, it is claimed, Rowe 'rarely mentioned any of her writings, even to her most intimate friends; nor ever discover'd the least elation at their great success, and the approbation they received from some of the finest writers of the age' (p. lxiii). This modesty is, of course, linked to a Christian contempt of riches and earthly glory. Here, however, it is used to underline further Rowe's amateur status:

> She could not be persuaded to publish her works by subscription, or even to accept the advantageous terms offered by the bookseller, if she would permit her scattered pieces to be collected and published together. She wrote no dedications to the great, and the name of no minister of state is to be found in her works.   (p. lxvii)

Rowe is thus removed from all the different manifestations of an economically driven literary culture. In this construction, she totally eschewed economic gain as well as avoided all forms of patronage and politics.

The biography also places great emphasis on Rowe's wish for anonymity which is again linked to her indifference to fame and her love of 'obscure solitude' (p. lxi). Theophilus denounces the practice of authorial prefaces and commendatory verses as examples of a love of glory. In contrast, Rowe 'wrote no prefaces to any of her works to pre-possess the publisher in their favour, nor suffered them to be accompanied with panegyrics of her friends. She would not, indeed, so much as allow her name to be prefixed to any of them' (p. lxix). In addition, any money Rowe did make from her writing is redirected for charitable ends. On first receiving money for her work, Rowe is said to have 'bestow'd the whole sum on a family in distress; and there is great reason to believe that she employed all the money she ever received on such an account in as generous a manner' (p. lxxix). Even the financial reward Rowe did receive from her writing is taken out of a professional context and used to reinforce her character of altruistic piety.

In its drive to present a version of female authorship as non-commercial, non-profit-oriented, modest, obscure and provincial, the biography is fundamentally contradictory, and frequent fissures appear in the attempt to maintain such an ideal image. In the first instance, the biography itself can be said to contradict the claims it makes as what it is doing is increasing Rowe's public visibility as a writer by commemorating her life and raising curiosity about the author and her work. The 'Life' is itself a commercial product designed to make Rowe's work attractive to the public. Indeed, Theophilus Rowe and/or the publishers must have been the primary recipients of any money that the collection generated. Throughout the biography it is also made clear that, albeit despite herself, Rowe was extremely successful as an author, and that the 'Life' is, in part, an extended advertisement for her works. Furthermore, the *Miscellaneous Works* provide precisely the sort of publicity that Rowe was said to shun. As well as the 'Life' and the portrait, the *Works* include commendatory verses by Isaac Watts, Henry Grove,

Joseph Standon and Thomas Amory as well as elegies by Elizabeth Carter and Nicholas Munckley.[46] Theophilus himself contributed two commemorative poems. The 'Life' was also serialized in *the Gentleman's Magazine* from May 1739 to February 1740 with other comments and letters about Rowe.[47] The biography was consistently republished in other editions of Rowe's works. From 1740 onwards, *Friendship in Death* (with *Letters Moral and Entertaining*) was often printed with 'an account of the author's life' which, when it appeared, was mentioned specifically in the title and was obviously an additional selling point.[48] Rowe's continuing popularity throughout the eighteenth century was due, in part, to the commercial appeal of the model of female authorship that the biography constructs. Although the biography attempts to obscure Rowe's fame and commercial success, the 'Life' actually increased her popular appeal.

An account of the life of Mrs Brereton

Jane Brereton's *Poems on Several Occasions by Mrs. Jane Brereton with Letters to her Friends and An Account of her Life* was published by Edward Cave, the editor of the *Gentleman's Magazine*, in 1744. Brereton had died in August 1740, and the poems were published by subscription probably to benefit her two remaining children Charlotte and Lucy. The life is most likely to have been written by Charlotte Brereton who, like her mother, was a poet, and had also contributed to Cave's *Magazine*. There are some striking similarities between the account of Brereton's life and the 1739 biography of Rowe which suggests that Charlotte was aware of the Grove–Rowe biography, as well as alert to the advantages of using Rowe's authorial image as a model for her mother. Given Charlotte's connections with the *Gentleman's Magazine*, this is extremely likely as Rowe was a popular topic in the journal and, as I have noted, the 'Life' of Rowe was also serialized in the *Magazine*. Jane Brereton herself also appears to have been a reader and avid admirer of Rowe and her work. One of the letters printed in the collection is an extended essay on Rowe's writing.[49] The inclusion of letters by the author in a poetry collection also stemmed from Rowe's works, which also printed a series of letters to and from Rowe before the text begins. What I want to argue here is not only that Charlotte Brereton, a writer herself, was directly influenced by the 1739 biography of Rowe, but also that the similarities between the two accounts demonstrates that the most marketable and popular image of the woman writer by the early 1740s was that offered by Rowe's example, as presented in the *Miscellaneous Works* of 1739.

The 'Account' begins, like many exemplary women's lives from the sixteenth and seventeenth centuries, by providing an account of Brereton's parents, Thomas and Anne Hughes of Bryn-Griffith near Mold in the county of Flint.[50] Like Rowe, Brereton showed an early aptitude for poetry:

> She soon discover'd a peculiar Genius for Poetry, which was her chief Amusement; and all her Acquaintance encouraged it by the Delight they took in whatever She composed. And, before she was Twenty, the Perfections of her Mind, the Amiableness of her Person, and Sprightliness of her Temper, render'd her generally admir'd.
>
> (p. ii)

Brereton's early inclinations for poetry are presented as an 'amusement' written for the delight of her friends rather than from any professional motive. In parallel with Rowe, she has a natural 'genius' for poetry which reflects the 'Perfections of her Mind'. In the absence of a portrait, Brereton's physical appearance is described in detail:

> Her Person was of a middle Stature, well shaped and easy; her Complexion inclining to Brown; her Hair a dark brown, a good Forehead, fine arch'd Eyebrows, small grey Eyes, a remarkable handsome Nose, an agreeable Mouth, and a fine set of Teeth. Her Face was well turn'd, an engaging Sweetness was diffused over her Countenance.
>
> (p. viii)

This is very similar to the description of Rowe in the 'Life' where the emphasis is on the woman writer's physical attractions but also her sweet disposition and softness:

> She was of a moderate stature, her hair of a fine auburn colour, and her eyes of a darkish grey inclining to blue, and full of fire. Her complexion was very fair, and a natural rosy blush glowed in her cheeks. She spoke gracefully, and her voice was exceeding sweet and harmonious, and perfectly suited to that gentle language which always flowed from her lips. But the softness and benevolence of her aspect is beyond all description. (p. lv)

These descriptions make the connections between a woman's character and her writing explicit. The 'Account' draws directly on the description of Rowe in the specific detail used for the portrait of Brereton, but also draws on broader rhetorical constructions which conflate a woman's character with the content of her texts. Not only do the exemplary lives of Rowe and Brereton provide a context for the reception of their writing, their physical appearance also confirms their virtue.

Brereton's marriage to Thomas Brereton, and her early married life in London, are passed over quickly in favour of a stress on her retired life in Wales, which is presented as comprising a respectable existence based on a close circle of friends. Her potentially scandalous separation from her husband is reconfigured here to endorse her virtue and her maternal concern. It is also stressed that she did not leave her husband of her own volition, but was acting on the advice of concerned friends:

> Mrs *Brereton* was advised, by all who had any regard for her, to separate from her Husband: But tho' all the Reason in the World pleaded for it, yet she express'd great Reluctance at it, especially unless she could have her children with her; and that being at last brought about, she left *London* about the Year 1721, and retired to her native country *Wales*, where she led a solitary life, seeing little Company, except some intimate Friends, Persons of great Merit; well knowing what a critical case it is to behave without the Censure of the World, when separated from a Husband. (p. iv)

Although very different in circumstance, Brereton's separation from her husband is presented here as a version of Rowe's virtuous widowhood when she returned to the 'recess' of Frome after the death of her husband. Thomas Brereton died shortly after the separation. On the death of her husband, Brereton could also be constructed as a virtuous widow dedicated to the proper upbringing of her two daughters.

After her husband's death, Brereton moved to Wrexham in Denbighshire. The 'Account' constructs a very particular image of Brereton's provincial life in Wrexham which is where she wrote most of her poetry, including her contributions to the *Gentleman's Magazine*. Wrexham is very carefully constructed as an ideal of a respectable provincial community in which Brereton made a number of close friends among the town's most prominent families:

> [She] was herself soon distinguish'd by the most considerable Families in and about the Town; And it must be allow'd by all, that that Neighbourhood is remarkable for Politeness, Taste and Hospita-

lity. She had the Happiness and Honour to commence a strict Friendship with some of the most eminent of both Sexes, which continued
till the time of her Death.   (p. vii)

The politeness and taste of Wrexham society endorses Brereton's character by the ease with which she was accepted into the life of the town.
Her notions of friendship are said to be of the strictest sort: 'she had the
most exalted notions of Friendship, and never in the smallest Article
swerv'd from its Rules' (p. x). For example, despite her 'stedfast Affection and Loyalty for the present Royal Family' she had 'great Charity
for all those of different Persuasions' (p. x), particularly if they were
'Ladies of Distinction'. Brereton's poetical name, 'Melissa', is said to
have been chosen for her by a gentleman of her acquaintance 'from
the Latin word *Mell*, as bearing some Allusion to the Sweetness of her
Numbers' (p. xii). Any further allusion to Brereton's use of 'Melissa' as
a politicized stance relating to her Welsh identity is carefully avoided.
Brereton's writing is also firmly presented as an amateur occupation.
Despite the inclusion of previously published work in the collection as
well as her contributions to the *Gentleman's Magazine*, Brereton is presented as being averse to publication, even by subscription, in a manner
reminiscent of Rowe's suggested attitude in the 1739 biography:

> Writing was her darling Entertainment, and was to her a Relaxation
> from her Cares; tho' she would not consent to have her Works
> publish'd by subscription, When proposed by a Gentleman, in a very
> pressing Manner.   (p. xii)

Further parallels can be drawn between the presentation of Brereton
and that of Elizabeth Rowe. Brereton is said to have been 'extremely
devout and observant of religious duties' (pp. ix–x). She 'was regular in
her own Devotions; and constantly twice a Day call'd her little Family
together for Prayers' (p. x). In contrast to the childless Rowe, however,
Brereton's Christian devotion also feeds into an ideal of motherhood:
'She was the most indulgent tender Parent, chusing to govern her
Children more by Love than Fear; and was particularly anxious about
her Daughters Education, and instilling into their Minds Religion and
Virtue' (p. ix). Whereas Rowe educates the general public in matters
of religion through her personal devotion to God and her writing,
Brereton directly influences her children through her example as a
mother. Like Rowe again, Brereton is also constructed as both pious and

charitable. She cared for her servants beyond the call of duty, and regularly used her own meagre income to give to the poor. Furthermore, like Rowe, 'She rejoyc'd at every Symptom of approaching Death, and was all Resignation' (p. viii).[51] The 'Account' concludes by stressing the various female roles that Brereton fulfilled as a model of virtue and respectability:

> It can only be added, that she was Aimiable in every Character of her Life, as the modest Maid, the chaste and prudent Wife, the tender and fond Parent, the decent Widow, the sincere and wise Friend, the indulgent Mistress, and the good, pious and exemplary Christian.
>
> (p. xv)

As was the case with the biography of Rowe, the reader is led to Brereton's poems via the exemplary portrait of virtuous Christian femininity offered by the 'Account'. The poems must then be read in the light of this construction of Brereton as an author. Like Rowe, Brereton is presented as an amateur, provincial writer who eschewed the publication of her work and remained secluded from the literary marketplace. Brereton is seen to be contented with the approbation of friends of merit and seeks no further satisfaction from the relaxing amusement of writing poetry. However, as was the case with the 'Life' of Rowe, the 'Account' also works in a commercial context. The account of Brereton's life not only validates its subject but also presents her in the most attractive light to a potential readership. The similarities between the two texts strongly suggest that the author of this memoir was very much aware of the commercial value, as well as the ideological power, of Rowe's posthumous image.

Models of female authorship

Much critical attention has been paid to the sexualized model of female authorship and how this construction plays on associations with the literary marketplace. From this perspective, the image of the professional woman novelist is one based on the notion of women writers as literary prostitutes, selling their bodies/texts on the open market. However, what is often neglected in such accounts is the simultaneous endorsement of women writers through collected editions of their work. Furthermore, it is possible to read the construction of the passionate woman writer of commendatory verse in a positive light, as a way of authorizing women's fiction rather than inviting satirical attack. As I have argued here, these collections also aim to elevate the woman writer to a position of canonical status. Eliza Haywood, for example, is often characterized as producing ephemeral texts for quick consumption. However, the appearance of two collections of her work within a year of each other suggests an attempt by her publishers to fix her status as an established author, not as a species of hackney scribbler. Even for women poets, these material presentations of the woman writer continued to be prominent. The publishers of Elizabeth Rowe's miscellaneous works draw on a set of marketing strategies for promoting the woman writer that had been in place since the late 1710s and early 1720s. As women became even more prominent in literary culture, strategies which emphasized a woman writer's canonical status and authorial *oeuvre* continued to be an effective way of presenting their work.

The view that constructions of female authorship became increasingly restrictive as the century progressed has also become something of a critical commonplace. Various studies of women's writing in this period trace a movement away from an openly sexual image of the woman writer towards a more circumscribed image of respectable femininity promulgated in particular through periodicals such as *The Spectator*. As Kathryn Shevelow has argued, for example, 'During the eighteenth century, as upper- and middle-class Englishwomen increasingly began to participate in the public realm of print culture, the representational practices of that culture were steadily enclosing them within the private sphere of the home.'[52] While it is important to note that increased access to print culture does not necessarily translate into greater freedom of expression, I would argue that the image of the woman writer beginning to predominate in the late 1730s is more complex than this 'domestic' model suggests. It is certainly true that the presentation of women writers from the mid-1730s was increasingly predicated on notions of respectable femininity such as piety, charity, sweetness, purity and modesty. Similarly, the ideal female author comes to represent ideals of eighteenth-century womanhood such as the perfect mother, the constant widow and the loving wife. At the same time, women became increasingly associated with poetry rather than fiction. The image of the woman writer penning occasional verses to family and friends with no view to financial reward was more acceptable than the professional woman writing novels for money. If a woman was known for writing fiction, as both Aubin and Rowe were, their fiction is given an explicitly moral purpose which reflects the piety of the woman writer herself.

Without doubt, then, this is a gendered model of authorship which posits women's writing as evidence of a woman's virtuous life in direct opposition to the conflation of a woman's own sexual intrigues with the amatory adventures presented in her novels. However, what is also apparent is that this image of respectable female authorship is also predicated on the Horatian model of retirement outlined in the previous chapter. The biographies of Rowe and Brereton place great emphasis on the provincial context of their subjects and their 'retreat' from the 'world'. What I want to suggest here is that, for women writers in particular, provincialism came to signify a range of meanings which complicate the picture of 'domestic' female authorship. First, a provincial context could serve to disassociate a woman writer from the literary marketplace. As a result, the woman writer could then be seen as modestly eschewing literary fame and any professional attitude to her literary career. A provincial life translates as a modest and respectable existence away from public scrutiny. This, in turn, informs the image of the woman poet as an accomplished amateur who chooses to circulate her verses among a close group of friends and distinguished acquaintances. Second, the image of the provincial woman writer links to the Horatian model of retirement from public life. For women, this authorial model is also gendered. In contrast to the male appropriation of Horatian retreat from public life, women's retirement signifies particularly feminine characteristics of modest self-effacement.

Despite the terms of this model being based on a rejection of the image of the woman writer as marketplace professional, I would argue that this construction of female authorship also has a commercial impetus which is often underplayed. The use of very similar material presentations, such as the publishing of women's 'Works' and the printing of portraits of the author, attests to the fact that writers like Rowe were also pitched in a commercial context. Furthermore, the constant foregrounding of a woman writer's provincial background in the title-pages to collections also suggests that a provincial identity, and all it implied, could be an effective selling point. A publisher as commercially minded as Edmund Curll certainly believed this to be the case. Therefore, just as the presentation of Aubin as a moral novelist was a bid to differentiate her fiction from rival publications circulating at the time, so too is the image of the virtuous, provincial woman writer, uninterested in literary fame and modest in persona, a marketing strategy employed to present the woman writer and her work in the most attractive light to a potential readership. As I argue in Chapters 5 and 6, the sentimental image of 'the pious Mrs. Rowe' does much to obscure

Rowe's actual literary practice and contemporary fame. Nevertheless, the respectable model she came to represent was, in fact, the most effective way to market her work and increase her popularity with the book-buying public. In the early eighteenth century, Elizabeth Rowe was as much, if not more, of a marketplace presence, as Eliza Haywood.

4
Making a Living: Booksellers, Patronage and Subscription

In the early eighteenth century there were three main routes to make money by writing. An author could engage directly with a bookseller, seek an influential and wealthy patron, or publish their work by subscription. Sale of copyright to the booksellers was the most obvious way an author could turn their writing into economic gain. However, despite the ongoing investment in women's writing from certain publishers, few writers were able to sustain a living from sale of copyright alone. Patronage therefore offered an alternative way of making money and supplementing income. As the century progressed, many women also took advantage of the financial benefit subscription publication seemed to offer. Writers such as Eliza Haywood, Elizabeth Boyd, Mary Barber and Mary Davys all used subscription publication to make money from their writing. Despite the opportunity for authorial independence that subscription could represent, this mode of publication involved a delicate balancing act, whereby the writer had to satisfy the desires of the patron-subscribers through a cautious use of authorial self-presentation. Patronage also involved complex social interactions which necessitated careful self-presentation by the writer and the adoption of various strategies of deference and flattery to persuade the patron to support a writer's work.

My approach in this chapter is two-fold. First, I offer an analysis of the practical engagement of women writers with the different economic systems at their disposal. In this context, I trace the association of particular booksellers with the production of women's texts and discuss the evidence for sale of copyright. With regard to the patronage system, I offer examples of various appeals to patrons which are motivated by the desire for economic advancement. Using the example of Elizabeth Boyd, I discuss the practicalities of arranging a subscription volume and what this entailed. Second, I am interested in how economic concerns could affect women's authorial self-representation and textual strategies. Using the examples offered by Eliza Haywood's dedications, I argue that women writers often employed gendered strategies to appeal to powerful patrons. These dedications provide insights into how women's relation to the economics of literary culture was mediated, and often compromised, by gender concerns. I end with a consideration of Mary Barber's involvement with the subscription system. Ostensibly, the publication of her poems by this method seemed to offer Barber some much-needed financial advancement. Nevertheless, her high level of self-consciousness about her dependence on the support of her patron-subscribers directly shaped her authorial self-fashioning, and her poetry, in ways that could be seen as limiting and reductive. Overall, this chapter aims to explore the motives behind the series of compromises that women were forced to make in their approach to writing for money in the early eighteenth century.

The London booksellers

Women novelists and their publishers

In the satirical text, *The Session of the Poets, Holden at the Foot of Parnassus-Hill July the 9th 1696*, Mary Pix is attacked in generalized terms as an example of an immodest female author. However, the commentary also refers specifically to her novel, *The Inhumane Cardinal; or, Innocence Betray'd* (1696), in the context of its perceived lack of market appeal: 'The very first Venture she expos'd unto public View was a Novel, a very barren Discourse, abounding with neither language nor Intrigue furnish'd out at the Bookseller's Charge, but I am very confident will not defray the expense of the Impression.'[1] This view of the fate of a woman's novel testifies not only to the low cultural status of the novel as a genre, but also displays a perception that the market for women's fiction was hardly a shrewd business venture for either the author or the bookseller. That the market for fiction was barely established at this time is shown by the fact that all three women who published fiction in 1696 (Manley, Pix and Trotter), found the theatre a much more lucrative way to earn money from writing. The market for women's writing at the turn of the century was indeed speculative. A bookseller's decision to publish a work of fiction by a woman in the late seventeenth century was, therefore, conjectural and potentially hazardous. As a result, many of the booksellers involved in the publication

of women writers were established figures in the trade whose speculation in the market for fiction was already cushioned by a substantial
backlist of authors and titles.[2] The risk of producing material of uncertain marketability was further reduced by the common practice of two
or more booksellers combining resources to spread the cost, and risk, of
publishing women's texts.

Despite the pessimistic view put forward in the *Session of the Poets*,
there is evidence of a nascent market for women's fiction in the late seventeenth century. It is apparent that certain booksellers were, even then,
particularly associated with the publication of women's texts. As noted
in Chapter 3, the fiction of Aphra Behn was one example to publishers
that women's fiction could sell. One important bookseller for the early
history of women's fiction was Samuel Briscoe. Briscoe had published
Behn's collected *Histories and Novels* in 1698 and was therefore aware of
the market potential for female-authored fiction.[3] Briscoe had also been
associated with the publication of Catherine Trotter's 1693 epistolary
fiction, *Olinda's Adventures; or, The Amours of a Young Lady*. *Olinda's
Adventures* first appeared as volume one of Briscoe's epistolary miscellany, entitled *Letters of Love and Gallantry and Several Other Subjects. All
Written by Ladies* (1693).[4] The second volume appeared in the following
year. The popularity of the collection was partly based, in this instance,
on the particular interests of the bookseller. As Robert Day notes,
between 1693 and 1718, 'Briscoe became something of a specialist in
popular epistolary miscellanies, perhaps because he was a principal
employer of Tom Brown, much of whose output consisted of original
and translated "'familiar letters"'.[5] In 1718 Briscoe capitalized on the
success of the original collections and published what Day identifies as
the 'most popular items' from a twenty-five-year career based on publishing miscellanies of this type. The 1718 edition of *Familiar Letters*
included *Olinda's Adventures*, as well as texts by Aphra Behn, Delarivier
Manley and Susanna Centlivre. Further editions appeared in 1720 and
1724, which suggests that the letters were popular and sold well. Briscoe
was one of the first publishers to specialize in women's fiction. His
success in this area demonstrates that his awareness of a market for
women's writing was well-founded.

There is a connection between Briscoe's publication and William
Chetwood, the publisher of Haywood's first novel *Love in Excess*. As I
have noted, Day records a 1720 edition (or re-issue) of *Familiar Letters*
advertised for Chetwood in 1720.[6] Through his connections with
Briscoe's publication, Chetwood must have been aware of a budding
market for women's writing. This practical knowledge must have made

Chetwood aware of the possibilities for Haywood's text. *Love in Excess* amply repaid Chetwood as this text not only made Haywood famous, but was also consistently reprinted throughout the eighteenth century.[7] Haywood's success can be said to have changed the face of the market-place for fiction dramatically. The decade following the publication of *Love in Excess* saw a remarkable increase in the publication of women's fiction. The fact that certain booksellers, such as Edmund Curll, Arthur Bettesworth, Samuel Chapman and Daniel Midwinter, consistently published work by women writers in this period also suggests that the commercial value of women writers was on the increase by the 1720s. Haywood's phenomenal rate of production in the 1720s contributed to the new market presence of both women writers and the novel. Although this 1720s vogue for fiction was not dominant in quantitative terms, in terms of marketability and sales appeal women's fiction in particular was perceived to be a popular, fashionable, and therefore lucrative sector of the market for books at this time. As William Warner has argued, 'Although they represented only a small part of print culture in the early decades of the eighteenth century, by the 1720s novels comprised one of the most high-profile, fashionable, and dynamic segments of the market.'[8] I would add here that women writers, and Haywood in particular, played a central role in this new development. Furthermore, many key booksellers in the trade were involved in the publication of women's fiction. Haywood must have been particularly useful for her booksellers given her rapid rate of production. Indeed, as Warner's comments suggest, the dominant characteristic of the market for fiction was its quick turnover. The constant need for new texts was also filled by the relative cheapness of the books themselves. Typically, novels by Haywood and her female contemporaries sold at around one shilling.[9] In this context, Haywood's rapid rate of production gave her publishers even more reason to perceive her novels as commercially attractive.

Haywood was published by a range of booksellers, but she can also be connected to some particular figures. Her fiction was repeatedly published by the partnership of Samuel Chapman and Daniel Browne, who were responsible for her two collections from 1724 and 1725.[10] Samuel Chapman became known as Haywood's main publisher.[11] Connections with the Aaron Hill circle can again be detected as Chapman also published Richard Savage's *Miscellaneous Poems and Translations* in 1728. In the various editions of *The Dunciad*, Haywood is directly connected with her booksellers. In *The Dunciad Variorum* (1729), Chetwood and Curll are pitted against each other as competitors for Haywood's favours or copy. In earlier editions of the poem, Samuel Chapman appeared as Curll's adversary.[12] In the public mind, then, a writer was often seen in direct relation to the booksellers who published their work. However, in the case of Haywood, what is also apparent is that her booksellers can be directly linked to the kind of literary circles she inhabited. Chetwood, for example, remained an important influence on her career. He collaborated with Browne and Chapman on texts including *The British Recluse* (1722), and *Idalia* (1723). Furthermore, the fact that Haywood consistently published with a certain number of booksellers suggests that they found her work profitable and that she was reasonably satisfied with her relationship with them. The fact that she also, at times, moved between different booksellers suggests that Haywood was successful in shopping around for the best deal.

Penelope Aubin was the other main producer of female fiction in the 1720s and, like Haywood, she was associated with particular booksellers. Aubin's publishing profile differs from Haywood's, however, in that the majority of her novels and translations were published by a conger of booksellers. As Terry Belanger has shown, the conger began as an association of booksellers who clubbed together 'to protect their investments from attack both from within the book trade, by pirates, and from without, by legislation'.[13] The conger could buy editions of a book collectively, which were then stored and distributed by them. As a result, the conger could provide a secure financial backing to cover the expense of producing new books, as well as for the reprinting of books already published. Although the original conger was a wholesaling initiative whose members did not necessarily own copyright, by the early eighteenth century variations on this initial group mainly comprised copyright-owning booksellers.[14] The booksellers involved in the congers of the early eighteenth century represented some of the most powerful figures in the trade. Membership of the congers was often passed on from father to son or through business associates. On one level, such combinations of business interests can be read as particularly valuable for publishers of women's fiction as they safeguarded a bookseller's involvement in a product of uncertain market appeal.[15]

The conger system was to prove invaluable for the publication of Aubin's novels. The majority of her fiction was published by a consortium of ten or more booksellers. The most common combination of names was: E. Bell, J. Darby, A. Bettesworth, F. Fayram, J. Pemberton, J. Hooke, C. Rivington, F. Clay, J. Batley and E. Symon.[16] Members of this collective were also responsible for publishing Aubin's translations. *The Prince of Clermont and Madam de Ravezan* (1722), *The History of Genghiz-*

can the Great (1722) and *The Doctrine of Morality* (1721) were published by J. Darby and E. Bell, as well as three members of the original whole-saling conger: William Taylor, William Innys and John Osborn. The same combination (without Bell) published *The Life of the Lady Lucy* (1726), and *The Life and Adventures of the Young Count Albertus* (1728). Aubin's *Collection of Entertaining Novels and Histories* (1739), was also published by a consortium of thirteen booksellers. As Cheryl Turner has noted, these collaborations for publishing women's fiction were good business practice given the relatively speculative market for such texts, especially in the early years of the century.[17] Furthermore, a writer's asso-ciation with the conger system could also suggest that the work of that writer was perceived to be potentially profitable. As Turner goes on to note, 'it is possible that, with some of this material, associations were the result of the traders' desire to remain or become involved with a good investment'.[18] It could also be the case that, given the huge success of *Love in Excess* and Haywood's novels, booksellers perceived women's fiction to be high on their list of marketable texts, despite the critical perception that novels by women constituted a culturally low genre. A women writer's involvement with the conger system could represent, then, not just a safety net for a risky business venture, but the safe-guarding of a valuable asset. Indeed, as Aubin's 1739 collection demon-strates, by this date at least, she was perceived to be a considerable market presence and an established commercial name. Despite the per-ception of women novelists as a commercial risk, many high-profile booksellers and congers saw women's writing as a useful and dynamic component of their business practice.

Edmund Curll and women's writing

One bookseller in particular who benefited from his involvement with women writers was, rather incongruously given his salacious reputation, Edmund Curll. William McBurney was the first scholar to make a connection between Curll and women writers.[19] More recently, Cheryl Turner has argued that Curll was 'an important force behind the early growth of women's fiction', and suggested that Curll, in fact, helped to raise the profile of a number of women writers.[20] Curll's first involve-ment with women's fiction was the publication of Jane Barker's *Love Intrigues* in 1713. Curll also published Barker's *Exilius; or, The Banish'd Roman* in 1715. In 1718 he joined forces with Charles Rivington to publish her Fénelon translation, *The Christian Pilgrimage*, and with Thomas Payne for the publication of *A Patch-Work Screen for the Ladies* in 1723.[21] Curll also published a number of plays by Susanna Centlivre, as well as another political romance in the style of Barker's *Exilius*, Sarah Butler's *Irish Tales; or, Instructive Histories for the Happy Conduct of Life* (1716).[22] Curll was notoriously connected with the poet Elizabeth Thomas who sold him private letters, some by Alexander Pope, for which she was dubbed 'Curll's Corinna' in *The Dunciad*. He also published Thomas' *Pylades and Corinna; Or, Memoirs of the Lives, Amours and Writings of Richard Gwinnet Esq. and Elizabeth Thomas* which includes 'The Life of Corinna. Written by Herself' (1731–2).[23] As the title of the previous text suggests, Curll's publications frequently reveal his interest in potentially scandalous letters and secret histories. A typical Curll title is the second edition of Lydia Grainger's *Modern Amours; or, A Secret History of the Adventures of some Persons of the First Rank. Faithfully related From the Author's own Knowledge of each Transaction*, which was advertised as printed for E. Curll in 1733.[24]

Curll's approach to the publication of women writers offers some insights into what he thought was marketable copy, and what he perceived to be the most commercial way of presenting a woman's work. As the publication of Thomas' life and the letters to and from her lover Richard Gwinnet suggest, Curll was particularly interested in texts which seemed to offer information about a woman writer's private life. His choice of women's texts shows a penchant for letters and autobiographies. As well as publishing Thomas' life and letters, he also published an unauthorized edition of Delarivier Manley's *Letters Written By Mrs. Manley* (1696) as *A Stage-Coach Journey to Exeter* (1725). In 1714, he published Manley's semi-autobiographical fiction *The Adventures of Rivella*.[25] Curll's further publications of this text play even more on the curiosity of the reader to know the personal details of Manley's life from her own mouth. The 1717 edition was titled *Memoirs of the Life of Mrs. Manley*, and the 1725 text appeared as *Mrs. Manley's History of Her Own Life and Times*. Further Curll publications continue to highlight the fascination about the lives of women writers. In 1732, he reprinted Martha Fowke Sansom's *The Epistles of Clio and Strephon*, based on letters between the author and William Bond. In 1729 he had brought out selections from this text as *Epistles and Poems by Clio and Strephon*. As I have shown, he later published an unauthorized edition of Rowe's poems in 1736, which included a life of the author and a letter supposedly by Rowe which hints that she in fact gave permission for Curll to print her work.[26] Curll is particularly significant in this respect because he was so obviously, and blatantly, commercial in his approach. His reliance on texts by women is a further indication of the marketability of women's writing.

Making money

It is clear, then, that as the century progressed women writers were becoming more prominent in literary culture. But how much money could a woman expect to earn from her writing? As I argued in Chapter 1, very few women writers could expect to earn a good living.[27] This situation was broadly true for male writers as well, with some notable exceptions such as Alexander Pope.[28] However, it is possible to make a distinction between the lower sort of hackney scribbler and an author like Eliza Haywood who was obviously profitable for her booksellers and, as I have shown, was able to move between different publishers. In his study *John Dunton and the English Book Trade*, Stephen Parks makes a useful distinction, based on Dunton's writing on this subject in *The Life and Errors of John Dunton* (1705), between hack writers and 'gentlemen-authors'.[29] Parks' description of the typical hack writer serves as a useful marker for realizing the sort of author which Haywood, for one, was certainly not: 'Few writers rose above the rank and file to achieve individual recognition. An unknown author was almost totally subject to the bookseller. Many never escaped anonymity.'[30] By contrast, the established author was 'not paid a shilling a sheet' but 'generally paid a sum for their work after negotiation, as well as with copies of their work'.[31] Therefore, writers like Haywood and Aubin can be seen to be somewhere between the lowly hacks and literary giants such as Pope. However, even if a writer was able to negotiate sale of complete copy with the booksellers, this was often a single payment with no further remuneration as the copyright of the book would be in the hands of the publisher or the conger. As many critics on the book trade in the early eighteenth century have pointed out, and as my analysis of women's literary careers in Chapter 1 suggested, it was extremely difficult to make a good living from writing in this period. Eliza Haywood survived mainly because she was able to produce a large body of work within a short space of time.

The evidence for sale of copyright for women's writing is scarce. Unfortunately, there are no figures for Haywood's 1720s fiction, but we do know that in 1734 Haywood sold the copyright of her *History of the British Theatre* to Francis Cogan and John Nourse for sixteen pounds and four shillings, with the following conditions: 'the said Eliza Haywood shall immediately assign over to them all the said Eliza Haywood's Right Title Interest & Claim Demand or pretence whatever'.[32] Haywood also sold the 'Sole Right and Property of the Second Volume of the Companion to the Theatre' for twenty pounds and five shillings in January

1746/7.[33] In March of 1746/7 Haywood had also made money by selling 'the sole Copy Right of the first part of a Translation Entitled Memoirs of a Man of Honour' to Nourse for seven pounds and seven shillings, and in April she received six pounds and six shillings for the second part of the memoirs.[34] When compared to the amount of money to be made in the theatre, the price for Haywood's copyrights are relatively low. Back in the 1710s, Susanna Centlivre, for example, had earned twenty-one pounds per play for selling the copyright to Edmund Curll.[35] However, in 1746/7 alone Haywood made a reasonable amount of money from her writing, but this was with the proviso that she would not have the chance to make any more money from the texts she had sold outright.[36]

Although there is no information concerning the original agreements for the sale of Penelope Aubin and Mary Davy's copyrights, there are figures for later sales of shares of the copyrights. On 28 February 1765, William Cater received two guineas from Thomas Lownds for 'the Copy Right of the Fruitless Enquiry after Happiness by Mrs. Davies of York'.[37] Lownds also sold one-tenth of the copyrights of Aubin's collection of novels, and her translation *The Illustrious French Lovers*, for two pounds, seven shillings on 1 June 1764.[38] The shares were bought by John Hinxman.[39] The overall copyright for each of Aubin's texts in the 1760s was therefore approximately twenty pounds, which suggests that by this date her fiction was at the lower end of the market. In their lifetimes, both Aubin and Davys must have made considerably more from the production of the one play they each wrote. In the preface to *The Lady's Tale* (written in 1700), Davys had claimed that she 'took three Guineas for the Brat of my Brain'.[40] She did considerably better from the third-night performance of *The Northern Heiress* in May 1716, from which she received twenty pounds and sixteen shillings in money, and fifty-one pounds and three shillings in third night receipts.[41] The actual figures for the performances of Aubin's comedy, *The Merry Masqueraders*, are not available, but the play was advertised on 11 December 1730 as benefiting the author.[42] Around this date Aubin must also have been making money from her oratory, where tickets were priced at two shillings and sixpence each.[43]

Throughout the early eighteenth century women writers were increasingly perceived to be of commercial value by the trade. The success of *Love in Excess*, and Haywood's high-profile presence in the marketplace, paved the way for women to be recognized as established authors whose work could be sold on the strength of a name.[44] Furthermore, many prominent booksellers were involved in the publication of women's writing and some, like William Chetwood and Edmund Curll, were directly responsible for bringing women writers to the attention of the reading public. Women writers themselves can also be seen to be alert to the exigencies of commercial publication. Many had ongoing connections with particular booksellers, and also benefited from their inclusion in literary circles which offered, by a variety of routes, introductions to appropriate members of the trade who could publish their work. Therefore, despite the common perception that to publish the work of women was a risky venture, it can be argued that by the 1720s women's writing had become an integral, if still relatively small, component of booksellers' lists.[45] However, this analysis of women's relations with the booksellers confirms my assertion in Chapter 1 that few women could expect to earn a comfortable living from their writing in the early eighteenth century, especially if they only relied on the direct sale of copyright. As is widely recognized, author–bookseller relations in the early eighteenth century privileged the copyright-holding bookseller not the writer. Once a writer had relinquished their copyright, no further money could be made from that text. The collections of women's fiction that proliferated in this period is only one example of the way in which booksellers could make further profit from the original purchase of copyright. This state of affairs accounts for the speed with which writers such as Aubin and Haywood produced new books, and suggests why many women diversified into other areas of literary activity to supplement the income from their printed books. The role played by patronage and subscription in the careers of women writers suggests that the author–bookseller combination was not the sole means by which the literary marketplace operated, nor was it the only way in which women writers could make a living and establish themselves as authors.

Women and the patronage system

Unless a writer was cushioned by personal wealth, the position of the literary author in society had always been one of dependency in different forms. In the late sixteenth and early seventeenth centuries authorial dependency was defined either by direct court patronage or the support of influential private patrons.[46] In these earlier periods patronage was systemic in the society and culture of the time and it is difficult to make a clear distinction between social and political patronage and literary patronage.[47] In the Elizabethan age, 'Authors dedicated books in order to gain support for a cause or to draw attention to their loyalty and personal expertise in an attempt to improve their own social position through "preferment".'[48] Such a state of affairs inevitably shaped styles of and approaches to authorship. As Arthur Marotti has noted of English Renaissance authorship in relation to the career of John Donne, 'Donne actually treated literature as an avocation rather than a vocation, as part of a style of life and career whose goals were the social prestige and preferment that successful exploitation of the patronage system could win.'[49] In effect, Marotti concludes, 'almost all English Renaissance literature is a literature of patronage'.[50] Such a claim certainly cannot be made for the literature of the early eighteenth century. Most critics agree that one of the main differences between Renaissance literary patronage and that of the Restoration and early eighteenth century is the decline of court influence.[51] This is not so much because the actual intervention of court and crown was substantially less than in earlier periods, but because the amount of authors who were writing had increased so dramatically. As such, authors had to find other ways than placements and direct patronage from the crown to support themselves. The burgeoning literary marketplace and the broadening readerships of the early eighteenth century provided a wealth of different avenues writers could follow in the quest for economic reward and critical recognition.

As Paul Korshin has argued, for those critics who focus on the development of the eighteenth-century literary marketplace, patronage often represents 'a dwindling leftover of Renaissance magnificence in an age of increasing democracy'.[52] As a result, the patronage system comes to signify an older tradition of dependency upon the crown and aristocracy which is replaced by a more democratic relationship between the author and their public. Taken in this way, eighteenth-century patronage is a residue of an antiquated and outmoded system at odds with the modernity of eighteenth-century culture. By contrast, Korshin and others have shown that patronage did not just persist in a similar, but diluted, form in the eighteenth century, but adapted in a variety of ways to the changed circumstances of the time. Far from becoming irrelevant, eighteenth-century literary patronage developed into 'a unique blending of free enterprise, commercial venture, private beneficence, and public or audience support'.[53] The reality of most authors' experience in the early eighteenth century was a joint reliance on the booksellers and market sales which included varying degrees of engagement with patronage in its adapted forms.[54] Given the inadequate rewards available for writers at this time it is not surprising that some reliance on patronage continued to be a component in the lives of many writers of the period. As I will demonstrate in a moment, even that consummate literary professional, Eliza Haywood, regarded patronage as an integral part of her authorial practice.

The perception that patronage became all but defunct in this period not only fails to recognize the different forms patronage could take – such as subscription publication – but also neglects the way in which the patronage system could interact with the literary marketplace. For example, the public endorsement of a writer's work by a famous and/or powerful name not only gave the author prestige by association, but could also, as Dustin Griffin has shown, increase the commercial appeal of a particular text, for booksellers as well as readers, by endorsing it with the 'authority' of the patron as an arbiter of taste.[55] As such, patrons provided the author and their work with 'symbolic capital' in addition to any more straightforward financial support. Patrons could also provide fledgling authors with important introductions to other literary figures, networks of writers, and useful booksellers. A patron could therefore act as an important link in the chain between an unknown author, the booksellers and a broad reading public. Similarly, prominent literary men, either writers such as Jonathan Swift or businessmen such as Edward Cave, could act as patrons of individual authors. Therefore, although the more traditional rewards of patronage such as government positions, ecclesiastical livings or court pensions did continue, early eighteenth-century literary patronage as a whole was much broader in its application than in earlier periods.

The material benefits that early eighteenth-century patronage could provide are amply, and poignantly, demonstrated in a letter by Elizabeth Thomas to a prominent literary patron, the Earl of Oxford (Robert Harley), which was written in 1730 when she was in Fleet prison for debt, in a state of 'painful malady, poverty and tatters'.[56] In this letter Thomas outlines the various ways she has benefited from patronage, especially that of titled women:

> Lady Frances Clifton clothed me, my Lord Delaware sent four guineas towards paying my prison debts [. . .] The Duchess of Somerset (who has been long a great support to me) had the bounty last week to give me a stock of stationary ware, and to buy of me after, with a gracious promise of future custom at her return. My Lady Delaware has given me leave to hope for a recommendation among her acquaintance, when I am out of this place; so that I now begin to hope I shall live by my honest industry; it being worse than death to me to receive favours and live idle.

Thomas' aristocratic patrons provide her with clothes, money, stock, custom and recommendations. They do not offer her an annual income or continuing support for her writing career. In fact, Thomas is in need of such support because she has failed to sustain herself as a writer. Thomas relates that she has enclosed a pamphlet for Harley which she has been unable to sell through the booksellers. Instead, she has to rely on the goodwill of her patrons to buy the books she received in lieu of payment. In order to raise further money to pay her prison debts, Thomas 'wrote the enclosed trifle, depending on two guineas for the copy, which is the market price for a sixpenny pamphlet, but through the deadness of trade could get no money; only an equivalent in books, which I humbly hope such friends as are inclined to buy will be so good as to purchase of me now, rather than of the shops when published'. Thomas received money and other forms of material support from her aristocratic supporters, but these gifts are not for her writing but because she is an object of charity. In the absence of buyers her work can only be of use to her in a patronage context: her income depends on the goodwill of wealthy friends and acquaintances rather than an anonymous reading public.

As Elizabeth Thomas' example indicates, issues of dependence are always central to any notion of patronage. In terms of literature, degrees of authorial dependence do not just involve personal or political loyalties, but also affect the style of authorship adopted and the content of a writer's work. In earlier periods, straightforward dependence on patrons was commonplace. Robert Folkenflick, for example, has described the Renaissance poet's position at court as 'a superior servant'.[57] Given the decline of formalized placements and court ties, it is tempting to characterize the early eighteenth century as offering writers a more independent style of authorship. As Paul Korshin suggests, 'According to this view, patronage, corrupt and corrupting, symbolizes the subservience and dependency of the writer upon a dominant aristocracy; the crumbling of the structure of patronage represents liberation for the man of letters from a financial tyranny and a timorous self-censorship.'[58] Korshin concludes that this view of eighteenth-century authorial release from dependence is 'a romantic ideal' which disguises the facts of continued reliance on favours and encouragement in the literary world. Robert Folkenflick, on the other hand, argues that, with the arrival of writers such as Gray and Collins on the literary scene in the later years of the century, the idea of authorial independence achieved through a rejection of patronage was well developed. This vision of authorship was fully expressed in the early eighteenth century through the authorial style of Alexander Pope and the role of patron-age in relation to authorial dependence was hotly contested at this time. Nevertheless, I would tend to agree with Korshin that, although patron-age did diversify, the traditions of flattery and the postures of authorial deference expected of dependent authors persisted, albeit in a different context. For example, Eliza Haywood's approaches to patrons were often speculative and it is apparent that she was not tied to any single patron for any length of time. Nevertheless, the tone and style of her dedica-tions are clearly implicated in notions of gratitude and deferential modesty.

Eliza Haywood and the language of dedications

In Elizabeth Thomas' case, it is clear that while she does receive support from a variety of aristocratic figures, this provision is not of the kind traditionally available to male writers fallen on hard times. As Dustin Griffin notes, 'a woman in the eighteenth century would not be named a private secretary to a peer, or set up as a political journalist, or appointed to a church living'.[59] On a basic level, then, some of the more conventional aspects of patronage were simply not available to women. However, it is overly pessimistic to conclude that women did not participate in, and sometimes benefit from, the varieties of patronage available in the early eighteenth century. Delarivier Manley's temporary control of Swift's political journal *The Examiner* is evidence that women sometimes could benefit from patronal encouragement.[60] Furthermore, as Thomas' example shows, women figured as patrons in this period as well as being recipients of patronage themselves.[61] Nevertheless, given women writers' relatively novel presence in print culture it is perhaps inevitable that female experience of patronage differed from systems of male preferment and homosocial encouragement. Unlike their male counterparts, women writers had to be aware of the potentially sala-cious implications of attracting male protection and support. For this reason, gender considerations and issues of dependency often converge in women's negotiations with the patronage system.

Eliza Haywood's participation in and use of patronage has often been overlooked in favour of recent assessments of her as working almost exclusively in the world of the booksellers and printers. Although Haywood did not benefit from the sustained support of any single patron, she did engage fully and variously in the patronage system in its early eighteenth-century incarnations. In fact, in contrast to her con-temporaries, Aubin and Davys, she writes fewer prefaces addressed to an anonymous reading public than she does dedications. As is to be expected, a good proportion of these dedications are addressed to male figures of rank. For example, *Lasselia* (1724) is dedicated to Edward Howard, *The Fatal Secret* (1724) to William Yonge, *Memoirs of the Baron de Brosse* (1725–6) to the Earl of Scarsdale, and *The Lady Philosopher's Stone* (1725) to Lord Herbert.[62] Haywood's early career in the theatre may have increased her awareness of the possible advantages of the patronage system. In the dedication to Lord Viscount Gage for her tragedy *The Fair Captive* (1721), for example, she states that 'the Noblest Performances stand in need of more than their own Merit to support 'em; and the most celebrated Authors, I mean of those whose *Muse* is their *Dependence*, are oblig'd to seek the Protection of some powerful Name'.[63] Here Haywood makes it clear that being a professional writer – 'those whose *Muse* is their *Dependence*' – does not exclude reliance on an influential patron. Scholars working on patronage agree that it is very difficult to gauge the exact rewards such 'protection' might yield. The financial gains for writing a dedication are also far from clear but the abundance of dedications in this period strongly suggests that some economic recompense was available. From the scant evidence we have, Korshin estimates that ten pounds was the average payment for a dedicatory address and that authors therefore only relied on this practice for 'incidental bounty' rather than sustained support.[64] However, given the rapid rate of Haywood's productions, and the fact that most of her novels carried dedications, if she was successful in securing money for each of her addresses this would be a significant addition to her income.

The incidental nature of this form of occasional patronage adds weight to the argument that authorship became more independent in this period as traditional patronage methods waned. In effect, an author could recoup their ten pounds and move swiftly on to the next potential patron without having to maintain the good graces of their original dedicatee. What is crucial to note here, however, is that, in the absence of concrete information, Haywood's approaches to her patrons must be seen as speculative ventures. Her uses of the dedication therefore provide us with a fascinating insight into her perception of the most successful way to make some money from a dedicatory address and her overall take on the position of the woman writer in relation to patronage. The practice of writing dedications may not have secured one single patron to whom the author was forever indebted and dependent, but it was, nonetheless, based on the author's ability to flatter and persuade. Indeed, although Haywood's authorial pronouncements in her dedications have received extended critical coverage, the context of patronage in which they were written has been all but ignored.[65] How, then, did Haywood present herself to her potential patrons? One term Haywood frequently uses to describe the function of patronage is 'Encouragement' which she compares, in the same dedication to Lord Gage, to the 'cold *Contempt*, and blasting *Scorn*' that unprotected writers have to face at the hands of critics. In contrast to this critical scorn, a writer who is supported by a patron can benefit 'by the warm Sun-shine of *Encouragement*', which might enable an author to 'tower to Heights deserving Admiration'. In Haywood's terms, patronage provides the warmth needed to bring an aspiring writer's literary aspirations to fruition.

This dedication shows Haywood to be well-versed in the conventional language of the dedicatory address. 'Encouragement' and 'Protection' were key words in the vocabulary of dedications and Haywood plays on the full range of meanings. 'Protection' suggests that the patron could shield the author from critical or personal attacks. 'Encouragement' similarly incorporates a sense of kindly support, but it could also signal financial reward, being a synonym for cash payment.[66] For women writers, however, the conventional phrases of dedications could accrue different meanings. The usual definition of 'protection', for example, could assume a new importance when used by a woman writer, who may be more vulnerable to attacks on her writing than men. Haywood certainly made this claim in the dedication to Lord Gage, where she refers specifically to the detractions she invites just by being a woman who writes for a living. Haywood also figures her patron as a kind of hero who takes pity on a suffering woman: 'It was in this Condition your Lordship's Pity found me; and by an Excess of Goodness, taught me that those very Misfortunes which wou'd *bar* the Gates of Favour against my Hopes, address'd to those of a less elevated Mind, were Pleas sufficient to *introduce* me here' (pp. viii–ix). Similarly, in the dedicatory address to the Earl of Scarsdale for the *Memoirs of the Baron de Brosse* (1925), Haywood uses the conventional dedicatory vocabulary to draw attention to her specifically female sufferings:

> It would be impossible to recount the numerous Difficulties a *Woman* has to struggle through in her Approach to *Fame*: If her writings are considerable enough to make any Figure in the World, Envy pursues her with unweary'd Diligence; and if, on the contrary, she only writes what is forgot, as soon as read, *Contempt* is all the Reward, her Wish to please, excites; and the cold Breath of Scorn chills the little Genius she has, and which, perhaps, cherished by Encouragement, might, in Time, grow to a Praise-worthy Height. (p. 5)

Such dedications as these play on Haywood's position as a vulnerable woman to frame her position in the patronage system. Women writers, Haywood suggests, are in even more need of patronal encouragement and protection, and it is an extraordinarily good-natured man who will take 'pity' on such suffering females and allow them to fulfil their true potential. Haywood is alert to the conventional language of dedications and she shapes these conventions to refer specifically to her position as a woman writer. The fact that she repeats these strategies on different occasions suggests that her approach was reasonably successful. However, these gendered dedicatory strategies could also be interpreted in a negative way to imply a sexual relation between the female author and the male patron. For example, in the early eighteenth century the word 'protection' could be 'a euphemism for sexual keeping'.[67] In her dedication to Captain John Rawlinson for her novel *The Female Deserters* (1719), Mary Hearne expresses precisely this anxiety:

I make not the least Question, but when the censorious World shall find your Name prefixed (as *Shakespear* calls it) to this *Woman's Toy*, they will presently apply a malicious Construction to the Favours which I here gratefully acknowledge to have received; though at the same time it gives me no small Pleasure to think, that the *Viper* will be employed in gnawing upon the File of Innocent *Friendship*, which, if truly placed, the Philosophers hold to be inseparable.

(pp. 2–3)

For women, the discourse of favours, protection and encouragement was fraught with sexual implications. As a result, in their dedications, many women either confront these issues directly, as Hearne does, or carefully rephrase their use of the terms available to them, in the manner of Haywood.

In addition to her printed dedications, there is also evidence of Haywood's direct appeals to patrons to support her work. In an undated letter to an unknown prospective patron, Haywood presented one of her tragedies for patronal support: 'The indifferent success this Tragedy met with, (not withstanding my great expectations on the account of the Theme) wou'd make me tremble to lay it at the feet of so good a Judge did I not know that truly great and generous minds are always most pleas'd to Confer favours where that are stood in need of.'[68] Haywood makes it clear that she is herself unknown to her potential benefactor ('Tho I am not happy enough to be personally known to you'), but she again emphasizes her position as an unprotected female by claiming that 'an unfortunate marriage has reduc'd me to the melan-cholly necessity of depending on my Pen for the Support of myself and two Children, the eldest of whom is no more than 7 years of age'. Haywood thus draws on her own particularly female misfortunes as a struggling mother, as well as a sense that she is of a good family fallen on hard times, to persuade the patron to support her work. She also draws on the sense that social rank is an indicator of taste by appealing to the good judgement of the patron she addresses. Haywood also recon-figures the term 'protection' to include a sense of the patron acting as a kind of surrogate husband. In the absence of the usual male protec-tion of a husband, Haywood suggests that the male patron can stand in for the figures of male authority lacking in her own life.

In two letters to patrons concerning her translation of Madame de Gomez's *La Belle Assemblée* (first published in 1724), Haywood is more expansive and fulsome in her praise of her patron and, in one of them at least, draws again on her own precarious position. The two letters are very similar in terms of the language used and, as one of them is inscribed to the Countess of Oxford and dated 15 April 1728, it is likely that the other letter is also from this date. There are some interesting distinctions to be made between the letter to an unknown male patron (addressed to 'Honoured Sir') and that to a female patron, the Countess of Oxford.[69] In the first letter Haywood reiterates the comments found in her published dedications concerning the role of patronage for the professional writer. She begins thus: 'Precarious as the condition of a person is whose only dependence is on the pen, to the name of Author wee are indebted for the privilege of imploring the protection of the *great* and *good*', and later she adds, '*Encouragement*, Sr, is the *Sun* by which *poets* thrive'. In the letter to the Countess of Oxford, which is considerably shorter, Haywood omits all mention of her general posi-tion as an author merely suggesting that the 'delicacy of the notions' expressed in the translation (the exact phrase used in the first letter), may appeal to a lady who is 'so much the ornament of her own sex and admiration of the other'. Furthermore, in the letter to the male patron, Haywood is more open about her hardships which play on the sympa-thy of the male protector: 'tho the Inclinations I ever had for writing be now converted to Necessity, by the Sudden Deaths of both a Father, and a Husband, at an age when I was little prepar'd to Stem the tide of Ill fortune, yet will it always be attended with pleasure, and a Justifiable pride, when I am permitted to hope what I write will be read by Your Honr'. There is an interesting gendered dynamic going on here whereby Haywood plays on her position as an 'unprotected' female figure, without the support of husband and father, in order to raise the sympathies of the male patron who is then seen as a surrogate protector for the struggling female writer. This strategy is completely absent from her, otherwise very similarly phrased, letter to the Countess of Oxford.[70]

In view of the potential indelicacy of female to male dedications, it is perhaps not surprising that women writers' choice of female patrons became more widespread as the century progressed. Eliza Haywood, for example, dedicated *The Injur'd Husband* (1723) to Lady Howe, *Philidore and Placentia* (1727) to Lady Abergavenny, *The City Widow* (1729) to a Mrs Burscoe and *The Rash Resolve* (1724) to Lady Romney.[71] Each of the four books of her periodical *The Female Spectator* (1744–6) is dedicated to a woman.[72] In her only dedicatory address, Jane Barker chose the Countess of Exeter as her patron.[73] Mary Davys also dedicates most of her fiction to women. *The Amours of Alcippus and Lucippe* (1704) is dedicated to Margaret Walker, *The Fugitive* (1705) to Esther Johnson (Swift's Stella), *The Cousins* (1725) to Lady Slingsby and her play *The Northern Heiress* (1716) to Princess Anne, the daughter of George I. What is particular about Davys' use of dedications to women is the way in which she uses the approach to a woman to reach the real object of her plea: the male relations or friends of the woman in question. This is shown in the dedication to Margaret Walker, who is clearly defined only in relation to her male relatives. She is described as 'Wife to Capt. Walker, And Daughter to the Late Honourable Sir John Jefferson, one of his late Majesty's Judges in Ireland'. The dedication to Esther Johnson clearly has Swift in mind, and the dedication to Princess Anne has been seen as Davys' 'most obvious attempt to reach the seat of power through a female member of it'.[74] Davys' dedications are also linked to her Irish background and to the period of time she spent in York: Lady Slingsby was from a notable Yorkshire family.[75] Penelope Aubin's dedications are fairly equally split between male and female patrons. *The Noble Slaves* (1722) is dedicated to Lady Coleraine, *The Life of the Countess de Gomez* (1729) to Mrs Guerin, *The Doctrine of Morality* (1721) to the Duchess of Ormonde and *The Life of Charlotta du Pont* (1723) to Mrs Rowe.[76] Her poem *The Stuarts* (1707) was appropriately dedicated to Queen Anne. Delarivier Manley had also addressed a female patron when she dedicated *The Power of Love* (1720) to Lady Lansdowne.

Whereas male patrons are more likely to be addressed as manly protectors, taking pity on poor suffering females, women patrons are often constructed as female paragons, whose specifically feminine virtues reflect back on the female author. However, the conventional language of dedications again poses problems for the woman writer even if the recipient is female. As commentators on Aphra Behn's dedicatory addresses to women have shown, the sexualized language of flattery employed by male writers to female patrons was often appropriated by women by, what Laura Runge terms as, a 'cross-gendered appropriation of gallantry'.[77] As Runge argues, on one level, a woman's praise of another woman avoids the suspicion of sexually motivated flattery contained in the compliments presented by a man. A woman can therefore claim to be more truthful in her praise of a female. In her dedication to *The Rash Resolve* (1724), addressed to Lady Rumney, Haywood addresses these issues:

> Flattery is a Vice so much in Fashion, and, I am sorry to say, so much encouraged, that there is nothing more difficult than to find a Patron who not expects, nor would be pleased with it: Where then should a Person, by Nature averse, and by Precept taught to shun it, make an Address of this Nature, but to a Lady, whose Character is so justly establish'd for all those Graces both of Mind and Body, which can be an Ornament to our Sex, that it would be needless as vain to attempt a Repetition of them.

Haywood here betrays an anxiety about the sycophantic nature of dedications which expose the mercenary motives of the author. In a dedication to Lady Howe for *The Injur'd Husband* (1723), Haywood had similarly tried to disassociate herself from any suspicion of naked materialism: 'the press is set to work only to gratifie a mercenary End, and He or She who is look'd on as a Person most likely to serve that Purpose is address'd and fulsome Praises and undeserv'd Encomiums generally answer the Design they are given for'. As well as trying not to appear excessively fulsome, it was also very difficult to avoid emphasizing the beauties of the woman being praised. Haywood, like Behn before her, thus becomes caught up in the masculine codes she is attempting to circumvent. She follows her remarks to Lady Rumney with a breathless account of her subject's charms: 'You, Madam! Are possess'd of Charms which the Soul only can describe! 'tis not Words to speak them. We all admire the Diamond's sparkling Lustre; but tho' we gaze never so long on the thousand differing colour'd Rays it casts, no Artist yet had ever skill to paint the Brightness of it.' Haywood's terms of praise here are perilously close to the language used to depict female fickleness by Pope in *The Rape of the Lock* and *Epistle: On the Characters of Women*.

Despite her inability to escape the masculine codes of fulsome praise, Haywood does manage to shift the emphasis of her flattery to promote a sense of Lady Rumney's mental abilities as well as her physical perfections: 'Those who are acquainted but with a part of those shining Qualities which make up the Character of your Ladyship, and consider you only as a Woman of Rank, admirable fine Sense, and the most discerning Judgement in the World; will, perhaps, be astonish'd at my Presumption in throwing at your Feet a Trifle so little capable of meriting your Regard.' As well as possessing taste, judgement and sense, Lady Rumney's mental qualities are also gendered feminine. She is described as having a 'Sweetness of Disposition' and is addressed as 'so Sweet a Judge'. As Haywood's emphasis on her patron's feminine sweetness suggests, female patrons were also useful for women writers as exemplars of virtuous femininity which could endorse the respectability of the woman writer herself. Haywood gains from her association with such a paragon of female virtue, and her fiction is similarly endorsed and authorized for her female readers who take the place of the sweet and virtuous primary recipient of the text. Just as the figure of the female author became increasingly domesticated as the century progressed, as shown by the examples of Rowe and Brereton, so too does the female patron come to assume the attributes of socially acceptable femininity. As Runge has shown in relation to Mary Pix's dedication to Princess Anne for *The Inhumane Cardinal* (1696), female patrons became increasingly associated with 'the proper female roles of wife and mother'.[78] This is most clearly shown in Aubin's dedication to Mrs Rowe for *The Life of Charlotta du Pont* (1723), where the recipient is described as 'the best Wife, the best Friend, the most prudent, most humble, and most accomplished Woman I ever met withal'. The use of female patrons by women writers, therefore, avoided the dangers expressed by Mary Hearne about the implications of a woman receiving male 'protection' and 'favours'. Women could use the feminine virtue of their patron to authorize their own positions as female authors, and also to make their fiction respectable by association. This strategy was particularly successful for Penelope Aubin. When Elizabeth Griffiths included Aubin's *The Noble Slaves* for a collection of novels she edited in 1777, she remarked of Aubin's association with Lady Coleraine, the projected patron of that novel, that 'This circumstance would certainly stamp her character as a decent and virtuous woman, if her writings had not already fixed her moral merits upon the firmest base.'[79]

As well as approaching members of the aristocracy or gentry, women writers also dedicated their work to other literary figures or participants in literary circles, sometimes male and sometimes female. Evidence of such interactions goes against Isobel's Grundy's sense that women were excluded from 'the new, mutual helping-hand system among professional colleagues' in the eighteenth century.[80] Haywood's bookseller, William Chetwood, acted as her 'introduction' to the literary world in his preface to *Love in Excess*, which is dedicated to the actress Ann Oldfield. Chetwood takes on the role of a paternal figure who is acting on behalf of an anonymous and anxious 'young lady'. Chetwood's choice was astute. Oldfield was an influential and extremely popular actress in the early eighteenth century who had a range of connections with theatre managers, writers and patrons. As David Oakleaf notes in his edition of *Love in Excess*, Oldfield 'moved in aristocratic circles as mistress of Brigadier General Charles Churchill (natural son of the Duke of Marlborough's brother); a potentially valuable patron who helped support Richard Savage'.[81] Haywood was soon in a position where she could choose her own patrons, and her choice was also astute. In 1724 she dedicated *The Surprise; or, Constancy Rewarded* to Richard Steele who, as Pat Rogers has shown, was one of the most popular recipients of dedications in the early eighteenth century.[82] Haywood's dedication to Steele would align her in print with one of the most high-profile literary figures of the day. Haywood is attempting to increase her own cultural capital by associating herself with a major literary figure and arbiter of taste; as she comments 'The next Step to having Merit one's self, is to admire it in another.' She goes on to emphasize her appreciation of Steele's writing in order to display her own taste, discrimination, and 'noble Sentiment':

> I no longer can refrain that publick Acknowledgement which is your Due from the whole World, whom your inimitable Writings have improv'd. Others may boast the instructive Art in some one Science to embellish Learning; but you refine the Mind, and make it fit for elevated Impressions. [. . .] You, Sir, teach us how to *Think* as well as *Act*; and by inspiring us with just and noble Sentiment, render it impossible to behave in a Manner contrary to them.

It is clear, then, that women writers were centrally involved in the patronage system and used it in sophisticated ways to increase their finances and to advance their reputations. However, as I have argued, women's use of patronage was also gendered, and dedicatory addresses written by women shift the terms of the conventional language of dedications to refer specifically to the position of women in literary culture. Furthermore, while it is clear that female patrons were a popular choice for women, the terms on which these women were addressed are often markedly different from appeals to male figures. Unlike their male counterparts, female patrons could offer women the 'protection' of feminine virtue. A recognition of the importance of patronage for women writers raises some important issues for thinking about female authorship in this period. First, it is apparent that women's involvement in the literary marketplace was not just based on an author–bookseller dynamic, but incorporated the patronage system in both an economic sense, as a way of raising income, and a symbolic sense, as a way of elevating a woman's status as a writer. Second, as the various dedications discussed in this section have demonstrated, a woman writer's reputation was based as much on the various connections she made, or claimed to make, with figures of rank and literary standing as it was on the sales of her texts. Overall, then, any account of female authorship in this period must incorporate the full range of literary contexts and practices available for the aspiring author. Women's participation in the literary marketplace was a complex amalgam of social networking and commercial pressure. This combination of sociable and economic practices come together most prominently in the final mode of authorship I discuss here: subscription publication.

Subscription publishing

Subscription publication is often identified as one of the innovations in literary patronage which flourished in the eighteenth century.[83] This mode of publication can be seen as a 'half-way house between dependence on a single patron to underwrite a book and reliance upon sales'.[84] The subscribers, usually drummed up by the author or friends of the author, financed the publication of a book by buying copies in advance of production, or, more typically, by paying half in advance and half on receipt. Ideally, an author could gain considerably more from this method of publication than from direct sale of copy. In addition, the list of names printed with the subscription edition acted as a public endorsement from an identified set of readers. Subscription is further evidence for the overlapping economies of patronage and marketplace in this period. The subscription system relies, in the first instance, on the support of well-known or aristocratic 'friends' of the author, whose public acknowledgement of the text provides a standard of taste by which the volume can be authorized. Aristocratic names are often placed first in the list of subscribers. In this sense, subscription conforms to the usual workings of patronage in that it provides the author with cultural capital in addition to economic reward. However, subscription also shifts the usual power balance between individual patron and author to a broader group dynamic where a variety of people all subscribe to one work. In contrast to previous forms of patronage again, the bulk of subscribers did not necessarily come from the higher ranks of society, but included a broader range of middling-class buyers and readers. These subscribers increasingly came to include those from the provinces as well as London[85] On one level, then, the subscription system represents a democratization of patronage in line with marketplace practices, whereby a more representative group of readers act as patrons in their public support and endorsement of the author and the text.

Alexander Pope's career demonstrates the extensive rewards subscription could bring for the author, if properly handled. However, Pope's experience of the system was exceptional. For the majority of authors, subscription was considerably less lucrative, especially if the author was less well-known and less well-connected; a more likely position for women writers to be in. Indeed, far from being conclusive evidence of the diminishing of the patronage system in this period, subscription as a mode of publication was still 'heavily dependent upon personal contact and the favour of individuals'.[86] Furthermore, as I will argue in relation to Mary Barber, the politics of subscription were still imbued with notions of dependency, sycophancy and gratitude, which continued to place the author in a subordinate position. However, many women benefited from subscription, and this method of publication was to become especially popular for women poets from the 1730s onwards. Subscription was particularly prominent as way of getting provincial women into print. Mary Masters' *Poems on Several Occasions* (1733) was the first volume of women's poetry published by this method. Masters hailed from Norwich, and a fair proportion of the subscribers to her work came from Norwich also.[87] Subscription therefore seems to have been an enabling mode of publication for the woman poet. Nevertheless, the terms upon which women entered print through subscription were often predicated on notions of charity and benevolence, rather than the encouragement or acknowledgement of literary talent. As Roger Lonsdale notes, 'The aim of such subscriptions was often less to encourage a woman writer to embark on a precarious literary career than to reward a "deserving" wife or mother and her family with some degree of financial security.'[88]

Although such presentations of the female author as objects of charity could be potentially limiting, they are also in keeping with broader constructions of the woman writer, which similarly emphasized virtuous and deserving femininity. As a publication practice, the subscription system chimed with ideological conceptions of the respectable woman writer that were beginning to become prominent around mid-century: domestic, feminine, private and provincial. Subscription, then, provides an interesting example of the way in which the material circumstances of publication directly affect broader constructions of female authorship. What it is also necessary to remember is the commercial impetus behind the construction of the virtuous woman writer. The presentation of the female author as the object of the subscribers' charity can also be read as an effective marketing ploy, designed to increase the number of names on the subscription list. A recognition of subscription as a significant part of women's publication practices also highlights the importance of social networks for female authorship in this period. Many subscription editions, such as those by Mary Masters and also Jane Brereton, were products of the authors' social circumstances and reflect the circles they inhabited and the original readers of their work. In the case of these two writers in particular, their provincial context is directly reflected in both the content of the poetry, and in the list of subscribers who encouraged the authors.

The women writers who published by subscription in the early eighteenth century use a variety of approaches, from the apparently self-organized subscription publication of Eliza Haywood's translation *Letters from a Lady of Quality to a Chevalier* (1721), to the extensive support of a male figure to enable the subscription, as in the case of Jonathan Swift's interventions on behalf of Mary Barber in the early 1730s. A pattern which became more common as the century progressed was the encouragement of a lower-class woman writer by women of higher status, as shown by Bridget Fremantle's activity on behalf of Mary Leapor, and later, in the promotion of Mary Jones by her aristocratic female friends Martha Lovelace, Lady Bowyer and Charlot Clayton.[89] Leapor's poems appeared in two subscription volumes in 1747 and 1751 respectively. Mary Jones' *Miscellanies in Prose and Verse* was published with a list of approximately 1400 subscribers in 1750. There are further examples of the support of social circles providing a net of potential subscribers. Mary Davys relied on the clientele of her coffee house in Cambridge as subscribers to her *Works* (1725) and *The Reform'd Coquet* (1724). Similarly, Elizabeth Boyd relied on the support of friends and acquaintances to subscribe to her novel *The Happy Unfortunate; or, The Female Page* (1732).

Women's fiction and subscription publication

In 1721 Haywood published a translation *Letters from a Lady of Quality to a Chevalier* by subscription. The timing of this edition implies that

Haywood was attempting to capitalize on the success of *Love in Excess* from the previous year.[90] Details of Haywood's attempts to secure subscribers for her edition can be gleaned from a letter dated 5 August 1720 to an unidentified male patron, from whom Haywood had previously received support. Haywood comments that 'I am Mistress of neither Words nor happy Turn of thought to Thank You as I ought for the many unmeritted favours you have Conferred on me.'[91] Haywood draws on the patron's past indulgence to persuade him to subscribe to the edition. She encloses the proposals for the book, and claims that as the stage has been unprofitable for her she has turned to novel writing and translation. She also capitalizes here on the success of *Love in Excess*:

> I have Printed some little things which have mett a better Reception than they Deserved, or I expected: and have now Ventur'd on a Translation to be done by Subscription, the Proposals whereof I take the Liberty to send you: I have been so much used to Receive favours from you that I can make no Doubt of yr forgiveness for this freedom great as it is, and that you will become one of those Persons whose Names are a Countenance to my Undertaking.

It is clear that Haywood perceived subscription to be a species of patronage. In the published preface to the *Letters*, Haywood draws attention to the subscription list to authorize her production. She plays on her 'humble' status as a writer to deflect criticism away from any suspicion of self-promotion, and instead foregrounds the 'judgement' and taste of the patron-subscribers as markers of the text's quality and worth. She also employs the conventional language of patronage, 'encouragement' and 'protection', to refer to the subscribers to her book:

> The Rush of Winds, which shake the aspiring *Cedar*, spare the humble *Reed*: I am too safe, in an insignificant Lowness, to fear the Blast of Envy, if the unquestionable Judgement of those Persons, who encourag'd me to undertake the Translation of the following Sheets, were not a sufficient Protection from whatever Malice or Ill-Nature might suggest.[92]

The subscribers include aristocratic figures, such as Lady Howard and Lady Herbert. The list also provides evidence of Haywood's involvement in London literary circles. Aaron Hill appears in the list as well as an intriguing entry under the name Mrs Barker. However, the list also includes a fair proportion of untitled names and a good quantity of women, upholding Cheryl Turner's claim that women's more general participation in print culture, 'as readers, as writers, and as patrons', was increasing in the early eighteenth century.[93] In terms of the status of the patrons, subscription was evidently part of a democratization process whereby the traditional structure of patronage was weakening. Whether or not this process extended to authors is considerably more difficult to determine. Haywood was not to use subscription as a publication method after this date. Catherine Ingrassia argues that this is due to Haywood's particular place in the literary marketplace as the consummate professional, who relied on 'her rapid rate of composition' and 'her ability to accommodate public taste, to create and respond to the desires of consumers, and to compete actively within print culture'.[94] Ingrassia concludes that subscription publication, which she views as more usually associated with more culturally valued publications (such as history and essays), was 'not consistent with Haywood's abilities or interests'. The most obvious reason for Haywood's rejection of subscription, however, is that it was not the most profitable or time-efficient way of publishing her work. She continued to use all the other available methods for attracting finance that were on offer for the professional author in the early eighteenth century and which were evidently more lucrative than subscription.

This is borne out by a quick glance at other women writers who employed subscription publication in the early eighteenth century, many of whom, like Haywood, only used subscription on a single occasion as a way of supplementing other methods of earning money from publication. In 1724, Mary Davys published *The Reform'd Coquet* by subscription, and a year later she published her *Works* in two volumes by the same method. In the preface to *The Reform'd Coquet*, Davys stresses the fact that she has male support and encouragement to publish, namely from the Cambridge undergraduates who frequented her coffee house. As I demonstrated in Chapter 2, Davys uses the increasingly familiar strategy of presenting herself as an impoverished widow in need of charitable support. She presents her position as a deserving object of charity as the main reason why people would wish to subscribe to her novel: 'it was not to the Book, but the Author, they subscribed'.[95] Despite Davys' self-effacement and the implication that her novel is not, in itself, of any artistic merit, the subscription list includes a fair number of aristocratic figures, as well as members of the London literary world. John Gay subscribed to *The Reform'd Coquet* and Alexander Pope to the *Works*.

The publication history of Elizabeth Boyd's novel *The Happy Unfortunate* provides some useful details on the practicalities of subscription publishing. A copy of Boyd's *Proposals for printing by subscription a novel Entitled, the Happy-Unfortunate; or The Female Page* (1732) are still in existence.[96] The proposals were printed after the book had gone into press, and included a list of names of those who had already subscribed. The subscription money was used to finance the production of the book: 'The Book being now in the Press, Subscription Money will be taken, that the Work may be forwarded with all possible Speed.' The proposals add that 'The Subscription will be carried on, whilst the Book is in the Press, till the Three Parts is compleatly printed.' The way in which the subscribers receive their books is also detailed: 'The Books when finish'd, will be carefully sent to the Subscribers Houses, or where they shall think proper to appoint, by the Author.' There are details of how much the book will cost, when the money should be paid, and to whom: 'The Price to the Subscribers will be Five Shillings; Half a Crown to be paid down, and Half a Crown on the Delivery of the Book in Sheets.' It is clear that both Elizabeth Boyd and her publishers were responsible for organizing and collecting subscriptions: 'And any Person, who will do the Author the Honour to Subscribe, are desir'd to send to her Lodgings, *viz.* to *Eliz. Boyd*, at Mr. *Wylder*'s, Coach-maker, in *Brewer's-Street*, by *Goldern-Square*, or to the Places under mention'd, where Subscriptions will be taken.' The undermentioned places are to the publisher Thomas Edlin and to two coffee houses: West-Saxon Coffee-House in Charing Cross and the German Coffee-House in St James Street. After the list of subscribers' names is a blank receipt that is to be filled in by Boyd, or her representatives, as proof of part-payment and future payment on the delivery of the printed sheets.

The printed version of the first part of *The Happy Unfortunate* was dedicated to John Campbell, Duke of Argyll and Greenwich, and acknowledged Campbell's patronage from an earlier date.[97] The preface outlines the reasons for the lateness of the appearance of the printed volume, and apologizes to the subscribers for the delay. Boyd gives 'a great Indisposition' as the reason for her lateness. In keeping with the dedication, Boyd claims that the novel was written 'when its Author was very young', and again gives ill-health as the reason why she has not corrected the text as far as she would have wished. Boyd also claims that she has no desire to please the 'little Splenetick Criticks', declaring that her 'sole Ambition' is 'to deserve my Subscriber's smiles'. Like Davys before her, Boyd casts the subscribers in the charitable role of a patron, and thanks them copiously for their help in raising her out of poverty. The subscribers are described as having 'in so genteel, and conspicious a Manner rais'd me from almost the lowest Condition of Fortune, and a worse State of Health'. Boyd adds that her 'most ardent Wishes' for the subscribers' 'continu'd Happiness' are felt 'with the deepest Sense of Gratitude'. In an advertisement added after the list of subscribers, Boyd states that she will set herself up 'in a Way of Trade', selling a variety of stationary goods in order to support her ailing mother. In a manner similar to Elizabeth Thomas' wish to avoid idleness, Boyd entreats her subscribers to continue their support by becoming her customers. Boyd claims that she has printed her manuscript, 'which otherwise I never had done', solely to provide for her mother. Therefore, Boyd presents her publication as enabling her subscribers to perform a charitable act to the deserving. She also suggests that she can build on her income from the book to support herself, and her family, by her own labour. As such, she removes herself from a professional context for writing and instead emphasizes her independent yet deserving nature.

The case of Mary Barber (c.1685–1755)

In the promotion of her subscription edition, Boyd draws heavily on the language of gratitude and dependency, despite her claim that her ultimate goal is to be self-supporting. This stance is also prominent in the authorial self-presentation of Mary Barber. In the case of Barber, however, the politics of subscription are more complex and are reflected in the content of her poetry as well as her authorial self-fashioning. The publication history of Barber's collection also provides a rather different set of circumstances by which to judge women's participation in the subscription system. Mary Barber was an impoverished Irishwoman, the wife of an unsuccessful draper in Dublin. By 1728, she was one of the circle of women writers around Swift, which also included Laetitia Pilkington and Constantia Grierson.[98] In 1730 Barber came to England where she settled in Bath. From the early 1730s plans were underway for a subscription edition of her poems, many of which had initially been written for her children. After a series of delays, *Poems on Several Occasions* eventually appeared in June 1735.[99]

Jonathan Swift was instrumental in arranging the subscription edition of Barber's 1735 poems. Swift intervened on Barber's behalf with his aristocratic friends and persuaded them to support Barber by subscribing. In a letter to the Earl of Oxford, dated 9 June 1731, Barber wrote from Soho in London to introduce herself by using Swift's name. She writes:

The Dean has desired Lord and Lady Oxford, Lady Margaret Harley, and Mr Harley and his son may be told 'tis his request she should be honoured with their names. She flattered herself from his Lordship's known humanity and love of arts that a woman, a stranger far from her friends and her country, who was recommended by one of the greatest genius's in the world who has so just an esteem of Lord Oxford, could not fail of his patronage.[100]

By 1733 it is clear that the subscription edition was well underway and that Swift's name had considerably smoothed its passage. In this year, Swift himself wrote to the Earl of Oxford from Dublin in a letter to be delivered by Barber:

> This letter will be delivered to you by Mrs. Mary Barber, who coming over hither last year on her private affairs was snapped by the gout, who made her such frequent visits that it prevented her return to London for several months. She is now well enough to undertake her voyage, and very easily prevailed with me to write in her favour to your Lordship. She is by far the best poet of her sex in England, and is a virtuous, modest gentlewoman, with a great deal of good sense, and a true poetical genius. Your Lordship must have often heard of her; for I believe you, or my Lady Oxford or Lady Margaret, have subscribed for her poetical works, which would have been published before this time, if she had not been so long confined by her illness here. My request is that all your family, friends and relations (who have not done it already) should by your commands immediately become her subscribers, and that my Lady Oxford and Lady Margaret shall be her particular protectors.[101]

Swift's postscript makes it clear that Barber had already received support from Lord and Lady Oxford: 'Since I writ this letter upon talking to Mrs. Barber, she told me with the greatest marks of gratitude, what honour and favour she received from your Lordship and my Lady Oxford.'[102] Barber benefited, then, considerably from her acquaintance with Swift, his energetic interventions on her behalf, and his genuine admiration for her poetry. The subscription list is extremely weighty, and, in the event, the Earl of Oxford subscribed for four books. The list also includes a high proportion of aristocratic names, as well as writers, including Mary Chandler, Elizabeth Rowe and, yet again, Alexander Pope. As Adam Budd calculates, '1,106 copies of her book were signed for by 918 subscribers, 249 of whom were aristocracy and other nobles representing 183 titled families – more than one-third of the entire British nobility and baronetage.'[103]

The printed format of Barber's *Poems on Several Occasions* draws on the context of its production. The reader has to wade through two dedications, a preface and three poems before reaching the collection proper. The major theme of this preliminary material is Barber's dependence on her patrons and her gratitude for their support, as well as the usual justifications concerning female authorship. In Barber's case, the two are clearly linked as her status as a female poet is inextricably bound up with her dependent status as an object of charity. The collection was dedicated by Barber to John Boyle, Earl of Orrery, but was authorized further by a letter from Swift to the Earl which acts as a preliminary dedication, serving to introduce Barber to her patron and her readers via the approval of a well-known and respected male literary figure.[104] Swift's dedication serves as a kind of meta-dedication, where he sketches out the kind of dedicatory address Barber should herself provide. The fact that Swift's dedication is placed before Barber's own gives it an authority which dictates the terms of her own commentary. The dedication also serves as an introduction by a well-known male figure to the work of an obscure woman poet. As I have noted, Chetwood's dedication to Ann Oldfield served a similar function for Eliza Haywood. Swift is concerned to point out that, in her sincere gratitude to her patron, Barber is raised above 'the common Herd of Dedicators'. Unlike most recipients of patronal support, Barber has 'an overflowing Spirit of Thankfulness', which is directly linked to 'the humble Opinion she hath of herself'. This view of Barber is continued in Swift's more general comments on her as a female poet. Swift suggests to Boyle that, 'she deserveth your Protection on account of her Wit and good Sense, as well as her Humility, her Gratitude, and many other Virtues'. Furthermore, the poems reflect the virtue of the poet as 'they generally contain something new and useful, tending to the Reproof of some Vice or Folly, or recommending some Virtue'. Swift continues his praise of Barber by drawing attention not only to her sex, but also her class position. She demonstrates a 'true poetical Genius, better cultivated than could well be expected, either from her Sex, or the Scene she hath acted in, as the Wife of a Citizen'. He concludes by stressing that her poetry has not detracted from her role as a good wife, by emphasizing her amateur status and her humility in deferring to the greater critical judgement of others: 'no Woman was ever more useful to her Husband in the Way of his Business. Poetry hath only been her favourite Amusement; for she hath one Qualification, that I wish all good Poets possess'd a Share of, I mean, that she is ready to take Advice, and submit to have her Verses corrected, by those who are generally allow'd to be the best Judges.'

Swift's dedication situates Barber in terms of her gender and class position as a citizen's wife to present her as a worthy object of patronage. Such characterizations also, of course, reflect back upon the virtue and charitableness of the subscribers who are endorsed by their support of the deserving woman poet. What is particularly interesting about Barber's collection, however, is the way in which Barber herself mediates these expectations in her own commentary on her position, and in her poems. In her own dedication, Barber presents Boyle as an exemplar of male domestic virtue. He is described as having 'an early Disposition to filial Piety', which was 'easily improv'd into conjugal Felicity and Affection'. Such a characterization of the male patronal figure serves to authorize Barber's own position as wife and mother; as she states, 'A good Son, and a good Husband, are Characters that include whatever is most amiable in human Nature; at least if Mothers and Wives, may be allowed for Judges.' This anticipates Barber's use of her own maternal authority as a way of framing her poetic voice in the poems to her children included in the collection. She claims in the preface that the aim of her poetry was principally 'to form the Minds of my Children'.[105] Barber is also expansive about her dependence on patronage. Like Haywood, she is aware of the economic benefits of patronage, but refigures these rewards by describing patronage as a kind of social and religious virtue:

> I have often thought, my Lord, when I have been reading Dedica-
> tions, that it was very odd in Authors, to confess they had already
> receiv'd great Favours, and yet request a greater, in desiring Protec-
> tion for their Writings: But since it has happen'd in my own Case, I
> now view it in another Light; and affirm, that nothing could shew a
> true Grandeur of Soul in the greatest of Mankind, than the support-
> ing the Dependence, which their Patronage encouraged.

Barber presents the position of the poet as one of absolute and ongoing dependence. This hierarchy of power is reinforced by Barber's expressed sense of the gratitude she feels by the encouragement of those of higher rank. She ends her dedication by stating that Boyle's patronage was of such a sort that those 'below' him 'think it a *Blessing*, to have *Superiors*'.

In the preface to the collection, Barber includes various vignettes which attest to the charitable nature of the different patrons she has been associated with. What is significant about her self-representation here is the way in which she presents herself as a dispenser of charity. Barber's first public act as a poet was a poem on behalf of an officer's widow, Mrs Gordon, in which Barber appealed for Lady Carteret's support. 'The Widow *Gordon's* Petition' is the third poem printed in the collection. In this poem, Barber adopts the voice of the grieving widow whose miseries are fully described:

> No Friendly Voice my lonely Mansion cheers,
> All fly th' Infection of the Widow's Tears:
> Ev'n those, whose Pity eas'd my Wants with Bread,
> Are now, O sad Reverse! My greatest Dread.
> My mournful Story will no more prevail,
> And ev'ry Hour I dread a dismal Jail:
> I start at each imaginary Sound, ·
> And *Horrors have encompass'd me around.* (17–24)

In the preface, Barber uses this poem as a way of deflecting attention away from any desire she may have to be a published poet. She claims that her verses were not written from a wish for literary fame but to instruct her children, and adds: 'Nor was I ever known to write upon any other Account, till the Distresses of an Officer's Widow set me upon drawing a Petition in Verse, having found that other Methods had proved ineffectual for her Relief.' Later in the preface, Barber expresses a similar sentiment with regard to the subscription edition of her poems. She states that she was 'encouraged to print them' only at the request of 'several Persons of Quality and Distinction, who generously offer'd to sollicit a Subscription for me'. It was only because of this, and the hope for 'some Advantage to my Family', that Barber was talked out of her 'Diffidence and Reluctance', and persuaded to publish.

Barber thus uses her own charitableness to increase her worth as an object of charity for others as well as authorizing herself as a writer. As Valerie Rumbold has argued, 'The origin of Barber's public writing in a vicarious appeal for charity is vital to the writing that follows.'[106] Indeed, the poems included in the collection are obsessed with charitable acts and the relief of economic distress. In a poem addressed to her son, 'A True Tale', for example, when asked by her son what she would bestow if she were queen, the maternal voice in the poem answers: 'What I'd bestow, says she, my Dear?/At least, *a thousand pounds a year*' (87–8). The context of this poem is her son's distress that so worthy a writer as John Gay, whose fables the mother has been reading to him, should go without reward. The son cries 'O dear Mamma, can he want Friends,/Who writes for such exalted Ends' (57–8), and declares that, if he were wealthy, Gay would have no reason to complain. This poem works on one level as an endorsement of one of Swift's friends and also serves as an appeal to Queen Caroline to patronize Gay. The mother comforts her son by assuring him that, 'He'll be the Care of Caroline', and adds, rather idealistically, that 'Poets, who write to mend the Mind,/A Royal Recompence shou'd find' (79–80). The poem also works, of course, as a vindication of Barber herself. In the final poem of the volume, 'To a Lady, who commanded me to send her an Account in Verse, how I succeeded in my *Subscription*', Barber presents a satirical account of all those who refused to subscribe to her poems. In the last stanza of the poem, Barber justifies herself, and those who did subscribe, by comparing an ideal female patron to the meanness of those who refused to support the collection:

> You, Madam, who your Sex adorn,
> Who Malice and Detraction scorn,
> Who with superior Sense are bless'd,
> Of ev'ry real Worth possess'd.   (119–22)

As an exemplar of the female sex the lady is praised for her specifically feminine qualities but also for her 'superior Sense' which allows her to recognize Barber's 'Faults' yet 'With Eye indulgent view my Lays' (123). Barber then goes on to defend herself by emphasizing her innocence and the altruistic motives behind her verses. She does not set up for a wit, but as a teacher and guide:

> One Merit I presume to boast,
> And dare to plead but one at most:
> The Muse I never have debas'd;
> My Lays are innocent at least;
> Were ever ardently design'd
> To mend and to enlarge the Mind.
> This must be own'd a virtuous Aim.
> The Praise of Wit – let others claim.   (127–34)

On one level, then, Barber's self-representation is very similar to the sentiments expressed by other women poets, especially Jane Brereton. For Barber, however, the context of patronage and subscription provide a further framework for her authorial construction as she consistently refers to her gratefully subordinate position in relation to her patrons and subscribers; a position of deference which is further enforced by her class position as the wife of a citizen. Barber's effusive expressions of gratitude raise problems for modern readers. What Pat Rogers has termed 'the poetics of dedication' are alienating for those not attuned to the rigid hierarchies of eighteenth-century society. As Rogers notes, 'we need a term which does not exist in social theory, to describe the prevailing note of sycophancy'.[107] This problem is exacerbated in the case of Mary Barber as it filters through to her actual poems as well as the usual dedicatory addresses. As two commentators on Barber's verse have noted, independently of each other, Barber's poetic authority is often severely compromised by her deferential stance. Valerie Rumbold and, more recently, Christopher Fanning, both argue that Barber's poetry is ultimately limited by her continual awareness of the context in which she was writing. Rumbold raises the question as to whether Barber's poetry is 'hopelessly vitiated by sycophancy', and Fanning suggests that Barber's technique of 'indirection' in her work, through the use of various poetic voices other than her own, ultimately 'requires a degree of self-effacement which obscures authority'.[108] In effect, in her desire to please her patrons and subscribers, Barber severely compromised the quality of her poetry.[109]

When read alongside her female contemporaries, however, Barber's attempt to balance public gratitude against individual expression may appear less compromised or, at least, the problems she encountered may seem less specific to her. Like many other writers at the time she is dependent on the favours of the great and the good and has to tailor her image accordingly. Barber's self-effacement was, perhaps, a necessary evil in that the subscription basis of her poems enforced a recognition of the subscribers' favours in the poems themselves. In one sense, then, Barber would have been ill-advised not to foreground her gratitude if she wished the volume to succeed. Deference could also be seen as a survival strategy, especially in view of Barber's class position. Barber also has to contend with the expectations about female authorship in general. Like her contemporaries again, Barber has to disguise her 'unfeminine' economic motives under the guise of charitable relief. Paradoxically, this stance also has a commercial basis in that it would make her poems, and her poetic persona, initially more attractive to potential readers/patrons of her work. However, in the most recent article on Barber, Adam Budd makes the case that the subscription project did not bring Barber the financial rewards she was hoping for. Budd argues that because Barber did not have a published record to draw on as a poet, and was therefore seen as an object of charity rather than of artistic merit, interest in her work inevitably waned during the delays between initial subscription and eventual publication. As a result, although the subscription list was ostensibly impressive, the subscribers' initial interest in Barber's plight may only have been cursory and did not, in the event, guarantee a financial reward for the poet. Barber was therefore in a no-win situation. Her only hope of attracting subscribers was to appeal to their charity. Yet it was because of this necessarily deferential stance, which also detracted from the value of her poetry, that her subscription edition failed to bring her the economic support she so badly needed.

As Valerie Rumbold suspects, Barber's collection of poems has much to tell us about 'gender, economics and the literary world'.[110] It is not enough to view women's participation in the literary marketplace only in relation to an author–bookseller dynamic which focuses primarily on the crude economic exchange of copy for copyright. Rather, the marketplace for books and publication practices in this period relied on a complex network of patrons and subscribers, as well as booksellers and printers. What Barber's example makes explicit, is the need to contextualize the material conditions under which women entered print if we are to understand fully the various influences, both social and economic, which shaped female authorship and female literary authority in this period. It was extremely difficult for a woman to have complete control over her authorial image, her poetic voice, or her texts, if she wanted to enter print and/or receive patronal support. Women writers' relations to print culture were compromised in a variety of ways, but it is important to be precise about why and how these compromises were enacted. One of the factors I have been emphasizing throughout this chapter is the economic side to female authorship in the early eighteenth century, and the commercial aspect of women's involvement in print culture. Just as women novelists had to be alert to the kind of fiction their booksellers found popular, so too does a woman like Mary Barber have to construct her authorial voice in line with the expectations of her patrons and subscribers. Although appeals to patrons frequently deflect attention away from any self-interested mercenary motives on the part of the author, it is clear that the construction of the woman writer as an object of charitable pity was also a bid to satisfy a consumer demand of a different kind: the expectations of the patrons and subscribers who financed – or appeared to finance – the production of the text.

Part III
The Literary Career of Elizabeth Singer Rowe

5
Gender, Authorship and Whig Poetics

Elizabeth Singer Rowe (1674–1737) was one of the most high-profile and popular women writers of her day. Yet her place in the history of women's writing has been relatively marginal. Why has this been the case? One reason is that Rowe has been assigned a very particular role in women's literary history which has narrowed assessments of her significance. Rowe's image has been one of sentimental piety and modest retirement: exactly the impression that her posthumous biography sought to imprint in the minds of her readers. In terms of the broader paradigms of women's literary history, Rowe serves as a rather dull example of what the woman writer would have to become in order to succeed: sentimental, spiritual, pious, virtuous and decidedly non-professional. In these final two chapters I aim to complicate this reductive portrait of Rowe by relocating her as a writer in terms of the different contexts – both discursive and geographical – in which she lived and wrote. First, I place her early publications and her first attempts at poetry in relation to the complex web of political and religious ideas within which Rowe was writing. By reading Rowe's poetry and authorial image through these contemporaneous discursive networks I demonstrate one way in which our understanding of Rowe can differ significantly from the posthumous portrait. In my final chapter I return to the question of location in a more direct sense. Rowe's habitation in Frome in Somersetshire was, I argue, integral to her authorial image and publication practices in ways other than a simple equation of provincial life with retired modesty might suggest. By focusing on questions of religion and politics as well as region, social circles, publication practices and individual circumstances, I present a different slant on Rowe's career than has been previously offered. In a broader sense, my case study of Rowe is an example of the way in which present understanding of the woman writer's relation to literary culture can be productively expanded by a detailed attention to the career of one writer.

In the present chapter, I analyse the terms of Rowe's first entry into print in the 1690s. Rowe's early poetry is evidence of a woman writing in support of 1688, both directly in her panegyrics to William III and her anti-Jacobite verse, and more indirectly in her general poetic practice. What I suggest here is that Rowe's 1690s poetry demonstrates a feminine version of the Whig poetic agenda practised by writers such as Charles Montagu, Joseph Addison and Richard Blackmore, and that Rowe herself based her authorial image and her literary authority on her whiggish politics. Second, I draw attention to the connections between the literary culture of nonconformity and the formation of a Whig poetic by focusing on Rowe's work in relation to that of Isaac Watts. I examine the way in which their work exemplifies, from a nonconformist angle, the critical theories outlined by John Dennis in the early 1700s. By focusing on Rowe's whiggish politics in relation to the culture of religious dissent this chapter provides a further dimension to constructions of female authorship in the early eighteenth century. Such a context for reading Rowe's poetry demonstrates the way in which female authorship was directly shaped by the wider literary and political debates of the period as well as by the commercial pressures of the marketplace and the patronage system.

Elizabeth Singer Rowe and the *Athenian Mercury*

Although Elizabeth Singer Rowe is now most famous for her popular epistolary fiction *Friendship in Death: In Twenty Letters from the Dead to the Living* (1728), her main output was poetry. Her first collection of poetry appeared in 1696 under the title *Poems on Several Occasions. Written by Philomela*, which was published by John Dunton. Rowe was known as Philomela throughout her writing life. This poetic pseudonym, typical of those used by many women writers, has obvious connections to the Greek myth of Tereus, Procne and Philomela, which found its most famous incarnation in Ovid's *Metamorphoses*. However, the use of Philomela to refer to Rowe seems to have less to do with the more gruesome elements of the mythic original than with that part of the story where Philomela turns into a nightingale. References to Rowe as Philomela consistently play on the connections between Rowe's maiden name Singer, the beautiful song of the nightingale, and her occupation as a poet.[1] After her experience as a periodical poet, Rowe continued to publish her poetry in a variety of miscellanies throughout the eighteenth century and her miscellaneous works appeared posthumously in 1739.[2] Rowe's background was firmly nonconformist. Her father was a Presbyterian who was imprisoned for his beliefs during the reign of Charles II, and Rowe retained strong links with her religious roots.[3] Rowe's first appearance in print was in John Dunton's popular questions and answer periodical, the *Athenian Mercury*, in the early 1690s. The choice of the *Mercury* was not arbitrary as Dunton was well-known for his nonconformist sympathies. A substantial part of his catalogue comprised works by dissenters.[4] Although not a dissenter himself, Dunton had strong connections with the community in London. He served his apprenticeship under the influential Presbyterian bookseller Thomas Parkhurst, and his first wife, Elizabeth, was the daughter of Samuel Annesley, one of the most distinguished dissenters in the capital.[5] The *Athenian Mercury* was launched in 1691 and ran until June 1697, with further offshoots from the original project continuing into the eighteenth century.[6] The Athenians were Dunton himself, his brother-in-law Richard Sault (later replaced by John Norris), and Samuel Wesley (father of the famous Methodists). The *Mercury* avoided any direct denominational label but displayed a strong allegiance to the Protestant reformed church, and a broad sympathy with the nonconformist position. In terms of politics, the *Mercury* was firmly Williamite and whiggish in its sentiments.

Rowe's poetry was to become central to the *Mercury*'s success. Her first appearance in the journal was in the issue for 1 December 1691, when she sent in a question for the Athenians to consider; the content of which signalled both her religious principles and her poetic agenda. The question runs thus:

> Whether Songs on Moral, Religious or Divine Subjects, compos'd by Persons of *Wit* and *Virtue*, and set to both grave and pleasant Tunes, wou'd not by the Charms of Poetry, and sweetness of Musick, make good Impression of Modesty and Sobriety on the Young and Noble [and . . .] make them really in Love with Virtue and Goodness, and prepare their minds for the design'd *Reformation*? and what are your Thoughts on the late Pastoral Poem?[7]

Rowe's query about the efficacy and appropriateness of poetry and songs on divine themes as a vehicle for moral and spiritual improvement anticipates her own poetic practice throughout her career. The question also prefigures Isaac Watts' later campaign to raise the stature of religious verse. For the moment, I wish to concentrate on the last, seemingly throwaway query, concerning the 'late Pastoral Poem'.[8] In their response to this question the Athenians home in particularly on this last remark, repeating it almost verbatim in their comment that, 'This Querist seems not only to be Poetically enclined but to desire our thoughts on the last pastoral poem.' The editorial commentary here serves to introduce a discussion of Rowe's explicitly political panegyric, 'Upon King William Passing the Boyn', which was never actually printed in the *Mercury*, but is referred to extensively by the Athenians, and appeared in Rowe's 1696 collection, also published by Dunton. The Athenians' extended poetical reply to Rowe's question, 'To the Author of the Late Famous Pastoral', clearly refers to Rowe's poem, and hints at the already wide circulation of the poem in manuscript.

'Upon King William Passing the Boyn'

The poem on King William is a clear example of a nascent Whig poetic. It is particularly interesting for being female-authored, as well as pre-dating other more extended Whig political panegyric, such as Joseph Addison's praise of Charles Montagu's poem on the same theme in his '*An* ACCOUNT *of the Greatest* ENGLISH POETS' (1694).[9] Rowe's poem obviously celebrates William's victory over James II at the Battle of the Boyne in 1690, a key event which assumed a symbolic status for Whig writers. What is also interesting in this respect is the way in which a popular journal responds almost immediately to events of political and national importance and presents them as suitable subjects for poetry. Rowe's poem offers an heroic and eulogistic compliment to William and figures him as victorious monarch and defender of 'Albion'. He is variously described as 'a Martial God', 'the Hero and the King', and 'the War-Like Prince'. In fact, Rowe's poem (not published until 1696, but obviously in circulation by at least 1691), incorporates many of the facets of the emergent Whig poetic that David Womersley has identified in his introduction to *Augustan Critical Writing*. The main effects of Addison's praise are to construct William's defeat of James as both political and literary triumph, and to imply that military and political events can constitute the main subject of, not just the impetus for, modern poetry. Both these effects can be seen in the opening lines of Rowe's poem:

> What *mighty genius* thus excites my Breast
> With flames too great to manage or resist;
> And prompts my humbler Muse at once to Sing
> (Unequal Task) the *Hero and the King*.

> *Oh were the potent inspiration less!*
> I might find words its Raptures to express;
> But now I neither can its force controul,
> Nor paint the *great Ideas* of my Soul.   (1–8)[10]

Rowe's invocation of her humble Muse to inspire her to write about military and heroic themes clearly links her poetic inspiration with an event of national political importance. Rowe's account of the inception of her poem similarly accords with, and pre-dates, Richard Blackmore's invocation of the Muse to sing in praise of Marlborough's military successes in *Advice to the Poets: a Poem* (1706). It is worth comparing these two poems as the striking parallels suggest that, even in the early 1690s, a common sense of a Whig poetics was taking shape which provided what was to become a familiar rhetoric for Whig poetry in the early years of the eighteenth century.

In her poem on William, Rowe describes her theme as 'potent', as raising 'Raptures' in the speaker, and as a 'force' that cannot be controlled. In relation to Marlborough, Blackmore refers to the 'raptures' and 'flames' raised by the praise of his military hero. As his poem reaches its apogee, the language Blackmore employs echoes Rowe's poem:

> 'Tis done. I've compass'd my ambitious Aim,
> The Hero's Fire restores the Poet's Flame.
> The Inspiration comes, my Bosom glows,
> I strive with strong Enthusiastic Throws.
> Oh! I am all in Rapture, all on Fire,
> Give me, to ease the Muse's Pangs, the Lyre.
> How can a Muse, that *Albion* loves, forbear
> To sing the Wonders of the glorious War?   (571–8)

The endings of the two poems also strike very similar notes. Like Blackmore, Rowe shifts the emphasis on to the divine protection given to the military successes of the Whig heroes. Rowe figures the heavenly powers as guiding and protecting William's actions. She thus places the triumph of 1688 on the side of heaven and presents the outcome of the Battle of the Boyne as an example of divine providence:

> Keep near him still, you *kind Aethereal Powers*,
> That Guard him, and are pleas'd, the Task is Yours.
> All the Ill Fate that threatens him oppose;

> Confound the Forces of his Foreign Foes,
> *And Treacherous Friends less generous than those;*
> May Heaven success to all his Actions give,
> *And long, and long, and long, let WILLIAM live.*   (36–42)

Rowe also takes a side swipe here at the French, those 'Foreign Foes' and those of her own nation less patriotic than herself. Blackmore's poem presents the Whig cause in comparable terms. However, he is considerably more expansive and effusive in his fanciful description of the flight to the celestial spheres, where the inhabitants of heaven are engaged in singing the praises of Whig military glory. An 'immortal Envoy', followed by the poetic speaker, ascends to the skies and arrives at 'Heav'n's Eternal gate'. The envoy then gives the happy tidings of Britain's defense against France:

> Hark! Now I hear the Shouts of Joy around,
> I hear the Triumph's multiplying Sound.
> Th'Angelic Acclamation grows, it fills
> All the blue Plains, and all the crystal Hills.
> They shew by this, repeated loud Applause,
> Those fight in Heav'n's, who fight in *Anna*'s Cause.   (128–33)

Although Queen Anne herself can not, of course, be lauded as military hero, by fighting in her cause Marlborough represents the masculine military might suggested by Rowe's William.

However, there are also some interesting differences in approach between the two poems. Like Blackmore, Rowe figures her Muse as inadequate to the task of singing William's praises. However, while Blackmore describes his Muse as 'unequal' (145) in strength to depict Marlborough's glory, and declares that 'Weak is thy Voice, and weary is thy Wing' (152), Rowe describes her voice in feminine terms, as 'Too soft' to speak of military action:

> Too soft's my Voice the *Hero* to express;
> Or, like himself, the War-like Prince to dress;
> Or, speak him Acting in the dreadful Field,
> As Brave Exploits as e'r the Sun beheld.   (11–14)[11]

Rowe depicts her poetic voice as too feminine to describe the bloody action of 'the dreadful field', and indeed her poem leaves William poised at the edge of the river. The poetic speaker declines to follow William into action, instead choosing to lament the danger he faces:

> No more – ah stay – though in a cause so good;
> 'Tis pitty to expend that Sacred Blood.
> Why wilt thou thus the boldest Dangers seek,
> *And foremost through the Hostile Squadrons break?*
> Why wilt thou thus so bravely venture all?
> Oh, where's the unhappy *Albion*, should'st thou fall?   (30–5)

Moreover, where Rowe refuses to witness the action of battle and turns away from the prospect of bloodshed ('Tis pitty to expend that Sacred Blood'), Blackmore is effusive and expansive about the horrors of warfare which are, rather disturbingly, celebrated as representing 'Britannia's' force. In contrast to Rowe's poem, the imagery of blood is central to his depiction of military glory:

> How red with Slaughter is *Ramillia's* Plain?
> How are the Mountains cover'd with the Slain?
> How deeply dy'd with *Gallic* Blood
> *Belgia's* polluted Rivers roll their Flood!   (693–6)

Such an emphasis on the bloody results of battle recalls, or fulfils, Addison's earlier comment in '*An* ACCOUNT *of the Greatest* ENGLISH POETS' that Edmund Waller (1606–87) was not able to depict the bloodshed of William's victory during his lifetime. If Waller had had the 'good fortune' to have witnessed the Boyne, Addison remarks, 'What scenes of death and horror had we view'd,/And how had *Boin's* wide current reek'd in blood'.[12] What Rowe adds, then, to the rhetorical strategies of the often war-mongering patriot Whig poetic speaker is a consideration of her sex. War is a distinctly unfeminine topic for a woman to broach, but Rowe has to negotiate this dilemma if she is to voice her appreciation and support of William's victorious status. Given the tone of later poems on Whig military victory, Rowe's remit is particularly difficult in that she has to negotiate a very masculinist emphasis on male heroic military achievement and the corresponding virulence of attacks on the French. Womersley's description of the poems of Charles Montagu, Joseph Addison and Richard Blackmore as 'Battle Hymns of the Junto Whigs', effectively encapsulates the problems Rowe was facing.[13]

A female patriot poet?

The attempts by post-1688 writers to construct an alternative tradition of Whig literary history are equally problematic for the woman writer. Montagu, Addison and Blackmore are all concerned to mount an appeal for the next national 'bard' who will be equal to the task of describing post-1688 culture. As Womersley argues, the 'advice to the poets' genre asks the question: What are the appropriate cultural models and exemplars for this nation?'[14] More specifically, the genre is also asking: *Who*, or what type of poet, is the appropriate model for articulating and representing a post-1688, whiggish literary and political culture? In all of the poems I have discussed, the model of the poet is male and the appropriate poetic agenda is, equally emphatically, masculine. Addison answers Montagu, and Montagu's poem uses the patron Charles Sackville, sixth Earl of Dorset as the exemplary male figure: 'Oh, DORSET! I am rais'd! I'm all on fire!'[15] In an even more exclusively androcentric move, Blackmore proposes a confederacy of bards – all men – who will work collectively to write the poetry of the nation. In *Advice to the Poets*, Blackmore's 'Master Bards' present an exclusively masculine model of the poet, and of poetry, whereby the manly subject matter must be met with a similar heroism on the part of the poets. Blackmore declares that 'The Poets, who assume this noble Theme,/Must have their Hero's Fire, their Hero's Flegm' (237–8), and adds with regard to his own poetic persona, 'Oh! Did a Portion of the noble Fire,/With which the Hero fought, my Breast inspire' (561–2). This army of poets, as it were, are also placed in a firmly paternal line of inheritance consisting of Matthew Prior, William Congreve, George Granville, William Walsh, George Stepney, John Somers, John Hughes and Charles Montagu. It is only this group of male poets who can effectively sing the praises of a variety of national heroes: 'For this great Task, let all these Sons of Art,/Their utmost Skill and Energy Exert' (149–50). It is perhaps little wonder, then, that so few women poets were drawn to this particular brand of Whig poetic. The masculinist nature of this poetic agenda could be said to exclude women as both speaking subject and poetic object, despite the move away from neo-classical formality to a more conversational style. Indeed, many women, including Rowe at a later stage in her career, found the poetry of Pope and Swift more congenial to their talents than the models offered by Addison and Blackmore.[16]

Within the pages of the *Mercury*, Rowe and the Athenians discuss the broader scope of a whiggish poetic agenda and the question of the attributes of a national bard. In contrast to Blackmore, however, there is also a consideration of the implications of a feminine version of Whig poetry practiced by a female patriot poet. The issue for December 1691, which included Rowe's question and the reference to her poem on William, offered a response by the Athenians to the poem, even though they chose not to print the poem itself. 'To the Author of the late Famous Pastoral Poem' is an extended reply to Rowe's poem as well as to the question she had posed. At this stage the Athenians seem to guess at Rowe's sex, although she had not, at this stage, revealed her identity to them. The Athenians' poetic response is fascinating, not only because it provides evidence of the immediate reception of Rowe's poem, but also because it makes gender issues central to the debates and concerns of Whig poetry. The initial praise of Rowe's poetry is couched in terms of amatory appreciation. Her verse is applauded in gendered terms for its seeming artlessness, pastoral softness, charm and virtue:

> Say, *Dear unknown!* What is't that charms me so?
> What secret Nectar through my lines does flow?
> What *Deathless Beauties* in thy Gardens grow?
> Immortal Wit in Natures *easiest* dress,
> A Paradice [sic] rais'd in a Wilderness
> Tho' harsh thy Subject, haggard & unkind,
> And rough, as bitter blasts of Northern Wind,
> Thy *Divine* Spirit corrects each ruder Sound
> And breaths delicious Zephirs all around.   (5–13)[17]

The productions of the female pen are seen in terms of cultured nature. Her subject may be as severe as 'bitter blasts of Northern Wind', but her treatment of it tempers the rudeness of untamed nature by transforming the cold winds to 'delicious Zephirs'. However, whereas the softness of Rowe's verse is praised for tempering the bleakness and severity of her theme, the Athenians do offer a criticism of Rowe's poem. Their more critical remarks foreground the difficulty of aligning the violence of war poetry with a pleasing feminine softness. The Athenians specifically pinpoint the fact that Rowe does not, as I have suggested, attempt to describe the horror of the battle she is referring to; descriptions of which are so central to the poetry of her male counterparts:

> But whilst I praise, I must accuse thee too,
> When thou hadst done so much, no more to do,

> When to the brink of the *Boyne* thy *Hero* came
> There to break off the *chase of him and Fame*.
> Where had bin Albion now, had he thus stood,
> But floating in another *Sea of Blood*?   (16–21)

What the Athenians criticize in Rowe's poem is the lack of engagement with the actual battle. She abandons her hero on 'the brink of the *Boyne*', which is the moment in her poem when the poetic speaker draws back from her description of military action to worry about the possibility of William being killed and to invoke the 'Aethereal Powers' to protect him. Despite the admirable softness of her verse, Rowe's poem does not quite fit the template for Whig poetry that was being adumbrated at this point in time. The Athenians' response suggests that, in refusing to describe military action, Rowe has ultimately failed to articulate fully the extent of William's glory. In doing so, they suggest, she also misses the opportunity to become glorified herself as the bard authorized to praise and commemorate the military success of both William and the nation:

> This! *Sweetest Bard*, hadst thou proceeding Sung,
> How had the *Woods*, how had the *Valleys* rung,
> And *Pollio*'s learned Muse, who sits above,
> The Shepherd's Admiration, and their Love,
> Had *deign'd* thee *Smiles*, as all the World esteem,
> Which dares not sure dislike what pleases him.   (32–7)[18]

Biblical models and the female bard

Two years later the Athenians' attitude to Rowe had undergone a substantial shift. In the issue for Saturday, 21 October 1693, the editors announce that they have received verses from an unknown woman, 'which, tho' they contain no Question, and are somewhat uncorrect, yet for the Honour of her Sex, and that uncommon Genius that Shines in 'em, we think not improper to insert in our *Mercury*'. The verses are Rowe's poems 'A Pindarick Poem on Habbakuk' and 'The Rapture', both of which were included in the 1696 collection. It is the poem on Habbakuk, and the Athenians' response to this poem, that I wish to focus on here. 'A Pindarick Poem on Habbakuk' plays on contemporary associations of Israel with England. In a continuation of her strategies in 'Upon King William', Rowe presents the power of God over the Chaldeans as symbolic of William's victories over the French and the Jacobites in defence of Protestant England. The representation of God in the poem is that of the Old Testament patriot and avenger:

> When God from *Teman* came,
>   And cloath'd in *Glory* from Mount-*Paran* shone,
>   Drest in th'insufferable *Flame*
>   That hides his *Dazling Throne*,
> His *Glory* soon *eclips'd* the once bright *Titan's Rays*,
> And fill'd the trembling *Earth* with *Terror* and *Amaze*.
>   Resplendent *Beams* did crown his *awful Head*,
>   And shining *brightness* all around him spread;
>   *Omnipotence* he graspt in his strong *Hand*,
> And *listning Death* stood waiting on his *dread Command*.   (1–10)

What Rowe can achieve in this poem through her use of biblical precedent is a closer approximation of the military action that was missing from the Boyne poem. Whereas the battle poetry of Montagu, Addison, Blackmore and the Athenians themselves is potentially alienating for women in its martial fervour, biblical paraphrase provides Rowe as a female poet with an enabling framework to articulate her politics. Rowe's God is distinctly martial and through her depiction of God's fury she can symbolically represent William's military glory. The closing lines of the poem make the political analogy explicit, and show Rowe, albeit in an allegorical fashion, depicting actual combat:

> Thy *threatening Arrows* gild their *flaming way*,
>   And at the *glittering* of thy *Spear* the *Heathen* dare not stay;
>   The very *sight* of thee did them *subdue*,
> And arm'd with *Fury* thou the *Vict'ry* didst pursue.
>   So now, great God, wrapt in avenging *Thunder*,
>   Meet thine and *William's Foes*, and tread them *groveling* under.

(43–8)

It was this poem which acted as the impetus for the Athenians to write and publish their own poem on William's martial exploits.[19] They begin by making the analogy between God's vengeance and national military glory even more explicit than Rowe had done in her poem. Yet in so doing they begin to claim for Rowe – who at this point they are aware is female – the status of the nation's bard:

> Sure thou by Heaven *inspir'd*, art sent
> To make the *Kings* and *Nations Foes* repent.
> To *melt* each *Stubborn Rebel* down,
> Or the Almighty's *hov'ring Vengeance* show,
> Arm'd with his *glittering Spear* and *dreadful Bow*,
> And yet *more dreadful Frown*.   (1–6)

The Athenians gesture towards Rowe's sex in the reference to the way in which her verse can 'melt' the rebels into submission. However, on this occasion they do not hesitate to suggest that a woman can articulate the themes necessary for commemorating William's glory, the focus of patriotic whiggish verse:

> Begin, begin thy *Noble Choice*,
> Great *William* claims thy Lyre, and claims thy *Voice*,
> All *like Himself* the *Hero* shew,
> Which *none* but *thou* canst do.   (7–10)

In the fourth stanza of the poem the Athenians go even further to praise Rowe in relation to the religious and political themes of her poetry:

> Thus sing, *bright Maid!* Thus and yet *louder sing*
> Thy *God* and *King*!
> *Cherish* That Noble *Flame* which warms thy *breast*,
> And be by *future Worlds admir'd and bless'd*.   (31–4)

As the last lines here show, the Athenians are now prepared to concede to Rowe the fame they hitherto denied her. They end by evoking Katherine Philips as a female poetic precursor who, it is implied, Rowe surpasses in her work. The Athenians imagine a 'Heaven of Poetry' where the 'glorious few' will be immortalized for their poetry:

> There Chaste *Orinda's* Soul shall meet with *thine*,
> More *Noble*, more *Divine*;
> And in the *Heaven of Poetry* forever shine;
>> There all the *glorious few*,
>> To *Loyalty* and *Virtue* true,
>> Like *her* and *you*.   (35–40)

The Athenians' construction of a poetic heaven inscribed with the names of female poets offers, then, a feminine version of Blackmore's male confederacy of whiggish bards in *Advice to the Poets*. Noble, divine, pious, chaste, loyal and virtuous, the female line of patriotic bards offers a very different version of the aggressive Whig poetic constructed by Montagu, Addison and Blackmore. Elizabeth Rowe, it is clear, is central to this alternative female tradition.[20]

Political authority and the female poet

In some of the questions she submitted to the Athenians, Rowe comments on her own poetic practice and authorial image. In the issue for 29 May 1694, she posed a 'Poetical Question' to the *Mercury* concerning the Jacobites. This question took the form of a short poem in which she openly reveals her political allegiance, and also comments on her own role as defender of 1688. Rowe declares that she has employed her 'Loyal Quill' to sing the praises of Whig heroes:

> Virtue, and our unequall'd Heroes praise!
> What Theams more glorious can exact my Lays?
> *William*! A Name my Lines grow proud to bear!
> A Prince as Great, and wondrous Good as e'er
> The sacred Burden of a Crown did wear.   (3–7)[21]

Rowe's literary authority is predicated on her glorious theme. The praise of William becomes the reason for writing her poetry and she also gleans a moral authority by drawing on the 'virtue' of whiggish political principles. The last lines of the poetical question directly confront the Jacobite enemies of William and his 'heroes', asking in an incredulous tone:

> Resolve me, then, *Athenians*, what are those,
> (Can there be any such?) You call his Foes?
> His Foes! Curst word; and why they'd pierce his Breast,
> Ungrateful Vipers! Where they warmly rest?   (9–12)

The Jacobite resistance to 1688 is figured by Rowe and the Athenians in their response as unnaturally evil. By contrast, in using William as her poetic theme and inspiration, Rowe is firmly positioned on the side of virtue. In her own construction of her poetic identity, then, Rowe firmly associates the virtuous female poet with a politically inflected sense of right government and rule.

In the second question which Rowe sent to this issue of the journal she again makes the analogy between the virtuous poet and support of William. Following the question I have just discussed, this second query, which concerns the nature of 'earthly fame' for the poet, is clearly contextualized in relation to her previous verses on the glory of William and the evil of Jacobite threat to his rule. Rowe asks:

> What if the Muses loudly sang my Fame,
> The barren Mountains ecchoing with my Name? (1–2)

In so doing, she is directly addressing the question of fame for the poet and the issue of the nature of the national bard. In answering her own question, which she goes on to do, Rowe shifts the register of the poem to a religious stress on the fleeting nature of earthly glory and a corresponding emphasis on the immortality that only virtue can provide:

> If o'er my Relicks Monuments they raise,
> And fill the World with Flattery, or with praise;
> What wou'd they all avail, if sink I must,
> My Soul to endless shades, my Body to the dust?
> Nothing, Ah Nothing! Vertue only gives,
> Immortal praise, that only ever Lives.
> What pains wait Vice, what endless Worlds of Woe,
> You know full well, but may you never know. (5–12)

Ostensibly this is an apolitical and in many ways conventional voicing of familiar religious sentiment. In the context of the previous question concerning the Jacobites and, as an introduction to the printing of Rowe's poem on Habbakuk, however, these verses have a distinctly political edge and a direct relation to the Whig poetics practiced by Blackmore in particular. Rowe combines the role of poet with that of prophet (Habbakuk) and speaker of religious truths with that of bard for the new age under William. The significance of 'Athenian' in *Athenian Mercury* is also brought into play here as Rowe includes in her construction of the role of the poet the Athenian sense of the poet as legislator as well as prophet. Shaun Irlam's recent discussion of Blackmore's vision of the 'primordial bard' provides the exact context in which to read Rowe's contemporaneous construction of her authority as a poet.[22]

In the pages of the *Athenian Mercury*, Rowe is quite pointedly working through Blackmore's conception of the poet, but from a female perspective. Blackmore's preface to *Prince Arthur, an Heroick Poem* (1695), for example, indicates the centrality of Rowe's views to the 1690s debates concerning the role of the nation's poets:

> 'Tis therefore no wonder that so wise a State as that of *Athens* should retain the *Poets* on the side of *Religion* and *Government*. [. . .] The *Poets* were look'd on as Divine, not only on account of that extraordinary Fury and Heat of Imagination wherewith they were thought to be inspir'd, but likewise upon the account of [. . .] their Business being to represent *Vice* as the most odious, and *Virtue* as the most desirable thing in the World.[23]

Rowe's political support of William and the principles of 1688 constitute both her poetical inspiration and her popularity with the Athenians. Throughout the succeeding issues of the *Mercury* – where Rowe's poetry becomes a staple of the material printed – her work diversifies into occasional verse and less explicitly political pastoral and biblical paraphrase. Yet it is the political verses in praise of William that the Athenians select to respond to with verses of their own. The Athenians deliberately foreground this aspect of Rowe's authorial persona to uphold their own political allegiances. The 'Pindarick on Habbakuk' serves particularly to introduce and, more importantly, to authorize and to contextualize, the Athenians' much more war-mongering and blatant articulation of Whig military glory. A section of their response to this poem includes a detailed description of the action of battle, for example:

> At *Landen* paint him, *Spears* and *Trophies* round,
> And *Twenty thousand Deaths* upon the slippery ground:
> Now, now the dreadful *Shock's* begun,
> Fierce *Luxemburgh* comes *Thundering* on;
> They *charge, retreat, return and fly*,
> *Advance, retire, kill, conquer, dye*! (Stanza III, 5–10)

Despite their own practice of a more virile version of Whig poetics, the construction of Rowe, and her poetry, as representing a female claim to the status of national bard is nonetheless significant. In effect, the Athenians present Rowe as a Protestant whiggish mascot to prove to the readers of the *Mercury* that virtue – specifically feminine virtue –

and Whig sentiments were not mutually exclusive. As Gilbert McEwan points out, 'For the Athenians, Rowe was a kind of female poet laureate, dedicated to defending King William in verse against all his enemies.'[24] What is extraordinary about this, I would argue, is that given the specifically manly agenda of the whiggish poetry in this period, and the pointedly male tradition of poets that is frequently evoked as worthy of representing Whig military glory in verse, the position of national bard was seen by the Athenians to be fulfilled by a woman. Rowe herself commented on the position to which the Athenians had raised her. In 'A Pindarick, to the Athenian Society' she describes how their construction of her has directly shaped her own sense of her 'heroic' poetic project:

> Untill by you,
> With more Heroick sentiments inspir'd
> I turn'd and *stood* the vigorous torrent too,
> And at my former *weak retreat admir'd*;
> So much was I by your *example fir'd*,
> So much the *heavenly* form did win:
> Which to my eyes *you'd painted virtue in.* (Stanza VI)[25]

Rowe brings together all the different components of the nascent Whig poetic in addition to a consideration of her sex. Spurred on by the praise of her male editors, Rowe presents herself as 'fir'd' by the 'Heroick sentiments' inspired by the Athenians. The female bard rejects her 'former *weak retreat*' and turns ready to face the 'vigorous torrent' in the name of religious faith and political virtue.

Elizabeth Rowe, John Dennis and Isaac Watts

Despite the overtly male agenda of much Whig war poetry there was another strand to the new poetics which was more appropriate for women poets, and especially for a nonconformist writer such as Rowe.[26] As I have shown, Rowe's use of carefully chosen biblical allegory in the poem on Habbakuk enabled her to articulate William's martial glory in fuller terms than in her poem on the Boyne. For early eighteenth-century readers, Rowe's sentiments, as expressed in the *Mercury*, would have exemplified the critical theories about religious verse championed, primarily, by John Dennis in *The Advancement and Reformation of Poetry* (1702) and *The Grounds of Criticism in Poetry* (1704), and practised by writers such as Blackmore, Aaron Hill, Isaac Watts and Edward Young. The reformation of poetry to didactic ends – which Rowe raised in her very first question to the Athenians – was supported by the argument that the Bible was the greatest source of poetical inspiration, as opposed to the classical (and pagan) epics of Homer and Virgil. Against the argument that the Bible was unpoetic, writers like Dennis and Watts insisted upon the utility of its literary qualities for inspiring both religious faith and moral sentiment. Consequently, poetry was given a direct didactic purpose through its Christian Protestant message, but was also annexed to early eighteenth-century social codes of politeness as propounded by Addison and Steele. As Shaun Irlam has argued, the debate about religious verse was played out against opposing notions that biblical verse betrayed a pernicious and threatening 'enthusiasm' with the negative connotations of extreme passion and irrationality.[27] Writers like Dennis and Watts countered these suspicions by claiming an explicitly reformist and moral agenda to frame the argument in favour of religious verse. Dennis, for example, made a careful distinction between the 'Enthusiastick Passions' and the 'Vulgar Passions' in *The Grounds of Criticism in Poetry*.[28] This agenda also had, of course, a political edge.[29] The debate about the aesthetic appeal and moral efficacy of religious verse was directly linked to the overall Whig poetic agenda of constructing an alternative poetic tradition to replace the Tory-inflected neo-classical canon. The post-1688 canon of poetry and poets took its cue not from Rome but from Milton, and was presented as not only a reformist mission, but also as a specifically British phenomenon.[30] Biblical verse was to be the saving of the nation and it was the duty of the nation's poets to participate in this national reformation. As Irlam argues in relation to Dennis' *Grounds of Criticism*, 'Dennis's treatise articulates the kind of millennial aspirations that motivate much earnest poetry in the mid-eighteenth century: an aspiration to accomplish nothing less than the moral rejuvenation of literature and modern society and the redemption of mankind from the consequences of the Fall.'[31] For Rowe, this was a framework which exactly accorded with her own religious and political beliefs as expressed in her poetry. And, as I shall argue, Rowe's authorial persona, her sex, and her poetry play a significant if neglected role in the formation and dissemination of these ideas in the early eighteenth century.

Rowe's poems in the *Athenian Mercury*, and in her 1696 collection, demonstrate that the main tenets of Dennis' theories on poetry were being practised before they were formalized. Rowe's choice of Habbakuk as a model for articulating her poetical agenda and her political and religious principles was especially appropriate and perhaps prescient. Many of Rowe's poetic subjects drawn from the Old Testament, Job, the Psalms, the songs of Judith, Judgement and the Last Day, were to be singled out by Dennis as constituting the major topics of contemporary poetry.[32] Dennis' comments on these models in *The Grounds of Criticism in Poetry* are useful, then, for making sense of Rowe's choice of biblical model, and also for further understanding the type of poet that she was beginning to represent for the Athenians. Dennis argues that:

> The most important Parts of the Old Testament to us, are the Prophecies; because without them we could never be satisfy'd that *Jesus* is the Messiah. For the Prophets were Poets by the Institution of their Order, and Poetry was one of the Prophetick Functions, which were chiefly three: 1. Predicting or foretelling things to come. 2. Declaring the Will of God to the People. And, 3. Praising God with Songs of the Prophets composing, accompany'd with the Harp and other Instrumental Musick.[33]

Dennis' comments here echo Rowe's first question to the *Mercury* in 1691 ('Whether Songs on Moral, Religious and Divine Subjects [. . .] set to both grave and pleasant Tunes' etc.), and provide a very specific context for reading her work and assessing her significance as a poet.

Rowe's next appearance in print after the 1696 poems was in a collection published in 1704. *Divine Hymns and Poems on Several Occasions* was obviously published with a view to further the reformation of poetry championed by Dennis in his critical writing.[34] The collection is dedicated to Richard Blackmore and draws attention to the moral agenda of the poems printed. Blackmore is seen as the figurehead of this reformist movement and is used to authorize the project by drawing on the concurrent debate about the reformation of the stage, headed by Jeremy Collier in the 1690s:

> Like a Zealous Friend to Religion, and Passionate Lover of your Country, you have express'd your just Concern for the Fatal Consequences of Loose and Profane Poetry, and with great Judgement have made it appear how vainly we hope for a Reformation of Manners, while the Abuses of the *English* Stage are left unreform'd.[35]

The unsigned preface continues in a similar vein. The 'degeneracy' of the age is lamented and seen as a result of the works of 'Loose and

Impious Authors'. In contrast, poetry inspired by virtue, such as Blackmore's work, will 'quench the Flames of Lust, and blow up the pure Flames of Devotion'.

Although she has been excluded from both a canon of Whig poets and discussions of religious poetry, such as Irlam's recent study, Rowe's significance for these debates in the early eighteenth century was clearly high. The title-page for the first edition of the collection foregrounds Rowe under her pseudonym Philomela, and specifically lists some of her poems included in the volume. The full title reads: *Divine Hymns and Poems on Several Occasions. Viz. A Pastoral on our Saviour's Nativity, The Wish, The Description of Heaven in Imitation of Mr. Milton. By Philomela and other Ingenious Persons.* The other contributors included Blackmore, Dennis and John Norris (Norris was one of the editors of the *Athenian Mercury*). Moreover, Rowe's poetry represents the majority of the material printed, and her work here shows the full range of hymns, paraphrases and translations on religious and biblical themes. In these poems Rowe rehearses all the important themes outlined by Dennis, and clearly situates her poetry in relation to the broader debates about the reformation of poetry, and through poetry, the nation. Her 'Hymn on Heaven', for example, clearly articulates the role of the poet in singing of God's glory and the unknowable aspects of Christian faith:

> What glorious things of thee, O glorious place!
> Shall my bold Muse in daring Numbers speak?
> While to immortal strains I tune my lyre,
> And warbling imitate angelic airs:
> While ecstasy bears up my soul aloft,
> And lively faith gives me a distant glimpse
> Of glories unreveal'd to human eyes.   (1–7)

The trembling modesty of the earlier Williamite poems is reproduced in a different context here. Rowe's muse is again 'bold' in its 'daring' attempt to depict the glories of heaven. Just as her virtuous defence of William eventually bolsters her poetic inspiration, here religious faith and ecstasy raises the poetic voice to a level capable of describing the magnificence of heaven. In 'A Description of Hell, in Imitation of Mr. Milton', Rowe again underlines the moral agenda of the collection as a whole. In the course of a graphic description of the terrors of Hell, she inserts the following warning to the profligate who, through reading Rowe's poem, has been shown the dreadful fate that awaits them:

> THE Libertine his folly here laments,
> His blind extravagance, that made him sell
> Unfading bliss, and everlasting crowns,
> Immortal transports, and celestial feasts,
> For the short pleasure of a sordid sin,
> For one fleet moment's despicable joy.   (37–42)

Rowe's poems simultaneously outline the role of the poet in singing of God's glory, and provide the moral framework in which they should be read. Her work is, therefore, central to the broader agenda facing poets in this period, and her poems encapsulate the theories offered by Dennis and others.

Another aspect of the Whig poetic in the early eighteenth century which has been relatively underplayed is the significant contribution of nonconformist writers to the issues raised by writers such as Dennis and Blackmore, as Rowe's contributions demonstrate. In contrast to the critical neglect of Rowe, the role played by Isaac Watts has been more fully acknowledged. However, the work of Rowe and Watts is very closely linked. These two writers provide important evidence of nonconformist intervention into the drive to construct a national poetics along different lines to the neo-classical and Tory tradition. Rowe was personally acquainted with Watts by 1706, but possibly even earlier.[36] Watts was to edit Rowe's posthumous *Devout Exercises of the Heart* in 1737, and has been seen to act as a champion of Rowe and her poetry. However, I would argue that the connections between the two writers were more evenly weighted, and that Rowe was in fact an influence on Watts. Indeed, her Athenian and Philomela poems pre-date Watts' writing on similar subjects. Through an analysis of Watts' commentary on poetry from the early eighteenth century, and his direct comments on Rowe's poetry, we can begin to reconstruct a further context for understanding the poetic agenda of the early eighteenth century, and for realizing Rowe's significance for her eighteenth-century readers.

The main point of comment about Watts' intervention into the debates I have been discussing is his preface to *Horae Lyricae*, which was added to the second edition of the collection in 1709 (first edition, 1706). In this preface, Watts shows he has the same agenda as Blackmore and Dennis. He refutes the assumption that 'the mysteries of Christianity are not capable of Gay Ornaments', and cites Cowley's *Davideis* and Blackmore's 'two *Arthurs*' as having 'experimentally confuted the vain pretence'. Like Rowe, Watts' views on poetry show the influence of Milton, and he focuses particularly on Dennis' insistence on sublimity in religious verse. Indeed, Watts emphasizes the need to inspire terror in the reader if the hoped-for reformation is to be effected, recalling Rowe's sentiments in 'A Description of Hell'. Watts argues that, the 'Scenes of Religion' and 'Heavenly Themes' should be 'Figures of Majesty, Beauty and Terror'. His extended description of how religious poetry should be written draws together this emphasis on sublimity with individual salvation. He also introduces the sense that poetry can be the national reformation of an increasingly secular and degenerate society:

> The Affairs of this Life with their reference to a Life to come, would shine bright in a Dramatick Description. The Anguish of inward Guilt, the secret Stings and Racks and Scourges of Conscience, the sweet retiring Hours and Seraphical Joys of Devotion, the Victory of a Resolved Soul over a Thousand Temptations, the inimitable Love and Passion of a dying God, the Awful Glories of the last Tribunal, the grand decisive Sentence from which there is no Appeal, and the Consequent Transports or Horrors of the two Eternal Worlds. How could such a Performance call back the dying Piety of the Nation to Life and Beauty: It would make Religion appear like itself, and confound the Blasphemies of a profligate World, ignorant of Pious Pleasures.

Rowe's poetry exemplifies Watts' critical comments and, I would argue, had a direct influence on his description of pious poetry. The first stanza of her 'A Description of Hell' is a striking example of Watts' emphasis on the terror, and, therefore, the repentance, that religious verse, properly managed, can inspire:

> DEEP, to unfathomable spaces deep,
> Descend the dark, detested paths of hell,
> The gulphs of execration and despair,
> Of pain, and rage, and pure unmingled woe;
> The realms of endless death, and seats of night,
> Uninterrupted night, which sees no dawn,
> Prodigious darkness! Which receives no light,
> But from the sickly blaze of sulph'rous flames,
> That cast a pale and dead reflection round,

> Disclosing all the desolate abyss,
> Dreadful beyond what human thought can form,
> Bounded with circling seas of liquid fire.   (1–12)

As Irlam points out, this is a very different poetic agenda from Pope's approach in *An Essay on Man* (1733–4): 'Know then thyself, presume not God to scan;/The proper study of Mankind is Man' (Epistle II, 1–2). Rowe's depiction of the unknown and 'unknowable' is vividly realized through poetry as a means to effect her moral purpose. Her 'Dramatick Description', to use Watts' phrase, of 'the dark, detested paths of hell' lit only by 'the sickly blaze of sulph'rous flames' clearly works as a metaphor for the lost soul of the 'profligate World' (Watts again) in need of reformation.

I want to conclude by looking at a very specific example of the mutual influence of Rowe and Watts, and to return to the more openly whiggish nature of their poetic agenda. What is also significant about Watts' poetry, which has been relatively ignored, is its patriotic aspect and his support of William in particular and the 1688 Revolution principles in general. As in Rowe's Athenian poems, there is a direct link between nonconformity and Whig politics. In a similar vein to Rowe's ode on William, Watts also wrote a series of poems which figure the king simultaneously as martial hero and religious saviour. In these poems salvation is also directly linked to William's domestic and foreign policies. *Horae Lyricae* includes Watts' poems 'An Hymn in Praise to the God of England for Three Great Salvations (viz.) From the Spanish Invasion, from the Gunpowder Plot, and from the Popery and Slavery by King William', and 'Epitaph on King William the Third of Glorious Memory: who dy'd March 8th 1701'. 'An Hymn in Praise to the God of England' draws a direct analogy between the will of Heaven and William's ascension to the throne of England, through a conjunction of the divine and the martial:

> Brigades of Angels lin'd the ways,
> And Guarded *William* to his Throne;
> There, ye Celestial Warriors, stay,
> And make his Palace like your Own.

All these strands come together when Watts included a poem to Rowe as the last set of verses in part two of the 1709 edition of *Horae Lyricae*: 'To Mrs. Singer; on the sight of some of her Divine Poems never

Printed'. From the context of this poem it is clear that the reader is being asked to read Rowe's poetry as an example of Watts' theoretical argument, and as inspiration for his own writing. The poetic voice is figured as reclining 'On the fair Banks of gentle *Thames*' (1) while singing to his harp about 'celestial Themes' (2) and 'everlasting Things' (6). As the poet drifts into a reverie, the sound of Philomela's voice glides by 'Sudden from *Albion*'s Western Coast'. In the presence of Philomela's 'superior Sweetness' of song, the poetic voice can only listen in admiration:

> 'Tis PHILOMELA's Voice, The neighb'ring Shepherd's cry;
> At once my Strings all silent lie,
> At once my fainting Muse was lost
> In the superior Sweetness drown'd.
> In vain I bid my Tuneful Powers unite;
> My Soul retir'd, and left my Tongue,
> I was all Ear, and PHILOMELA's Song
> Was all Divine Delight.   (10–17)

The welcome intrusion of Philomela's song into the private daydream of the poetic speaker serves as a way of authorizing Rowe's poetry as the prime example of a successful and moving use of religious and devotional themes for contemporary poetry. The poet admits that he has already rejected neo-classical precedent in favour of religious verse:

> 'Twas long ago
> I bid adieu to mortal Things,
> To *Grecian* Tales, and wars of *Rome*,
> 'Twas long ago I broke all but th'immortal Strings.   (19–22)

However, the superior skill of Philomela's poetry and her ability to 'tune the Notes of Heav'n, and propagate the Joy' of religious devotion renders the poet's similar attempts redundant. Rather than reaching the heights of devotion through his own outpourings, the poet rises to the heights of joy through listening to the beauties of Philomela's song:

> Now these immortal Strings have no employ
> Since a fair Angel dwells below
> To tune the Notes of Heav'n , and propagate the Joy.

> Let all my Powers with thee profound
> While PHILOMELA sings
> Attend the Rapture of the Sound,
> And my Devotion rise on her Seraphic Wings.   (23–9)

Rowe read and responded to this elaborate compliment from Watts. In the 1727 edition of *Horae Lyricae*, Watts included a poem by Rowe, dated 1706, which comprises the response by her to Watts' work. In this poem Rowe returns Watts' compliment. She figures herself as rejecting the use of pastoral in her poetry and, through the influence of Watts, as turning exclusively to celestial themes:

> No gay *Alexis* in the grove
>   Shall be my future theme;
> I burn with an immortal love,
>   And sing a purer flame.   (9–12)

However, although Rowe echoes Watts' original poem, the poetic voice here is not seen to reject her own literary efforts but instead is described as gathering new momentum through Watts' example.

> Seraphic heights I seem to gain
>   And sacred Transports feel;
> While WATTS, to thy celestial strain
>   Supriz'd I listen still.   (13–16)[37]

Just as in Watts' poem where Philomela is depicted with 'Seraphic Wings', Rowe figures herself as gaining 'Seraphic Heights' in her poetry. As such, although she seems merely to echo Watts' compliments, she also claims her own poetic authority as an angelic being who inspires fervent devotion and ecstatic joy in her listeners/readers. As in her poems to the Athenians, here we see Rowe responding directly to the reactions to her work voiced by male readers and adapting her poetic identity, and her poetry, in accordance with these views. However, this is not a passive capitulation to male expectation. Rowe and Watts are in dialogue with each other. Watts' own conception of his poetic project was as much informed by Rowe's example as she was inspired by him. In fact, in terms of this particular exchange it is apparent that Rowe's poetry is seen as transcending Watts' own efforts. Nevertheless, the two-way discussion between Watts and Rowe further enables Rowe to make sense of her role as a female poet, and to claim a measure of authority for her writing. Moreover, reading her poetry in relation to Watts and his ideas provides a further context for reassessing Rowe's significance for the literary culture of her day.

Elizabeth Singer Rowe and women's literary history

Rowe was central to the poetics being practised by Blackmore and other Whig writers in the early eighteenth century. She was also seen by the Athenians and Isaac Watts as exemplifying the virtuous piety that was needed in a national poet dedicated to singing the praises of Whig military glory and, later, to furthering the project for a poetic tradition based on the Bible rather than the pagan epics.[38] In this, I would argue, the fact that she is a female poet assumes central importance not only for broadening our sense of the Whig poetic project, but also for refiguring Rowe's place in the history of women's writing. As I have noted, Rowe's significance has been read only in terms of her iconic status as a much admired pious and virtuous woman poet; an image which has proved remarkably enduring. Despite its ideological and commercial force, I would argue that this sentimental reading of Rowe and her poetry is incomplete. The accepted image of Rowe obscures the aspects of her authorial persona for which she was initially applauded and brought to public attention: her political and religious affiliations. Rowe did, indeed, become almost canonized as a saint among women writers, as Watts' poems clearly demonstrate, but it is important to remember that it was her overtly Williamite poems that first brought her to the attention of the male critical establishment. Indeed, although Watts' description of Rowe as 'a fair Angel' could be read as excessive, patronizing and ultimately limiting, his poem also places her at the centre of a network of politically inflected ideas about the nation's poetry and the nation's poets. Furthermore, the 'seraphic' nature of Rowe's poetry and persona serves this broader agenda rather than simply endorsing her cultural value as an 'angel' among women. We can, then, begin to construct another context in which to read Rowe's poetry and to assess her significance as a female poet. From an analysis of the content and reception of her early poetry, it is clear that she served a very useful purpose as a feminine version of an otherwise aggressively masculine poetic tradition. Later generations of editors and critics have all but erased the political meaning of her image and overall career as a writer. Nonetheless, it is necessary to keep in mind that Rowe's entry into print was predicated on a deliberate and self-conscious construction of feminine virtue along the lines of a specifically whiggish and nonconformist literary agenda. What is equally important is that Rowe herself found this agenda enabling and used it to shape not only the content of her poetry, but also to stamp her authority as a poet.

6

Provincial Networks, Dissenting Connections and Noble Friends

'Twas only out of regard to Mr. Rowe, that with his society she was willing to bear London during the winter season; and as soon after his decease as her affairs would permit, she indulged her unconquerable inclinations to solitude, by returning to Frome in Somersetshire, in the neighbourhood of which place the greater part of her estate lay. When she forsook the town, she determined to return to it no more, but to conceal the remainder of her life in absolute retirement.[1]

Despite her politicized identity in the 1690s, the image of Rowe presented here and elsewhere by her biographers is of a pious and modest woman more interested in works of charity than literary fame, a lover of 'absolute solitude' who eschewed the bustle of the town in preference for a virtuous rural retirement. This image of Rowe as modest and retiring was extremely influential and did much to establish her reputation as a pious exemplar as well as to increase the popularity of her writing. Rowe did live most of her life apart from the centre of print culture and instead lived and worked in the provincial town of Frome in Somerset. She was born in Ilchester on 11 September 1674, but the family moved to Frome around 1692 when Rowe was eighteen. Rowe spent her brief married life (1710–15) in London; but after Thomas Rowe's early death in 1715, she returned to Frome and remained there. However, the presentation in the above quotation of Frome as an isolated backwater is misleading and does little to explain how Rowe's provincial background actually shaped her career as a writer. In fact, as a thriving market town, late seventeenth- and early eighteenth-century Frome was very different from the impression given of it by the 'Life'. In *A Tour Through the Whole Island of Great Britain* (1724–6), for example,

Daniel Defoe notes that by the early eighteenth century some of the market towns of Wiltshire and Somerset were 'equal to cities in bigness, and superior to them in numbers of people'; and he includes Frome as one of the 'principal clothing towns' of the area:

> The town of Froom, or, as it is written in our maps, Frome Sellwood, [...] is so prodigiously increased within these last twenty or thirty years, that they have built a new church, and so many streets of houses, and those houses are so full of inhabitants, that Frome is now reckoned to have more people in it, than the city of Bath, and some say, even Salisbury itself, and if their trade continues to increase for a few years more, as it has done for those past, it is very likely to be one of the greatest and wealthiest inland towns in England. [...] Its trade is wholly clothing, and the cloths they make, are, generally speaking, all conveyed to London [...] and if we may believe common fame, there are above ten thousand people in Frome now, more than lived in it twenty years ago, and yet it was a considerable town then too. Here are, also, several large meeting houses, as well as churches, as there are generally, in all manufacturing and trading towns in England, especially in the western counties.[2]

Defoe's description of Frome is backed up by historical scholarship concerning provincial towns in the eighteenth century. As Peter Borsay, Rosemary Sweet and others have shown, from the late seventeenth century onwards, provincial towns expanded dramatically and built up strong trading and cultural links with the capital.[3] The west country in particular was an area of increasing wealth in this period as shown by the development of both Bath and Bristol as cultural centres.[4] As Defoe notes, Frome was particularly associated with the textile industry which was the main source of local wealth: Rowe's father was a clothier, her family were reasonably affluent, and she was financially independent after her father's death in 1719, as she inherited his entire estate. As atypically fortunate as her economic circumstance was, Rowe to a degree represents an emergent form of middle-class authorship which neither fits an urban model of dependence on the literary marketplace, nor the older model of the financially independent literary gentleman. Furthermore, as the provinces continued to develop both economically and culturally so too did the opportunities for writers to live and work there rather than having to gravitate towards London. Nevertheless, Rowe's provinciality also allowed her to foster what was, in many ways, a quite artificial image of herself as uninterested in literary fame and as actively repudiating the literary marketplace. As I have already noted, although this image has often been emphasized as part of Rowe's authorial persona as a modest lady, what has been ignored is the way in which Rowe's provincial context centrally informs this aspect of her persona. In what follows, I explore how Rowe's provinciality directly shaped her career as a writer. What I emphasize here is not only how Rowe's provincial background actually enabled her career as a writer in a practical sense, but also how her provincial image and reputation for retirement directly shaped the image of female authorship she came to represent.

The provinces and the periodical press

Although Rowe physically avoided London, she did not repudiate literary fame; nor was she completely isolated from London literary culture. As I demonstrated in the previous chapter, her first appearance in print was in a London journal: John Dunton's *Athenian Mercury*. Rowe's contributions to Dunton's journal led to the London publication of her collected *Poems on Several Occasions by Philomela*. Also, the commercial success of the *Mercury*, one of the most widely read Whig periodicals of the late seventeenth century, which was distributed through the coffee houses and for the period of its success was the key to Dunton's commercial survival, owed a great deal to Rowe's contributions.[5] From 19 May 1694 onward, the majority of its poetical content was Rowe's. As well as the political verse on William and the Jacobites, the *Mercury* printed a range of her verse, from paraphrases of the Canticles (5 June 1694) to the lighthearted 'To one that perswades me to leave the Muses' (18 June 1695). Even more striking than the consistent foregrounding of Rowe's work is the fact that the whole of the fifteenth volume is dedicated to 'the Pindarical Lady' (Rowe's early pseudonym). Furthermore, on 18 June 1695, five poems by Rowe appeared which comprise the entire paper. The editors' comments on this occasion suggest the popularity of Rowe's verses was so great that she can sustain a whole issue independently: 'We thought we could not more oblige our *Readers* then by Printing *all together* in one *Mercury*, the following *POEMS*, they being all written by the ingenious *Pindarick Lady*, and printed *Verbatim*, as we receiv'd 'em from her.'[6] A substantial amount of her work also appeared in the eighteenth and nineteenth volumes.[7] The 9 July 1695 number prints her 'A Pindarick, to the *Athenian Society*' and, as in volume fifteen, praises her: 'All the *Poems* written by the ingenious *Pindarick Lady* having a peculiar Delicacy of *Stile* and Majesty of *Verse*, as does distinguish 'em from all others.'

Clearly, as I argued in the previous chapter, Rowe was perceived by the *Mercury* as central to its success. Throughout the life of the paper, Dunton never met Rowe but made a variety of attempts to contact the unknown Pindarick Lady; and there is evidence of an ongoing correspondence between the journal and its protégé. In the 6 October 1694 issue, a letter states that the 'Ingenious *Pindarick Lady* who formerly sent many *Poetical Questions* to the *Athenian Society*, is desir'd now to send all those Poems she formerly mention'd – Directed to our *Bookseller* at the *Raven* in *Jewen Street*'. On 8 January 1695, Dunton notes that 'The Poems sent by the *Pindarick Lady* were received', and asks her to send in details of 'how a Letter may be Directed to her'. It is clear that Rowe responded to these requests for more poems and also that Dunton's idea to publish a collection of her poetry was already under negotiation.[8] Accordingly, *Poems on Several Occasions. Written by Philomela* was printed for Dunton in 1696 to capitalize on the interest shown in Rowe.

Provincial writers could, then, interact with the literary world of London through its periodicals.[9] The postal service necessary to this interaction proved increasingly valuable, and London journals circulated in the provinces throughout the eighteenth century. As John Feather has noted, some London papers timed publication for the days on which the mail left the capital for the main provincial towns.[10] Periodicals were also available through the post for individual readers, and the *Athenian Mercury* in particular was bound in volumes with supplements for the benefit of provincial readers who could not access the paper as soon as it appeared.[11] As the century progressed, the London periodical press was to rely more and more upon a provincial, and, increasingly, a national, readership. It is typical of Dunton's commercial acumen that he was one of the first to exploit the potential of the periodical market. For the purposes of my argument here, Rowe's involvement with the *Mercury* – as reader as well as writer – is further evidence that the provinces were not culturally isolated from the capital in this period. The postal system and the periodical press linked the metropolis and the provinces together in ways that overcame geographical distance and the need for writers to live in London. Rowe sent her contributions to the *Mercury* by post, and she also negotiated the publication of her collection of poetry without meeting Dunton in person or travelling to London.[12] In this instance, it is the London readers of the *Mercury* who are consuming literary culture from the provinces. At a moment in history when the metropolitan nature of literary culture is constantly emphasized, and an urban model of authorship is seen as increasingly dominant, it is important to note that another influential strand of literary culture and authorial practice was being created at the beginning of the eighteenth century: the provincial middle-class woman writer who used the periodical press as the means to publish her poetry and establish herself as a writer.

Dissenting connections

Rowe's choice of the *Athenian Mercury* was based on its accessibility for provincial readers, but, as I argued in the previous chapter, she must also have been attracted by the nonconformist and whiggish bias of the journal. Rowe's father was Presbyterian and she retained strong links with her dissenting background in terms of her marriage, her circles of friends, her politics and the subject and style of her poetry. As well as showing the importance of the periodical press for connecting London and the provinces, Rowe's appearance in the *Mercury* points to another context in which to evaluate provincial–metropolitan interaction: the culture of nonconformity. Although there is clear evidence of large nonconformist populations concentrated in certain regions, it has been argued that nonconformists in provincial areas actually interacted more extensively with the capital than communities centred around the established church. As Rosemary Sweet has suggested, dissenting culture had a less narrowly localized identity than provincial Anglicanism due to a shared sense of victimization and difference: 'Dissent created supra-local allegiances between members of the same denomination, fore-shadowing the national identity of class, whereas the strength of the Anglican parish was as a focal point for the local community.'[13] These broad links between metropolitan and provincial dissenters inevitably led to cultural and literary ideas being passed back and forth more readily. As Defoe's comment on the proliferation of meeting-houses implies, dissent was a strong presence in Frome and the west country; and to be a provincial dissenter was by definition to have strong links with the capital.[14]

Rowe's being a dissenter in the provinces may actively have enabled her career as a writer, therefore. Throughout her writing life she relied on a network of nonconformist writers, ministers and intellectuals who had connections in and between London and the west country. Rowe's appearance in *Divine Hymns and Poems on Several Occasions* (1704), shows the influence of these 'supra-local' cultural networks. This collection of religious verse, which includes a weighty selection of Rowe's poems, was dedicated to Sir Richard Blackmore and was obviously tailored to add fuel to the movement for the reformation of poetry which

I discussed in the previous chapter. Rowe's poetry clearly and consistently demonstrates the key elements associated with this school of poets. Although not all of the proponents of divine poetry were dissenters, the attraction of such critical sentiments for a nonconformist writer are clear. Among the other contributors to this collection are one John Bowden and one Mr Wesley. Before 1700, John Bowden was an assistant to the minister in Frome (Humphrey Philips) and became sole minister on Philips' death. Rook Lane chapel in Frome, of which Rowe was a member, was built for Bowden in 1707, and that is where he preached Rowe's funeral sermon in 1737.[15] The appearance of a local nonconformist minister in a London-produced collection of poetry points to the way in which dissenting circles had a wide sphere of influence beyond a specific area or region. However, it may have been Rowe who facilitated Bowden's entry into print through her earlier connections with the *Athenian Mercury*. Indeed, Samuel Wesley was one of the editors of the journal alongside John Norris, whose work also appears in *Divine Hymns and Poems*. At this point, Frome and London can be seen to interact in two ways – via Rowe's previous links with a sympathetically edited periodical as well as through the way in which nonconformist ministers, in particular, had strong connections with the metropolis.

The dissenting academies in London played a crucial role in connecting the metropolis to the provinces. Many of the significant literary acquaintances Rowe made stemmed from the connections between the academy at Newington Green in London and the west country. The central figure who connects this intricate, and often confusing, network of nonconformist writers was Rowe's husband Thomas, whose uncle (also called Thomas Rowe) was a tutor at the academy and numbered Henry Grove, John Hughes and Isaac Watts among his pupils. Even before Rowe's marriage, the network of writers who attended the elder Thomas Rowe's academy can be seen in operation. Henry Grove is the figure who most exemplifies the provincial–metropolitan connections maintained by dissenting ministers. Grove, who had begun writing Rowe's biography shortly before his death in 1738, was born in Taunton in Somerset and moved back to the west country after a two-year stay in London when he attended Thomas Rowe's academy and became acquainted with Isaac Watts. Grove became the tutor at the Taunton Academy in 1706, and numbered John Bowden among his tutees. Both these men appeared in miscellanies with Elizabeth Rowe in the early eighteenth century. As Rowe's poetry had already appeared in print – both in the *Mercury* and in her single-authored collection of 1696 – it is likely that Rowe was the lynch-pin of this literary network, and that she used her London connections and publishing profile to help her friends into print.

The most influential contact Rowe made from her nonconformist background in Frome was, of course, Isaac Watts, who may have been introduced to her through Henry Grove, possibly via John Bowden. Watts may, in turn, have introduced Rowe to her future husband (the couple supposedly met at Bath in 1709). Thomas Rowe's father and uncle were both present at Watts' 'acceptance ceremony' at Mark Lane Church in 1702, where he was a minister and educator.[16] Rowe met Watts in about 1706, but possibly even earlier. As I have shown, Watts' views on poetry accord with Rowe's poetic practice, and it is clear that they admired each other's work. Moreover, the fourth edition of *Horae Lyricae* (1726) included a number of commendatory poems to Watts which correspond to the provincial literary circles Rowe inhabited: poems appear by Rowe, Henry Grove and Joseph Standon (also a dissenting minister in the west country). All these poems are dated 1706, and point, therefore, to a coterie group of writers exchanging verses in a provincial context many years prior to their appearance in print.

The importance of this network of writers continued throughout Rowe's career. Therefore, although Rowe had published a collection of poetry and various other examples of her work in periodicals and miscellanies before she met Isaac Watts, it is nevertheless clear that she inhabited a supportive network of like-minded writers who encouraged and read her work, as she did theirs. The sense that Rowe may also have helped her male friends into print points to her active engagement in these literary networks and suggests that she was not just a passive recipient of male encouragement. The connections she made in London through Grove, Watts and her husband, also facilitated the literary links between Frome and the metropolis, which further enabled her as a writer. For example, her husband (a historian) knew Richard Steele, and in 1714 (when the Rowes were living in London), examples of Rowe's work appeared in Steele's *Poetical Miscellanies*, which also included the work of Alexander Pope and John Gay, among others.[17] Even when she was no longer in London, and her husband no longer alive, the early nonconformist connections still proved invaluable to her progress as a writer. Rowe's name was to be linked to Pope in another context; this time after her husband's death in 1715, on which occasion she wrote her most famous poem, 'On the Death of Mr. Thomas Rowe'. The elegy appeared with Pope's poetry on two occasions: it was published in *Poems on Several Occasions* published by Bernard Lintot in 1717 and then again with the second edition of *Eloisa to Abelard* in 1720. John Hughes, who translated the medieval text on which Pope based his poem, was educated with Isaac Watts at Thomas Rowe's dissenting academy, and numbered Addison, Steele and Richard Blackmore, as well as Rowe, among his literary associates. Clearly, the cultural traffic between London and the provinces was not only complex and extensive, but also extremely vital and productive.

Noble friends: Longleat and the Hertford circle

In many respects, Frome was ideally situated in relation to a number of provincial centres in the early eighteenth century. Not only was the town near to Bath and Bristol, it was also within seven miles of Longleat, the country estate of the Weymouth family. The Weymouths acted as patrons and supporters of the young Elizabeth Rowe. According to the 1739 'Life', Rowe's father became acquainted with Henry Thynne (son of 1st Viscount Weymouth), who admired some of Rowe's juvenile verse and responded by teaching her French and Italian:

> What first introduced her into the notice of the noble family at Longleat, was a little copy of verses of her's, with which they were so highly delighted as to express a curiosity to see her and the friendship which commenc'd from that time, subsisted ever after; not more to her honour, which was the favourite of persons so much superior to her in the outward directions of life, than to the praise of their judgement and taste who knew how to prize, and took a pleasure to cherish such blooming worth. She was not then twenty.[18]

As a result of this initial encouragement and notice, by the early eighteenth century Rowe had become a kind of companion to Henry Thynne's daughter Frances (1699–1754), later countess of Hertford. Despite being twenty-five years apart in age, they developed a lifelong friendship. This friendship was to play a central part in Rowe's later writing life not only because Frances, as Lady Hertford, was to become a well-known literary patron who cultivated her own literary circle of poets and writers which included Rowe, but also because their letters to each other formed the basis for Rowe's popular epistolary fictions of the late 1720s and early 1730s, *Friendship in Death* (1728) and *Letters Moral and Entertaining* (3 vols, 1729–33).

On one level, then, the proximity of Longleat to Frome and the presence of a literary-minded family at the nearby country estate was geographical coincidence. Nonetheless, the Thynnes' encouragement of Rowe exemplifies the way in which the country house could serve as a centre for provincial literary culture and patronage. Furthermore, due to the inevitable links between the court and aristocratic families such as the Weymouths, the country house could serve as a focal point for exchange between provincial, metropolitan and court life.[19] The proximity of Longleat to Frome helped Rowe specifically as a writer in two major ways. First, she met aristocratic circles of writers and intellectuals with whom, as a middle-class dissenter, it would have been unlikely she could have made contact under other circumstances. Second, due to her lifelong friendship with Lady Hertford she was a participant in an extended literary circle which focused on Lady Hertford's activities as a patron and encourager of the arts. Due to Lady Hertford's activities she came into contact – either in person, by letter or by association – with many literary figures of the time.

The significance of Longleat for Rowe's early literary career can be traced in a suprisingly direct way. In 1703, the poet and diplomat Matthew Prior spent two weeks at Longleat where he met Rowe, became interested in her poetry, and pursued a short correspondence with her beginning in the autumn of that year.[20] One topic of this correspondence is the printing of Rowe's poems in Tonson's *Poetical Miscellanies: the Fifth Part*, published in 1704. The miscellany included a selection of Rowe's verse (eight poems in all), and thirteen poems by Prior, who had appeared in the 1694 Dryden/Tonson miscellany also. Part of an ongoing project which had been collated by Dryden before his death, and which included only 'the most eminent hands', Tonson's fifth miscellany included Prior's response to Rowe's 'A Pastoral Inscrib'd to the Honourable Mrs ——' which was entitled, 'To the Author of the Pastoral Printed, Page 378', and another poem which may allude to Rowe, 'Disputing with a Lady who left me in the Argument'. In the correspondence between Rowe and Prior (we only have Prior's side), it is clear that she was very much involved with the publication of her work, but it is also clear that his initial interest in Rowe's work was sparked by reading her poetry in manuscript. Writing from Westminster on 14 October 1703, in terms of playful coquetry, Prior mentions that Rowe has given him a translation of Tasso to comment upon:

> To give you an account of the Poetical Commission with which you entrusted me, I should make bold to break through all the Prose Business which I find at my return to London, But Tonson is not yet come from Holland, and I shal have time enough to look over your

ENCHANTED FORREST, not that it will ever be so good as ARMINDA'S GARDENS, For tho' I could Judge or Correct pritty well when I was with you, I am stupid and Senceless at fourscore miles distance, and the little Wit I had is not owing to Nature but Inspiration.[21]

The correspondence between Prior and Rowe shows how Rowe's participation in the sociable literary circles at Longleat enabled her as a writer and increased her status as an author. On one level, this literary circle operates as a coterie group, as Rowe obviously sent Prior copies of her poems in manuscript for his comments and suggestions, and he sent his own verses to her. However, it is also clear that Rowe used Prior for her negotiations with Tonson, and as a way of receiving the printed text of her poems. For example, Prior promises to send her a copy of the fifth miscellany on its publication (25 November 1703), and in a letter of 24 June 1704, he mentions that Rowe has asked him to negotiate with Tonson to include some of her friend's poems in the next miscellany: 'Jacob Tonson does not intend us an other Miscellany this great while, when he does your Friends shal be sure to have a place kept.' Accordingly, the sixth miscellany includes two poems by Grove, Rowe's biographer. Here the different strands of Rowe's provincial context come together through the intersection of her nonconformist connections and the aristocratic Longleat circle.

Overall, then, Rowe's entry into print is helped considerably by her acquaintance with influential patrons from the Longleat circle who aided her publication and actively encouraged her writing. She also gained considerable cultural status from her appearance in collections which contained the work of Prior, Alexander Pope, John Dryden and Anne Finch, Countess of Winchelsea. Thus, far from being marginalized because of her provincial existence, the early connections she made at Longleat gave Rowe access to one of the most prestigious forms of publication, and also the approval of some of the most influential and famous literary men and women of her time. Indeed, despite the rather facetious tone of Prior's letters, it is apparent that his approval of her work was genuine. In 1709, Tonson printed Prior's *Poems on Several Occasions* which included the pastoral printed in the fifth miscellany, with the new title 'Love and Friendship', as well as Prior's responses, 'To the Author of the Foregoing Pastoral' and 'To a Lady: She refusing to continue a Dispute with me, and leaving me in the Argument. An Ode'. In the preface, Prior specifically mentions 'Mrs. Singer' by name, and thanks her for giving him 'leave to Print a Pastoral of her Writing; That Poem having produced the verses immediately following it'. The fact that Rowe was mentioned in the preface to Prior's works indicates the high profile and respect she enjoyed at the start of her writing career. This prestige must have been strengthened by the handsome subscription folio edition of Prior's poems published in 1718, which retained the original preface and poems. Another edition of the poems was published in 1721, which also included Rowe's poem. The literary circle behind the publication of the 1718 folio edition is clearly mapped out in the list of subscribers, which included Lady Hertford, the Earl of Hertford, and the Earl and Countess of Winchelsea.[22]

As the century progressed, Rowe became more associated with Lady Hertford in particular, rather than with the family at Longleat. After her marriage, Lady Hertford was no longer based at Longleat, of course, but divided her time between London and her husband's various country estates.[23] Rowe benefited as a writer from Lady Hertford's position as an influential female patron of a number of predominantly male poets, including James Thomson, John Dyer, Stephen Duck, Richard Savage and George Shenstone. Although Rowe did not benefit financially from her associations with Lady Hertford, her ongoing acquaintance and correspondence with the countess brought her to the attention of the literary circles surrounding Lady Hertford throughout the 1720s and 1730s. One poet whom Rowe came into contact with, in writing and in person, through Lady Hertford was James Thomson. Thomson dedicated 'Spring' to Lady Hertford in 1728, and it has been suggested that he wrote the majority of the poem when he visited one of her country seats, Marlborough Castle in Wiltshire, during the summer of 1727.[24] Both women subscribed to the first edition of *The Seasons* on its publication in 1728. Rowe's place in this circle of writers is shown by the way in which she corresponded with Thomson through Lady Hertford. Rowe's poem 'To Mr. Thomson. On the Countess of ——'s praising his Poems', was sent in a letter to Lady Hertford and eventually printed in Rowe's posthumous *Works*. Thomson himself clearly saw Rowe as an integral part of Lady Hertford's coterie. In various early versions of his 'Hymn on Solitude', Rowe is mentioned in relation to Lady Hertford under her literary pseudonym, Philomela:

> A Lover now, with all the Grace
> Of that sweet Passion in your Face!
> Then, soft-divided, you assume
> The gentle-looking H——d's Bloom,
> As with her PHILOMELA, she,
> (Her PHILOMELA fond of thee)

> Amid the long, withdrawing Vale,
> Awakes the rival'd Nightingale.[25]

Although Rowe did visit Marlborough on a few occasions, the literary circle she participated in through Lady Hertford was primarily an epistolary one.[26] The extensive correspondence between Rowe and Hertford illuminates how literary circles operated in the early eighteenth century: poems were exchanged, ideas shared, and books and writers recommended. One frequent topic of discussion between Rowe and Lady Hertford was Isaac Watts. In a letter dating from 1725, Rowe alludes to a missed opportunity of a meeting between Lady Hertford and Watts, and in further letters it is clear that Rowe's attempts to interest her friend in Watts' work were successful.[27] Rowe received some commendatory verses, 'Written in a blank leaf of Mr. Watts's Poems', written by Lady Hertford for Watts, and promised to forward them, adding that ''twill give him new inspiration; he'll be a proud of them as if an angel had given him a wreath of immortal amaranthus'.[28]

The example of Watts' work which Lady Hertford so admired was the fourth edition of *Horae Lyricae* (1726). Watts acknowledged the compliment in the fifth edition for 1727, by including one of Lady Hertford's poems under the name 'Eusebia' as part of a series of commendatory verses by Rowe, Joseph Standon and Henry Grove. Watts sealed his connection with Lady Hertford by dedicating the 1734 edition of *Reliquiae Juveniles* to her and also, albeit anonymously, the posthumous edition of Rowe's *Devout Exercises of the Heart* (1737). The preface to *Reliquiae Juveniles* includes an elaborate compliment to Rowe, where her work is compared to Pope's *Messiah* and Edward Young's paraphrase of the Book of Job:

> Could I imitate those admirable Representations of Human Nature and Passion which that ingenious Pen has given us, who wrote the late volumes of *Epistles from the Dead to the Living*, and *Letters Moral and Entertaining*, I should then hope for happier Success in my Endeavours to provide innocent and improving Diversions for polite Youth.[29]

In a similar vein, the dedication to Lady Hertford praises her piety, taste and politeness, which anticipate the praise of Rowe's writing:

> Your Ladyship's known Character and Taste for everything that is Pious and Polite, give an honourable Sanction to those Writings

which stand Recommended by Your Name and Approbation; 'tis no Wonder then that these ESSAYS should seek the Favour of such a Patronage.

(p. iv)

The connections between Rowe, Lady Hertford and Watts are significant for two reasons. First, for the way in which Rowe's nonconformist background intersects with her aristocratic connections through her encouragement of Lady Hertford's interest in Watts. Rowe's interventions on Watts' behalf resulted in him benefiting from the support of a well-known patron of the arts. The second point of interest is the way in which the patronage relationship between Lady Hertford and Rowe is reconfigured by Watts as a form of virtuous female friendship based on shared interests and values. Watts continues the association of the two women by using the form of a letter, 'To Philomela', to frame his own verse compliment to the Countess, 'Piety in a Court'. As the title suggests, 'Piety in a Court' contrasts Lady Hertford's love of rural life with the senseless round of court pleasures:

> Is there a Soul at Court that seeks the Grove
> Or lovely Hill to muse on heavenly love;
> And when to crowds and state her Hour descends,
> She keeps her Conscience and her God her Friends?

The narrative frame which Watts employs provides a textual representation of the literary circles inhabited by Rowe and Lady Hertford. The letter to Philomela describes a select company of 'a few intimate Friends' (p. 273), who read the poems to and by Lady Hertford out loud. The company agree that Lady Hertford exemplifies Watts' conception of piety at court, and one of the fictional characters, Alethina, passes Lady Hertford's manuscript poems to the 'Isaac Watts' figure in the group:

> I know Eusebia's modesty, said she, and a Blush will easily be raised in the Face of so much Virtue: yet I don't think the Writer hath mistook her character; in my Opinion 'tis just and sincere. [. . .] I have been favour'd with some of the Fruits of her retir'd Meditations, and as I have long had the Happiness of her Acquaintance, I dare pronounce that she lives what she writes. It so happens at present, that I can give you a Taste of her Piety and her Acquaintance with the Muses together, for I have had Leave to transcribe three or four copies with which I have been much entertained, and I'm persuaded you'll thank me for the Entertainment they give you.

(p. 273)

In effect, Watts is dramatizing the coterie production of Lady Hertford's poems, and the manner in which her literary circle operated. Watts' dramatization of this provincial circle accords with the practice of such groups, shown by the use of pastoral pseudonyms and the transcription of manuscript poems. Like many other women writers, Lady Hertford's poetry is said to reflect her virtuous character. The production of her poetry is seen in relation to a close group of intimate female friends who read her poems as evidence of her piety. Rowe's place in this group is clear. Rather than being set in a position of grateful dependency on her patron, in the manner of Mary Barber, Rowe's relationship with Lady Hertford is one of friendly intimacy. In the dedication to *Devout Exercises of the Heart*, Watts continues the association of Rowe and Hertford. The dedication is addressed to 'An intimate Friend of Mrs. ROWE', and foregrounds the friendship between the two women:

> If these pious MEDITATIONS, of so sublime a genius should be inscribed to any name, there is none but your's must have stood in front of them. That long and constant intimacy of friendship with which you delighted to honour her, that high esteem and veneration you are pleased to pay her memory, and the sacred likeness and sympathy between two kindred souls, absolutely determine where this respect should be paid.   (p. iii)

Watts ends the dedication by imagining the two friends reunited in heaven: 'There you may join with your beloved PHILOMELA, in paying celestial worship, in exalted and unknown forms, to her GOD and your GOD; and may the harmony of the place be assisted by your united songs to JESUS, your common Saviour!' (p. v). Although Watts alludes to the discrepancy in rank and religion between the two women, he also attempts to smooth over these differences in his presentation of Rowe and Lady Hertford as 'kindred souls'. The power balance inherent in the patron–author relation has thus almost completely vanished.

The most significant manifestation of Rowe's connections with Lady Hertford can be seen in her most well-known publications: *Friendship in Death* and *Letters Moral and Entertaining*. When *Friendship in Death* was published anonymously in 1728 it was at first thought possible that the author was Lady Hertford. Rowe herself rather mischievously encouraged speculation as to the authorship of the book. In a letter to the countess, Rowe remarked: 'I wish the letters from the Dead were your Ladyship's but be they whose they will I have the utmost importance to see them.'[30] Although partly fictionalized, the letters that comprise *Friendship in Death*, and the speculation over their authorship, foreground the association of Rowe with Lady Hertford, and build on their actual correspondence. This association of Rowe and Lady Hertford was furthered by the publication of *Letters Moral and Entertaining*, the first part of which (1729) includes letters from the genuine correspondence between the two women under the titles, 'Letters to Cleora' (Rowe's letters), and 'Letters to the Author' (Lady Hertford's). What is significant here is that the market success of Rowe's epistolary fiction was predicated on Rowe's provincial background and the acquaintances she made originally at Longleat: in fact, the content of her most popular texts came from that context. Furthermore, the correspondence printed in *Letters Moral and Entertaining* also celebrates the friendship between the two women in ways that enforce both their piety and their preference for rural retirement. Letter I, 'To Cleora', contrasts 'Hyde-Park and the Opera' with life in 'some rural abode'. The letter concludes that 'such a retreat as disengages the mind from those interests and passions which mankind generally pursue, appear to me the most certain way to happiness'. Cleora's reply 'To the Author', alludes to biblical precedent to back up her assertion that it is easy to be virtuous in retirement: 'I cannot praise your virtue in becoming a recluse, and getting the victory by a cowardly flight. I would have you raise your character, by venturing into this wicked town, and by despising the world in the midst of its dazzling temptations.' However, Cleora soon reveals her own preference for the countryside and her agreement with her friend's mode of existence: 'But my comparisons are so much to the advantage of the country, that I am afraid you will suspect my advice to be the effect of envy; and I had as good throw off the disguise, and own that at present my way of living is a series of impertinence.' Accordingly, Letter III describes Cleora in the gardens of her country estate planting 'her perfect wilderness of sweets'.

Lady Hertford did indeed have a reputation for piety and a preference for rural life as opposed to her court duties. She tried to spend most of her time at her various country seats: Marlborough Castle in Wiltshire, St Leonard's Hill in Windsor Forest, and at Percy Lodge near Colnbrook. It was at Percy Lodge that she cultivated her garden in the fashionable wilderness style of the day to evoke a symbolic atmosphere of solitude and virtuous retirement. She also had a hermitage built in the gardens of St Leonard's Hill.[31] Lady Hertford's image was extremely useful for Rowe. Other women writers construct their female patrons as virtuous exemplars in order to reflect back upon themselves, but it was the similarities between Rowe and Hertford which were continually played on by various commentators, as well as forming the basis of *Letters Moral and Entertaining*. Although, as I have shown, Rowe's relation with Lady Hertford and her family followed the familiar trajectory of the support of a lower-class writer by literary-minded figures of high rank, the usual dynamic between author and patron is consistently elided with regard to Rowe. As such, although Rowe's own letters to Lady Hertford are alert to the social differences between them, the way in which their relationship is presented avoids the connotations of sycophantic dependency or effusive gratitude. This was due in part to Rowe's economic independence, but it was also connected to the symbolic use of Lady Hertford's character to enforce Rowe's image as a writer dedicated to virtue, piety and rural retirement. One later example of this reconfiguration of the patronage relation as a form of virtuous friendship can be found in John Duncombe's *The Feminiad; or, Female Genius* (1754). Written with the intention of praising female poets and bestowing immortality upon them, Duncombe's work clearly reveals what was expected of a woman writer by the mid-century. She had to be modest, retiring and not neglectful of domestic duties in her service of the Muses. Rowe is constructed as an angelic spirit whose exemplary life is rewarded with a joyful death and existence in heaven. In a reversal of the usual relationship between patron and author, where the author gains by association with a noble patron, the description of Rowe's 'illustrious friend and patroness', Lady Hertford, comes after the praise of Rowe. The description of Lady Hertford is clearly framed by Rowe's example:

> Nor can her noble Friend escape unseen
> Or, from the Muse her modest virtue screen;
> Here, sweetly blended, to our wand'ring eyes,
> The Peeress, Poetess and Christian rise.   (167–70)

Elizabeth Rowe and the literary marketplace

Despite the strenuous attempts made by various commentators to reconfigure Lady Hertford's patronage as a form of virtuous female friendship, Rowe's connections with such a high-profile figure must have added to the popularity and marketability of her work. The commercial value of her association with Lady Hertford is shown by the success of the printed version of their letters. Furthermore, despite her reputation as modest and retiring, Rowe's epistolary fiction *Friendship in Death* (1728), was remarkably successful. It was printed for the bookseller Thomas Worrall, and reached four editions before Rowe's death in 1737, with a fifth edition in 1738. The immediate success of the book is indicated by the printing of the second edition as early as 1729, a year after its first print run. Like her female contemporaries, Rowe also had to negotiate with the London booksellers. As was the case with many other women writers, Rowe's choice of bookseller reflects her particular interests and style of authorship. From the evidence of the advertisement listing 'Books printed for, and Sold by THO. WORRALL, at the Judge's Head, against St. Dunstan's-Church in Fleet-Street', printed in *Friendship in Death*, Worrall's publications show a marked bias towards sermons and works of morality, although the list is typically eclectic.[32]

In contrast to most prose fiction by women in the period, both *Friendship in Death* and *Letters Moral and Entertaining* were initially anonymous. However, by the time the first part of the *Letters* were published in 1729 it must have been clear that the author was Rowe.[33] Rowe's control over her the publication of her work in this respect is strongly suggested by the fact that is only after her death that her name begins to appear on the title-page. Rowe dedicated *Friendship in Death* to Edward Young, in 'gratitude for the pleasure and advantage I have received from your Poem on the LAST JUDGMENT, and the PARA-PHRASE on part of the Book of Job'. Young responded by providing a preface.[34] Therefore, although she chose to remain anonymous, Rowe also employed the strategy of aligning herself in public with an established male writer to authorize her work. In this case, Rowe guides the reader into associating her text with religious verse. In the dedication, Rowe also emphasizes her lack of economic motivation for writing, and declares that she has no intention of courting fame: 'The author of these Letters is above any view of interest; and can have no prospect of reputation, resolving to be concealed.' Rowe betrays an anxiety here that the publication of her work will result in accusations of mercenary motives. She constructs herself as an independent author who does not have to rely on the sales of her book, the demands of a patron, or political bias. She is 'above any view of interest'. 'Interest' here denotes a range of meanings as Rowe's strategies are designed to disassociate herself from all forms of dependence, both commercial and patronal. In the manner of Pope, for example, Rowe suggests that she is different from those writers who depended on the booksellers for survival, as well as distinguishable from the fawning sycophancy associated with a reliance on patronal favours, or the taste of subscribers. Rowe's anonymity is not, therefore, based on a notion of feminine modesty, but on a lofty removal of herself from any kind of economic pressures.[35]

This symbolic authorial stance relies, of course, on actual financial security. Due to the legacy from her father, Rowe did not have to rely on writing for her livelihood and therefore her adoption of the stance of the disinterested amateur rests on a firm economic basis. In her own comments on her economic circumstances, Rowe uses the loaded term 'dependence' to distinguish her own position as an author. In a letter to Mrs Arabella Marrow, a Warwickshire friend, Rowe declares that she is 'above all dependence', and remarks that, 'I have ease and plenty to the extent of my wishes and could form no desires but what my fathers [*sic*] indulgence would procure'.[36] In a letter to Lady Hertford, Rowe connects her independence to her wish to remain anonymous. In a similar stance to that adopted by Mary Barber and Jane Brereton, the publication of *The History of Joseph* is presented as a result of friendly encouragement by those private acquaintances who have enjoyed the poem in manuscript:

> By the partiality of some of my Acquaintances the Poem of Joseph has been so often transcribed & got into so many Hands that I been flatter'd or teaz'd into a Consent to let it be Publish'd on Condition the author is never known nor nam'd as for success I have no manner of vanity or Concern I am as Proud of adjusting a Tulip or Butterfly in a right position on a screen as of writing Heroicks.[37]

Here Rowe presents a gendered version of the disinterested amateur author. She reconfigures her writing as a form of feminine accomplishment, and suggests that any pride she may have in her work is comparable to the private satisfactions of minor domestic achievements. Rowe's authorial pronouncements must be read, however, in the light of her economic independence. She could, quite literally, afford the luxury of denouncing an economic motive for writing. In Rowe's case, the stance of the private, modest lady amateur is based on a firm financial footing.

Even though Rowe was economically independent, her claim to 'have no prospect of reputation' is disingenuous, despite her anonymity. In the same letter to Lady Hertford, Rowe betrays a more professional interest in the mechanics of publication. She describes her (unsuccessful) attempt to design a 'romantick scene' for the frontispiece of an edition of *Letters Moral and Entertaining*: 'The Reason of this Disign [*sic*] was, hearing that Mr Worral [*sic*] intended to put a Frontice peice [*sic*] before Letters Moral & entertaining the next Edition. If I could have pleas'd my Self I should have given him the Plan.' Furthermore, like Frances

Burney's secret glee at the commendations she heard about *Evelina* when it was published anonymously in 1778, Rowe delights in the praise her published work receives. In another letter to Lady Hertford, Rowe expresses her approval of *Friendship in Death*, recommended to her by the countess, and adds that such a book could 'tempt me to wish I had writt it myself if I had the least ambition of being an author'.[38] Just before the publication of *Letters Moral and Entertaining*, Rowe expresses her pleasure to Lady Hertford that their correspondence will appear in print: 'I long to see them publisht as they soon will bee [sic].'[39]

Conclusions: rethinking women's literary history

When viewed in the light of a model of female authorship which focuses exclusively on the London marketplace and the economic relations between author, bookseller and reading public, Rowe's career might seem anomalous. Furthermore, if the commercial success of her fiction is coupled with Rowe's disclaimers about literary ambition and her intimate relations with her patron, her career might seem to represent two conflicting approaches to authorship. On the one hand, because of her popularity with a wide-ranging readership, shown by the various editions of her work, Rowe can be placed in a commercial context and her texts in direct competition with other works of fiction on the market. Indeed, although Rowe professed disinterest in the financial rewards writing could offer, she nevertheless must have received payment for her work. On the other hand, Rowe's career demonstrates the large part a provincial context and private circles of acquaintance could play in a woman writer's public success. In addition, her career is evidence of the continuing importance of various forms of patronage and aristocratic encouragement. Moreover, Rowe's provinciality actually enabled her as a writer and became a key component of her commercial success. Rather than viewing Rowe as anomalous, therefore, it is more useful to broaden out the accepted paradigms of female authorship to include a writer as prominent as Rowe. Rowe's career demonstrates that in order to be a popular writer in the period it was not necessary to live in London and work directly in the literary marketplace. However, it is also clear that Rowe does not represent an alternative model of private, amateur and coterie production. Rowe's success was predicated on a combination of negotiation with London booksellers, such as John Dunton, Jacob Tonson and Thomas Worrall, as well as the support of aristocratic and influential friends who effectively act as patrons in their encouragement and support of Rowe's work. Added to this is Rowe's particular place as a dissenting woman writer who caught the attention of influential men of similar beliefs and political allegiances. Rowe's career can be said to combine the commercial impulses of the London trade and the older tradition of patronage and friendly encouragement. However, far from being anomalous, her pattern of literary production is, in fact, more representative of early eighteenth-century female authorship than the image of the scandalous prostitute of the pen churning out copy at the demands of an avaricious bookseller.

What my analysis of Rowe's career suggests in a broader sense is that the current concentration on 'Grub Street' as the only context which produced popular writing by women is overly narrow. For Rowe, and a variety of other women writers, it is clear that local and regional networks of support were equally important to their literary careers. As well as providing an insight into the operation of provincial literary culture, Rowe's career represents a form of authorship which is often neglected in accounts of the eighteenth-century literary marketplace. While it is indisputable that London was the centre of publishing in this period, the role played by the provinces in shaping literary culture and modes of cultural transmission has often been overlooked. In many ways, therefore, the accepted narrative of the rise of the 'professional' author in this period is remarkably one-sided. As Rowe's example has shown, the dominant version of eighteenth-century authorship as London-centred and market-led is not sufficient to describe the full range of authorial practices and networks which informed literary culture at this point in history. In terms of women's literary history, it is clear that existing models of women's writing do not accurately or fully describe female literary practice in the years from 1690 to 1740. By contrast, the 'pluralist' model of women's literary history which I have followed in this book suggests one way in which we can 'relocate' women's place in literary culture. A close attention to the different contexts in which women were writing – be they geographical, political, religious, patronal, coterie or commercial – opens up the remarkable range of activity which characterizes women's literary production at this time. Such a model not only broadens our sense of the opportunities as well as the struggles women faced as authors, but also allows a fuller appreciation of the richness and diversity of women's participation in the literary culture of their day.

Notes

Introduction

1. See, for example, C. Gallagher, *Nobody's Story: the Vanishing Acts of Women Writers in the Marketplace, 1670–1820* (Oxford: Clarendon Press, 1994) and C. Ingrassia, *Authorship, Commerce, and Gender in Early Eighteenth-Century England: a Culture of Paper Credit* (Cambridge: Cambridge University Press, 1998). Until recently, most general studies of eighteenth-century women writers concentrated on fiction. See, for example, R. Ballaster, *Seductive Forms: Women's Amatory Fiction from 1684 to 1740* (Oxford: Clarendon Press, 1992); J. Spencer, *The Rise of the Woman Novelist: From Aphra Behn to Jane Austen* (Oxford: Blackwell, 1986); J. Todd, *The Sign of Angellica: Women, Writing and Fiction, 1660–1800* (London: Virago, 1989).
2. A. Kernan, *Samuel Johnson and the Impact of Print* (Princeton: Princeton University Press, 1987) and M. Rose, *Authors and Owners: the Invention of Copyright* (Cambridge: Harvard University Press, 1993).
3. Kernan, *Samuel Johnson and the Impact of Print*, p. 5.
4. D. Griffin, *Literary Patronage in England, 1650–1800* (Cambridge: Cambridge University Press, 1996) and M. J. M. Ezell, *Social Authorship and the Advent of Print* (Baltimore and London: Johns Hopkins University Press, 1999).
5. B. Hammond, *Professional Imaginative Writing in England, 1670–1740: 'Hackney for Bread'* (Oxford: Clarendon Press, 1997), p. 5.
6. See, for example, M. Duffy, *The Passionate Shepherdess: Aphra Behn 1640–1689* (London: Jonathan Cape, 1977) and A. Goreau, *Reconstructing Aphra: a Social Biography of Aphra Behn* (Oxford: Oxford University Press, 1980).
7. Gallagher, *Nobody's Story*, p. 4.
8. V. Woolf, *A Room of One's Own* (London: Penguin Books, 1945), p. 64.
9. Woolf, *A Room of One's Own*, p. 65.
10. See especially, Goreau, *Reconstructing Aphra*.
11. K. R. King, 'Elizabeth Singer Rowe's Tactical Use of Print and Manuscript', in *Women's Writing and the Circulation of Ideas: Manuscript Publication in England, 1550–1800*, edited by G. L. Justice and N. Tinker (Cambridge: Cambridge University Press, 2002), pp. 158–81, p. 175.
12. N. Cotton, *Women Playwrights in England c. 1363–1750* (London and Toronto: Bucknell University Press, 1980), pp. 200–1.
13. Todd, *The Sign of Angellica*, p. 41.
14. Todd, *The Sign of Angellica*, p. 41.
15. M. L. Williamson, *Raising Their Voices: British Women Writers, 1650–1750* (Detroit: Wayne State University Press, 1990). Williamson's approach is heavily indebted to Nancy Cotton's earlier characterization of eighteenth-

century women writers as 'Astreas' or 'Orindas'. See Nancy Cotton, *Women Playwrights in England*.

16. J. Medoff, 'The Daughters of Behn and the Problem of Reputation', in *Women, Writing, History 1640–1740*, edited by I. Grundy and S. Wiseman (London: Batsford, 1992), pp. 33–54.

17. J. J. Richetti, *Popular Fiction Before Richardson: Narrative Patterns 1700–1739* (Oxford: Clarendon Press, 1969).

18. P. R. Backscheider, *Spectacular Politics: Theatrical Power and Mass Culture in Early Modern England* (Baltimore and London: Johns Hopkins University Press, 1993), p. 81.

19. M. J. M. Ezell, *Writing Women's Literary History* (Baltimore and London: Johns Hopkins University Press, 1993), p. 11.

20. See E. Hobby, *Virtue of Necessity: English Women's Writing 1649–88* (London: Virago, 1988) and ' "Discourse So Unsavoury": Women's Published Writings of the 1650s', in *Women, Writing, History 1640–1740*, pp. 16–32. See also Ezell's chapter on Quaker women's writing in *Writing Women's Literary History*.

21. J. Spencer, *Aphra Behn's Afterlife* (Oxford: Oxford University Press, 2000).

22. K. R. King, *Jane Barker, Exile. A Literary Career 1675–1725* (Oxford: Clarendon Press, 2000).

23. C. Barash, *English Women's Poetry, 1649–1714: Politics, Community, and Linguistic Authority* (Oxford: Clarendon Press, 1996).

24. P. McDowell, *The Women of Grub Street: Press, Politics, and Gender in the London Literary Marketplace* (Oxford: Clarendon Press, 1988).

25. Ezell, *Social Authorship and the Advent of Print*.

26. J. Phillips Stanton, 'Statistical Profile of Women Writing in English from 1660 to 1800', in *Eighteenth-Century Women and the Arts*, edited by F. M. Keener and S. E. Lorsch (New York: Greenwood Press, 1988), pp. 247–61, p. 248.

27. Hobby, ' "Discourse So Unsavoury" ', p. 16.

28. Hobby, *Virtue of Necessity*, p. 1.

29. Hobby, *Virtue of Necessity*, p. 26.

30. Stanton, 'Statistical Profile of Women Writing in English from 1660 to 1800', p. 248.

31. Stanton, 'Statistical Profile of Women Writing in English from 1660 to 1800', Table 24.2, p. 251.

32. For an analysis of Haywood's significance in statistical terms, see C. Turner, *Living by the Pen: Women Writers in the Eighteenth Century* (London: Routledge, 1992), p. 38.

33. For a discussion of early eighteenth-century women's fiction which makes this point, see J. C. Beasley, 'Politics and Moral Idealism: the Achievement of Some Early Women Novelists', in *Fetter'd or Free? British Women Novelists, 1670–1815*, edited by M. A. Schofield and C. Macheski (Ohio: Ohio University Press, 1986), pp. 216–36.

34. For a study of the intermixture of old and new forms of publishing methods in the seventeenth century, see H. Love, *Scribal Publication in Seventeenth-Century England* (Oxford: Clarendon Press, 1993).

35. Ezell, *Social Authorship and the Advent of Print*, p. 7.

1. Authorship for women

1. P. Rogers, *Hacks and Dunces: Pope, Swift and Grub Street* (London and New York: Methuen, 1980), p. 3.
2. Turner, *Living by the Pen*, p. 60.
3. F. Donoghue, *The Fame Machine: Book Reviewing and Eighteenth-Century Literary Careers* (Stanford: Stanford University Press, 1996), p. 160.
4. Backscheider, *Spectacular Politics*, p. 71.
5. Backscheider, *Spectacular Politics*, p. 72. See also, D. Roberts, *The Ladies: Female Patronage of Restoration Drama, 1660–1700* (Oxford: Clarendon Press, 1989).
6. S. Fyge Egerton, *The Female Advocate; or, An Answer to a Late Satyr Against the Pride, Lust, and Inconstancy of Women* (1686); M. Astell, *A Serious Proposal to the Ladies* (1694); J. Drake, *An Essay in Defense of the Female Sex* (1696).
7. R. D. Hume, *Henry Fielding and the London Theatre 1727–1737* (Oxford: Clarendon Press, 1988), p. 27. As Hume notes, the dominance of the patent monopoly of Drury Lane and Lincoln's Inn Fields resulted in few opportunities for new playwrights. Previously unperformed plays involved an unwelcome expenditure of time and money. Hume calculates that in the repertory for Drury Lane in 1726–7, only '8 per cent of the plays staged had been written within the previous twenty years, and thirty-seven of them (57 per cent) were more than thirty years old', p. 15.
8. For the growth of women's fiction in the 1720s, see Turner, *Living by the Pen*, pp. 34–9.
9. For a recent treatment of Haywood's professional career, see Ingrassia, *Authorship, Commerce, and Gender*.
10. For discussion of Haywood's career in the theatre, see W. S. Clark, *The Early Irish Stage: the Beginnings to 1720* (Oxford: Clarendon Press, 1920), J. R. Elwood, 'The Stage Career of Eliza Haywood', *Theatre Survey*, 5.2 (1964), 107–16 and 'Henry Fielding and Eliza Haywood: a Twenty Year War', *Albion*, 5 (1973), 184–92, and M. Heinemann, 'Eliza Haywood's Career in the Theatre', *Notes and Queries*, 20.1 (1973), 9–13.
11. State Papers Hanoverian: SP35 22/54.
12. For Haywood's connections with the theatre in the 1730s, see Ingrassia, *Authorship, Commerce, and Gender*, pp. 105–7. For her connections with Henry Fielding's company in this period, see Elwood, 'Henry Fielding and Eliza Haywood: a Twenty Year War' and Hume, *Henry Fielding and the London Theatre*.
13. Birch Add MS 4293 ff. 81–82, c.1730, f. 81. Christine Blouch dates this letter as nearer to 1728 by its similarity to another letter written to the Countess of Oxford. I discuss this letter in Chapter 4. See C. Blouch, 'Eliza Haywood and the Romance of Obscurity', *Studies in English Literature*, 31 (1991), 535–51, p. 548, note 26.
14. Birch Add MS 4293 f.82 c.1730.
15. P. Aubin, *A Collection of Entertaining Histories and Novels*, 3 vols (London, 1739).
16. W. H. McBurney 'Mrs Penelope Aubin and the Early Eighteenth-Century English Novel', *Huntington Library Quarterly*, 20 (1956–7), 245–67. Joel H.

Baer, 'Penelope Aubin and the Pirates of Madagascar: Biographical Notes and Documents', in *Eighteenth-Century Women. Studies in Their Lives, Work, and Culture*, Vol. 1., edited by L. V. Troost (New York: AMS Press, Inc., 2001), pp. 49–62.

17. Baer, 'Penelope Aubin and the Pirates of Madagascar', p. 55.

18. For information on Henley, see G. Midgley, *The Life of Orator Henley* (Oxford: Clarendon Press, 1973).

19. McBurney, 'Mrs Penelope Aubin', p. 245, note 3. The original issue of the *Universal Spectator* is in the Burney Collection of Newspapers (British Library, 270b). Aubin is recorded as having participated in similar events on two earlier occasions: 19 April 1729 and 22 April 1729. See *The London Stage 1660–1800: a Calender of Plays, Entertainments and Afterpieces Together with Casts, Box-Receipts and Contemporary Comment*, Part 2, 1700–29, edited by E. L. Avery (Carbondale: Southern Illinois University Press, 1960). For further details, see volume one of *A Biographical Dictionary of Actors, Actresses, Musicians, Dancers, Managers and Other Stage Personnel in London, 1660–1800*, edited by P. H. Highfill, Jnr., K. A. Burnim and E. A. Langhans (Carbondale and Edwardsville: Southern Illinois Press, 1973). The editors note that Aubin 'was apparently the first woman to take advantage of the vogue for public oratory', p. 175.

20. See, for example, Spencer, *The Rise of the Woman Novelist*, p. 86. For a previous discussion of Aubin and the oratory which argues against this view, see S. Prescott, 'Penelope Aubin and *The Doctrine of Morality*: a Reassessment of the Pious Woman Novelist', *Women's Writing*, 1.1 (1994), 99–112.

21. Abbé Antoine François Prévost d'Exiles, *Le Pour et Contre: ouvrage periodique d'un gout nouveau*, 20 vols (Paris: Chez Didot, 1733–40), 4. lviii (1734), pp. 294–7.

22. 'Aventure d'un Manuscrit de Mistress Aubin', in *Le Pour et Contre* 10. cxli (1736), pp. 125–8.

23. *The London Stage*, Part 3. 1729–1747, edited by A. H. Scouten (1961), p. 101. Details from *The London Stage* suggest that this was not Aubin's first encounter with the theatre. A performance of *The Spanish Fryar* at Lincoln's Inn Fields was held to benefit Aubin on 2 January 1724. Money taken was £55 10s. Tickets were £17 3s. *The London Stage*, Part 2, p. 273.

24. See, for example, Richetti, *Popular Fiction*, and Williamson, *Raising Their Voices*.

25. K. R. King, 'Galesia, Jane Barker and a Coming to Authorship,' in *Anxious Power: Reading, Writing and Ambivalence in Narratives by Women*, edited by C. J. Singley and S. E. Sweeney, SUNY Series in Feminist Criticism and Theory (Albany: State University of New York Press, 1993): pp. 91–104.

26. K. R. King with the assistance of J. Medoff, 'Jane Barker and her Life (1652–1732): the Documentary Record', *Eighteenth-Century Life*, 21, NS. 3 (1997), 16–38, p. 25.

27. For details of these communities, see King, *Jane Barker, Exile*.

28. King, *Jane Barker, Exile*, pp. 13–15.

29. King, *Jane Barker, Exile*, chapter 4.

30. For biographical details on Davys, see the introduction to *The Reform'd Coquet, Familiar Letters Betwixt a Gentleman and a Lady*, and *The Accomplish'd*

Rake, edited by M. F. Bowden, Eighteenth-Century Novels by Women (Lexington: University Press of Kentucky, 1999), p. xvii.

31. Bowden, *The Reform'd Coquet*, pp. xviii–xix.

32. Bowden, *The Reform'd Coquet*, p. xxiii.

33. E. Boyd, *The Happy-Unfortunate; or, The Female Page* (1732), edited by W. Graves (New York and London: Garland Publishing, Inc., 1972).

34. For details of Haywood's other activities and her later fiction, see Ingrassia, *Authorship, Commerce, and Gender*, chapter 4.

35. See R. Perry, *The Celebrated Mary Astell: an Early English Feminist* (Chicago and London: University of Chicago Press, 1986), p. 58.

36. Perry, *The Celebrated Mary Astell*, pp. 63–4.

37. Perry, *The Celebrated Mary Astell*, p. 263.

38. As quoted by Perry, *The Celebrated Mary Astell*, p. 66.

39. Perry, *The Celebrated Mary Astell*, p. 68.

40. Perry, *The Celebrated Mary Astell*, p. 69.

41. For Hill's biography see D. Brewster, *Aaron Hill: Poet, Dramatist, Projector* (New York: Columbia University Press, 1913). For further discussion of the Hill circle, see C. Tracy, *The Artificial Bastard: a Biography of Richard Savage* (Toronto: University of Toronto Press, 1953), and J. Bowyer, *The Celebrated Mrs Centlivre* (Durham, NC: Duke University Press, 1952).

42. Haywood's *Poems on Several Occasions* were published in the fourth volume of *The Works of Mrs. Eliza Haywood* (1724). The titles of the poems give a clear indication of their coterie origin: 'An irregular Ode, To Mr. Walter Bowman, Professor of the *Mathematicks*. Occasion'd by his objecting against my giving the Name of Hillarius to Aaron Hill Esq'; 'To HILLARUS, on his sending some VERSES, sign'd M. S.'; 'To DIANA, On her asking me how I lik'd a fine Poem of Mr Hill's'. Martha Fowke Sansom, *Clio; or, A Secret History of the Life and Amours of the Late Celebrated Mrs. S-n-m* (London, 1752), edited by P. J. Guskin as *Clio: The Autobiography of Martha Fowke Sansom (1689–1736)* (Newark: University of Delaware Press, 1997), p. 57.

43. For details of Sansom's background, see Guskin, *Clio*, p. 20.

44. See P. J. Guskin, ' "Not Originally Intended for the Press": Martha Fowke Sansom's Poems in the *Barbadoes Gazette*', *Eighteenth-Century Studies*, 34.1 (2000), 61–91.

45. Guskin, *Clio*, pp. 37–8.

46. For a discussion of Haywood's involvement with Duncan Campbell and the Campbell group in general, see F. A. Nussbaum, 'Speechless: Haywood's Deaf and Dumb Projector,' in *The Passionate Fictions of Eliza Haywood: Essays on her Life and Work*, edited by K. T. Saxton and R. P. Bocchicchio (Lexington: University Press of Kentucky, 2000), pp. 194–216. See also, Guskin, *Clio*, p. 28.

47. See Brewster, *Aaron Hill*, p. 187, note 90.

48. For discussion of the distinction between poetry and fiction for women's careers, see Barash, *English Women's Poetry*, p. 54. For an analysis of the different genres professional women used, see Turner, *Living By the Pen*, especially chapter 4: 'Professional Authorship: the Alternatives for Women'.

49. Barash, *English Women's Poetry*, p. 20.

50. Both Barash, *English Women's Poetry*, and King, *Jane Barker, Exile*, discuss the

importance of different communities for the production of women's writing.

51. See, for example, R. D. Havens, 'Changing Tastes in the Eighteenth Century: a Study of Dryden's and Dodsley's Miscellanies', *PMLA*, 44 (1929), 515–34.
52. *The Poems and Prose of Mary, Lady Chudleigh*, edited by M. Ezell (New York and Oxford: Oxford University Press, 1993), p. xxvi.
53. For biographical details on Chudleigh see Ezell's introduction to *The Poems and Prose of Mary, Lady Chudleigh*.
54. Ezell, *Poems and Prose*, p. xxviii.
55. Ezell, *Poems and Prose*, p. xxviii.
56. Ezell, *Social Authorship*, p. 89.
57. See Barash, *English Women's Poetry*, p. 263, for the different manuscript and print versions of this poem.
58. For biographical details on Finch, see B. McGovern, *Anne Finch and Her Poetry: a Critical Biography* (Athens: University of Georgia Press, 1992).
59. McGovern, *Anne Finch*, pp. 93–103. C. Gildon (ed.), *A New Collection of Poems for Several Occasions* (London, 1701); *Poetical Miscellanies: Consisting of Original Poems and Translations. By the Best Hands* (London, 1714), edited by R. Steele; *Poetical Miscellanies: The Sixth Part, containing a Collection of Original Poems with Several New Translations by the Most Eminent Hands*, compiled by J. Tonson (London, 1709).
60. Donoghue estimates that the circulation of 'The Mag', as it was known, was 3500 copies a month, which gives an idea of the audience that these women poets were reaching. *The Fame Machine*, p. 3.
61. These provincial women include, Jane Brereton, Charlotte Brereton, the anonymous 'Ophelia', Anna Seward, Elizabeth Teft and Mary Whateley (Darwell). See Lonsdale, *Eighteenth-Century Women Poets*, p. xxvi.
62. Lonsdale, *Eighteenth-Century Women Poets*, p. 78.
63. For biographical details on Brereton, see the memoir which was published with her *Poems on Several Occasions* (1744).
64. There is evidence that Jane Brereton used other methods as well as writing to earn a living. There are letters and poems dating from 1729 to 1731 in the Flintshire Record Office to John Mellor of Erddig, near Wrexham. Some of these letters concern Brereton's attempt to sell bottles of medicinal 'spirits', for which enterprise Mellor appears to have acted as a patron. Flintshire Record Office, Hawarden. Call no: D/E/871, 7 letters. Call no: D/E/1542/42 &100a, 2 poems.
65. See Ariosto, *Orlando Furioso*, translated by B. Reynolds (Harmondsworth: Penguin Books Ltd, 1975), vol. 1, Canto III, 8–15, pp. 160–1. I am grateful to Andrew Hadfield for locating this reference. For a discussion of Brereton's poems to Caroline, see J. Colton, 'Merlin's Cave and Queen Caroline: Garden Art as Political Propaganda', *Eighteenth-Century Studies*, 10.1 (1976), 1–20 and C. Gerrard, *The Patriot Opposition to Walpole: Politics, Poetry, and National Myth 1725–1742* (Oxford: Clarendon Press, 1994).
66. See Lonsdale, *Eighteenth-Century Women Poets*, p. 519, for details of Brereton's contributions to *The Gentleman's Magazine*.
67. Lonsdale, *Eighteenth-Century Women Poets*, p. 79.
68. Lonsdale, as above.
69. Peter Borsay, 'The London Connection: Cultural Diffusion and the

Eighteenth-Century Provincial Town', *The London Journal*, 19.1 (1994), 21–35, p. 27.
70. Borsay, as above, p. 31.

2. Negotiating Authorship

1. J. Paul Hunter, *Before Novels: the Cultural Contexts of Eighteenth-Century English Fiction* (New York and London: W. W. Norton, 1990), p. 76.
2. C. N. Thomas, *Alexander Pope and His Eighteenth-Century Women Readers* (Carbondale and Edwardsville: Southern Illinois University Press, 1994), pp. 194–5.
3. L. Colley, *Britons: Forging the Nation 1707–1837* (London: Pimlico, 1992), p. 14.
4. Bowden, *The Reform'd Coquet*, p. xiv. All further references to Davys' works are from this edition and included in parenthesis in the text.
5. L. L. Runge, *Gender and Language in British Literary Criticism, 1660–1790* (Cambridge: Cambridge University Press, 1997), p. 83.
6. For a discussion of this issue, see J. Spencer, 'Women Writers and the Eighteenth-Century Novel', in *The Cambridge Companion to the Eighteenth-Century Novel*, edited by J. Richetti (Cambridge: Cambridge University Press, 1996), pp. 212–35.
7. For a discussion of similar strategies in the prefaces to French romances, see Runge, *Gender and Language in British Literary Criticism*, pp. 91–2.
8. Runge, *Gender and Language in British Literary Criticism*, p. 91.
9. Mary Davys, *The Works of Mrs. Davys*, 2 vols (London: 1725), Bowden, *The Reform'd Coquet*, p. 87.
10. See, for example, Congreve's preface to *Incognita; or, Love and Duty Reconciled* (1692), and D. Defoe, *The Life and Strange Surprizing Adventures of Robinson Crusoe* (1719).
11. Davys expands on this sense of the fashionable gentleman as reader of her novels in the dedication to *The Accomplish'd Rake* (1727), which is addressed to 'The Beaus of Great-Britain'. As the title suggests, the novel concerns the adventures of a profligate man of fashion who reforms at the end of the novel. The text is a humorous male version of her *Reform'd Coquet*, which focused on the sentimental education of a young woman, Amoranda.
12. *The Noble Slaves* (London, 1722), in *A Collection of Entertaining Novels*, 3 vols (London, 1739), I, p. viii.
13. *The Life of Charlotta du Pont* (London, 1723), in *A Collection of Entertaining Novels*, III, p. vi.
14. *The Life and Adventures of the Lady Lucy* (London, 1726), pp. 130–1.
15. Hunter, *Before Novels*, pp. 280–1.
16. *The Life of Madam de Beaumont* (London, 1721), in *A Collection of Entertaining Novels*, III, pp. 233–4.
17. For a discussion of anti-novel discourse of this type, see W. Warner, *Licensing Entertainment: the Elevation of Novel Reading in Britain, 1684–1750* (Berkeley: University of California Press, 1998), ch. 4.
18. For a recent discussion of *The Life of Madam de Beaumont* in relation to both

its Welsh setting and its political and religious content see M. Dearnley, *Distant Fields: Eighteenth-Century Fictions of Wales* (Cardiff: University of Wales Press, 2001), ch. 2.

19. Warner, *Licensing Entertainment*, p. 150.

20. Despite her pronouncements, Aubin's fiction can be directly compared to that of Eliza Haywood. See S. Prescott, 'The Debt to Pleasure: Eliza Haywood's *Love in Excess* and Women's Fiction of the 1720s', *Women's Writing*, 7.3 (2000), 427–45.

21. For a discussion of the different perceptions of poetry and the novel in the early eighteenth century, see Hunter, *Before Novels*, p. 87

22. See, for example, Todd, *The Sign of Angellica*, ch. 7, 'The Modest Muse: Women Writers of the Mid-Eighteenth Century'.

23. For a discussion of this poem, see A. Messenger, *Pastoral Tradition and the Female Talent* (New York: AMS Press, Inc., 2001), pp. 86–7.

24. Ezell, *The Poems and Prose*, p. 80 (17–20). All further references are to this edition and included in the text.

25. In *Poems on Several Occasions by Mrs. Jane Brereton* (London, 1744), pp. 30–6.

26. This poem is dated 1718. Given that Haywood only published her first novel in 1719, the poem may have a later date. Alternatively, Haywood's work may have been circulated prior to its publication. Lonsdale identifies the 'Heywood' of this poem as Eliza Haywood, *Eighteenth-Century Women Poets*, p. 519.

27. Biographical detail is taken from the memoir to Brereton's *Poems on Several Occasions* (1744).

28. Some of Brereton's poems are very strongly pro-Hanoverian. See, for example, *The Fifth ODE of the Fourth Book of Horace Imitated, and Apply'd to the King*, 1716, which contains the lines, 'Religion, Liberty, we owe/To great Nassau, and greater You!' (iv, 3–4), *Poems* (1744), pp. 20–2, p. 22.

29. G. A. Williams, *When Was Wales? A History of the Welsh* (London: Penguin Books, 1985), p. 85. For details of the forms English colonization of Wales took see ch. 5, 'The Last Prince'.

30. G. Jenkins, *The Foundations of Modern Wales, 1642–1780* (Oxford: Oxford University Press, 1993).

31. For a discussion of the ways in which the native Welsh laws benefited women, see J. Davies, *A History of Wales* (London: Penguin Books, 1990), pp. 88 and 92–3. Although he emphasizes the positive aspects of the Welsh law for women, Davies also notes the inequality between the sexes in relation to land inheritance.

32. R. R. Davies, *The Age of Conquest: Wales 1063–1415* (Oxford: Oxford University Press, 1987), p. 369. For a detailed comparison of Welsh and English law in relation to women and the Welsh context, see R. R. Davies, 'The Status of Women and the Practice of Marriage in Late Medieval Wales', in *The Welsh Law of Women*, ed. D. Jenkins and M. E. Owen (Cardiff: University of Wales Press, 1980), pp. 43–114.

33. For a discussion of Anne Finch's use of the Apollo trope, see Spencer, *Aphra Behn's Afterlife*, pp. 157–60.

34. For discussions of Brereton's poetry and Queen Caroline's pavilions, see Colton, 'Merlin's Cave and Queen Caroline' and Gerrard, *The Patriot Opposition to Walpole*.

35. For Caroline's activities as a patron, see R. L. Arkell, *Caroline of Ansbach: George the Second's Queen* (London: Oxford University Press, 1939), ch. 10, 'Born to Encourage'. Caroline famously patronized Stephen Duck, but she also helped Richard Savage, and offered John Gay a sinecure.

36. *The Bible, Authorized King James Version*, ed. R. Carroll and S. Prickett (Oxford: Oxford University Press, 1997), *The New Testament of our Lord and Saviour Jesus Christ*, p. 106.

37. Brereton's choice of patron was appropriate as Caroline had a grotto, 'Merlin's Cave', built in her gardens at Richmond. Merlin's Cave contained a wax figure of Merlin at a table. Arkell, *Caroline of Ansbach*, p. 247. See also Colton, 'Merlin's Cave and Queen Caroline' and Gerrard, *The Patriot Opposition to Walpole*.

3. Marketing the Woman Writer

1. See, for example, Ballaster, *Seductive Forms*.

2. See, for example, M. J. M. Ezell, 'The Posthumous Publication of Women's Manuscripts and the History of Authorship', in *Women's Writing and the Circulation of Ideas: Manuscript Publication in England, 1550–1800*, ed. G. Justice and N. Tinker, pp. 121–36.

3. For a similar argument to mine, but in relation to anthologies of the 'Lives' of women poets, see P. McDowell, 'Consuming Women: the Life of the "Literary Lady" as Popular Culture in Eighteenth-Century England', *Genre*, 26 (1993), 219–52. As McDowell notes, 'Early literary lives were an entrepreneurial technique – designed primarily to encourage interest in, and boost sales of, an author's *works*', p. 222.

4. Spencer, *Aphra Behn's Afterlife*, p. 87.

5. Spencer, *Aphra Behn's Afterlife*, p. 87.

6. For publication details of Behn's fiction, including eighteenth-century reprints, see Spencer, *Aphra Behn's Afterlife*, pp. 87–9. For a discussion of collected work of male dramatists, as well as the use of portraits of the author, see Paulina Kewes, *Authorship and Appropriation: Writing for the Stage in England, 1660–1710* (Oxford: Clarendon Press, 1998).

7. Kewes, *Authorship and Appropriation*, pp. 198–9.

8. Kewes, *Authorship and Appropriation*, p. 198.

9. As Kewes notes, 'Organized around the figure of the author, and designated "Works", these little stitched-up volumes at once reflected and contributed to the emergence of a new literary hierarchy.' *Authorship and Appropriation*, p. 200.

10. For details of further editions and reprints, see King, *Jane Barker, Exile*, note 26, pp. 189–90. King suggests that the reprinting of Barker's fiction was, perhaps, an attempt to 'move slowly selling material', and that the 'new' editions were more likely to be reissues of the 1719 imprint. In 1736 Curll published a 'third edition' of Barker's fiction entitled *The Entertaining Novels of Mrs. Jane Barker of Wilsthorp in Northamptonshire*.

11. *The Amours of Alcippus and Lucippe* (1704) was reprinted in *The Works* as *The Lady's Tale*. *The False Friend; or, The Treacherous Portugueze* (written c. 1700–4) was printed for the first time in the *Works* as *The Cousins*. *Familiar Letters*

Betwixt a Gentleman and a Lady, The Self Rival (an unacted play), and 'The Modern Poet' appeared here for the first time.

12. All these texts, except *Love in Excess* and *The Fair Captive*, were also published in single-volume format by Browne and Chapman. William Chetwood, the publisher of *Love in Excess*, joined forces with Browne and Chapman on the publication of *The British Recluse, Idalia* and *The Injur'd Husband*. The publishers of *The Fair Captive* were T. Jauncy and H. Cole.

13. *The Secret History of the Present Intrigues of the Court of Caramania* (London, 1727).

14. 'Fair as before her *works* she stands confess'd,/In flow'r'd brocade by bounteous Kirkall dress'd' (151–2), *The Dunciad* (1728) (my italics). Pope also singles out *Memoirs of Utopia* and *Caramania*, Haywood's two scandal narratives.

15. For a discussion of Pope's 1717 *Works*, see M. Mack, *Alexander Pope: a Life* (New Haven and London: Yale University Press, 1985), pp. 331–6.

16. As always, Pope was more involved in the professional marketplace than he ever admitted. As Mack notes, the 1717 *Works* appears to have been mostly the work of Bernard Lintot in an effort 'to compensate for the somewhat less than hoped return that his part in the Homer, the folio without plates, had brought in'. *Pope*, pp. 333–4.

17. The portrait by Vertue is, as far as I am aware, the only extant portrait of Haywood. In *The Dunciad*, as the lines above imply, Pope claims that the *Works* (1724) contained a portrait by Kirkall. Scriblerius notes, '*Kirkall*, the Name of a Graver. This Lady's Works were printed in four Volumes *duod*. with her picture thus dress'd up, before them', Book II, note 152. This is upheld by G. Whicher, *The Life and Romances of Mrs. Eliza Haywood* (New York: Columbia University Press, 1915), p. 121, and the *Dictionary of National Biography*, XXXI, entry on Kirkall. I am unable to locate a portrait of Haywood by Kirkall. *The Works* (1724) do not contain a portrait, and the print room at the British Museum could not locate a Haywood portrait among Kirkall's engravings. Pope is therefore likely to be referring to the portrait by Vertue, which appeared in all the editions of *Secret Histories, Novels, and Poems* from 1725 to 1742. The portrait (Figure 1), does not conform to Pope's description, except for a solitary flower in Haywood's hair. It is extremely similar to Vertue's engraving of Elizabeth Rowe for her *Miscellaneous Works* (1739), which points to a specific style in female portraits (Figure 2). However, in *A Biographical Dictionary; Containing an Historical Account of all the Engravings from the Earliest Period of the Art of Engraving to the Present Time* (London, 1785–6), J. Strutt lists a reference to a Kirkall portrait by Haywood: 'Period 1703–1727, Class IX "Gentlewomen": Eliza Haywood Literat. 1727. Design by Paramentier – G. Vertue 12mo.', Kirkall 12 mo.', p. 310. The date of 1727 is too late for either the *Works* or the *Secret Histories*, although Whicher does catalogue a two-volume edition of *Secret Histories* for 1727, printed for D. Browne, p. 77. I have been unable to locate this edition, and Whicher only refers to it via advertisement details from the *Daily Post*, 2 November 1727. In addition, Pope specifically refers to four volumes. For a discussion of Pope's portrait for the 1717 *Works*, see Mack, *Pope*, pp. 331–3.

18. The bibliographical details we have currently for Haywood are confusing. I

have also used a two-volume edition of the *Secret Histories* in the British Library (12614 c.14) from 1725 which seems to be a reprint of volumes two and four of the four-volume 1725 collection. The two-volume 1727 edition of *Secret Histories*, as cited by Whicher, has completely different texts from those in the 1725 collection.

19. For information on Defoe's professional career, see P. R. Backscheider, *Daniel Defoe: His Life* (Baltimore and London: Johns Hopkins University Press, 1989).
20. For Barker's incongruous connections with Curll, see King, *Jane Barker, Exile.*
21. For information on Sewell and Curll's business practices, see R. Strauss, *The Unspeakable Curll: Being Some Account of Edmund Curll, Bookseller To Which is Added a Full List of His Books* (New York: Augustus M. Kelly Publishers, 1970), pp. 41, 44, 77, 103, 119.
22. In *The Galesia Trilogy and Selected Manuscript Poems of Jane Barker*, edited by C. Shiner Wilson, Women Writers in English, 1350–1850 (Oxford: Oxford University Press, 1997), pp. 5–6.
23. The poems appeared at the beginning of volume two. They are reprinted in Eliza Haywood, *Love in Excess; or, The Fatal Enquiry*, edited by D. Oakleaf (Ontario: Broadview Press, 2000).
24. The poem is reprinted in Oakleaf, *Love in Excess*, pp. 277–9. For discussions of the representation of Haywood in this poem, see Ballaster, *Seductive Forms*, pp. 165–6, and Richetti, *Popular Fiction Before Richardson*, pp. 180–3.
25. *The Ladies Journal* (1727), in the microfilm collection *Women Advising Women*: Part 1: 'Early Women's Journals c. 1700–1832' (Marlborough: Adam Matthew Publications, 1992), Reel II, 1–22. The original is in the Hope Collection in the Bodleian Library.
26. See *The Lover's Week* and *The Female Deserters* by Mary Hearne; *Love Intrigues* by Jane Barker, edited by J. Grieder (New York: Garland Publishing, Inc., 1973).
27. There are currently no biographical details about Mary Hearne.
28. Grieder, *The Lover's Week*, pp. 1–2 of unnumbered dedication. *The Lover's Week* also included a commendatory poem to Hearne, 'To the Fair and Ingenious Author of the LOVER'S Week', by 'Joseph Gay'. This poem is very similar to the approach taken in the verses on Haywood. For example, 'Thy fluent, skillful Lines this Truth may prove, That best a *Woman* knows to write of *Love*', 39–40 (italics reversed).
29. This is actually a quotation from Finch's poem 'The Progress of Life', which is presented in *The New Atalantis* as the work of 'the proudest woman in Atalantis'. See Delarivier Manley, *The New Atalantis*, edited by R. Ballaster (London: Penguin Books, 1992), pp. 91–2.
30. Prescott, 'Penelope Aubin and *The Doctrine of Morality*'.
31. See W. Zach, 'Mrs Aubin and Richardson's Earliest Literary Manifesto', *English Studies*, 62 (1981), 271–85.
32. Zach, 'Mrs Aubin and Richardson's Earliest Manifesto', p. 274.
33. For a detailed analysis of these parallels see Zach, 'Mrs Aubin and Richardson's Earliest Manifesto'.
34. For Warner's discussion of this preface, see *Licensing Entertainment*, pp. 183–6.

35. For a discussion of the Killigrew and Monck collections and a general overview of posthumous publication for women, see Ezell, 'The Posthumous Publication of Women's Manuscripts and the History of Authorship'.

36. Medoff, 'The Daughters of Behn', p. 47.

37. *The Miscellaneous Works in Prose and Verse of Mrs. Elizabeth Rowe*, 2 vols (London, 1739). All page references to the 'Life' are cited parenthetically in the text.

38. The 'Devotions' refer to *Devout Exercises of the Heart, In Meditation and Soliloquy, Prayer and Praise* (London, 1737). This is also a posthumous publication which was edited by Isaac Watts.

39. S. Trill, 'Religion and the Construction of Femininity', in *Women and Literature in Britain, 1500–1700* ed. H. Wilcox (Cambridge: Cambridge University Press, 1996), pp. 30–55, p. 33. For an accessible modern reprint of Stubbes' memoir, see *Renaissance Woman: a Sourcebook. Constructions of Femininity in England*, ed. K. Aughterson (London and New York: Routledge, 1995).

40. Trill, 'Religion and the Construction of Femininity', p. 33. A comparable text from the later seventeenth century is Henry Wilkinson's account of 'The Life and Death of Mrs. *Margaret Corbet*, who died *Anno Christi, 1656'*, in Samuel Clarke's *A Collection of the Lives of Ten Eminent Divines* (1662). Reprinted in *Lay by Your Needles Ladies, Take the Pen: Writing Women in England, 1500–1700*, ed. S. Trill, K. Chedgzoy and M. Osborne (London: Arnold, 1997), pp. 211–17.

41. Stubbes, *A Crystall Glasse, for Christian Women*, in Aughterson, *Renaissance Woman*, p. 238.

42. For details of the publication of Rowe's poem in various collections, see H. F. Stecher, *Elizabeth Singer Rowe, the Poetess of Frome. A Study in Eighteenth-Century English Pietism* (Berne: Herbert Lang, 1973), Appendix C.

43. John Dunton had also used this poem in his *The Life and Errors of John Dunton* where he selects lines from the poem to refer to his own reaction to Rowe's writing: 'In vain, alas! in vain my Fate I shun,/I read and sigh, and Love, and am undone'. *The Life and Errors of John Dunton Late Citizen of London; Written by Himself* (London, 1705), p. 251.

44. For a recent discussion of Rowe's dealings with John Dunton and the embarrassment this may have caused her in later life, see King, 'Elizabeth Singer Rowe's Tactical Use of Print and Manuscript', pp. 158–81.

45. M. R. Hansen makes a similar point in 'The Pious Mrs. Rowe', *English Studies*, 1 (1995), 34–51.

46. For biographical details on these figures see Stecher, *Elizabeth Singer Rowe*, 'Register of Names', pp. 13–15.

47. For a discussion of the presentation of Rowe in the *Gentleman's Magazine* see Hansen, 'The Pious Mrs. Rowe'.

48. See, for example, the 1755 Edinburgh edition, *Friendship in Death in Twenty Letters From the Dead to the Living. To Which are Added, Letters Moral and Entertaining, in Prose and Verse. By Mrs. Elizabeth Singer Rowe. To Which is Prefix'd, An Account of the Author's Life.* See also, editions for Dublin, 1760; Glasgow, 1760; Edinburgh 1763; London 1764; Glasgow 1764; Edinburgh 1768; London 1770; London 1775; Edinburgh 1776; London 1780; London 1783; London 1789; Boston 1792; London, 1793. The 'Life'

was also printed with later editions of Rowe's *Poems on Several Occasions* in 1759 and 1778.

49. Letter IV, 'To Miss ••, in answer to hers of March 22, 1739', in *Poems on Several Occasions*.

50. Brereton is said to have had a sister who died when she was fourteen. Rowe also had a sister whose early death is recorded in the 'Life'.

51. Parallels can again be drawn to Katherine Stubbes who, according to her husband, was so 'desirous [. . .] to be with the Lord' that she constantly cried out 'I desire to be dissolved and to be with Christ [. . .] Come, quickly Lord Jesus, come quickly', in Aughterson, *Renaissance Woman*, p. 240.

52. K. Shevelow, *Women and Print Culture: the Construction of Femininity in the Early Periodical* (London and New York: Routledge, 1989), p. 1.

4. Making a Living

1. Quoted by C. Clark, introduction to *The Inhumane Cardinal (1696)* (New York: Scholars' Facsimiles & Reprints, 1984), p. v.

2. See Turner, *Living by the Pen*, ch. 5, 'Women Novelists and Their Publishers', for an account of those publishers associated with women writers in the eighteenth century as a whole.

3. *All the Histories and Novels written by the Late Ingenious Mrs. Behn, Entire in One Volume. The Third Edition, with Large Additions* (London: Samuel Briscoe, 1698).

4. See R. Adams Day's introduction to *Olinda's Adventures; or, The Amours of a Young Lady*, The Augustan Reprint Society. Publication Number 138 (University of California, Los Angeles: William Andrews Clark Memorial Library, 1969), p. i.

5. Day, *Olinda's Adventures*, p. ii.

6. Day, *Olinda's Adventures*, p. ii.

7. The edition of *Love in Excess* in the *Works* (1724) was advertised as 'the fifth edition'. This novel also appeared in *Secret Histories* for 1725, 1732 and 1742.

8. Warner, *Licensing Entertainment*, p. 6.

9. For a comparative analysis of retail prices for women's fiction in the first half of the eighteenth century, see Turner, *Living by the Pen*, p. 143.

10. Daniel Browne had also been involved with the publication of Behn's fiction. In 1718 he was one of a number of booksellers who published the two-volume *Seventeen Histories and Novels Written by the Late Ingenious Mrs. Behn*.

11. H. R. Plomer, G. H. Bushell and E. R. McC. Dix, *A Dictionary of the Printers and Booksellers Who Were At Work in England, Scotland and Ireland from 1726 to 1775* (Printed for the Bibliographical Society at the Oxford University Press, 1932 (for 1930)), p. 50.

12. *The Dunciad in Four Books*, ed. by V. Rumbold (Essex: Pearson Education Limited, 1999), pp. 173–4. In this edition of the poem Thomas Osborne replaced Chetwood and Chapman. Significantly for Pope, Chapman committed a double error by not only publishing Haywood's *Works*, but also Lewis Theobald's *Shakespeare Restor'd* in 1728.

13. T. Belanger, 'Publishers and Writers In Eighteenth-Century England,' in *Books and their Readers in Eighteenth-Century England*, ed. I. Rivers (Leicester: Leicester University Press, 1982), pp. 5–25, p. 13.

14. See Belanger, 'Publishers and Writers', for the way in which the original wholesaling conger diversified.

15. For a discussion of congers and women's writing, see Turner, *Living by the Pen*, pp. 88–9.

16. Bettesworth had also been involved with Behn's publications. See *The Land of Love. A Poem* (London: H. Meere and A. Bettesworth, 1717).

17. Turner, *Living by the Pen*, p. 88.

18. Turner, *Living by the Pen*, p. 88.

19. W. H. McBurney, 'Edmund Curll, Mrs Jane Barker and the English Novel', *Philological Quarterly*, 35.2 (1958), 385–99.

20. Turner, *Living by the Pen*, p. 90.

21. There is some overlap between Aubin and Barker's publishers. Arthur Bettesworth published Barker's *The Lining of the Patch-Work Screen* (1726). Both Bettesworth and Rivington were part of the Aubin consortium.

22. Kathryn King has convincingly argued that Curll deliberately marketed *Exilius* to a provincial Jacobite readership. See *Jane Barker, Exile*, p. 170. King also makes the connection between the coded Jacobitism of Barker's text and Butler's *Irish Tales*. For a further reading of Butler's text, see I. Campbell Ross, ' "One of the Principal Nations in Europe": the Representation of Ireland in Sarah Butler's *Irish Tales*', *Eighteenth-Century Fiction*, 7.1 (1994), 1–16. Nothing is known about the life of Sarah Butler.

23. The two volumes of this text were posthumous. For a discussion of Curll and Thomas, see A. McWhir, 'Elizabeth Thomas and the Two Corinnas: Giving the Woman Writer a Bad Name', *English Literary History*, 62 (1995), 105–19.

24. For details of this publication, see W. H. McBurney, *A Check List of English Prose Fiction 1700–1739* (Cambridge, Massachusetts: Harvard University Press, 1960), p. 93.

25. For a discussion of the publication history of *Rivella*, see Katherine Zelinsky's introduction to *The Adventures of Rivella* (Ontario: Broadview Press Ltd, 1999). The appendix to this edition also reprints Curll's preface to his 1725 edition of the text, entitled *Mrs. Manley's History of Her Own Life and Times*, which prints Manley's letters to Curll concerning the writing of *Rivella*. Curll uses these letters to prove to the reader that Manley was indeed 'the genuine author' of her own life, p. 117.

26. This claim is extremely unlikely. Rowe commented on Curll's edition in a letter to Lady Hertford. This letter makes it clear that his edition was unauthorized. Rowe states, 'I am in pain till you know I am entirely Ignorant of Curll's romance of my Life & Writings only what I have seen in an Advertisement', Alnwick 110, ff. 359–60.

27. For a useful summary of the cost of living in the period, see Hammond, *Professional Imaginative Writing*, p. 52.

28. For an informative discussion of the economic rewards writing could offer, both for the Grub Street hack and higher-status writers, see M. Foss, *The Age of Patronage: the Arts in England 1660–1750* (New York: Cornell University Press, 1971), pp. 83–8.

29. S. Parks, *John Dunton and the English Book Trade: a Study of His Career with a*

Checklist of his Publications (New York and London: Garland Publishing Inc, 1976).

30. Parks, *John Dunton and the English Book Trade*, p. 190.
31. Parks, *John Dunton and the English Book Trade*, p. 191.
32. Upcott Collection, 'Original Assignments of Mss between Authors and Publishers, principally for dramatic works, from the year 1703–1810', vol. 1. BL Add MS 38, 728 ff. 112–13. In 1745 Cogan sold his share of the copyright to Nourse for two pounds, four shillings. See also, Blouch, 'Eliza Haywood and the Romance of Obscurity'.
33. BL Add MS 38, 728 f. 113
34. BL Add MS 38, 728 f. 113
35. Hammond, *Professional Imaginative Writing*, p. 75.
36. Hammond estimates that £50 per annum would secure a relatively good living for a family at the turn of the century (*Professional Imaginative Writing*, p. 52). Haywood made at least approximately £30 from the sale of her copyrights in the mid-1740s. While not exceptional, when put in relation to other sums she may have made at this time from her writing, she would have been able to survive, albeit in a very modest fashion.
37. Upcott Collection, vol. 3. BL Add MS 38, 730 f. 37.
38. BL. Add MS 38, 730 f. 88.
39. Hinxman was the publisher of *Tristram Shandy*. See J. Feather, 'The Commerce of Letters: the Study of the Eighteenth-Century Book Trade', *Eighteenth-Century Studies*, 17 (1983–4), 405–24, p. 421. Hinxman was a former apprentice of Dodsley.
40. Bowden, *The Reform'd Coquet*, p. 87.
41. *The London Stage 1660–1800*, Part 2, 1700–29, ed. E. L. Avery (1960), p. 400. The previous two performances of Davys' play were on 27 April and 28 April 1716.
42. *The London Stage*, Part 3, 1729–47, ed. A. H. Scouten, p. 101.
43. *The London Stage*, Part 2, p. 1026. Two further 'concerts' were advertised at Mrs Aubin's 'Ladies Oratory' in the York Buildings, pp. 1026 and 1030.
44. For a discussion of the use of Haywood's name to sell her subsequent books, see Ingrassia, *Authorship, Commerce, and Gender*, pp. 83–4.
45. As Belanger argues in 'Publishers and Writers', the real money in the trade lay in the copyrights of dictionaries.
46. See, for example, J. van Dorsten, 'Literary Patrons in Elizabethan England', in *Patronage in the Renaissance*, ed. G. Fitch Lytle and S. Orgel (Princeton: Princeton University Press, 1981), pp. 191–206.
47. See A. F. Marotti, 'John Donne and the Rewards of Patronage', in *Patronage in the Renaissance*, pp. 207–34, p. 207.
48. Van Dorsten, 'Literary Patrons in Elizabethan England', p. 192.
49. Marotti, 'John Donne and the Rewards of Patronage', p. 208.
50. Marotti, 'John Donne and the Rewards of Patronage', p. 207.
51. See, for example, R. Folkenflik, 'Patronage and the Poet-Hero', *Huntington Library Quarterly*, 48 (1985), 363–79, P. Korshin, 'Types of Eighteenth-Century Literary Patronage', *Eighteenth-Century Studies*, 7 (1974), 453–73, p. 463, and Michael Foss, *The Age of Patronage*, p. 87.
52. Korshin, 'Types of Eighteenth-Century Literary Patronage', p. 454.
53. Korshin, 'Types of Eighteenth-Century Literary Patronage', p. 473.

54. For a discussion of male writers' experience of more traditional forms of aristocratic patronage in the early eighteenth century (including Prior, Pope, Gay and Addison), see Foss, *The Age of Patronage*, ch. 6, 'New Prospects'.
55. Griffin, *Literary Patronage in England*, p. 24.
56. *Report on the Manuscripts of his Grace The Duke of Portland, K.G., Preserved at Welbeck Abbey*, vol. VI (London: His Majesty's Stationary Office, 1901). Harley Letters and Papers, 'Mrs. E[lizabeth] Thomas ("Corinna") to [the Earl of Oxford]', 5 June 1730, Fleet Prison, p. 29.
57. Folkenflik, 'Patronage and the Poet-Hero', p. 369.
58. Korshin, 'Types of Eighteenth-Century Literary Patronage', p. 454.
59. Griffin, *Literary Patronage in England*, p. 189.
60. See McDowell, *The Women of Grub Street*, for a discussion of Manley and the patronage system.
61. For a discussion of women patrons in the Renaissance, see D. M. Bergeron, 'Women as Patrons of English Renaissance Drama', in *Patronage in the Renaissance*, pp. 274–90.
62. Edward Howard (1672–1731) was the eighth Earl of Suffolk and a prominent Whig patron. See J. C. Beasley, *The Injur'd Husband; or, The Mistaken Resentment* and *Lasselia; or, The Self-Abandon'd* (Lexington: University of Kentucky Press, 1999), p. 156, note 1. The 4th Earl of Scarsdale was Nicholas Leake (1682?–1736). See *The Official Baronage of England, Showing the Succession, Dignities, and Offices of every Peer from 1066 to 1885*, 3 vols, ed. J. E. Doyle (London: Longmans, Green and Co, 1886), vol. iii, p. 288. Sir William Yonge (d. 1755) was a baronet and Whig politician. He was very pro-Walpole. See *DNB*, xxi, p. 1246. Lord Herbert is Henry Herbert (1693–1751), 9th Earl of Pembroke.
63. Dedication to *The Fair Captive: a Tragedy* (London, 1721), p. vii.
64. Korshin, 'Types of Eighteenth-Century Literary Patronage', p. 467.
65. See, for example, Ballaster's analysis of Haywood's self-presentation in *Seductive Forms*.
66. See Griffin, *Literary Patronage in England*, pp. 19–20: ' "Encouragement" [. . .] was convertible into financial gain. By the 1720s the terms was quantifiable in cash. Mallet writes in 1723 of a tutorship for which "My encouragement is £30." In 1725 Pope was granted £200 "as his Matys Encouragement" of his translation of the *Odyssey*', p. 20.
67. Griffin, *Literary Patronage in England*, p. 189.
68. BL Add MS 4293, 109, f. 82. G. M. Firmager suggests that Haywood is referring to *The Fair Captive*: 'Eliza Haywood: Some Further Light on her Background', *Notes and Queries*, 38.2 (1991), 181–3. Blouch, 'The Romance of Obscurity', suggests that, as the date of the letter is c.1730, the play is more likely to be *Frederick, Duke of Brunswick-Lunenburgh* (1729), p. 549, note 26.
69. The letter to the male patron is BL Birch Add MS 4293, 109, ff. 81–2. c.1730, f. 81. The letter to the Countess of Oxford can be found in *Report on the Manuscripts of his Grace The Duke of Portland, K.G., Preserved at Welbeck Abbey*, vol. VI (London: His Majesty's Stationary Office, 1901). Harley Letters and Papers, 'Eliza Haywood to the Countess of Oxford', p. 21.
70. *La Belle Assemblée: Being a curious collection of some very Remarkable incidents which happen'd to Persons of the First Quality in France* (1724 and further edi-

tions), was extremely popular and must have been a staple of Haywood's income. It does not have a dedication, but as the manuscript letters suggest, Haywood did seek patronal support even for those texts which do not have printed dedications. The popularity of this text is shown by the fact that Haywood produced a sequel: *L'Entretian des Beaux Espirits, Being the Sequel to the Belle Assmblée*, 2 vols (London, 1734). This was dedicated 'To the High Puissant and most noble Prince, Charles Seymour, Duke of Somerset, Earl of Hertford', and signed Eliza Haywood. The dedication implies that Lord Hertford has helped Haywood on previous occasions: 'Thanksgivings are the only Tribute in my little Power to pay to that transcendent Goodness which has vouchsafed to rank me among the Number it has obliged.'

71. Lady Abergavenny was Catherine (Tatton) Nevill, the wife of William Nevill, cousin of Edward IV and Baron of Abergavenny (*The Official Baronage of England*, vol. i, p. 8). Lady Howe was Mary Sophia Charlotte (1695–1782), wife of Emanuel Scrope (Howe), Viscount Howe. She was Lady of the Bedchamber to the Princess of Wales. See Beasley *The Injur'd Husband* and *Lasselia*, p. 151, note 1. Lady Romney was Elizabeth Masham, wife of Robert Masham (1685–1724). She died in 1732 (*The Official Baronage of England*, vol. iii, p. 174).

72. Volume 1 was dedicated to Mary, the Duchess of Leeds (d. 1764), who was married to Thomas Osborne, a high-profile politician, volume 2 to the Duchess of Bedford, volume 3 to the Duchess of Queensberry and Dover, and volume 4 to the Duchess of Manchester.

73. See King, *Jane Barker, Exile*, pp. 182–5.

74. Bowden, *The Reform'd Coquet*, p. xix. The use of an address to a female member of a family to reach a male figure was also common in the Renaissance. Bergeron gives the example of Philip Massinger's address to Katherine Stanhope for his play *The Duke of Milan* (1623). Stanhope was the sister of the Earl of Huntingdon who was probably the real target. Huntington was Fletcher's patron. See, 'Women as Patrons of English Drama', p. 280, note 23.

75. Bowden, *The Reform'd Coquet*, p. xviii.

76. Aubin's male patrons are: a Dr Smithson for *The Illustrious French Lovers*, the Prince of Wales for *Genehizcan the Great*, Lord Coleraine for *Lady Lucy*.

77. Runge, *Gender and Language in British Literary Criticism*, p. 102.

78. Runge, *Gender and Language in British Literary Criticism*, p. 103.

79. *A Collection of Novels, Selected and Revised by Mrs Griffiths*, vol. ii (London, 1777), preface 'Of the Author' attached to *The Noble Slaves*.

80. I. Grundy, 'Samuel Johnson as Patron of Women', *The Age of Johnson*, I (1987), 59–77, p. 62.

81. Oakleaf, *Love in Excess*, p. 38, note 1.

82. P. Rogers, 'Book Dedications in Britain 1700–1799: a Preliminary Survey', *British Journal for Eighteenth-Century Studies*, 16.2 (1993), 213–33, p. 222.

83. See both Folkenflik, 'Patronage and the Poet-Hero', pp. 366–7, and Korshin, 'Types of Eighteenth-Century Literary Patronage', pp. 463–4.

84. W. A. Speck, 'Politicians, Peers, and Publication by Subscription 1700–50', in *Books and their Readers*, pp. 47–68, pp. 47–8.

85. Turner, *Living by the Pen*, p. 112. As Turner notes, women subscribers became increasingly common.

86. Turner, *Living by the Pen*, p. 110.

87. Mary Barber's collection was the second volume of women's poetry to be published by subscription. See A. Budd, '"Merit in Distress": the Troubled Success of Mary Barber', *Review of English Studies*, 53.210 (2002), 204–27, p. 205, note 3.

88. Lonsdale, *Eighteenth-Century Women Poets*, p. xxvi.

89. For details of Mary Leapor, see Richard Greene, *Mary Leapor: a Study in Eighteenth-Century Women's Poetry* (Oxford: Clarendon Press, 1993). For details of Mary Jones see the head-note to her poems in *Eighteenth-Century Poetry: an Annotated Anthology*, ed. D. Fairer and C. Gerrard (Oxford: Blackwell Publishers, Ltd, 1999), p. 275.

90. Ingrassia, *Authorship, Commerce, and Gender*, p. 80.

91. State Papers Domestic, 35. 22/54.

92. Preface to *Letters from a Lady of Quality to a Chevalier* (London, 1721), pp. iii–iv.

93. Turner, *Living by the Pen*, p. 112.

94. Ingrassia, *Authorship, Commerce, and Gender*, p. 81.

95. Bowden, *The Reform'd Coquet*, p. 5.

96. The original proposals are in the Houghton Library, Harvard University: EC7. B6924.732p.

97. John Campbell (1678–1743) was a military hero who had fought at Ramilies in 1706, and Malplaquet in 1709. He was known for his love of reading. See *DNB*, vol. iii, p. 821.

98. For details of this group, and Swift's encouragement of women writers, see M. A. Doody, 'Swift Among the Women', *The Yearbook of English Studies*, vol. 18 (1988), 68–92. A Special Number: Pope, Swift and their Circle, ed. C. J. Rawson and J. Mezciems.

99. As Adam Budd has noted, the title-page of Barber's poems gives the date as 1734. An advertisement in the *Daily Courant*, however, points to a date of early June 1735. See Budd, '"Merit in Distress": the Troubled Success of Mary Barber', p. 205, note 3.

100. *Report on the Manuscripts of his Grace The Duke of Portland, K.G., Preserved at Welbeck Abbey*, vol. vi, pp. 38–9.

101. *Report on the Manuscripts of his Grace The Duke of Portland*, p. 46.

102. *Report on the Manuscripts of his Grace The Duke of Portland*, p. 47.

103. Budd, '"Merit in Distress": the Troubled Success of Mary Barber', pp. 205–6.

104. John Boyle, Earl of Cork and Orrery (1706/7–1762), was known for his *Remarks on Swift*. He was a friend of Swift and a poet. He spent a large part of his life in Ireland. See A. Webb, *A Compendium of Irish Biography* (Dublin: M. H. Gill & Son, 1878), p. 32.

105. On Barber's use of maternal authority in her poetry, see Doody, 'Swift Among the Women'.

106. Valerie Rumbold, 'Negotiating Patronage: Mary Barber's *Poems on Several Occasions* (1734)', an unpublished paper delivered at the 'Rethinking Women's Poetry, 1730–1930' conference, Birkbeck College, University of London, July 1995, p. 3. I am grateful to Dr Rumbold for allowing me access to her paper.

107. Rogers, 'Book Dedications in Britain', p. 230.
108. See Rumbold, 'Negotiating Patronage', p. 1, and C. Fanning, 'The Voice of the Dependent Poet: the Case of Mary Barber', *Women's Writing*, 8.1 (2001), 81–98, p. 82.
109. Both Fanning and Rumbold do, however, claim a measure of independence in Barber's verse.
110. Rumbold, 'Negotiating Patronage', p. 1.

5. Gender, Authorship and Whig Poetics

1. Kathryn King has recently argued that Rowe adopted the name Philomela when she turned her back on the commercial print-based world of the *Mercury* and moved more towards 'the exclusive manuscript society' centred on Lady Hertford. Given the fact that Philomela was used in the title of her 1696 poems – published by Dunton himself – and that the pseudonym was also used to refer to Rowe's other print publications in the miscellanies this seems unlikely. See 'Elizabeth Rowe's Tactical Use of Print and Manuscript', p. 166.
2. The miscellanies include *Divine Hymns and Poems on Several Occasions* (London, 1704); *Poetical Miscellanies, Consisting of Original Poems and Translations. By the best Hands. Publish'd by Mr. Steele* (London, 1714); Bernard Lintot's *Poems on Several Occasions* (London, 1717); and the fifth and sixth parts of Jacob Tonson's *Poetical Miscellanies* (London, 1704, 1709). Examples of Rowe's work also appeared in Matthew Prior's *Poems on Several Occasions* (London, 1709). The famous elegy on the death of her husband, 'On the Death of Mr. Thomas Rowe', was printed in the Lintot *Poems* (1717), and with *Eloisa to Abelard written by Mr. Pope. The second edition* (London, 1720). Rowe's posthumous works were edited by Henry Grove and Theophilus Rowe as *The Miscellaneous Works in Prose and Verse of Mrs. Elizabeth Rowe*, 2 vols (London, 1739).
3. For Rowe's background, see Stecher, *Elizabeth Singer Rowe*.
4. See G. D. McEwan, *The Oracle of the Coffee-House: John Dunton's Athenian Mercury* (California: Huntington Library, 1972), p. 6. See also Parks, *John Dunton and the English Book Trade*.
5. McEwan, *The Oracle of the Coffee-House*, p. 4.
6. These include: *The Athenian Oracle: being an Entire Collection of all the Valuable Questions and Answers in the old Athenian Mercuries* (London, 1703–10), and *The Athenian Spy* (London, 1704).
7. *Athenian Mercury*, Tuesday, 1 December 1691.
8. The use of pastoral for political purposes has a long history. See, for example, H. Cooper, *Pastoral: Mediaeval into Renaissance* (Ipswich: Brewer, 1977), D. Norbrook, *Poetry and Politics in the English Renaissance* (London: Routledge & Kegan Paul, 1984), and A. Patterson, *Pastoral and Ideology: Virgil to Valéry* (Berkeley: University of California Press, 1987).
9. See *Augustan Critical Writing*, ed. D. Womersley (London: Penguin Books, 1997), pp. xviii–xix. It may have been that Rowe substantially revised her poem in the light of Addison's commentary on Montagu, but we can, nevertheless, assume that the foundation for the poem, as printed in 1696,

was in place by 1691 by the response offered by the Athenians in that year. Montagu's poem on the Boyne is 'An EPISTLE To the Right Honourable CHARLES Earl of Dorset and Middlesex. Occasion'd by His Majesty's Victory in Ireland', published posthumously in *The Works and Life of . . . Charles, late Earl of Halifax* (London, 1715).

10. Poem 30 in *Poems on Several Occasions. Written By Philomela* (London, 1696).
11. Montagu's 'Epistle' uses similar language to refer to Mary who is able to 'Soften War's Horror with her lovely Face'.
12. J. Addison, *'An ACCOUNT of the Greatest ENGLISH POETS'* (1694). Quoted by Womersley, *Augustan Critical Writing*, p. xviii.
13. Womersley, *Augustan Critical Writing*, p. xxiii.
14. Womersley, *Augustan Critical Writing*, p. xxii
15. Womersley, *Augustan Critical Writing*, p. xxvi.
16. See, for example, Thomas, *Alexander Pope and His Eighteenth-Century Female Readers*, and *Pope, Swift, and Women Writers*, ed. Donald C. Mell (Newark: University of Delaware Press, 1996).
17. The use of 'paradice' here is an obvious allusion to Milton and plays off the broader mythologizing of William's victory as divinely sanctioned. There is perhaps an additional sense that Rowe is atoning for the sins of Eve.
18. These lines allude to the Pollio celebrated by Virgil in his 4th and 8th Eclogues. Rowe consistently uses pastoral and pindaric forms (the Athenians called her 'The Pindarick Lady'), and is clearly being read in a pastoral context. The use of pastoral and pindaric was rejected by Blackmore in *Advice to the Poets*. His remarks on this subject, and on the imitation of Milton, are intriguing as a possible negative reaction to Rowe's feminized version of Whig poetry: 'Away, ye Triflers, who all Rule disdain./Who in *Pindaric* sing *Philander's* Pain,/ And Camps, and Arms, in *Paster-Fido's* Strain' (199–201). Rowe wrote many pastoral poems, including 'A PASTORAL on the nativity of our SAVIOUR. In imitation of an Italian PASTORAL' (1704), as well as imitations of Milton.
19. The poem was reprinted in the 1696 collection as 'The Athenians to the Compiler of the Pindarick now Recited'.
20. Katherine Philips was a Royalist and wrote a number of political poems. The Athenians elide Philips' political identity in favour of her image as 'the matchless Orinda'. A similar depoliticizing process was applied to Rowe herself later in the eighteenth century. Here two female poets of differing political persuasions are grouped together under the common rubric of 'female virtue'. However, it is important not to overstate the gender issues here. As Blackmore's poetry also shows, the construction of a whig literary tradition was not tied exclusively to specifically Whig writers. Rowe herself at different times expressed her admiration for both Dryden and Pope.
21. This poem was reprinted in the 1696 collection as 'A Pindarick Question concerning the Jacobites, sent to the Athenians'.
22. S. Irlam, *The Poetics of Enthusiasm in Eighteenth-Century Britain: Elations* (Stanford, California: Stanford University Press, 1999), pp. 57–8.
23. Quoted by Irlam, *The Poetics of Enthusiasm*, p. 58.
24. McEwan, *The Oracle of the Coffee-House*, p. 107
25. This poem appeared in the issue for Tuesday 9 July, 1695. It was also printed in the 1696 collection.

26. Rowe was working from a long tradition of women who used the Bible as inspiration and authorization. Examples include Mary Sidney's *The Psalms* (*c.* 1586–1599), and Aemilia Lanyer, *Salve Deus Rex Judaeorum* (1611).
27. See Irlam, *The Poetics of Enthusiasm*, Chapter 1, 'Enthusiasm in the Seventeenth Century: The Vicissitudes of an Image'.
28. *The Grounds of Criticism*, in *Augustan Critical Writing*, pp. 155–6.
29. As Dennis remarks, 'But since the final End of Poetry is to reform the Manners, nothing can be according to the true Art of it, which is against Religion, or which runs counter to moral Virtue, or to the true Politicks, and to the Liberty of Mankind', *Augustan Critical Writing*, p. 151.
30. For the replacement of Virgil and Homer by Milton, see Dennis, 'Being the Substance of what will be said in the Beginning of the Criticism upon Milton', *The Grounds of Criticism in Poetry*, in *Augustan Critical Writing*, p. 147. See also D. Fairer, 'Creating a National Poetry: the Tradition of Spenser and Milton', *The Cambridge Companion to Eighteenth-Century Poetry*, ed. J. Sitter (Cambridge: Cambridge University Press, 2001), pp. 177–201.
31. Irlam, *The Poetics of Enthusiasm*, p. 65.
32. For two broad accounts of the popularity of these subjects with seventeenth and eighteenth-century writers, see N. H. Keeble, *The Literary Culture of Nonconformity in Later Seventeenth-Century England* (Athens: University of Georgia Press, 1987), and D. B. Morris, *The Religious Sublime: Christian Poetry and Critical Tradition in 18th-Century England* (Lexington: University Press of Kentucky, 1972).
33. *Augustan Critical Writing*, p. 172.
34. There were further editions of this collection (which also included poems by Katherine Philips and John Dryden), in 1709 and 1719.
35. Dedication, sig. A3.
36. The first printed evidence for a connection between Rowe and Watts is in the second edition of Watts' *Horae Lyricae* (London, 1709). As I will discuss, a poem by Watts addressed to Rowe in this volume is dated 19 July 1706.
37. The title of Watts' poem shows that he is referring to manuscript copies of unpublished poems. The 1727 edition of *Horae Lyricae* dates Rowe's poems as July 1706, and the 1709 edition dates Watts' poem as 19 July 1706. The two poems were obviously circulated in manuscript between Rowe and Watts before publication, and were written in the same month. The two poets were therefore obviously in dialogue in verse, and probably in person as well.
38. Rowe published her own biblical verse epic. *The History of Joseph: a Poem* (in ten books) was published in 1736.

6. Provincial Networks, Dissenting Connections and Noble Friends

1. 'The Life of Mrs. Elizabeth Rowe', in *The Miscellaneous Works*, p. xxxiii.
2. D. Defoe, *A Tour Through the Whole Island of Great Britain* (1724–6), introduced by G. D. H. Cole and D. C. Browning, 2 vols (London: Dent, 1962), vol. I, pp. 279–80.

3. P. Borsay, *The English Urban Renaissance: Culture and Society in the Provincial Town 1660–1770* (Oxford: Clarendon Press, 1989), pp. 26, 46, 98–9. R. Sweet, *The English Town, 1680–1840: Government, Society and Culture* (New York: Pearson Education Limited, 1999).

4. See W. E. Minchinton, 'Bristol – Metropolis of the West in the Eighteenth Century', in *The Early Modern Town: a Reader*, ed. P. Clark (London: Longman, 1976), pp. 297–313, and R. S. Neale, *Bath 1680–1850: a Social History* (London: Routledge & Kegan Paul, 1981).

5. Rowe must also have received some economic reward for her contributions, although there is no evidence of any payments she may have received. Indeed, information about payment to writers from periodicals is scarce. Brean Hammond estimates that authors would receive, on average, '1 to 6 guineas' for a prose essay, 'one of the most significant aspects of authorial income in the eighteenth century', *Professional Imaginative Writing*, p. 73. Walter Graham similarly hints at lucrative 'stipends' for periodical writers, but does not give any figures or sources, *English Literary Periodicals* (New York: Octagon Books, Inc, 1966), p. 20.

6. The poems are: 'To one that perswades me to leave the Muses'; 'To Sir Thomas Travel'; 'Occasioned by the Report of the Queen's Death'; 'John 21.17'; 'Canticles 5.6'.

7. Vol. 18, no. 4, Saturday 27 July 1695: 2 poems ('To Codrus' and 'A Pastoral Elegy'); no. 11, Tuesday 20 August 1695: 2 poems ('To Despair' and 'To Orestes); no. 16, Saturday, 7 September 1695: 4 poems ('Revelations, Chap I from v.13 to v.18', 'To a very Young Gentleman at a Dancing-School', 'To the same Gentleman', 'A Pastoral'); no. 22, Saturday, 28 September 1695: 2 poems: ('To Celinda' and 'Thoughts on Death'). Vol. 19, no. 17, Tuesday, 24 December 1695: 4 poems ('Platonick Love', 'To Mutius', 'To Strephon', 'Malachy 3.14'); no. 18, Saturday, 28 December 1695: 1 poem ('On Mrs Rebecka'); no. 21, Tuesday, 7 January 1696: 3 poems ('Canticles 7.11', 'Micha. 6.6.7', 'The Reflection').

8. It is tempting to speculate that the Athenians may have commissioned the substantial examples of Rowe's poetry that they printed, but as it is clear that, even by 1695, they are unaware of her identity, this is unlikely. However, the evidence in the *Mercury* of a correspondence between Rowe and the Athenians suggests that they did commission the later poems that appeared towards the end of the *Mercury*'s life, as well as her 1696 collection.

9. By the 1730s, literary entrepreneurs, such as Edward Cave of *The Gentleman's Magazine*, had realized the market potential of the provinces more fully, and, as I have shown, provincial women like Jane Brereton and Rowe are well represented. See J. Feather, *The Provincial Book Trade in Eighteenth-Century England* (Cambridge: Cambridge University Press, 1985), pp. 19–21. For discussion of a later woman writer whose career provides some interesting parallels to Rowe, see John Brewer's chapter on Anna Seward, the 'Swan of Lichfield', in *The Pleasures of the Imagination: English Culture in the Eighteenth Century* (London: HarperCollins, 1997), pp. 573–612.

10. Feather, *The Provincial Book Trade*, p. 47.

11. McEwan, *The Oracle of the Coffee-House*, p. 46.

12. For a discussion of the role of the Post Office in newspaper distribution, see Feather, *The Provincial Book Trade*, pp. 37–8, 47–8.
13. Sweet, *The English Town*, p. 189.
14. See M. R. Watts, *The Dissenters from the Reformation to the French Revolution* (Oxford: Clarendon Press, 1978), p. 278. Watts estimates that Taunton had the largest dissenting population in Britain in this period. In Frome, the Presbyterians had a congregation of approximately 1000.
15. John Bowden's brother, Samuel (fl. 1732–61), was the author of two volumes of poems published from 1733–5, and a contributor to *The Gentleman's Magazine*. Samuel Bowden belonged to the same communion as Rowe in Frome. See *DNB*, vol. ii, p. 948.
16. Stecher, *Elizabeth Singer Rowe*, p. 88.
17. For information on Thomas Rowe, see *DNB*, vol. xvii, p. 338.
18. 'The Life of Mrs. Elizabeth Rowe', pp. xvii–xviii.
19. Lady Hertford earned £500 a year for her office as Lady of Our Bedchamber in Ordinary to Queen Caroline. She served the court from 1723 until Caroline's death in 1737. Lord Hertford entered Parliament in 1722 as Baron de Percy, Lord Lieutenant of Northumberland. See H. Sard Hughes, *The Gentle Hertford* (New York: Macmillan Company, 1940), pp. 42–4.
20. Prior was Viscount Weymouth's colleague on the Board of Trade and Plantations. See H. Bunker Wright, 'Matthew Prior and Elizabeth Singer', *Philological Quarterly*, 24.1 (January 1945), 71–82, p. 71. Wright reprints the correspondence between Rowe and Prior in this article. All references to the letters are to this article.
21. Wright, 'Matthew Prior and Elizabeth Singer', pp. 73–4. The translations of Tasso did appear in the 1704 miscellany.
22. The Winchelseas were friends of the Weymouths.
23. These estates included Marlborough Castle in Wiltshire, St Leonard's Hill in Windsor Forest and Percy Lodge, near Colnbrook. Lady Hertford's country seats were the subject of various country house poems in the eighteenth century, which reflects her status as a well-known patron. See D. Hill Radcliffe, 'Genre and Social Order in Country House Poems of the Eighteenth Century: Four Views of Percy Lodge', *Studies in English Literature*, 30 (1990), 445–65.
24. For Lady Hertford's links with Thomson, see the articles by H. Sard Hughes, 'Thomson and the Countess of Hertford', *Modern Philology*, 25 (1928), 439–68, and 'Thomson and Lady Hertford Again', *Modern Philology*, 28 (1931), 468–70.
25. See Hughes, 'Thomson and the Countess of Hertford' for printed and manuscript versions of Thomson's 'Hymn'.
26. From her letters it is clear that Rowe visited Marlborough, for example, and that Lady Hertford even visited Frome. Selection of Rowe's letters are printed in *Miscellaneous Works* (1739), but manuscript copies also survive in a bound volume in Lady Hertford's hand in the Duke of Northumberland's collection at Alnwick Castle, Alnwick MS 110. I am grateful to the Duke of Northumberland for permission to consult this volume, and to the archivist, Colin Shrimpton, for his assistance. See Alnwick MS 110, ff. 182–3, for a letter from Rowe to a friend, Arabella Marrow, which describes her visit to Lady Hertford. The letter is undated. See also, H. Sard

Hughes, 'Elizabeth Rowe and the Countess of Hertford', *PMLA*, 59 (1944), 726–46.

27. Alnwick MS 110, f. 151.

28. Alnwick MS 110, f. 120.

29. I. Watts, *Reliquiae Juveniles: Miscellaneous Thoughts in Prose and Verse on Natural, Moral, and Divine Subjects; written chiefly in Younger Years* (London, 1734), Preface, p. xii.

30. Alnwick MS 110, f. 248.

31. Hughes, *The Gentle Hertford*, p. 97.

32. Examples of Worrall's other publications include, *A Vindication of PROVI-DENCE: Or, a true Estimate of Human Life*, by E. Young; Dr William Sherlock's sermons in two volumes; *Reform'd Devotions, in Meditations, Hymns, and Petitions for every Day in the Week, and every Holiday in the Year*, by Theophilus Doddington, Rector of Wittersham in Kent; as well as *The History of the Amours of the Marshal de BOUFLERS: Or, a true Account of his Love Intrigues*.

33. The *Letters* were advertised as being by the author of *Friendship in Death*, and were usually bound together.

34. Rowe's poetry was influenced by Young. Her letters show her knowledge and approval of his work. See, for example, Alnwick MS 110, f. 154. Young also mentions Rowe's work in his letters. See *The Correspondence of Edward Young, 1683–1765*, ed. H. Pettit (Oxford: Clarendon Press, 1971), pp. 72–5.

35. For a discussion of male authors who used similar strategies to distance themselves from any form of 'dependence', see D. Griffin, 'Fictions of Eighteenth-Century Authorship', *Essays in Criticism*, 43.3 (1993), 181–94. Pope's independent stance, of course, was enabled by the money he had made from his translations of Homer.

36. Alnwick MS 110, f. 79.

37. Alnwick MS 110, f. 357. Rowe's use of a familiar feminine accomplishment to 'screen' her literary ambition is similar to Jane Barker's use of a 'Patch-Work Screen' to frame her novelistic tales. *The History of Joseph* was also published by Worrall, as well as further editions up to 1744 (second edition, 1737; third edition, 1741; fourth edition, 1744).

38. Alnwick MS 110, ff. 195–6.

39. Alnwick MS 110, f. 237.

Bibliography

Manuscript sources

Alnwick MS 110. Alnwick Castle, Northumberland.
British Library Birch Additional MS 4293, 109 ff. 81–2. C. 1730.
British Library Sloane MS 4059 f. 144.
Flintshire Record Office, Hawarden. Letters and Poems by Jane Brereton. D/E/871, 7 letters. D/E1542/42 &100a, 2 poems.
State Papers Hanoverian. SP35 22/54.
Upcott Collection. Original Assignments of Mss between Authors and Publishers, principally for dramatic works, from the year 1703–1810. British Library Additional MS 387, 28 and British Library Additional MS 387, 30

Primary sources

Anon. *The Session of the Poets, Holden at the Foot of Parnassus-Hill July the 9th, 1696.*
Arisoto, *Orlando Furioso.* Trans. Barbara Reynolds. 2 vols. Harmondsworth: Penguin Books Ltd., 1975.
'Ariadne', pseud. *She Venture and He Wins. A Comedy.* London, 1696.
Astell, Mary. *A Serious Proposal to the Ladies.* London, 1694. Ed. Patricia Springborg. London: Pickering & Chatto, 1997.
Aubin, Penelope. *The Stuarts: a Pindarique Ode.* London, 1707.
The Strange Adventures of the Count de Vinevil and His Family. London, 1721.
The Life of Madam de Beaumont, a French Lady. London, 1721.
The Noble Slaves; or, The Adventures of Two Lords and Two Ladies. London, 1722.
Trans. François Pétis de la Croix (the Elder). *The History of Genghizcan the Great, First Emperor of the Antient Moguls and Tartars.* London, 1722.
Trans. Louise Gomez de Vasconcelles. *The Prince of Clermont and Madam de Ravezan.* London, 1722.
The Life of Charlotta du Pont, an English Lady. London, 1723.
The Life and Adventures of the Lady Lucy. London, 1726.
Trans. Robert Challes. *The Illustrious French Lovers: being the True Histories of the Amours of Several French Persons of Quality.* London, 1727.
Trans. Marguerite de Lussan. *The Life of the Countess de Gomez.* London, 1729.
The Merry Masqueraders; or, The Humorous Cuckold. London, 1730.
A Collection of Entertaining Novels and Histories Designed to Promote the Cause of Virtue and Honour. 3 vols. London, 1739.
Baker, David Erskine. *Biographica Dramatica; or, The Companion to the Playhouse.* 2 vols. London, 1782. Originally published as *The Companion to the Playhouse; or, An Historical Account of all the Dramatic Writers (and their Works) that have appeared in Great Britain and Ireland.* 2 vols. London, 1764.

Ballard, George. *Memoirs of Several Ladies of Great Britain.* London, 1752.

Barber, Mary. *Poems on Several Occasions.* London, 1734.

Barker, Jane. *The Galesia Triology and Selected Manuscript Poems of Jane Barker.* Ed. Carol Shiner Wilson. Women Writers in English, 1350–1850. Oxford: Oxford University Press, 1997.

Poetical Recreations: Consisting of Original Poems, Songs, Odes, &c. With Several New Translations. London, 1688.

Love Intrigues; or, The Amours of Bosvil and Galesia. London and Cambridge, 1713.

Exilius; or, The Banish'd Roman: a New Romance: In Two Parts. Written after the Manner of Telemachus, For the Instruction of Some Young Ladies of Quality. London, 1715.

The Christian Pilgrimage; or, A Companion for the Holy Season of Lent. London, 1718.

The Entertaining Novels of Mrs. Jane Barker. 2 vols. London, 1719.

A Patch-Work Screen for the Ladies; or, Love and Virtue Recommended: In a Collection of Instructive Novels. London, 1723.

The Lining of the Patch-Work Screen; Design'd for the Farther Entertainment of the Ladies. London, 1726.

Behn, Aphra. *All the Histories and Novels written by the Late Ingenious Mrs. Behn.* London, 1698.

Seventeen Histories and Novels Written by the Late Ingenious Mrs. Behn. London, 1717.

The Land of Love. A Poem. London, 1717.

The Bible, Authorized King James Version. Ed. Robert Carroll and Stephen Prickett. Oxford: Oxford University Press, 1997.

Birch, Thomas, ed. *The Works of Mrs. Catherine Cockburn, Theological, Moral, Dramatic, and Poetical.* 2 vols. London, 1751.

Boyd, Elizabeth. *Proposals for Printing by Subscription A Novel. Entitled The Happy-Unfortunate; or, The Female Page. In Three Parts. By Louisa.* London, 1732.

The Happy-Unfortunate; or, The Female Page. London, 1732. Ed. William Graves. New York and London: Garland Publishing Inc, 1972.

Brereton, Jane. *The Fifth Ode of the Fourth Book of Horace, Imitated.* London, 1716.

An Expostulary Epistle to Sir Richard Steele Upon the Death of Mr. Addison. London, 1720.

Merlin: a Poem. London, 1735.

Poems on Several Occasions by Mrs. Jane Brereton. London, 1744.

Briscoe, Samuel, ed. *Familiar Letters of Love, Gallantry and Several Occasions.* 2 vols. London, 1718.

Butler, Sarah. *Irish Tales; or, Instructive Histories for the Happy Conduct of Life.* London, 1716.

Centlivre, Susanna. *The Busy Body.* London, 1709.

Chudleigh, Lady Mary. *The Poems and Prose of Mary, Lady Chudleigh.* Ed. Margaret Ezell. New York and Oxford: Oxford University Press, 1993.

Cibber, Colley. *Lives of the Poets of Great Britain and Ireland.* London, 1753.

Congreve, William. *Incognita; or, Love and Duty Reconciled.* London, 1692. In *An Anthology of Seventeenth-Century Fiction.* Ed. Paul Salzman. Oxford: Oxford University Press, 1991.

Davys, Mary. *The Northern Heiress; or, The Humours of York.* London, 1716.

The Amours of Alcippus and Lucippe. London, 1704. Rpt as *The Lady's Tale*. 1725.

The Fugitive. London, 1705.

The Works of Mrs. Davys. 2 vols. London, 1725.

The Reform'd Coquet, Familiar Letters Betwixt a Gentleman and a Lady, and *The Accomplish'd Rake*. Ed. Martha F. Bowden. Eighteenth-Century Novels by Women. Lexington: University Press of Kentucky, 1999.

The False Friend; or, The Treacherous Portugueze. London, 1732.

Defoe, Daniel. *The Life and Strange Surprizing Adventures of Robinson Crusoe*. London, 1719.

A Tour Through the Whole Island of Great Britain. Introduced by G. D. H. Cole and D. C. Browning. 2 vols. London: Dent, 1962.

Drake, Judith. *An Essay in Defense of the Female Sex*. London, 1696.

Duncombe, John. *The Feminiad; or, Female Genius*. London, 1754.

Dunton, John, ed. *The Athenian Mercury*. 20 vols. London, March 1690–June 1697.

Ed. *The Athenian Oracle: Being an Entire Collection of the Valuable Questions and Answers in the Old Athenian Mercuries*. 3 vols. London, 1704.

The Life and Errors of John Dunton Late Citizen of London; Written by Himself. London, 1705.

Ed. *The Athenian Spy: Discovering the Secret Letters which were sent to the Athenian Society by the most Ingenious Ladies of the Three Kingdoms*. London, 1709.

Egerton, Sarah Fyge. *The Female Advocate; or, An Answer to a Late Satyr Against the Pride, Lust, and Inconstancy of Women*. London, 1686.

Gildon, Charles, ed. *A New Collection of Poems for Several Occasions*. London, 1701.

Grainger, Lydia. *Modern Amours; or, A Secret History of the Adventures of some Persons of the First Rank*. London, 1733.

Griffith, Elizabeth. *A Collection of Novels, Selected and Revised by Mrs. Griffith*. 3 vols. London, 1777.

Hammond, Anthony, ed. *A New Miscellany of Original Translations and Imitations. By the most Eminent Hands*. London, 1720.

Haywood, Eliza. *Love in Excess; or, The Fatal Enquiry*. London, 1719–20. Ed. David Oakleaf. Ontario: Broadview Press Ltd., 2000.

The Fair Captive: A Tragedy. London, 1721.

Letters from a Lady of Quality to a Chevalier. London, 1721.

The British Recluse; or, The Secret History of Cleomira, Suppos'd Dead. London, 1722.

Idalia; or, The Unfortunate Mistress. London, 1723.

The Masqueraders; or, Fatal Curiosity. London, 1724.

The Fatal Secret; or, Constancy in Distress. London. 1724.

The Surprize; or, Constancy Rewarded. London, 1724.

The Tea-Table; or, A Conversation Between Some Polite Persons of Both Sexes at a Lady's Visiting Days. London, 1724.

The Works of Mrs. Eliza Haywood. 4 vols. London, 1724.

Poems on Several Occasions. London, 1724.

The Rash Resolve; or, The Untimely Discovery. London, 1724.

La Belle Assemblée: Being a curious collection of some very Remarkable incidents which happen'd to Persons of the First Quality in France. London, 1724.

The Injur'd Husband; or, The Mistaken Resentment and *Lasselia; or, The Self-*

Abandon'd. Ed. Jerry C. Beasley. *Eighteenth-Century Novels by Women.* Lexington: University of Kentucky Press, 1999.

Secret Histories, Novels and Poems. 4 vols. London, 1725.

The Force of Nature; or, The Lucky Disappointment. London, 1725.

Fantomina; or, Love in a Maze. London, 1725.

The Lady's Philosopher's Stone; or, The Caprices of Love and Destiny. London, 1725.

Memoirs of the Baron de Brosse, Who Was Broke on the Wheel in the Reign of Lewis XIV. London, 1725–6.

Memoirs of a Certain Island Adjacent to the Kingdom of Utopia. Written by a Celebrated Author of that Country. 2 vols. London, 1725–6.

The City Jilt; or, The Alderman Turn'd Beau. London, 1726.

The Secret History of the Present Intrigues of the Court of Caramania. London, 1727.

Philidore and Placentia; or, L'Amour Trop Delicat. London, 1729.

L'Entretian des Beaux Espirits, Being the Sequel to the Belle Assemblée. 2 vols. London, 1734.

The Dramatic Historiographer; or, The British Theatre Delineated. London, 1735.

The Adventures of Eovaai, Princess of Ijaveo: A Pre-Adamatical History. Ed. Earla Willputte. Ontario: Broadview Press, 1999.

The Female Spectator. 4 vols. London, 1744–6.

Hearne, Mary. *The Lover's Week* and *The Female Deserters.* Ed. Josephine Grieder. New York: Garland Publishing, Inc., 1973.

Hill, Aaron. *The Plain Dealer: Being Select Essays on Several Curious Subjects. Relating to Friendship . . . Poetry and Other Branches of Polite Literature. Publish'd Originally in the Year 1724.* 2 vols. London, 1730.

Leapor, Mary. *Poems Upon Several Occasions.* London, 1748.

Lintot, Bernard, ed. *Poems on Several Occasions.* London, 1717.

Manley, Delarivier. *Letters Written By Mrs. Manley.* London, 1696. Rpt *A Stage Coach Journey to Exeter.* London, 1725.

The Lost Lover; or, The Jealous Husband: A Comedy. London, 1696.

The Royal Mischief. A Tragedy. London, 1696.

The Secret History of Queen Zara and the Zarazians. London, 1705.

Almyna; or, The Arabian Vow. London, 1707.

The New Atalantis. Ed. Ros Ballaster. London: Penguin Books, 1992.

Memoirs of Europe Towards the Close of the Eighth Century. London, 1710.

The Adventures of Rivella. Ed. Katherine Zelinsky. Ontario: Broadview Press Ltd, 1999.

Lucius, the First Christian King of Britain. London, 1717.

The Power of Love in Seven Novels. London, 1720.

Masters, Mary. *Familiar Letters and Poems on Several Occasions.* London, 1755.

Montagu, Charles. *The Works and Life of . . . Charles, late Earl of Halifax.* London, 1715.

Philips, Katherine. *The Collected Works of Katherine Philips: The Matchless Orinda.* 3 vols. Ed. Patrick Thomas. Essex: Stump Cross Books, 1990.

Pix, Mary. *The Inhumane Cardinal (1696).* Ed. Constance Clark. New York: Scholars' Facsimiles & Reprints, 1984.

The Spanish Wives. A Farce. London, 1696.

Ibrahim, the Thirteenth Emperor of the Turks: A Tragedy. London, 1696.

Pope, Alexander. *The Rape of the Lock.* London, 1714.

Eloisa to Abelard written by Mr. Pope. The second edition. London, 1720.

The Dunciad. In *The Twickenham Edition of the Works of Alexander Pope*. Vol. V. Ed. John Sutherland. London: Methuen, 1953.

The Dunciad in Four Books. Ed. Valerie Rumbold. Essex: Pearson Education Limited, 1999.

An Essay on Man. London, 1733–4.

Moral Essays. Epistle II. To a Lady. London, 1735.

Prévost, Abbé François d'Exiles, *Le Pour et Contre: ouvrage periodique d'un gout nouveau*. 20 vols. Paris: Chez Didot, 1733–40.

Prior, Matthew. *Poems on Several Occasions*. London, 1709.

Richardson, Samuel. *Pamela; or, Virtue Rewarded*. Ed. Peter Sabor. London: Penguin Books, 1985.

Roscommon, Wentworth Dillon. *Divine Hymns and Poems on Several Occasions*. London 1704.

Rowe, Elizabeth Singer. *Poems on Several Occasions. Written by Philomela*. London, 1696.

Friendship in Death. In Twenty Letters From the Dead to the Living. London, 1728.

Letters Moral and Entertaining in Prose and Verse. 3 vols. London, 1729–33.

The History of Joseph: a Poem. London, 1736.

Devout Exercises of the Heart, In Meditation and Soliloquy, Prayer and Praise. London, 1737.

The Miscellaneous Works in Prose and Verse of Mrs. Elizabeth Rowe. 2 vols. London, 1739.

Sansom, Martha Fowke. *Epistles of Clio and Strephon*. London, 1720.

Clio; or, A Secret History of the Life and Amours of the Late Celebrated Mrs. S-n-m. London, 1752.

Savage, Richard, ed. *Miscellaneous Poems and Translations. By Several Hands. Publish'd by Richard Savage, Son of the Late Earl Rivers*. London, 1726.

The Authors of the Town. A Satire. Inscribed to the Author of the Universal Passion. London, 1735.

Steele, Richard, ed. *Poetical Miscellanies: Consisting of Original Poems and Translations. By the Best Hands*. London, 1714.

Strutt, Joseph. *A Biographical Dictionary; Containing an Historical Account of all the Engravings from the Earliest Period of the Art of Engraving to the Present Time*. London, 1785–6.

Thomas, Elizabeth. *Miscellaneous Poems on Several Subjects*. London, 1722.

Pylades and Corinna; or, Memoirs of the Lives, Amours, and Writings of Richard Gwinnet Esq; . . . and Elizabeth Thomas, . . . To which is prefixed, The Life of Corinna. Written by Herself. London, 1731–2.

Tonson, Jacob, ed. *Poetical Miscellanies: the Fifth Part, containing a Collection of Original Poems with Several New Translations by the Most Eminent Hands*. London, 1704.

Poetical Miscellanies: the Sixth Part, containing a Collection of Original Poems with Several New Translations by the Most Eminent Hands. London, 1709.

Trotter, Catherine. *Olinda's Adventures; or, The Amours of a Young Lady*. Ed. Robert Adams Day. The Augustan Reprint Society. Publication Number 138. University of California, Los Angeles: William Andrews Clark Memorial Library, 1969.

Agnes de Castro. A Tragedy. London, 1696.

The Fatal Friendship. A Tragedy. London, 1698.

Watts, Isaac. *Horae Lyricae*. London, 1709.

Reliquiae Juveniles: Miscellaneous Thoughts in Prose and Verse on Natural, Moral, and Divine Subjects; written chiefly in Younger Years. London, 1734.

Winchelsea, Anne Finch. Countess of. *An Elegy on the Death of K. James. By a Lady.* London, 1701.

Miscellany Poems, On Several Occasions. By a Lady. London, 1713.

Young, Edward. *Complete Works.* London, 1854.

The Correspondence of Edward Young, 1683–1765. Ed. Henry Pettit. Oxford: Clarendon Press, 1971.

Secondary sources

Arkell, R. L. *Caroline of Ansbach: George the Second's Queen.* London: Oxford University Press, 1939.

Aughterson, Kate, ed. *Renaissance Woman: a Sourcebook. Constructions of Femininity in England.* London and New York: Routledge, 1995.

Backscheider, Paula R. *Daniel Defoe: His Life.* Baltimore and London: Johns Hopkins University Press, 1989.

Spectacular Politics: Theatrical Power and Mass Culture in Early Modern England. Baltimore and London: Johns Hopkins University Press, 1993.

Baer, Joel. H. 'Penelope Aubin and the Pirates of Madagascar: Biographical Notes and Documents.' In *Eighteenth-Century Women.* Ed. Troost. 49–62.

Ballaster, Ros. *Seductive Forms: Women's Amatory Fiction from 1684 to 1740.* Oxford: Clarendon Press, 1992.

'Seizing the Means of Seduction: Fiction and Feminine Identity in Aphra Behn and Delarivier Manley'. In *Women, Writing, History.* Ed. Grundy and Wiseman. 93–108.

Barash, Carol. *English Women's Poetry, 1649–1714: Politics, Community, and Linguistic Authority.* Oxford: Clarendon Press, 1996.

'Gender, Authority and the "Life" of an Eighteenth-century Women Writer: Delarivier Manley's *Adventures of Rivella'. Women's Studies International Forum,* 10.2 (1987): 165–9.

Beasley, Jerry C. 'Politics and Moral Idealism: the Achievement of Some Early Women Novelists'. In *Fetter'd or Free?* Ed. Schofield and Macheski. 216–36.

Belanger, Terry. 'Publishers and Writers in Eighteenth-Century England'. In *Books and their Readers.* Ed. Isabel Rivers. 5–25.

Bergeron, David M. 'Women as Patrons of English Renaissance Drama'. In *Patronage in the Renaissance.* Ed. Lytle and Orgel. 274–90.

Blouch, Christine. 'Eliza Haywood and the Romance of Obscurity'. *Studies in English Literature,* 31 (1991): 535–51.

Borsay, Peter. 'The London Connection: Cultural Diffusion and the Eighteenth-Century Provincial Town'. *The London Journal,* 19.1 (1994): 21–35.

The English Urban Renaissance: Culture and Society in the Provincial Town 1660–1770. Oxford: Clarendon Press, 1989.

Bowyer, John. *The Celebrated Mrs Centlivre.* Durham, NC: Duke University Press, 1952.

Brewer, David. '"Haywood", Secret History, and the Politics of Attribution'. In *The Passionate Fictions of Eliza Haywood.* Ed. Saxton and Bocchicchio. 217–39.

Brewer, John. *The Pleasures of the Imagination: English Culture in the Eighteenth Century*. London: HarperCollins, 1997.

Brewster, Dorothy. *Aaron Hill: Poet, Dramatist, Projector*. New York: Columbia University Press, 1913.

Budd, Adam. ' "Merit in Distress": the Troubled Success of Mary Barber'. *Review of English Studies*, 53.210 (2002): 204–27.

Clark, Peter, ed. *The Early Modern Town: a Reader*. London: Longman, 1976.

Clark, William Smith. *The Early Irish Stage: the Beginnings to 1720*. Oxford: Clarendon Press, 1920.

Clarke, Norma. 'Soft Passions and Darling Themes: from Elizabeth Singer Rowe (1674–1737) to Elizabeth Carter (1717–1806)'. *Women's Writing*, 7.3 (2000): 353–71.

Colley, Linda. *Britons: Forging the Nation 1707–1837*. London: Pimlico, 1992.

Colton, Judith. 'Merlin's Cave and Queen Caroline: Garden Art as Political Propaganda'. *Eighteenth-Century Studies*, 10.1 (1976): 1–20.

Cooper, Helen. *Pastoral: Mediaeval into Renaissance*. Ipswich: Brewer, 1977.

Cotton, Nancy. *Women Playwrights in England c. 1363–1750*. London and Toronto: Bucknell University Press, 1980.

Davies, John. *A History of Wales*. London: Penguin Books, 1990.

Davies, R. R. *The Age of Conquest: Wales 1063–1415*. Oxford: Oxford University Press, 1987.

'The Status of Women and the Practice of Marriage in Late Medieval Wales'. In *The Welsh Law of Women*. Ed. Jenkins and Owen. 43–114.

Dearnley, Moira. *Distant Fields: Eighteenth-Century Fictions of Wales*. Cardiff: University of Wales Press, 2001.

Donoghue, Frank. *The Fame Machine: Book Reviewing and Eighteenth-Century Literary Careers*. Stanford: Stanford University Press, 1996.

Doody, Margaret Anne. 'Swift Among the Women'. *The Yearbook of English Studies*, 18. A Special Number: Pope, Swift and their Circle. Ed. C. J. Rawson and Jenny Mezciems (1988): 68–92.

Doyle, James E. ed. *The Official Baronage of England, Showing the Succession, Dignities, and Offices of every Peer from 1066 to 1885*. 3 vols. London: Longmans, Green and Co., 1886.

Duffy, Maureen. *The Passionate Shepherdess: Aphra Behn 1640–1689*. London: Jonathan Cape Limited, 1977.

Earle, Peter. *The Making of the English Middle Class: Business, Society and Family Life in London, 1660–1730*. Berkeley and Los Angeles: University of California Press, 1989.

Elwood, John R. 'Henry Fielding and Eliza Haywood: a Twenty Year War'. *Albion*, 5 (1973): 184–92.

'The Stage Career of Eliza Haywood'. *Theatre Survey*, 5.2 (1964): 107–16.

Ezell, Margaret J. M. 'The Posthumous Publication of Women's Manuscripts and the History of Authorship'. In *Women's Writing and the Circulation of Ideas*. Ed. Justice and Tinker. 121–36.

Social Authorship and the Advent of Print. Baltimore and London: Johns Hopkins University Press, 1999.

Writing Women's Literary History. Baltimore and London: Johns Hopkins University Press, 1993.

Fairer, David. 'Creating a National Poetry: the Tradition of Spenser and

Milton'. In *The Cambridge Companion to Eighteenth-Century Poetry*. Ed. Sitter. 177–201.

Fairer, David and Christine Gerrard, eds. *Eighteenth-Century Poetry: an Annotated Anthology*. Oxford: Blackwell Publishers, Ltd., 1999.

Fanning, Christopher. 'The Voice of the Dependent Poet: the Case of Mary Barber'. *Women's Writing*, 8.1 (2001): 81–98.

Feather, John. *A History of British Publishing*. London and New York: Routledge, 1988.

   The Provincial Book Trade in Eighteenth-Century England. Cambridge: Cambridge University Press, 1985.

   'The Commerce of Letters: the Study of the Eighteenth-Century Book Trade'. *Eighteenth-Century Studies*, 17 (1983–4): 405–24.

Firmager, Gabrielle M. 'Eliza Haywood: Some Further Light on her Background'. *Notes & Queries*, 38.2 (1991): 181–3.

Folkenflik, Robert. 'Patronage and the Poet-Hero'. *Huntington Library Quarterly*, 48 (1985): 363–79.

Foss, Michael. *The Age of Patronage: the Arts in England 1660–1750*. New York: Cornell University Press, 1971.

Gallagher, Catherine. *Nobody's Story: the Vanishing Acts of Women Writers in the Marketplace, 1670–1820*. Oxford: Clarendon Press, 1994.

   'Embracing the Absolute: the Politics of the Female Subject in Seventeenth-Century England'. *Genders*, 1 (1988): 24–39.

Gerrard, Christine. *The Patriot Opposition to Walpole: Politics, Poetry, and National Myth 1725–1742*. Oxford: Clarendon Press, 1994.

Goreau, Angeline. *Reconstructing Aphra: a Social Biography of Aphra Behn*. Oxford: Oxford University Press, 1980.

Graham, Walter. *English Literary Periodicals*. New York: Octagon Books, Inc, 1966.

Greene, Richard. *Mary Leapor: a Study in Eighteenth-Century Women's Poetry*. Oxford: Clarendon Press, 1993.

Greer, Germaine et al., eds. *Kissing the Rod: an Anthology of 17th-century Women's Verse*. London: Virago Press, 1988.

Griffin, Dustin. *Literary Patronage in England, 1650–1800*. Cambridge: Cambridge University Press, 1996.

   'Fictions of Eighteenth-Century Authorship'. *Essays in Criticism*, 43.3 (1993): 181–94.

Grundy, Isobel. 'Samuel Johnson as Patron of Women'. *The Age of Johnson*, vol. 1 (1987): 59–77.

Grundy, Isobel and Susan Wiseman, eds. *Women, Writing, History, 1640–1740*. London: Batsford, 1992.

Guskin, Phyllis J. '"Not Originally Intended for the Press": Martha Fowke Sansom's Poems in the *Barbadoes Gazette*'. *Eighteenth-Century Studies*, 34.1 (2000): 61–91.

   Ed. *Clio: the Autobiography of Martha Fowke Sansom (1689–1736)*. Newark: University of Delaware Press, 1997.

Hammond, Brean S. *Professional Imaginative Writing in England, 1670–1740: 'Hackney for Bread'*. Oxford: Clarendon Press, 1997.

Hansen, Marlene R. 'The Pious Mrs. Rowe'. *English Studies*, 1 (1995): 34–51.

Havens, Raymond D. 'Changing Tastes in the Eighteenth Century: a Study of Dryden's and Dodsley's Miscellanies.' *PMLA*, 44 (1929): 515–34.

Heinemann, Marcia. 'Eliza Haywood's Career in the Theatre.' *Notes and Queries*, 20.1 (1973): 9–13.

Helgerson, Richard. *Self-Crowned Laureates: Spenser, Jonson, and the Literary System*. Berkeley and London: University of California Press, 1983.

Highfill, Philip H., Jr., Kalman A. Burnim, and Edward A. Langhans. *A Biographical Dictionary of Actors, Actresses, Musicians, Dancers, Managers and Other Stage Personnel in London, 1660–1800*. 14 vols. Carbondale and Edwardsville: Southern Illinois University Press, 1973.

Hobby, Elaine. *Virtue of Necessity: English Women's Writing 1649–88*. London: Virago Press Limited, 1988.

' "Discourse So Unsavoury": Women's Published Writings of the 1650s'. In *Women, Writing, History 1640–1740*. Ed. Grundy and Wiseman. 16–32.

Hughes, Helen Sard. 'Elizabeth Rowe and the Countess of Hertford'. *PMLA*, 59 (1944): 726–46.

The Gentle Hertford. New York: Macmillan Company, 1940.

'Thomson and Lady Hertford Again'. *Modern Philology*, 28 (1931): 468–70.

'Thomson and the Countess of Hertford'. *Modern Philology*, 25 (1928): 439–68.

Hume, Robert D. *Henry Fielding and the London Theatre 1727–1737*. Oxford: Clarendon Press, 1988.

Hunter, J. Paul. *Before Novels: the Cultural Contexts of Eighteenth-Century English Fiction*. New York & London: W. W. Norton, 1990.

Ingrassia, Catherine. *Authorship, Commerce, and Gender in Early Eighteenth-Century England: a Culture of Paper Credit*. Cambridge: Cambridge University Press, 1998.

Irlam, Shaun. *The Poetics of Enthusiasm in Eighteenth-Century Britain*. Stanford, California: Stanford University Press, 1999.

Jenkins, Dafydd and Morfydd E. Owen, eds. *The Welsh Law of Women*. Cardiff: University of Wales Press, 1980.

Jenkins, Geraint. *The Foundations of Modern Wales, 1642–1780*. Oxford: Oxford University Press, 1993.

Justice, George. *The Manufacturers of Literature: Writing and the Literary Market-place in Eighteenth-Century England*. Newark: University of Delaware Press, 2002.

Justice, George and Nathan Tinker, eds. *Women's Writing and the Circulation of Ideas: Manuscript Publication in England, 1550–1800*. Cambridge: Cambridge University Press, 2002.

Kairoff, Claudia Thomas. 'Eighteenth-century Women Poets and Readers'. In *The Cambridge Companion to Eighteenth-Century Poetry*. Ed. Sitter. 157–76.

Keeble, N. H. *The Literary Culture of Nonconformity in Later Seventeenth-Century England*. Athens: University of Georgia Press, 1987.

Keener, Frederick M. and Susan E. Lorsch, eds. *Eighteenth-Century Women and the Arts*. New York, Connecticut: Greenwood Press, 1988.

Kernan, Alvin. *Samuel Johnson and the Impact of Print*. Princeton: Princeton University Press, 1987.

Kewes, Paulina. *Authorship and Appropriation: Writing for the Stage in England, 1660–1710*. Oxford: Clarendon Press, 1998.

King, Kathryn R. 'Elizabeth Singer Rowe's Tactical Use of Print and Manuscript'. In *Women's Writing and the Circulation of Ideas: Manuscript Publication in England, 1550–1800*. Ed. Justice and Tinker. 158–81.

Jane Barker, Exile. A Literary Career 1675–1725. Oxford: Clarendon Press, 2000.

With the assistance of Jeslyn Medoff. 'Jane Barker and her Life (1652–1732): the Documentary Record'. *Eighteenth-Century Life*, 21.3 (1997): 16–38.

'Galesia, Jane Barker and a Coming to Authorship'. In *Anxious Power*. Ed. Singley and Sweeney. 91–104.

Korshin, Paul. 'Types of Eighteenth-Century Literary Patronage'. *Eighteenth-Century Studies*, 7 (1974): 453–73.

Langford, Paul, *A Polite and Commercial People: England 1727–1782*. Oxford: Oxford University Press, 1992.

LeGates, Marlene. 'The Cult of Womanhood in Eighteenth-Century Thought'. *Eighteenth-Century Studies*, 10 (1976–7): 21–39.

The London Stage, 1660–1800: a Calendar of Plays, Entertainments and Afterpieces etc. Part 2. 1700–1727. Ed. Emmett L. Avery. 2 vols. Carbondale: Southern Illinois University Press, 1960. Part 3. 1729–1747. Ed. Arthur H. Scouten. Carbondale: Southern Illinois University Press, 1961.

Lonsdale, Roger, ed. *Eighteenth-Century Women Poets: an Oxford Anthology*. Oxford: Oxford University Press, 1990.

Love, Harold. *Scribal Publication in Seventeenth-Century England*. Oxford: Clarendon Press, 1993.

Lytle, Guy Fitch and Stephen Orgel, eds. *Patronage in the Renaissance*. Princeton: Princeton University Press, 1981.

Mack, Maynard. *Alexander Pope: a Life*. New Haven and London: Yale University Press, 1985.

Marotti, Arthur F. 'John Donne and the Rewards of Patronage'. In *Patronage in the Renaissance*. Ed. Lytle and Orgel. 207–34.

Marsden, Jean L. 'Mary Pix's *Ibrahim*: the Woman Writer as Commercial Playwright'. *Studies in the Literary Imagination*, 32.2 (1999): 33–44.

McBurney, William H. *A Check List of English Prose Fiction 1700–1739*. Cambridge, Massachusetts: Harvard University Press, 1960.

'Edmund Curll, Jane Barker and the English Novel'. *Philological Quarterly*, 35.2 (1958): 385–99.

'Mrs Penelope Aubin and the Early Eighteenth-Century English Novel'. *Huntington Library Quarterly*, 20 (1956–7): 245–67.

McDowell, Paula. *The Women of Grub Street: Press, Politics, and Gender in the London Literary Marketplace*. Oxford: Clarendon Press, 1998.

'Consuming Women: the Life of the "Literary Lady" as Popular Culture in Eighteenth-Century England'. *Genre*, 26 (1993): 219–52.

McEwan, Gilbert D. *The Oracle of the Coffee-House: John Dunton's Athenian Mercury*. California: Huntington Library, 1972.

McGovern, Barbara. *Anne Finch and Her Poetry: a Critical Biography*. Athens: University of Georgia Press, 1992.

McKillop, Alan D. 'Letters from Aaron Hill to Richard Savage'. *Notes & Queries*, 199 (1954): 388–9.

McLaren, Juliet. 'Presumptuous Poetess, Pen-Feathered Muse: the Comedies of Mary Pix'. In *Gender at Work*. Ed. Messenger. 77–113.

McWhir, Anne. 'Elizabeth Thomas and the Two Corinnas: Giving the Woman Writer a Bad Name'. *English Literary History* 62 (1995): 105–19.

Medoff, Jeslyn. 'The Daughters of Behn and the Problem of Reputation'. In *Women, Writing, History*. Ed. Grundy and Wiseman. 253–8.

Messenger, Ann. *Pastoral Tradition and the Female Talent*. Studies in Augustan Poetry. New York: AMS Press Inc, 2001.

Ed. *Gender at Work: Four Women Writers of the Eighteenth Century*. Detroit: Wayne State University Press, 1990.

Midgley, Graham. *The Life of Orator Henley*. Oxford: Clarendon Press, 1973.

Minchinton, W. E. 'Bristol – Metropolis of the West in the Eighteenth Century'. In *The Early Modern Town*. Ed. Clark. 297–313.

Morgan, Fidelis. *A Woman of No Character: an Autobiography of Mrs. Manley*. London: Faber & Faber, 1986.

Ed. *The Female Wits: Women Playwrights on the London Stage 1660–1720*. London: Virago Press Ltd, 1981.

Morris, David B. *The Religious Sublime: Christian Poetry and the Critical Tradition in 18th-Century England*. Lexington: University Press of Kentucky, 1972.

Neale, R. S. *Bath 1680–1850: a Social History*. London: Routledge & Kegan Paul, 1981.

Needham, G. B. 'Mary de la Riviere Manley: Tory Defender'. *Huntington Library Quarterly*, 12 (1949): 253–88.

Norbrook, David. *Poetry and Politics in the English Renaissance*. London: Routledge & Kegan Paul, 1984.

Nussbaum, Felicity A. 'Speechless: Haywood's Deaf and Dumb Projector'. In *The Passionate Fictions of Eliza Haywood: Essays on her Life and Work*. Ed. Saxton and Bocchicchio. 194–216.

Paloma, Dolores. 'A Woman Writer and the Scholars: a Review of Mrs. Manley's Reputation'. *Women and Literature*, 6.1 (1978): 36–46.

Parks, Stephen. *John Dunton and the English Book Trade: a Study of His Career with a Checklist of his Publications*. London and New York: Garland Publishing Inc, 1976.

Patterson, Annabel. *Pastoral and Ideology: Virgil to Valéry*. Berkeley: University of California Press, 1987.

Payne, Deborah C. '"And Poets Shall by Patron Princes Live": Aphra Behn and Patronage'. In *Curtain Calls*. Ed. Schofield and Macheski. 105–19.

Perry, Ruth. *The Celebrated Mary Astell: an Early English Feminist*. Chicago and London: University of Chicago Press, 1986.

Plomer, H. R., G. H. Bushell and E. R. McC. Dix, *A Dictionary of the Printers and Booksellers Who Were at Work in England, Scotland and Ireland from 1726 to 1775*. Printed for the Bibliographical Society at the Oxford University Press, 1932 for 1930.

Prescott, Sarah. 'Provincial Networks, Dissenting Connections, and Noble Friends: Elizabeth Singer Rowe and Female Authorship in Early Eighteenth-Century England'. *Eighteenth-Century Life*, 25 (2001): 29–42.

'The Debt to Pleasure: Eliza Haywood's *Love in Excess* and Women's Fiction of the 1720s.' *Women's Writing*, 7.3 (2000): 427–45.

'Penelope Aubin and *The Doctrine of Morality*: a Reassessment of the Pious Woman Novelist'. *Women's Writing*, 1.1 (1994): 99–112.

'Feminist Literary History and British Women Novelists of the 1720s'. Ph.D. thesis. University of Exeter, 1997.

Radcliffe, David Hill. 'Genre and Social Order in Country House Poems of the Eighteenth Century: Four Views of Percy Lodge.' *Studies in English Literature*, 30 (1990): 445–65.

Report on the Manuscripts of his Grace The Duke of Portland, K. G. Preserved at Welbeck Abbey. London: His Majesty's Stationary Office, 1901.

Richetti, John J., ed. *The Cambridge Companion to the Eighteenth-Century Novel*. Cambridge: Cambridge University Press, 1996.

   Popular Fiction Before Richardson: Narrative Patterns 1700–1739. Oxford: Clarendon Press. First published 1969; rpt. 1992.

Rivers, Isobel, ed. *Books and their Readers in Eighteenth-Century England*. Leicester: Leicester University Press, 1982.

Roberts, David. *The Ladies: Female Patronage of Restoration Drama, 1660–1700*. Oxford: Clarendon Press, 1989.

Rogers, Pat. 'Book Dedications in Britain 1700–1799: a Preliminary Survey.' *British Journal for Eighteenth-Century Studies*, 16.2 (1993): 213–33.

   Hacks and Dunces: Pope, Swift and Grub Street. London and New York: Methuen, 1980.

Rose, Mark. *Authors and Owners: the Invention of Copyright*. Cambridge, Mass.: Harvard University Press, 1993.

Ross, Ian Campbell. ' "One of the Principal Nations in Europe": the Representation of Ireland in Sarah Butler's *Irish Tales*'. *Eighteenth-Century Fiction*, 7.1 (1994): 1–16.

Røstvig, Maren-Sofie. *The Happy Man: Studies in the Metamorphoses of a Classical Ideal*. 2 vols. Oslo and Oxford: Akademisk Forlag and Blackwell, 1955–8.

Rumbold, Valerie. 'Negotiating Patronage: Mary Barber's *Poems on Several Occasions* (1734)'. An unpublished paper delivered at the 'Rethinking Women's Poetry, 1730–1930' conference, Birkbeck College, University of London, 1995.

   Women's Place in Pope's World. Cambridge Studies in Eighteenth-Century Literature and Thought 2. Cambridge: Cambridge University Press, 1989.

Runge, Laura L. *Gender and Language in British Literary Criticism, 1660–1790*, Cambridge: Cambridge University Press, 1997.

Saxton Kirsten T. and Rebecca P. Bocchicchio, eds. *The Passionate Fictions of Eliza Haywood: Essays on her Life and Work*. Lexington: University Press of Kentucky, 2000.

Schofield, Mary Anne and Cecilia Macheski, eds. *Curtain Calls: British and American Women and the Theater, 1660–1820*. Ohio: Ohio University Press, 1992.

   Eds. *Fetter'd or Free? British Women Novelists, 1670–1815*. Ohio: Ohio University Press, 1986.

Shevelow, Kathryn. *Women and Print Culture: the Construction of Femininity in the Early Periodical*. London and New York: Routledge, 1989.

Singley, Carol J. and Susan E. Sweeney, eds. *Anxious Power: Reading, Writing and Ambivalence in Narratives by Women*. SUNY Series in Feminist Criticism and Theory. Albany: State University of New York Press, 1993.

Sitter, John, ed. *The Cambridge Companion to Eighteenth-Century Poetry*. Cambridge: Cambridge University Press, 2001.

Spencer, Jane. *Aphra Behn's Afterlife*. Oxford: Oxford University Press, 2000.

   'Women Writers and the Eighteenth-Century Novel.' In *The Cambridge Companion to the Eighteenth-Century Novel*. Ed. Richetti. 212–35.

The Rise of the Woman Novelist: From Aphra Behn to Jane Austen. Oxford: Blackwell, 1986.

Stanton, Judith Phillips. 'Statistical Profile of Women Writing in English from 1660 to 1800'. In *Eighteenth-Century Women and the Arts*. Ed. Keener and Lorsch. 247–61.

Stecher, Henry F. *Elizabeth Singer Rowe, the Poetess of Frome. A Study in Eighteenth-Century English Pietism*. European University Papers 14. Berne: Herbert Lang, 1973.

Steeves, Edna L., ed. *The Plays of Mary Pix and Catherine Trotter*. 2 vols. New York & London: Garland Publishing Inc., 1982.

Strauss, Ralph. *The Unspeakable Curll: Being Some Account of Edmund Curll, Bookseller To Which is Added a Full List of His Books*. New York: Augustus M. Kelly Publishers, 1970.

Sweet, Rosemary. *The English Town, 1680–1840: Government, Society and Culture*. New York: Pearson Education Limited, 1999.

Thomas, Claudia N. *Alexander Pope and His Eighteenth-Century Women Readers*. Carbondale and Edwardsville: Southern Illinois University Press, 1994.

Tracy, Clarence. *The Artificial Bastard: a Biography of Richard Savage*. Toronto: University of Toronto Press, 1953.

Treadwell, Michael. 'London Trade Publishers 1675–1750'. *The Library*, Sixth Series 4.2 (1982): 99–134.

Trill, Suzanne. 'Religion and the Construction of Femininity'. In *Women and Literature*. Ed. Wilcox. 30–55.

Trill, Suzanne, Kate Chedgzoy and Melanie Osborne, eds. *Lay by Your Needles Ladies, Take the Pen: Writing Women in England, 1500–1700*. London: Arnold, 1997.

Todd, Janet. *The Secret Life of Aphra Behn*. London: André Deutsch, 1996.
  The Sign of Angellica: Women, Writing and Fiction, 1660–1800. London: Virago Press, 1989.
  Ed. *A Dictionary of British Women Writers*. London: Routledge, 1989.
  'Life after Sex: the Fictional Autobiography of Delarivier Manley'. *Women's Studies*, 15 (1988): 43–55.

Troost, Linda V., ed. *Eighteenth-Century Women. Studies in Their Lives, Work, and Culture*. Vol. 1. New York: AMS Press, Inc, 2001.

Turner, Cheryl. *Living By the Pen: Women Writers in the Eighteenth Century*. London: Routledge, 1992.

Van Dorsten, Jan. 'Literary Patrons in Elizabethan England'. In *Patronage in the Renaissance*. Ed. Lytle and Orgel. 191–206.

Waldron, Mary. 'Ann Yearsley and the Clifton Records'. *The Age of Johnson*, 3 (1990): 301–29.

Warner, William. *Licensing Entertainment: the Elevation of Novel Reading in Britain, 1684–1750*. Berkeley and Los Angeles: University of California Press, 1998.

Watts, Michael R. *The Dissenters from the Reformation to the French Revolution*. Oxford: Clarendon Press, 1978.

Webb, Alfred. *A Compendium of Irish Biography: Comprising Sketches of Distinguished Irishmen, and of Eminent Persons connected with Ireland by Office or by Their Writings*. Dublin: M. H. Gill & Son, 1878.

Whicher, George. *The Life and Romances of Mrs. Eliza Haywood*. New York: Columbia University Press, 1915.

Wilcox, Helen, ed. *Women and literature in Britain, 1500–1700*. Cambridge: Cambridge University Press, 1996.

Williams, Gwyn A. *When Was Wales? A History of the Welsh*. London: Penguin Books, 1985.

Williamson, Marilyn L. *Raising Their Voices: British Women Writers, 1650–1750*. Detroit: Wayne State University Press, 1990.

Wright, H. Bunker. 'Matthew Prior and Elizabeth Singer'. *Philological Quarterly*, 24.1 (1945): 71–82.

Womersley, David, ed. *Augustan Critical Writing*. London: Penguin Books, 1997.

Woolf, Virginia. *A Room of One's Own*. London: Penguin Books, 1945.

Zach, Wolfgang. 'Mrs Aubin and Richardson's Earliest Literary Manifesto'. *English Studies*, 62 (1981): 271–85.

Index

Printed by Printforce, United Kingdom